T0246380

"*The Summer of Love and Death* offers page-turning suspense of how the legacy of murder can continue, leaving more than death in its wake." —**Nina Wachsman, author of *The Courtesan's Secret***

"*The Summer of Love and Death* is an engrossing, clever, and propulsive read guaranteed to keep you turning pages . . . Add this to your TBRs now." —**Mandy McHugh, bestselling author of *Chloe Cates Is Missing* and *It Takes Monsters***

"Vividly set in the Catskills, *The Summer of Love and Death* is excellent fun, chock full of murder, theater, and a diverse and devious cast of suspects." —**Emilya Naymark, author of *Behind the Lie***

"Marcy McCreary's *The Summer of Love and Death* is a fiendishly smart modern who-dunnit with clever characters and a mystery that keeps you guessing." —**Elise Hart Kipness, author of *Lights Out***

"*The Summer of Love and Death* is an intricately plotted mystery loaded with colorful characters, tricky red herrings, and whiplash-inducing twists . . . This book had me guessing until the end!" —**K. T. Nguyen, author of *You Know What You Did***

"A moving exploration of intergenerational trauma and family bonds, wrapped up in a classic whodunnit. *The Summer of Love and Death* will have you rooting for Detective Susan Ford, trying to unravel knot after knot, feverishly flipping pages right up to the end." —**I. S. Berry, author of *The Peacock and the Sparrow***

"*The Summer of Love and Death* breaks the mold of the classic whodunit with characters that jump off the pages right into your living room . . . This is a rollercoaster mystery ride that will keep you guessing until the very end." —**J. M. Adams, author of *Second Term***

THE SUMMER OF LOVE AND DEATH

THE SUMMER OF LOVE AND DEATH

❧ A FORD FAMILY MYSTERY ❧

MARCY McCREARY

CamCat
Books

CamCat Publishing, LLC
Fort Collins, Colorado 80524
camcatpublishing.com

Hardcover ISBN 9780744310597
Paperback ISBN 9780744310610
Large-Print Paperback ISBN 9780744310641
eBook ISBN 9780744310634
Audiobook ISBN 9780744310658

Library of Congress Control Number: 2023952392

Book and cover design by Maryann Appel
Interior artwork by Md Saidur Rahman, Moorsky, Sylverarts, Theerakit

5   3   1   2   4

FOR MOM

Feel free to rip this page out of the book and
hang on your refrigerator. I win.

1

YOU KNOW that jittery, gut-roiling feeling you get when heading out on a blind date? That brew of nerves, anxiety, anticipation—plus a hint of dread. That pretty much summed up my morning. Today was the day, and standing at the front door, it finally hit me. I was no longer flying solo. A new partner was waiting for me down at the station.

My fingers twitchy, I fumbled with the zipper of my yellow slicker as I stood in front of the framed poster—an illustration of a white dove perched on a blue guitar neck, gripped by ivory fingers against a bright red background—touting three days of peace and music. Usually, I paid it no mind. But today it captured my attention. A signal, perhaps, that everything would turn out just fine, like it did exactly fifty years ago when four hundred thousand idealistic hippies descended upon this town. A projected disaster that ended up being a glorious experience. The legendary summer of love.

The Woodstock Music and Art Fair didn't take place in Woodstock, New York. The residents of Woodstock were not keen on having the initially projected fifty thousand hippies traipsing through their town. The concert promoters eventually secured Max Yasgur's dairy farm in Bethel, New York—fifty-eight miles from Woodstock and six miles from where I live now. I was four at the time. I have no memory of it. Mom said I was sicker than sick that weekend. Ear infection. Fever escalating to 104 degrees. She tried to take me to a doctor, but the roads were clogged with festival revelers, so she had to postpone my appointment until Tuesday. But by then, the worst of it was over.

Fifty years. Those teenagers were in their sixties and seventies now. The older ones in their eighties. How many of them were still idealistic? How many were still into peace, love, and understanding? How many "dropped out" and berated "the man," only later to find themselves the beneficiaries of capitalism? Becoming "the man."

I leaned over slightly as I reached for the doorknob. The door swung open unexpectedly, smacking me in the forehead. "Whoa." I ran my fingertips along my hairline. No bump. For now.

"Sorry, babe." Ray's voice drew Moxie's attention. Our thirteen-year-old lab mix moseyed into the foyer, tail in full swing. Moseying was really all Moxie could muster these days. "Didn't realize you were standing there."

Ray had left the house an hour earlier. I peered over his shoulder at the running Jeep. "Forget something?"

"Yeah. My wallet." Ray stepped inside, dripping. Moxie stared up at him, waiting. He squatted and rubbed her ears. "Raining cats and dogs out there. No offense, Moxie." He glanced up at the poster. "Just like fifty years ago." He sighed.

Ray's parents were married at the festival by a traveling minister. One-year-old Ray in tow (earning him bragging rights as one of the youngest people to attend Woodstock). Tomorrow would have been their fiftieth wedding anniversary. Their death, at the hand of a drunk driver twelve years ago, spawned a program called Better Mad Than Sad—a class baked into the local drivers-ed curriculum that Ray (and the drunk driver's girlfriend, Marisa) created ten years ago. Parents would join their kids for a fifty-minute session in which they pledged to pick up their kids or their kid's friends, no questions asked, no judgment passed.

Last month, Ray reached out to a few of his and his parents' friends asking if they would be up for a "celebration of life" vigil at the Woodstock festival site this evening. Nothing formal. Just twenty or so folks standing around, reminiscing and shooting the shit about his parents.

Ray shook the rain off his jacket. "Met your new partner this morning."

"Yeah?"

"He's very good-looking." He smirked, then added, "Movie star good-looking."

I leaned back and gave Ray the once-over. "I'm more into the rough-around-the-edges type."

"So I got nothing to worry about?"

"Not as long as you treat me right." I smiled coyly.

I had been without an official partner for a little over a year, since July 2018. My ex-partner bought a small farm in Vermont. He told me not to take it personally, but he was on the verge of a nervous breakdown. I still wondered if I contributed to his anxiety in some small way. Then I got shot in the thigh that August. So hiring a new partner was put on hold. Upon my return to active duty in October of 2018, I was assigned an under-the-radar cold case with my dad brought on as consulting partner. By the time the Trudy Solomon case was resolved, in December 2018, Chief Eldridge still hadn't found a suitable replacement. Small-town policing isn't everyone's cup of tea. So for the better part of 2019, it was just me and my shadow. Dad and Ray assisted on the Madison Garcia case, but the chief made it clear that protocol called for two detectives working a case, and my partnerless days were numbered. Don't get me wrong. It's not like I didn't want a partner. I did. I just wished I had a say in who it was.

❀ ❀ ❀

THE DREADED handshake awaited me as I walked into the precinct. I thought about using the "I-have-a-cold" excuse, but lying to Detective John Tomelli on Day One seemed like a dishonest way to kick off what should be a trusting partnership.

"There she is," Eldridge called out, motioning me over to where he and Detective Tomelli were standing.

John thrust his right hand forward.

"Ford doesn't do handshakes," Eldridge said.

"Oh, oh," John said, furrowing his brow and drawing his hand back to his side.

"Just getting over a cold," I said with wavering conviction. Which wasn't entirely a lie, as I spent all of July on antibiotics for a sinus infection.

"Well, I'll let you two get to know each other," Eldridge said, backing away toward his office.

"So, John—"

"Jack."

"Jack?"

"Yeah, everyone calls me Jack."

I nodded. "Okay."

"My dad's name is John. So to avoid confusion . . . y'know." He eyed my right hand. "What's with the no handshakes?"

"Well, *Jack*, I have a weird medical malady called *palmar hyperhidrosis*. Ever hear of it?"

He shook his head.

I held up my palms and wiggled my fingers. "Sweaty palms. Uncontrollably clammy hands."

"Does it affect your ability to handle a gun?"

And this was why I didn't tell anyone.

"No," I said curtly. "It doesn't," I added for good measure.

Nothing like getting off on the wrong foot on the first day. I had to admit, he was *very* good-looking (Ray was right about that). But John/ Jack wasn't my type—I wasn't blowing smoke when I told Ray I like my men rough around the edges, and this guy was as smooth as they came, right down to his perfectly coifed jet-black hair. It was going to take more than his chiseled jaw and dimpled cheeks to win me over after that barb.

"Ford! Tomelli!" Eldridge shouted before *Jack* had a chance to say anything else on the matter.

Jack led the way. At the door, he stepped aside and waved me in. Instead of being appreciative of the gesture, I wondered if I was a guy if he would have proffered the same courtesy. Was this a "ladies first" move or was he merely deferring to my seniority? I didn't know what was pissing me off most—his Hollywood good looks, that gun remark, or the fact that he just treated me like his date. *Shake it off, Susan.*

"I just got a call from dispatch," Eldridge said as we lingered in front of his desk. "Possible homicide at the Monticello Playhouse. Paramedics are there now. Pronounced dead at the scene. Mark and Gloria are on their way. As is CSI."

"Mark and Gloria?" Jack asked.

"Mark Sheffield is the county's medical examiner and Gloria Weinberg is our crime scene photographer," I explained.

Jack turned to Eldridge. "Who's the victim?"

Eldridge peered down at the paper on his desk. "The woman who called it in said it was one of the actors. Didn't say which one."

Jack turned to me and smirked. "I'll drive."

My blood started to boil. Mom had a theory about exceedingly handsome men, especially those who knew they were. They strut like peacocks and puff out their chests to draw attention to themselves, then, after they get what they want, they shimmy over to the next shiny new object, and you're left wondering if it was something you said, something you did, or that you're just not special enough. Mom was

Miss Sullivan County 1961 and had her fair share of good-looking beaux, including my dad. So, perhaps she did speak from experience. Although a grain of salt was always needed when it came to Mom's doctrines. Was Jack one of *these* guys? Big ego, take charge, deliberately making me feel fragile compared to his manly-man bullshit.

Or was I making a big-ass mountain out of a pint-sized molehill?

THE MONTICELLO Playhouse was situated a mile down the road from the Holiday Mountain Ski and Fun Park—a seven-slope ski area with an elevation of thirteen hundred feet and a vertical drop of four hundred feet. I spent many youthful days zipping down their trails. Back then, you had to rely on Mother Nature for a good coating, and most winters delivered what was needed. These days, the owners relied on snowmaking machines—it was the only way for the ski area to survive the warming winters of climate change.

Jack lifted his hand from the steering wheel and pointed toward the windshield. "Ski area?" he asked as we passed the entrance sign. "Looks open."

"Yeah. It doubles as an amusement park in the summer. Arcades, rock climbing wall, bumper boats. That kinda thing." I side-eyed Jack. "You should take your kids."

He frowned and shook his head. "Don't have kids. You? You have kids?"

"One kid. Adult kid. Natalie."

I waited for him to ask a follow-up question. *How old? What does she do for a living? Grandkids?* But he just tapped his thumbs on the leather-encased steering wheel of his fancy Volvo. I thought about volunteering more info, get a conversation going, get to know each other better, but he seemed tucked away in his own thoughts. Neither of us said another word.

We pulled into the parking lot of the theater. Jack swiveled his head from side to side, then swung his car to the right and parked below a canopy of trees, a good ways away from the hubbub of activity. Above our heads, birds tweeted in melodious call-and-response chirps.

I spotted Mark's silver Honda Accord and Gloria's Chevy pickup truck. "Gang's all here."

Jack popped open the trunk and grabbed his crime scene kit, a duffel containing personal protective gear, evidence markers, and evidence-collection equipment.

As Jack and I strode up the stone walkway toward the entrance of the playhouse, Officer Sally McIver and her partner appeared from around the side of the building. Sally jogged over to us.

"You must be the new guy," Sally said. "Detective John Tomelli?"

"You can call me Jack."

"Jack it is." Sally held out her hand and Jack shook it firmly. She turned to her right. "This is my partner, Officer Ron Wallace."

Ron stepped forward. "About time they filled the position," he said, pumping Jack's hand.

"You guys first on scene?" I asked.

"Yeah. I just surveyed the ground under the windows," Ron said, twisting around toward the theater. "Nothing obvious, but I took photos, just in case. Hopefully, Gloria can get some pro shots before the rain starts up again." He paused. "All the windows lock from the inside."

Sally picked up the thread. "I checked inside the building and all the windows were locked. Doesn't mean someone didn't crawl through an open window, lock it from the inside, and then exit through one of the doors, but that's for you two to figure out."

I glanced over at the actors' dormitory, situated about twenty yards from the theater. A small crowd had gathered outside, craning their necks and whispering among themselves. Three officers stood between them and us, keeping them at bay.

"Mounted cameras anywhere?" I asked Ron and Sally, remembering how an obscure CCTV camera helped get my ass out of trouble a year ago.

"Nothing obvious," Sally replied. "But they could be hidden. I'll look around."

"Let's get a perimeter going," I said to Ron, scanning the vast outdoor area around the theater. "Fifteen yards out from the theater. Also, set up a single entry/exit point over there. I'll get one of the other officers to log who comes and goes."

I turned to Sally. "Who found the victim?"

Sally flipped open her notebook. "Jean Cranmore, the woman in charge of costumes. She's over there." Sally pointed to a fiftysomething redheaded woman sitting on a nearby bench, her hands tucked between her knees, rocking back and forth. Her blue windbreaker zipped up to her chin. "I took her statement when I first arrived. She said she's seen enough cop shows to know not to let anyone near the body or say anything to anyone, so at least we know the crime scene hasn't been contaminated."

"Eldridge said it's one of the actors," Jack said. "Did she say which one?"

"Actually, the director." Sally scanned her notes. "Adam Kincaid. She said she was freaked out and must have said actor by mistake when she called 9-1-1."

"Let her know I'll speak to her after I've surveyed the crime scene." I noted that a scowl formed on Jack's face when I used the word *I* instead of *we*. Perhaps I should have explained that it was merely a habit from not having a partner for a while. But I let the moment pass.

Sally jutted her chin toward the walkway that separated the dormitory from the theater. "What about the lookie-loos over there?"

"Interview them as well. That'll help me sort out who I need to talk to first." Oops. Did it again.

Sally flipped her notebook closed. "Will do."

"You saw the body?" I asked.

"Yeah. It's a weird one," Sally hinted, knowing full well that I preferred to assess the crime scene without exposition. "You'll see."

THE MONTICELLO Playhouse used to be a Catholic church. It sat abandoned for fifteen years, until Malcolm Slater bought it six years ago. Yeah, *that* Malcolm Slater . . . lead singer of Blueberry Fields, an alternative rock band that dominated the radio airwaves in the nineties. After calling it quits with his bandmates in the mid-aughts, he drifted over to the production side of the business and opened a recording studio in the neighboring town of Forestburgh, New York. The guy was a bit of a celebrity around here. Rumor had it he was also a prima donna.

Malcolm Slater not only invested in the property, but he installed himself as the theater's executive director, providing the bulk of the funding for the summer stock productions. Some called it philanthropy, a gift to revitalize the area. Others believed he had an ulterior motive . . . to give his girlfriend, Shana Lowry, a stage and a starring role.

I gazed up at the white gable-roofed building, the narrow bell tower shooting straight up over the entrance. Slater did a heck of a job transforming it from a rundown church to a refurbished theater. I'd give him that.

Jack raced by me, taking two steps at a time as he ascended the ten steps to the porch landing. He stood in front of the wooden double doors. I sucked in my breath, then slowly exhaled before climbing the stairs.

He unzipped the duffel and extracted two plastic bags containing Tyvek coveralls, booties, and a pair of blue latex gloves. He tossed one of the bags in my direction. We quickly donned our PPE. Jack opened the door and, once again, stepped aside and waved me through. With a tight-lipped smile, I hurried into the foyer, then up the aisle toward the stage. Mark was center stage, leaning over the body. Gloria was in the orchestra pit, hunched over her camera equipment. She looked up and waved me over. I glanced over my shoulder and saw Jack making his way up the aisle.

"Bring me up to speed," I said to Gloria.

"Just took the global photos. Waiting on you for midrange and close-up." Gloria tipped her head toward the dead body. "I've photographed a lot of crime scenes in my day, but this one takes the proverbial cake."

As I mounted the steps to the stage, I heard Jack introduce himself to Gloria.

Mark stepped away from the body and walked toward me. When Jack caught up to me, I initiated the introductions. "Jack, meet Mark Sheffield, Sullivan County's death investigator and medical examiner and, in my nobody-gives-a-shit opinion, one of the best in the business."

"Good to meet you, Mark."

"Likewise. Ready?"

Mark led the way to the center of the stage where the body was situated. Jack remained behind me but close on my heels. *Was this deference or a case of nerves?*

I wasn't sure what to expect, but it wasn't what I saw. No one prepares you for that.

A MAN, roughly late twenties, lay in a narrow platform bed.

I sucked in my breath, holding it for a few moments, then expelled a puff of air. *Holy shit* were the only two words that came to mind. I was so entranced, I wasn't even sure I uttered them out loud. I looked over at Jack. His mouth was agape. I turned back to the body and inventoried the scene.

The victim's wrists and ankles bound by rough-hewn rope. Fancy nautical knots. Naked. And that wasn't the worst part of this tableau. His face was caked in smeared makeup. Lips bright red. Cheeks pink with blush. Eyelids powdery blue. A white pillow—placed below the feet of the deceased—was also smeared in makeup, looking like a second-rate Vasily Kandinsky knockoff. And if this gruesome display wasn't enough to throw me for a loop, the killer had laid a dazzling peace sign necklace over his heart. Shimmering hues of blue, green, and yellow stained glass soldered between the copper foil lines creating the peace symbol.

Jack swayed, shifting his weight from his right foot to his left. "What the—?"

Well, we shared that sentiment. I bent over to get a better look at the man's face, somehow thinking a close-up view would explain this twisted scene. But all I could make out was a pale face under swirls of garish color.

Someone, quite possibly associated with this theater, went to a whole heck of a lot of trouble to stage this body in this grotesque manner. *A message? A warning? A clown fetish? And what's with the stained glass necklace? The killer's calling card, perhaps?* I closed my eyes to ground myself and focus on what else seemed out of place. A large makeup case sat on the floor at the side of the bed. I looked around for clothes, but there was not a stitch of discarded clothing anywhere on the stage. Jack was now hovering at my side, angling to get a better look, so I stepped aside. He wheezed slightly but remained silent as he took in the scene.

I turned to face Mark. "Approximate time of death?"

"It was called in at nine fifteen this morning. Based on rigor and lividity, I'd say between eight last night and eight this morning. Hopefully someone can tell you when he was last seen alive . . . help you narrow that down."

"Cause of death?"

"Possible asphyxiation," he said, pointing to the pillow. "There's some bruising around his nose and mouth. But until I get him back to the morgue I won't know for sure. Didn't put up much of a fight, so I'm thinking drugged, then smothered. Tox panel will give a fuller picture."

"Can you make this a priority?"

"It's not up to me," Mark replied with a sigh. "But a bizarre murder like this will get the brass's attention."

I moved to the foot of the bed to inspect the body from a different angle. If I thought this vantage point would make the sight of this spectacle easier to stomach, I was dead wrong. "Well, we've got to make this a priority. Something this outlandish tells me we have a madman in our midst. I'm hoping our vic here was specifically targeted, but we could be looking at something more sinister."

"A serial killer?" Jack offered. "Shit. Perhaps everyone in the cast are sitting ducks."

That thought crossed my mind, but I wasn't ready to jump to any conclusions. That was how Dad operated. I tend to hold off on assumptions until I've amassed more facts. But if we were dealing with a serial killer with a penchant for dolling up his victims, I feared we were going to need outside help.

I could just picture the attention-grabbing moniker the press would give our perp: the Makeup Murderer of Monticello or the Peace Sign Perp or some such nonsense. Was Jack right? Was it possible that the cast were sitting ducks? "Let's hope you're wrong about that," I finally said.

Jack glanced over his shoulder. "Is this bed part of the set?"

"Yeah," Gloria chimed in, then turned to me. "You're gonna love this, Susan . . . they've been rehearsing Agatha's Christie's *Murder on the Orient Express.* Supposed to open tonight."

"*Murder on the Orient Express* is a play?" I was familiar with the book and movie (Ray and I watched the movie about a year ago, when we were both waylaid with a stomach bug. His first viewing, my second), but I had no idea it was adapted for the stage.

Mark straightened up. All six foot six of him in full view now. "Yeah, in fact I had tickets to the Sunday show."

"Well, I hope you can get a refund, because I'm pretty sure there won't be a Sunday show. It's going to take a while to process and clear the scene." I surveyed the stage for anything else out of the ordinary. But nothing leaped out at me. "They'll be lucky if they open on Monday . . . if at all."

My phone rang. It was Sally. I walked to stage right. Or was it stage left? I could never remember if the wings were from the actor's perspective or the audience's perspective. "Yeah."

"I got Malcolm Slater out here. He's demanding to go inside."

"He can demand until the cows come home. Tell him I'll be out to talk to him when I'm done in here."

A man's voice erupted through the line. "Give me the phone!"

Sally abruptly ended the call. She's no shrinking violet. If anyone can handle that guy, she can. An aging rocker versus a no-nonsense police officer with two tours in Iraq under her belt. I got my money on Sally. Even so, I did not appreciate being rushed, but suddenly felt somewhat obliged to speak with Malcolm Slater sooner rather than later. I rejoined our little group and conferred with Gloria on the mid-range and close-up shots. Jack simply nodded as I spoke. The side door opened and a sudden burst of light illuminated the stage. Three county CSIs entered and strode toward us.

"Let's use this pathway for getting on and off the stage," I said, motioning with my arms a narrow passage from where we were all standing to the steps. "Jack, can you mark the path with the cones? There should be some in the CSK. Feel free to confer with CSI. I'm going outside to chat with the theater's executive director."

Before Jack could object or offer a different strategy, I turned away from him. I flashed a smile at Gloria, and she winked back. She knew exactly what I was doing. Establishing my dominance. Making sure Jack knew who was in charge.

BEFORE LEAVING the theater, I lingered in the lobby. I had hurried through this area when first arriving with Jack and didn't get a chance to see if anything was amiss in here. Along the wall to my right were three evenly spaced five-foot-long wooden benches—a seating area for patrons to wait for the theater doors to open or perhaps chat with fellow theatergoers during intermission. On the wall to my left hung eleven-by-fourteen framed photographs of all the troupes—cast and crew—who had performed in the theater over the years. I walked over to the photograph closest to the door: the first troupe to perform in 2014. I strolled down to the last photograph. Engraved on a gold-plated plaque above this photograph were the words: *Cast and Crew of Mousetrap and Murder on the Orient Express, Summer 2019.* I surveyed the faces of the people who were about to be shocked to hear the news about their director.

When I exited the theater, I beelined it to Sally, who was standing at the designated entry/exit point. Pacing behind the yellow crime tape was none other than Malcolm Slater —tall and wiry, with hair too dark and too long for a man his age, which I pegged at about fifty. He charged toward me.

"I've been standing out here in the rain for a fucking hour!" he screamed, tilting his large black umbrella slightly backward. "I'll have your badge! Your supervisor will be hearing about this. Chief Cliff Eldridge, right?"

"You're free to file a complaint," I said, doing my best to sound cordial. Well, somewhat cordial. I glanced around looking for shelter and spotted a large shed at the edge of the tree line. "We haven't cleared that shed over there, but we can talk under the overhang."

As we strode toward the shed, plump droplets replaced the gentle mist. By the time we reached the overhang, the rain intensified, and all I could think about was all the outdoor evidence being washed away.

"I have a right to know what's going on in my theater." Malcom lowered his umbrella, shook off the water, and pulled it shut. "Was there an accident? Or something . . . worse?"

"There's been a murder. The body has been identified by a witness, so until we notify next of kin, there is not much more I can tell you."

He stepped closer to me. "What witness? Who?" he demanded, waving his free hand around.

"You need to calm down, Mr. Slater." I said in my firm, steady, kindergarten-teacher voice.

"This is bullshit! Utter bullshit!" He shook the umbrella, causing it to open slightly. He grabbed the little strap and secured it around the middle. "Was it someone in the cast or crew? At least tell me that much."

"Mr. Slater, I have an investigation to run. I will not risk fucking this up just because you threaten to 'speak to my superior' or 'have my badge.' Got it?"

Malcolm stepped back. He opened his mouth, but quickly snapped it shut.

I took a baby step toward him, closing the gap. I also knew a thing or two about intimidation. "Who has access to your theater at night?"

Malcolm rocked slightly back on his heel but maintained his position. "Ricky is responsible for locking the front and side doors after rehearsals and shows, but there are a few people who have keys to the side door."

"Ricky?"

"Ricky Saunders. Our maintenance guy."

"Okay. I'll need a list of everyone who has a key."

I thought this demand would be met with resistance, but he merely scowled, then quickly said, "Sure."

I thought about stepping back, giving him more space, but decided to stand my ground, not give an inch, make it crystal clear I was not taking his guff.

"Are there security cameras on the premises?"

Malcolm sniffed derisively. "I find them to be invasions of privacy. And I don't want my actors to think I'm spying on them."

That's understandable, given his previous profession. In his heyday, the paparazzi were relentless. He'd leaned heavily into the "sex, drugs, and rock 'n' roll" stereotype. Although I always felt some of his shenanigans seemed manufactured, played up for publicity.

"Who lives in the old rectory?"

Malcolm tilted his head to the right, craning over my shoulder to glimpse the building. "The Equity actors and a few department heads live on the first and second floors. The non-Equity actors live on the third, fourth, and fifth floors. There's a smaller building behind the rectory that houses the crew."

"And those bungalows?" I asked, pointing to the edge of the property abutting the woods.

Malcolm's eyes followed my finger to the cluster of bungalows; he squinted, then turned back toward me. "That's where the musicians live."

"So, the entire cast and crew live on-site?"

"No. Not everyone. Some department heads are scattered around the area. I bought a few small bungalows around Smallwood and Sackett Lake to house them during the summer. This way I can attract top talent from around the country." He cleared his throat. "Now that I've given you the lay of the land, I would appreciate you telling me who has been murdered."

"I've already told you more than I should have. Now, I suggest you tell your cast and crew to cooperate." I leaned forward, lifting my heels slightly off the ground. "In fact, the more you cooperate with me, the more I will cooperate with you. Do I make myself clear?"

Malcolm whipped open his umbrella and stormed away just as a crack of lightning lit up the gray midmorning sky.

TO SHIELD our witness from the rain, Sally had escorted Jean Cranmore, the costume director, to the gift shop—a one-story stand-alone building about forty feet from the theater's side exit door. Sally had asked Malcolm to unlock it when he arrived on scene so CSI could do a sweep of the place. When given the all clear, Sally asked Jean to wait in there. A tinkle announced my entrance. Jean was seated on a stool among the mugs, T-shirts, keychains, refrigerator magnets and other touristy tchotchkes branded with the Monticello Playhouse logo. I quickly scanned the shop for stained glass peace sign necklaces but saw nothing of the sort.

"How are you holding up?" I looked around for another stool or chair, but there was none, so I leaned against the glass counter.

She sniffled and ran her sleeve across her nose. Her eyelashes were moist and mascara smudges lined the area beneath her eyes. She inhaled deeply, then let out a long breath.

"Just want to confirm that the man you saw in the theater is the director, Adam Kincaid?"

"Yes, I'm sure. Even with the way he looked"—she shivered, then wrapped her arms tightly around her torso—"I could tell it was Adam."

"Right now you're the only one who knows. And until we reach his next of kin, I would appreciate you keeping it to yourself."

"But they are going to ask me. The cast. They're waiting for me. They're going to badger me." She fingered the small cross that hung around her neck. "What do I say?"

"I can take you to a motel if you'd like. Adam Kincaid's parents live about fifty miles from here. I'll be talking to them this afternoon."

She nodded reluctantly. "Okay."

"Tell me about this morning. What were you doing in the theater that early?"

A tear slipped down her cheek, which she swatted away when it hit her chin. She cocked her head, closed her eyes for a few seconds, then snapped them open. "I usually don't get up early, but with the show opening tonight, I wanted to get a jump on things. There were a few costumes that needed adjustments. Some issues with fitting were brought up during the tech rehearsal last night, and Nathan was livid."

"Nathan?"

"Nathan Fowler. Our production manager." She shivered, perhaps still feeling stung by his wrath. Or maybe it was the air-conditioning.

"Is Nathan easily angered?"

"Not really. He's just a stickler for detail." She frowned. "He makes his displeasure known."

"How did you get into the theater this morning?"

"I have a key to the side door nearest the dorms."

"So the door was locked?"

"Yes."

"Did you see anyone enter or exit the theater before you went in?"

She looked down at her lap and gently shook her head. "Tech rehearsal ran late so I imagine most people slept in this morning."

"How late?"

"We wrapped at one in the morning. I left the theater shortly after that and went straight to bed. But a few people hung around."

"Was Adam Kincaid among those who hung around?"

"No. He actually left before me." She ran her fingertips under her eyes, smudging the mascara residue. "He wasn't well-liked. Adam."

I glanced up from my notepad. "Yeah?"

"He was just . . . a tad intense. He could dress you down pretty severely if he wasn't pleased with a scene. He was all about the play, not the camaraderie. Don't get me wrong . . . he's super talented. The aggravation is worth it when you see the final product."

"Could you think of a reason why someone would kill him?"

She straightened up a bit and squinted. "Well, there is a rumor going around that Adam was having an affair with Malcom Slater's girlfriend."

"Shana Lowry?"

"The one and only. The *star* of our show." She snorted derisively. "And she never let you forget it." Jean gazed around the gift shop, making sure we were still alone. "Rumor has it, Adam just broke it off with her. And she was none too pleased."

"Okay. Good to know. Anything else you can think of?"

She looked past me, gazing into space. When she turned back toward me, her eyes were glassy. "It's just . . . I mean, the way he looked. That's definitely some level of crazy. I can't imagine anyone doing something like that to Adam. You would think things like this only happen in the city. But here? Never in my wildest dreams would I think that . . ."

I waited a few seconds for her sentence to resolve, but she just stared down at her clasped hands. When she finally looked up, she whispered, "You know what's also weird? That necklace on his chest. I mean, he never wore jewelry. I couldn't imagine him owning a gaudy piece like that."

I didn't realize Jean had gotten that close. "You saw that?"

She nodded. "Hard to miss."

"So you don't think it was Adam's?"

She shrugged. "Well, I've never seen him wear it before."

"Was it a prop?"

She touched her own necklace. "I don't think so, but you can talk to Libby. Libby Wright. She's the prop mistress."

I scribbled down Libby's name, along with a note to assign Sally the initial interview.

Then I asked Jean to follow me outside, where I handed her over to Sally to drive her to a motel.

JACK AND I headed west to the village of Hancock, New York—situated just east of the Pennsylvania border along the Delaware River—to break the news to Adam Kincaid's parents, Jason and Lynn. A fifty-minute scenic drive along Route 17 West.

"Fucking bird crap on my car," Jack snarled as he deployed the windshield wipers.

"Probably shouldn't have parked under the trees," I said as I rolled down the window and inhaled the pine scent of the evergreens. My ears popped as the car crested a hill.

Instead of using this time to reset the relationship with Jack, I slipped on my earbuds and listened to an episode of *My Favorite Murder*. He glanced at me once in a while but made no indication that he wanted to chat. I couldn't tell if he was reticent by nature or deliberately being aloof. I knew I could've been the bigger person in this situation, strike up a conversation, but I ignored him.

At two on the dot we pulled into the driveway of 39 Millhouse Lane. There was no worse part of this job than telling next of kin that their loved one was gone, murdered. Jack insisted on taking lead on this, and I was fine conceding this particular task to him. I will be the first to admit, projecting sympathy does not come naturally to me. I can turn it on when I need to, but I've always sensed it coming across forced and stilted. When I say to a complete stranger, "I'm so sorry for your loss," it rings hollow in my ears and tugs superficially on my heartstrings.

As we made our way up the brick walkway, I surveyed the Kincaids' modest home. A split-level probably built in the sixties or seventies. Neatly trimmed rhododendron bushes, bursting with purple flowers, flanked the front door. A well-maintained front lawn sloped gently toward the sidewalk. No flower beds or decorative lawn ornaments. Tidy but devoid of personality.

A knot formed in my stomach as I rang the doorbell. I glanced over at Jack, and he was slowly breathing in and out, cracking his neck, and shaking his arms, as though he was loosening up before taking his spot on a racetrack starting line.

Jason Kincaid opened the door. I glimpsed Lynn Kincaid leaning over the railing of the upper level. "Who is it?" she called out. When she made eye contact with the two strangers standing in her doorway, she scurried down the stairs to join her husband.

Jack displayed his shield. "I'm Detective Jack Tomelli and this is my partner, Detective Susan Ford. May we come in?"

Lynn spread her fingers out over her heart, and pressed gently. "Is it Adam? Did something happen to Adam?"

"If we can come inside?" Jack said gently.

They backed away slightly, but the entryway was too small for the four of us. Lynn retreated up the six steps to the upper landing, visibly shaking as she waited for the rest of us to join her there. A quick glance around revealed dated furniture in decent shape. The room tidy and comfortable with crocheted throws on the sofa and recliner. Glass trinkets sat atop doilies on the end tables.

Jack broke the news.

Their reactions were textbook.

Lynn collapsed to the floor like an imploding building, straight down. She stuffed her fist into her mouth, attempting to stifle the wails. But she eventually lowered her clenched hand to her lap and allowed her cries to fill the room. Jason Kincaid squatted next to her in an attempt to console her as she swayed back and forth. He eventually managed to take hold of her elbow and waist, lift her gently, and guide her to the couch. Jason repeatedly asked, "Are you sure it's Adam?"

"Someone at the theater identified your son," Jack said, as he maneuvered his way around the furniture to an armchair opposite the sofa.

There were no other seating options, so I stood to the right of Jack.

"Do you have a picture?" Jason draped his arm around Lynn's shoulder; she buried her face in her hands. Her sobbing subsided into a soft whimper. "So we can be sure it's him."

Lynn lifted her head, her eyes lit up with a glimmer of hope that we might have gotten it wrong. That a photograph would prove otherwise. We had no intention of showing them a photograph of their dead son in his current condition, with makeup slathered all over his face.

"We're sure it's him," Jack said gently. He leaned forward, his forearms rested on his thighs, his hands clasped. "However, we will need a next-of-kin positive identification from one of you. We can accompany you to the morgue now or we can set up a video feed, if you prefer."

Jason and Lynn exchanged glances. Without verbally conferring, Jason said, "We'll both go."

Lynn rubbed her eyes, smudging her black mascara and eyeliner to the outskirts of her eyelids. "How?" she asked, her voice cracking. "Why?" she whispered.

Jack tilted his head toward me, eyebrows raised, discreetly asking me how much we should disclose.

I jumped in to answer. "Until we have all the facts—"

"No! I want to know now." Lynn rocked forward dislodging her husband's arm from around her shoulder. "I *need* to know."

Jack cleared his throat. "Ms. Kincaid. The cause of death is still under investigation. All we can tell you is that Adam was murdered at the Monticello Playhouse sometime between one o'clock and nine o'clock this morning. Detective Ford and I have made Adam's case a top priority. We will leave no stone unturned. You have our word."

As he spoke, Lynn shifted her gaze from Jack to me, to the photographs that hung on the wall just off my right shoulder.

I turned toward the annual family portraits—lined up in chronological order—along the wall leading to the bedroom level. In the first photo, a smiling baby boy sat on Lynn's lap. In the second year, the boy was joined by a baby girl. By the fourth year, the girl was no longer in any of the pictures. I'm guessing this was their second heartbreak.

Jason must have noticed me eyeing the portraits. "Twice now," he said. "No one should have to bury their children."

"I'm so sorry for your loss." I gulped down a knot forming in my throat. This situation hitting me harder than usual. This family had seen its fair share of hard knocks and bad luck. Future holidays and birthdays fraught with reminders of what has been lost. No weddings. No family gatherings. No backyards filled with grandchildren and mischief. I thought of how truly lucky, even blessed I have been. No real heartaches. No tragedies. Dysfunction aplenty. But, I'll take that over what these folks have endured.

Lynn pinched her lips into a thin line and shuddered. "Emily was only four. Leukemia. We do two good deeds and still get punished." She started to weep. "If you'll excuse me," she croaked out before she launched off the sofa and ran up the four steps to the bedroom level. A few seconds later we heard a door close.

I turned to Jason. "What did she mean by 'two good deeds'?"

Jason glimpsed the stairs, then back to me. "We adopted Emily and Adam. Lynn wanted Adam to have a baby sister. We thought about adopting again, but Lynn didn't want to go through any more heartache. Not to mention, a few adoptions fell through before we got Adam, and I didn't think she was up for the rigmarole of it all. I know I wasn't." He sighed.

We sat quietly for a few moments, then Jack got back to business. "We'll need the address of Adam's primary residence."

Jason blinked a couple of times, as though mentally shifting gears in response to Jack's request. "Um, Adam was in between apartments, so he was crashing here . . . in his old bedroom. But he hasn't been here in weeks—he's been living at the theater, in an apartment there."

I glanced at Jack. "We'd like to take a quick look around his bedroom."

"It's the second door on the right," Jason said, jutting his chin toward the stairs. "If you'll excuse me, I'll let Lynn know we'll be leaving soon."

Jack and I entered the small and tidy bedroom. The closet and dresser drawers were filled with men's winter clothing. Definitely Adam's, as the style was more suited to a millennial than a boomer. His summer clothes were probably in the playhouse apartment. I leafed through a few wire-bound notebooks filled with directing notes. Jack rummaged through the desk drawers. Nothing related to his murder jumped out at us during this cursory sweep. CSI would confiscate his possessions for closer inspection.

"Find anything?" Jason asked as we emerged from the bedroom. Lynn stood close to his side.

"Nothing obvious, but we'll need you to stay out of that room until we can get someone out here to collect his things. Oh, almost forgot . . ." I pulled out my phone and scrolled to the photograph I took of the stained glass necklace. I held it up. "Is this Adam's necklace?"

Jason pulled a pair of readers from his shirt pocket and stared at my phone for a few seconds. "If it is, I've never seen it before."

"That's not something Adam would wear. He was a conservative dresser." Lynn tilted her head. "Why do you ask?"

I hesitated, thinking how best to phrase the answer, then said, "It was found at the scene."

Jason blinked rapidly, but could not prevent a few tears from escaping. "So it belonged to . . . to the person who killed my son?"

"We don't know, Mr. Kincaid. It's evidence. And we'd like to find its owner, that's all."

AS JACK pulled away from the curb, my phone dinged with a text message from Sally.

Ron and I finished interviews. Check your email for my report.

I opened my email. "Sally sent over her interview notes."

"And?" There was an edge to his voice I hadn't heard before.

"And, you know the saying, 'Patience is a virtue, possess it if you can. Seldom women have it, but never does a man.' Give me a sec to pull it up."

Jack drummed his fingers on the steering wheel. He glanced up at the rearview mirror, probably making sure the Kincaids were still tailing us. His energy was different. Maybe it was the encounter with the Kincaids. Maybe he didn't like my quote about being impatient. I think we were both rattled, neither of us expecting to get an earful about another dead child.

I scanned Sally's report. "Interesting. There are two sets of cast and crew that alternate throughout the summer season, a musical troupe and a drama troupe. The musical troupe just wrapped *A Walk on the Moon* and went to a party in Manhattan, which was arranged by Malcolm Slater. He chartered a bus and booked them a hotel. They will start rehearsals on Monday. *Little Shop of Horrors.*"

"So while one group is performing at night, the other group is rehearsing during the day?"

"Yeah. Which means all the musicians were also in the city the night of the murder. Each show runs for two weeks, starting on a Friday night and ending on a Thursday matinee. They also hold a matinee on the Wednesday of the second week."

"So eight performances per week running for two weeks?" Jack let out a low whistle. "They sure do pack in a lot of performances over that two-week time frame. And I thought our job was grueling."

I spun the knob on the radio to lower the volume. "First piece of business when we get back is to confirm that everyone who said they went to the city actually went to the city. I can put Ron on that. Unfortunately, that still leaves us the entire cast and crew of *Orient Express* to clear."

"Maybe they all did it, like in the book. Life imitating art."

"That's one heck of a theory you got there, Inspector Poirot." I wasn't ready to entertain the possibility that we had more than one sicko on our hands.

"Just saying it feels a bit like a reenactment."

That thought crossed my mind as well, but it felt too premature to start theorizing. That might be his style, but it wasn't mine. I let the evidence tell the story.

And the evidence had yet to tell me this was a reenactment of the plot of the play they were all performing. That seemed incredibly far-fetched. And even a bit too on the nose. I closed my eyes in an attempt to stave off an impending headache.

My phone pinged again. Another message from Sally. I read aloud to Jack.

"CSI swept through Adam's apartment. Retrieved phone from the nightstand. There's also a laptop."

"Phone on nightstand tells me he left his place in a hurry," Jack said.

"Maybe. It's also possible he was just groggy."

This morning I woke up thinking Ray's anniversary tribute to his parents would be the most thrilling part of the day. But this bizarre murder and a less-than-auspicious start to a new partnership had upstaged Ray's get-together.

The swish of the Volvo's windshield wipers abruptly stopped and I cracked open my eyes. The clouds were dissipating and the sun was inching toward a clear patch of blue.

I leaned my head against the headrest, searching for my own patch of blue sky. The bright side: Ray's planned gathering of friends and family could be just the antidote needed to counter this awful day. Clear the old noggin, because tomorrow was going to be equally brutal—questioning a bunch of temperamental actors who had the skills to deceive us.

THE SUN was setting as I ascended the knoll to the Woodstock monument—a gray rectangular slab of concrete featuring a raised sculpture mimicking the dove with the guitar and fingers from the poster, and two bronze plaques with the names of all the bands that performed. Concrete benches flanked the monument on either side. I spotted Ray chatting with his mother's best friend, Phoebe, and her husband, Paul. A quick headcount put the crowd at sixteen. I was a bit surprised to see my parents in the mix.

As I sidled up to Ray, he smiled and whispered in my ear: "Glad you could make it."

I slapped him playfully on the arm. "Sorry I'm late. Had to stick around the morgue until the Kincaids left."

He kissed me on the cheek, then turned to face the group. "Okay, everyone gather around," Ray shouted, as he moved closer to the monument. "As you all know, today would have been my parents' fiftieth wedding anniversary. And I appreciate y'all coming out on this drizzly night to honor and toast their enduring love." He flashed me a mischievous grin and a conspiratorial wink. "But that's not the only reason why I called you all here this evening."

Ray suddenly dropped to his knee. Then gazed up at me. "Susan, will you marry me?" He unfurled his fist, revealing a little black box in the palm of his left hand. He lifted the lid.

Wasn't expecting this. Nope. Not in a million years. I stood stock-still. But my heart was racing like a son of a gun. A fiery sensation burned in my lungs, then started radiating outward. *That's good, right?* My brain was about two steps behind my emotions. I couldn't speak. I stammered, tried to say something, then I thought, *Wait, is this some kind of* Candid Camera *stunt?* I glanced around. But everyone was smiling, definitely in on whatever Ray had cooked up. Dad had the biggest grin on his face.

Even Mom cracked a rare smile.

I turned away from Mom and leaned over to inspect the contents of the velvet box. A square-cut sapphire ring stared back at me. Ray's father gave that ring to his mother on their twenty-fifth wedding anniversary. "Uh, yes?" I found Ray's eyes. "Um, I mean, yes. Yes, I'll marry you."

Ray jumped up, nearly bowling me over. He wrapped his arms around me, squeezing tight like a boa constrictor and lifting me slightly off the ground. He laughed as he released me, his eyes glassy and bright.

"So, you gonna do the honors?" I said, holding out my left hand.

He plucked the ring out of the velvet box and slipped it on my finger.

I admired it for a moment, then grabbed Ray's collar and kissed him. Our embrace was interrupted when everyone rushed toward me.

"Mazel tov," Paul yelled. "It's about time!"

The fiery sensation that ripped through my lungs earlier had now settled comfortably into my chest. And that warmth more than made up for my shitty day.

A FEW moments later I steered Dad away from the revelers toward the open field. "So you knew about this?"

"We all did. Ray may act all tough and shit, but he's a romantic." Dad peered over my shoulder. "You got a good one there."

"I have to say, I'm oddly excited. Getting married at fifty-four, who woulda thunk." I held up my left hand and stared at the ring. "Just don't want to ruin what we have. I know that's silly, seeing nothing will change, but still."

"Look, I'm not one to give advice about marriage, but I know a good thing when I see it. Under that exterior of yours I can tell you're as giddy as a, well, a younger bride-to-be. So, tie the knot. Make it official. Besides, you'll get a better tax break. And his social security benefits and pension when he kicks the bucket."

"Jeez, Dad. That's morbid." As that word tumbled out of my mouth, I sucked in my breath as today's grisly events crept into my brain. I was hoping this joyous moment would override it, momentarily erase what I had witnessed at the theater. I knew what Ray would say: *leave it at the precinct doorstep.* It always amazed me how well Ray compartmentalized, while I perseverated about my cases after clocking out—my professional and personal life bleeding into one another like a watercolor painting. Without the capacity (or willingness) to just let it go, I turned to Dad and said, "The murder scene I attended today was like something out of a bad B movie. The guy's ankles and wrists tied with coarse rope. Naked."

Dad grunted. "I've seen worse." He started walking further into the field, so I fell in step with him.

"The murder victim's face was covered in makeup. Caked on like Bette Davis in *Whatever Happened to Baby Jane?*"

Dad stopped abruptly and spun toward me, his earlier plastered-on smile replaced with a twisted grimace. "Was he smothered with a pillow?"

"Um, yeah."

He pointed to the ground. "Was the pillow at the feet of the victim?"

Bells were going off in my head. And they were not wedding bells. "Who told you about this?"

Dad started pacing. He ran his hands through his mane of gray hair, forcing it to stand on end. Couple that with the wild look in his eye and he looked like a caged tiger ready to take out whoever got in the cage with him. "That's the MO of Mac Gardner. Ankles and wrists tied with rope. Naked on a bed. Caked makeup on the face. Pillow placed at victim's feet." Dad stopped pacing and rubbed the back of his neck as though tamping down raised hairs. "Susan, it was my first case working as a detective in the summer of 1969."

"Holy shit," I exclaimed, although the words got caught in the back of my windpipe and escaped as a hoarse whisper. I coughed into my fist to clear my throat, and my head. "Was there a stained glass peace sign necklace placed on your victim's chest?"

"Peace sign necklace?" Dad scratched the side of his forehead. His head started bobbing up and down. "Yeah, yeah. But not stained glass. Carved out of wood, dangling on a leather cord."

Maybe Jack was right about this being a reenactment. Except for one detail: this murder was not a reenactment of the play but a reenactment of a fifty-year-old murder. "What else do you remember?"

"I'm a little fuzzy on the details." Dad poked at the dirt with the tip of his right loafer. "There were three murders with the same MO."

"Wait. There was more than one murder? Are you saying this guy was a serial killer?"

"Yeah. The victim in our jurisdiction was a guy named Sam Blackstone. He was a waiter at one of the hotels. His wife's name was either Ellen or Helen. They had two, maybe three kids." Dad scratched his chin. "I might not remember the details, but I sure as heck remember how my partner Jimmy solved the case."

"I'm all ears."

"Jimmy was hailed a hero after quickly piecing together the evidence that led to the arrest of Mac Gardner," Dad began. "The dominoes started falling when Jimmy recalled a newspaper article about a similar murder a month earlier up in Kingston. He then called around to the surrounding counties and got wind of a similar murder in Ellenville, confirming his suspicions that we were dealing with a psycho."

"So, three look-alike murders over a three-month period?"

"Yeah. And I even remember the victims' names and the dates they were murdered . . . that, somehow, got etched in my brain." Dad raised his hand and ticked off his fingers. "Sam Blackstone on July fifth in Monticello. Robert Sherman on June seventh in Kingston. And Kenneth Waterman on May second in Ellenville. All male victims in their early twenties."

"Shit. So, how did Jimmy figure out it was Mac Gardner?"

"Well, a little bit of luck helped him nab the killer. A fingerprint left at the Kingston crime scene matched an old arrest record in Ellenville. From there it was easy to locate Mac Gardner. Lived in Liberty with his wife and daughter. He was a truck driver for a commercial bakery that supplied bagels, bread, and other baked goods to half the hotels in the region." Dad sighed. "I remember meeting Jimmy in a diner the day we went to interview Mac's wife like it was yesterday."

"Yeah? What made that so memorable?"

"It was the day after the Apollo 11 moon landing and there was just this sense of promise and progress in the air. Like the world was a better place." Dad guffawed. "And that son-of-a-bitch ruined it."

DETECTIVE WILL FORD

July 21, 1969

I was nearing the bottom of my mug when my partner, Detective Jimmy Tillman, finally walked through the door.

Jimmy had asked me to meet him at the Monticello Diner for a quick cup of joe before heading over to Liberty to interview Mac Gardner's wife.

"Watch the moon walk last night?" Jimmy asked as he slid into the booth. Although, it was more like a squeeze given the size of his protruding beer belly.

"Yeah. That was some—"

Gladys appeared before I had a chance to say anything further about it. "Hey darlin', whatcha having?"

Jimmy eyed the cup of coffee and Danish on my side of the table. "What he's having."

She tucked her pad into her apron pocket, slid her pencil above her ear, and sauntered away.

"She's got a shine for you."

"She's young enough to be my daughter." He coolly observed Gladys in the corner of the diner as she poured coffee into a mug from a glass carafe. "So, how's your daughter—Susie, right?"

I nodded. "Already reading. She's quite smart for her age. Gets that from Vera, not me." I felt a proud-papa grin erupt across my face—a reflex I still couldn't control like when the doctor smacks your knee with the little rubber hammer. "She begged me to watch the moon landing, so I let her stay up, but she fell asleep curled in my lap."

"And Vera?"

"I let her stay up too." I waited a beat, then added, "She crawled up into my lap later."

"Mr. Funny Man. Really, how's she doin'?"

"Now that Susie's in nursery school, she's clamoring to get a day job. She's looking into the open librarian position at the elementary school."

"Well, you got it made, Will. Gorgeous wife. Cute kid. Detective at twenty-eight. You want my advice? Don't fuck it up."

"Keen advice. I'll try not to forget it."

Gladys set the Danish and cup of coffee in front of Jimmy. "Anything else, gentlemen?"

"All set," Jimmy said, eyeing the pastry.

Gladys adjusted her bra strap. "Okay. Holler if you need me."

"What the hell does she see in me? I'm bald, grumpy, and paunchy," he said, patting his bowling-ball stomach.

"It's those baby-blue eyes. Maybe you remind her of Paul Newman."

"Speaking of blue eyes . . . Mac Gardner. Shit, it was like staring at a frozen tundra. I've never seen eyes so icy and intense." Jimmy shuddered. "You know me. Takes a lot to rattle my cage, but talking to that guy yesterday was unsettling. Especially knowing he's got a wife and three-year-old daughter at home." He shook his head. "And he said nothing about the makeup on his victims. Probably gonna need a top-notch headshrinker to get to the bottom of that business."

"Yeah, well, at least he's off the streets . . . thanks to you."

Jimmy slurped the last bit of coffee, reached into his trousers, then threw a few bills on the table. "On me."

One heck of a first case, *I thought, as I slid out of the booth to interview the wife of a psychopath.*

2

SATURDAY | AUGUST 17, 2019

DAD SAT across from Chief Eldridge. I stood, leaning against the closed office door.

"Go ahead. Tell him what you told me." I wanted Eldridge to hear the story directly from Dad. It was his case. His memory.

"Fifty years ago, I was the rookie detective in the department. My partner at the time was Jimmy Tillman."

"Yeah, I remember Jimmy," Eldridge said. "My first year was his last."

"Susan told me about the murder in the theater. I think you got a copycat, Cliff. Mac Gardner killed three young men, same MO as your director. Back then we didn't use the term *serial killer*, but that's what he was. But Mac committed suicide before the trial. So we never really learned what was behind the makeup business. We solved the *who* but never the *why*. Neither why he done it and why these victims."

"I think we should dig up the old files," I said. "See if something from that case is connected to this one."

Eldridge swiveled his head from me to Dad, then back to me. "So you think Adam Kincaid's murder is somehow connected to a string of 1969 murders. That was the summer of love, y'know."

"Sounds like it was the summer of death." I chortled.

"This isn't funny." Dad frowned. "Did you ever think that you're the one being targeted, Susan? Maybe someone knows you're my daughter and thinks this is some kind of twisted game—"

"Shit . . ." Eldridge cut in, squeezing his temples. "I hope you're wrong about that, Will."

"Look, Chief. I could really use Dad's help on this. In an unofficial capacity. Bring him the facts as we uncover them. See if we can't dislodge some memories."

Eldridge folded his arms against his chest. I knew him well enough to know he was calculating the pros and cons—and risks—of involving Dad.

He leaned forward and glared at Dad. "What else can you tell us about your case, Will?"

"I wish I could tell you more, but honestly, I'm pretty fuzzy on details. I was just learning the ropes but what stuck with me was the condition in which the victim was found. Because, I'll tell you, that was pretty memorable."

I pushed off from the wall and sat down next to Dad. "I'm going to call around to surrounding jurisdictions. See if there's been a similar murder."

Eldridge grunted. "For now, let's keep this between us and these four walls, okay? The press gets ahold of this and, well, y'know." He drummed his fingertips on the desk. "Susan, see if you can find the old evidence files or put Jack on it."

"Jack? I thought you just said to keep this between us and the four walls."

"Susan, whether you like it or not, he's your partner. I suggest you figure out a way to get back on track with him. Not sure why you got a bee in your bonnet." He held up his palm as I started to speak. "I don't want to hear. Just do it."

I GOT word that Jean Cranmore, the costume director who found Adam Kincaid, was waiting for me in the lobby. I had asked her to come to the precinct to give a formal statement. Jack was already in the lobby, casually chatting with her. He glanced at his watch, then back at me.

"Ready?" he asked.

It took every fiber of my being not to yank that watch off his wrist and fling it across the room.

We escorted Jean to the nicer of the two interrogation rooms. And by nicer, I meant less smelly. "Thank you for coming in this morning," I said to Jean.

"No problem, really, but is this necessary? I thought I answered all your questions yesterday."

"Standard operating procedure, that's all. Because you found Adam Kincaid, we need a formal written and verbal record of what you witnessed."

Jean proceeded to tell us exactly what she'd told me yesterday when I interviewed her in the gift shop, from the moment she entered the theater to when she laid eyes on the director, to running outside and dialing 9-1-1.

"You mentioned that you didn't notice Adam until *after* you gathered up the costumes that needed alterations. Why is that?"

Jean's gaze darted around the room a bit before settling on her clasped hands. After a few seconds, she looked up to address us. "Well, when I first got there, I did think it odd that the bed was moved to the dead center of the stage." She raised her hand to her neck and winced. "Oh dear, no pun intended."

"No worries. Humor helps us deal with situations like this," Jack said, presumably to put her at ease. "Then what happened?"

She lowered her hand back to her lap. "Well, after I retrieved what I needed, I thought, perhaps, a couple of actors must have been, um, goofing around and fell asleep on the bed. I knew Malcolm would be livid, so I thought it best to wake them up and tell them to skedaddle. It took just a few steps to see . . . to see"—she gulped, then sniffled—"that it was just one body. That it was Adam in that horrible state." She dabbed the corner of her eye with her knuckle. "Come to think of it, I probably would've seen that it was just Adam on that bed when I first arrived, but the ghost light was off."

Jack tilted his head. "The ghost light?"

"Yeah. It's that tall lamp with the exposed lightbulb near the rear of the stage. It's theater superstition that it be left on at night. A courtesy for the theater ghosts." Jean cracked a thin smile, then cleared her throat. "But there's a practical reason also. Actors' Equity requires a stage light on at all times, for safety reasons. The last person to leave the theater usually turns it on."

"Interesting," Jack said. "We'll check the switch for fingerprints."

"I'm sure lots of people have touched it," Jean said. She bowed her head and murmured, "Including myself."

"We understand." I smiled reassuringly. The last thing I needed was our key witness clamming up or asking for a lawyer. "Are you sure you saw no one enter or exit the theater yesterday morning, or perhaps someone lurking about outdoors?"

Jean squeezed her eyes shut for a moment. "There was no one around." She raised her fingertips to her lips. "Although—and I don't know if this is important, but the makeup case on the floor next to the bed belongs to one of the actresses. Leslie Brattle."

The name rang a bell. She was one of the cast members Sally had flagged for further interrogation. Sally had the niggling feeling she was hiding something. *Cagey* is how she described Leslie. I've seen a lot of careless moves by criminals, but leaving her personal makeup case at the scene of a murder would earn her the dumbest-murderer-of-the-year award. The fingerprints alone would have revealed her as the owner of the case.

"And you know this how?" Jack asked.

"It's a very expensive kit—all the top brands—and she carries it around with her, afraid someone is going to steal her stuff. And honestly, I don't blame her. Everyone is nice enough, but you never know with some people." Jean leaned across the table and lowered her voice. "But I can't imagine in a million years that Leslie would do such a thing to Adam. Someone must have gotten ahold of her case."

The murder itself was meticulously executed. I doubted the perp would leave a key piece of evidence behind. Was it there to frame Leslie or was Leslie trying to make herself look innocent by deliberately leaving an item that would point directly to her so she can claim she was being framed? I pressed Jean for anything else she thought was out of the ordinary, but she couldn't think of anything specific.

As we escorted Jean back to the lobby of the precinct, my phone pinged.

I turned to Jack. "Mark Sheffield is ready for us. Autopsy time."

NO LONGER slathered in makeup, Adam Kincaid's face was quite angelic. Delicate blond eyelashes below white-blond eyebrows added to the effect. I could tell he was quite handsome, with defined cheekbones and a strong jawline. A white sheet, pulled up to his mid-torso, covered the rest of him.

With only coffee in my system, lightheadedness set in. I held a tissue over my nose and mouth in a futile attempt to block the stench of death, made worse by the chemical odors permeating the room. Rarely did a crime scene affect me like this. But when it came to viewing a dead body on a metal slab, I always felt two minutes away from barfing up whatever I last ate. On a scale of one to ten (with one looking like our victim was merely asleep and ten being a victim who was viciously attacked), we were in three-to-four territory. That helped keep my roiling stomach at bay.

I glanced at Jack. He stood still, unbothered. Composed and casual as if we were merely waiting for a table at a restaurant. I waited for him to make some snide comment about my tissue, but he just smiled politely at me and nodded.

Mark cleared his throat. "As suspected, asphyxiation by pillow." He pulled down the overhead lamp and directed it at Kincaid's mouth. "Subcutaneous contusions around the nose and mouth as well as fibers from the pillow found in his nasal cavity. And according to the lab report, the DNA on the pillowcase is a match to our victim."

"Anybody else's DNA on the pillow or pillowcase?" I asked, which reminded me to check with the lab regarding DNA on the necklace. I'm sure I would have heard from my contact there if the results came back, but it never hurt to light a fire under those guys.

"Just the victim's DNA," Mark replied.

"So new pillow and pillowcase?"

"Would seem so." Mark turned Adam's palm skyward. The letter "S" was inked on his palm. "It's faint, probably written with a ballpoint pen. Adam could have done this himself. Or maybe it's a message from the unsub."

"Interesting," Jack said.

I leaned over, lowering my tissue slightly to get a better look, and immediately regretted doing so. I clamped the tissue back over my nose and mouth, then backed up. I made a mental note to ask Dad if he recalls any letters written on the palms of the 1969 victims.

Mark turned Adam's palm downward. "Tox panel came back clean. But I know why he didn't put up much of a fight." Mark turned to his assistant. "Wayne, can you help me?" Together they pulled the body toward them, revealing Kincaid's back. "A nonlethal blow to the back of his head—here, behind the right ear— knocked him out cold. It appears to be a cylindrical blunt object, like a baton. The measurements and photographs will be in the final autopsy report."

"So it would have taken a strong person to deliver the blow," Jack said.

"Not to mention move him and lift him onto the bed," Mark said, gently lowering the corpse back to a prone position.

Jack raised an eyebrow. "Or multiple people working together."

SHANA LOWRY answered the door in her bathrobe. A silky coral number that just, and I mean just, covered her derriere. I glanced at Jack, whose eyes were darting left and right, trying his darnedest not to give her the once-over. Shana batted her fake eyelashes at Jack in a blatant attempt to capture his full attention.

Malcolm Slater suddenly appeared behind her. "For Christ's sakes Shana, get dressed."

Shana turned on her heel and fluttered her fingers. "Be right back," she said coyly.

Jack lowered his gaze briefly before Malcolm stepped sideways, deliberately blocking his view.

"Thought you might want to chat here, as opposed to down at the station," I said.

He swung open the door. "This is a freaking nightmare. I got the board of directors calling me, the sponsors, the ticket holders, the cast, the crew. The goddamn media. I need that theater cleaned up and cleared out ASAP."

"Your director was murdered last night," Jack said, with a whiff of hostility. "The theater is an active crime scene. And all you can think about is your show?"

I cleared my throat in an attempt to defuse the tense atmosphere. "Mr. Slater, I'm not going to make any promises, but we should be done by end of day tomorrow. However, you'll have to arrange for cleanup. And, if you're worried about the cost, I believe your insurance company will cover it. Depends on your insurance, of course." I glanced up at the darkening skies. "Can we please come in?"

Malcolm backed up, giving us just enough space to enter. "Follow me. And close the door behind you," he said gruffly.

As we followed Malcolm down a rather long hallway, we passed an identical set of the cast and crew photographs I had spied at the theater. Jack stopped in front of *Murder on the Orient Express*, eyeing the photo briefly before falling back in line behind me.

I expected to see a living room adorned with awards and accolades, hanging guitars and other musical paraphernalia, but it was rather mundane, a mix of midcentury pieces and modern touches. Bland artwork on white walls. The entire space devoid of any character or charm.

He stopped abruptly and spun around. "Are you going to tell me what the hell happened?"

Before I could answer, Shana waltzed in and plopped down on the oatmeal couch. Sally had told me she'd just turned twenty-eight. A Barbie doll came to mind. Platinum-blond hair cascaded down her back, culminating in perfectly twirled curls. Adroitly applied black eyeliner accentuated her green saucer-shaped eyes. She wore a simple blue-and-white gingham dress, giving off a Dorothy of Kansas vibe. Her ten-minute transformation from the seductress we met at the door to the ingenue splayed out on the sofa was quite impressive.

She raised her hand to her heart and ran her fire-engine-red fingernails across her collarbone. "I've been shaking all night." Her voice quivered for maximum effect. Either she was doing her best Katherine Hepburn impersonation or she was genuinely frightened. And the frustrating thing was, I couldn't get a read on her. After a beat, she continued: "So terrible, what happened to Adam. Do you have any idea who could have done this?"

"We're still in the early stages of the investigation," I replied. "Right now we're interviewing everyone associated with the theater. Not as suspects. Just to get background. And to rule people out. Standard procedure."

"So, like, you want our DNA?" Shana withdrew her hand from her collarbone and ran her palms along the lap of her dress, from her upper thighs to her knees and back again.

"Well, yes, but at this point it's voluntary. I can take a swab now or you can come down to the station. We'll also need your fingerprints." I noted their concerned expression, and added, "At this point, it's strictly for elimination. We expect your fingerprints will be found at the scene. Our goal is to find a fingerprint of someone who did not have access to the stage and backstage area. It will simply make our jobs easier by having everyone's prints on file."

Shana glanced at her perfectly manicured fingernails.

"I have a mobile scanner with me—no need for ink," I said.

Malcolm and Shana exchanged quick glances.

"Fine. Let's do it and get it over with," Malcolm said.

"I . . . I'd like to wait. Um, talk to my dad's lawyer. If that's okay?"

"Sure." I reached into my backpack and pulled out one swab kit and the mobile scanner. After collecting Malcolm's saliva and scanning his fingertips, I sat back down and put the next question to both of them. "What we need to know is where you two were last night between the time tech rehearsal ended at one a.m. and nine o'clock Friday morning."

"Our alibis?" Malcolm asked. "You think one of us had something to do with this? First of all, Shana was in Manhattan Thursday night . . . with the cast and crew of *A Walk on the Moon*. I put everyone up at the Elevate Hotel, and I booked Shana a private suite. She took a car service back up here last night to be with me during this ordeal."

I turned to Shana. "Is that so? Because according to your cast-mates, you weren't among them."

Malcolm's eyebrows inched closer to each other. His stoic expression morphed to confusion as it dawned on him that she might not have been totally forthcoming about her whereabouts Thursday night.

"If you weren't in the city, where were you?" I continued.

Not so subtly, Malcolm inched away from Shana.

"I can explain." The last word came out as a squeak. "I wasn't feeling well and I didn't want Malcolm to worry." She glanced at Malcolm, whose face was pinched in controlled anger. "So, I asked Claudette—"

"Claudette?" Jack asked.

"Claudette is one of the lead actresses in the musicals—I asked her if I could stay in her Smallwood bungalow for the night, and she gave me her key." Her eyelashes fluttered as she twisted away from Malcolm. "And . . . and Malcolm thinks it's important I hang around with everyone, and I didn't want him to know that I bagged out."

I waited for an outburst from Malcolm, but he sat absolutely still, his eyebrows knitted in malice.

"So, you were alone Thursday night into Friday morning? With no one to corroborate your story?" Jack asked.

Shana squinted at Jack as she lifted the back of her hand to her forehead. "If by 'story' you mean made-up, that's just not so. It's what I did." Her body and voice morphed from ingenue to that of distressed damsel as those words tumbled from her pouty lips.

Maybe it was her dramatic affectation, but I got the sense Shana was hiding something. I wanted to ask her about the rumor regarding her relationship with Adam Kincaid, but thought better of accusing her of infidelity in front of her clearly agitated boyfriend. Besides, without evidence to prove the dalliance, we could be opening a can of worms that we had no business prying open—at least for now. That conversation would be better left to when we could chat with them separately. Today was just preliminary. Get their alibis, suss out their perception of what happened.

But Jack didn't give it a second thought. He forged right ahead. "How would you describe your relationship with Adam Kincaid?"

I quickly tried to soften the insinuation. "In other words, my partner would like to know, how the two of you got on with Adam." I turned to Malcolm. "Were you friends with him? Or was it just a business arrangement?"

"We weren't friends. Nathan Fowler, our production manager, brought him to my attention. I hired Adam because he's good—no, he's great—at what he does. He's a bit of a pain in the ass, some might even say a prick, but we got along just fine. He's a perfectionist, demanding. He's also damn creative." He looked away for a moment, then back at me. "Was. He was all those things."

"I didn't work with Adam," Shana said. "He was directing the plays I wasn't in. I would say we were friends. Got together for coffee or lunch once in a while." She shrugged her shoulders nonchalantly to emphasize what she was telling us was no big deal. It had the opposite effect.

"Can you think of any reason why someone would want him dead?" Jack asked.

Shana dropped her chin to her chest and shook her head.

Malcolm vigorously shook his. "I know he wasn't well-liked among the cast and crew, but kill him because he berated you or made you practice a scene over and over? No way. No fucking way. If that was the case, half the directors on Broadway would be murdered."

"I had a feeling something like this was going to happen," Shana said to Malcolm. "I heard the ghost light wasn't on last night." She turned to face me. "And Adam told me that George Zettler, the actor who plays Hercule Poirot, uttered the word"—she paused, then whispered—"*Macbeth* during rehearsal."

Jack and I looked at each other, and in unison, said, "So?"

Malcolm rolled his eyes. "It's bad luck to say that name in a theater if you're not rehearsing or performing the play. Instead, we call it The Scottish Play."

"Adam made George go through the ritual of reversing the curse," Shana said.

"Ritual?" I asked.

Shana sighed like she couldn't believe she had to explain this. "Adam sent George outside to spin around three times, spit over his shoulder, and then knock on the front door to be let back in."

That sounded humiliating. "Was he upset at having to do that?"

"Not at all. It has to be done," Shana exclaimed. "Otherwise bad stuff will happen." She scrunched her face. "Oh dear, maybe he didn't do it right."

"Let's table the supernatural for now," I said. "Mr. Slater, we haven't yet established where you were Thursday night into Friday morning."

He let out a puff of air, clearly signaling that he thought this interrogation was beneath him and a total waste of his time. "I stopped in during tech rehearsal, watched for about an hour. Left sometime around midnight. I'm pretty sure Ricky—I told you about him, our maintenance guy—saw me drive off. I spotted him smoking a cigarette near one of the picnic tables."

"So you came right back here and never left?" Jack asked.

"Yes. You want a play-by-play? I read a few emails that did not need my immediate attention, so I went to bed. That would've been around one o'clock. I woke at six, like I always do. I rode my stationary bike for forty-five minutes, showered, then settled into my home office. I reviewed a marketing plan for one of my newly signed bands. Then I answered a bunch of emails. At around ten fifteen, I got a call from Grant Holcomb, one of the actors, who informed me there was a police presence at the theater. I immediately jumped into my car and raced over there."

"You mentioned that several people have keys to the theater and you would get me a list," I said. "Do you have that?"

"Yeah. It's on my desk." Malcolm rolled his eyes, then launched himself from the sofa like he was doing me an enormous favor.

In his absence, we all sat silently. He returned holding up a sheet of paper.

"Here," he said, thrusting the paper at me. "The keys are DND keys, meaning they cannot be duplicated. They only work on the side door near the dormitory. I distribute them to four people in each troupe at the start of the season, and they are returned to me at the end of the season. So, a total of eight keys, plus Ricky's. Except for me, Ricky is the only one with a full set for all the doors."

"So, no key, no entry. If you want to get into the theater, you have to find a key holder to let you in?" Jack asked.

"Correct. We had several break-ins and thefts a few years ago. And then there was this time, before I issued DND keys, when an actor cut a copy of a key and gave it to a buddy of his, who took up residence in the storage room in the basement. For insurance reasons, and peace of mind, I decided to step up security by limiting the number of people who get a DND key. And if you're wondering about the keys held by the musical troupe, I confiscated them before they went to party in the city—the last thing I need is someone to get drunk and lose it. And up until Thursday night, my system worked. No thefts. No squatters. Hence, no need for security cameras."

I scanned the paper and folded it down the middle. I noted that Adam was one of the four key holders.

"You didn't tell me how Adam was killed," Malcolm said, rejoining Shana on the couch.

"Asphyxiation."

"He was strangled?"

"Suffocated," I replied. "And that's all I can say right now."

"I have a right to know what—"

Jack slapped his hands on his thighs, then rose. "Well, I think that's it for now." He swiveled his head toward me. "Unless Detective Ford has another question."

"One last question." I scrolled through my phone until I landed on the photograph of the stained glass peace sign necklace. I held it up. "Ever see this before?"

They leaned in closer. Then they glanced at each other.

"No," Malcolm said emphatically.

"I've never seen that," Shana scoffed. "Besides, I wouldn't be caught dead wearing a piece of costume jewelry."

"Well, then, all set," I said, rising. "If you think of anything, please be in touch."

"Sure." Malcolm glared at Shana, who was staring at her nails. He was visibly miffed. Although hard to tell if it was because she didn't join her castmates in Manhattan or that she lied to him about it, or perhaps it was because she wasn't fully cooperating with our request for DNA and fingerprints. Then he directed his ire toward us. "Whatever you need," he snapped. "I'll do whatever it takes to get that yellow tape off my property." He stood abruptly. "Shana, please show the detectives out." He turned on his heel and marched into his office.

Jackass.

I PEERED over the roof of Jack's Volvo. "What was that all about? Asking Shana about her relationship with Adam Kincaid?"

"I think it's important we know whether that rumor had any truth to it. Don't you?"

I got in and slammed the door. I waited until Jack buckled up. "Sure, but there's a time and place for that line of questioning. Let's run down the rumor, get more intel on the situation, then confront her, okay? We can't catch her in a lie if we don't yet know the truth."

"Fine. I get it." He sucked in his breath and tapped the steering wheel. "What next?"

"There's something I need to tell you."

"Yeah? What?"

I laid out what Dad had told me about the 1969 case.

"Holy hell. Why didn't you tell me earlier?"

I shrugged. "I needed to run it by Eldridge. And then we got busy interviewing. It's hush-hush for the time being."

Jack's knuckles whitened as he gripped the wheel even tighter. "What does your dad remember about the case?"

"Unfortunately, not much. But there are old case files we can read through, and they're stored at a local warehouse." I plugged the address into Jack's GPS, then filled him in on what Dad remembered about his case.

I could have sworn I saw his jaw twitch. "You should've told me, Susan."

He's right. I should have.

CLOSED-CASE EVIDENCE boxes and files were stored in two secure warehouses (unsolved cold case files remained in the basement of the precinct). Eldridge believed the old warehouse on Canter Road was where I would find what I was looking for, seeing that Dad's case predated 1985, when the new warehouse was built.

"This feels like a waste of time," Jack said as we pulled up in front of the warehouse. "Instead of researching some old case, I think our priority should be taking statements from cast and crew. Someone at that theater knows something."

"This will only take a few minutes." Dad's memory of the fifty-year-old case had faded like an aging Polaroid, and I was certain these files would provide some clarity. "Someone went through the trouble to reenact a fifty-year-old serial killer case and the more we know about it, the better armed we'll be when we investigate and interrogate. Besides, Sally set up all the interviews for tomorrow morning, so this is not a waste of time. It's a good use of our time."

Jack held up his hands in surrender.

We fast-walked across the small parking lot to the two-story warehouse. It was smaller than I expected, about fifteen hundred square feet per floor. I glanced up at the CCTV camera aimed at me from above the entrance, then unlocked the door.

The air inside was stale and musty. In-flight dust particles were illuminated by the shaft of sunlight coming through the one narrow window above the entranceway. A fine layer of dust had settled on everything—the metal shelving, the tops of cardboard boxes, the gunmetal file cabinets. A few cobwebs were suspended between boxes and evident in corners.

CCTV cameras were mounted on the ceiling. I walked up the first aisle, shelving on both sides of me. I peered at the markings on the boxes. "There doesn't seem to be any rhyme or reason to the filing system," I shouted, unaware of where Jack had gone.

He came up behind me. "Man, it's dusty in here," he said, raking his finger along a shelf.

"We're going to have to walk every aisle. The case number is sixteen eighty-two. If the database is correct, there are two boxes."

"Got it. I'll start on the other side and we'll meet in the middle."

I walked slowly up the aisle, eyeing each case number as I passed by. As I made my way down the second aisle, Jack yelled, "Found one of the boxes! Sixteen-eighty-two dash two!"

Turning the corner, I saw Jack pointing his flashlight toward a box on the top shelf. I grabbed the stepladder that was leaning against the back wall and set it up in front of the column of boxes. Once Jack got positioned at the top of the ladder, he shimmied the box out of its spot, kicking up just enough dust to make him wheeze.

Once the box was firmly in his grip, he leaned over. "Here you go."

I reached up and grabbed the box, careful not to breathe in the dust that clung to its top and sides. It was light—too light. As Jack folded the ladder, I lifted the lid.

"You might want to reopen the ladder," I said, peering into the box. "There's only one skinny file folder in here." I pulled a green folder out of the box. The only thing inside was a Kingston newspaper clipping dated June 8, 1969: a two-column article recounting bits and pieces of the second murder. The who, what, where—but scant on the details.

"That's it?" Jack asked, peering into the empty box.

"Afraid so."

We spent another half hour searching for the other box, but came up empty-handed.

When I stepped outside, my phone pinged. A message from Eldridge. I also noticed an email from the lab. I opened the email first, hoping it was the DNA results from the necklace. The good news: it was. The bad news: no traces of DNA on the necklace. Wiped clean. I relayed the news to Jack, then proceeded to read Eldridge's message out loud: "Tech guys downloaded data from Kincaid's laptop and phone. Thumb drive on your desk. I'm told there is a ton of shit on there. Be prepared to pull an all-nighter."

"Now we're getting somewhere," Jack said as we headed over to the car, seemingly excited to spend the night at the station.

"Let's hope Adam's killer sent him a threatening message," I said. Of course, it never, ever worked that way.

RAY WAS mid-whisk when I entered the kitchen. "Breakfast for dinner!" he exclaimed. "I'm making scrambled eggs, bacon, and English muffins. I can throw in two more."

"Sounds good," I replied, reaching for the glass of wine Ray had already poured for me.

"Sit your butt down there," he said, pointing the whisk at the barstool tucked under the island. "So, I see you still have the ring on. Guess you haven't changed your mind."

"Either that or you've resized it too tight and I can't pull it off," I said, fake-tugging it.

"Caught me dead to rights." He chuckled.

I smiled, then sighed.

Ray leaned over the island and gently squeezed my clenched fist. "Tough day at the office?"

"That's putting it mildly."

"Find anything on Adam's laptop or phone that sheds any light on his murder?" Ray asked as he sprinkled shredded cheese onto my eggs.

"No obvious smoking gun, but there's a lot to mine—emails, apps, text messages, and tons and tons of documents about plays and directing. Plus, the guy used Snapchat for texting, so we'll never recover those messages."

Ray plated my eggs, bacon, and toasted English muffin and set it in front of me. "It'll take us a while to dig through it all. Jack's still at it. I needed this dinner break." I so desperately wanted to tell him about Dad's old case, get his take, thoughts, theories. I fully understood Eldridge's desire to keep this piece of information on a need-to-know basis. The less people who know, the less likely to leak. It's not that I didn't trust Ray to keep it under his hat—he would—but not following orders would land me in the doghouse, or worse—off the case.

Besides, Ray had his hands full with a case that was going nowhere fast. A case that rankled him more than usual because it involved the murder of a young woman. Two weeks ago, a Sullivan County Community College student named Brandy Johnson was found in a shallow grave in the woods behind a bungalow colony. Ray had no solid leads, no obvious motive. All he knew was that a twenty-year-old woman sustained a fatal head injury—a single blow caused by a sharp object—and was haphazardly buried in the dirt. Ray was hoping Brandy's best friend, who was currently traipsing around Europe, could fill him in on what was going on in Brandy's life. But with this friend on another continent, his case remained at a standstill.

The doorbell rang. We both twisted our heads toward the sound.

"You expecting someone?" Ray asked.

"No, you?"

"I'll get it. You finish up your dinner."

I could hear muffled sounds at the door and a few moments later Ray reappeared with Dad in tow.

"Eggs?" Ray asked.

"I'm good. Had dinner a while ago."

"Beer?" Ray asked.

"Now, that I could go for," Dad replied. He pulled out the barstool next to mine and sat.

"So, what brings you around?" Ray asked, handing Dad the bottle.

"Nothing in particular. I was passing by . . . thought I'd give you a proper congratulations."

Ray chuckled. "Well, thanks Will, but why do I get the sense there's another motive for this pop in? You're not the only one with Spidey senses." Ray leaned across the island and grabbed my empty plate. "Does this have something to do with your visit to the station this morning? The one where the two of you and Eldridge met behind closed doors?"

Dad and I exchanged glances.

"I saw that!" Ray exclaimed. "You two are definitely up to something. Either of you care to spill the beans?"

"The beans need to remain in the can for just a while longer," Dad said.

I shifted slightly in my chair, mildly uncomfortable with keeping a secret from my soon-to-be husband. Of course, there were degrees of secrets. This was not on the magnitude of the secrets my mother harbored from my father, making me feel a tad better about keeping my lips sealed. "We're sorting out an oddity with the theater case, and Eldridge has sworn us to secrecy until we, well, sort it out."

Ray threw up his hands, palms out. "Fine, I get it." He turned to Dad, who was eyeing the open carton of eggs on the island. "You sure you don't want scrambled or fried eggs, Will?"

"Y'know, since you're insisting, sure. I like 'em sunny side up with a side of toast, if you got it."

I was itching to ask Dad if he knew anything about the missing case files. But it would have to wait until Ray finished cleaning up. Meanwhile, I watched Dad gleefully scarf down his eggs and bacon, washing it down with an IPA, and yakking about Horizon Meadows' new pickleball club.

DAD AND I settled in the living room after dinner while Ray headed upstairs to shower.

"Before you bring me up to speed with your case, I have to ask you about something." Dad paused and I immediately thought he might be having second thoughts about me getting married. "Have you spent any time with your mother lately?"

I hesitated, partly because I was caught a bit off guard by his question and partly because I had a bad feeling as to where this was going. "No, not really. Why?"

"Hmm. I'm probably wrong—well, I hope I'm wrong—but I think she's drinking again."

"What makes you think that?" I said, even though the thought had crossed my mind. There was something off about Mom, but I couldn't quite put my finger on it. Since returning one week ago from a one-week Alaskan cruise—a gift Dad and I chipped in on so she could escape her house while her kitchen was being renovated—she'd been a bit of a recluse, coming up with lame excuses not to get together. "*Headache. But nothing a few Advils can't fix.*" Or "*Knee acting up. Don't want to overexert myself.*" And this weird one: "*My tooth hurts. I can't talk right now.*"

"It's just that something happened the other day." Dad clicked his tongue against his teeth. "Never mind."

"You can't drop a bomb like that and then say 'never mind.' What happened?"

"We were supposed to meet for lunch the other day. But she never showed up. And when I went over to her house, she told me I had the dates wrong."

"Okay, so she mixed up the dates. Did you smell liquor on her breath? Was she slurring her words? Did she seem tipsy?"

"No. None of those things. But she got belligerent and accused me of gaslighting her. Which, if you remember, Susan, is how she would react when she was drinking."

"Let's not jump to conclusions. Maybe she's just jet-lagged from her trip."

"Yeah, I guess that could be it," Dad said with as little conviction as I'd felt when I suggested it.

"Tell you what. I'll check in with her tomorrow. Sort out what's going on. Okay?"

"Okay." Dad leaned against the cushions. "Now tell me what you found in the case file boxes."

I brought Dad up to speed on what Jack and I discovered in the warehouse. Well, actually what we didn't discover. Dad thought he might know where the missing case files ended up. He vaguely recalled a detective from Kingston requesting the evidence boxes for a book he was planning to write about the case. Sometime in the late eighties. Although that didn't explain why we found one box that merely contained a newspaper clipping of one of the three murders.

"Rules were a bit loosey-goosey back then. If the guy wanted the files, he probably took them home. The case was closed, the perp was dead, it wasn't like anyone thought we would ever need them again. Maybe someone consolidated the two boxes, and that one folder got stuck at the bottom of the box."

"Is it worth a trip to the Kingston PD . . . perhaps ask around if anyone knows anything about this guy who took the files?"

"If there's a chance we can recover them, then yes." Dad drummed his fingers on the cocktail table. He stood suddenly and started pacing. "I'm telling you there is a connection between my case and yours." He stopped and gazed intently at me. "I know it. I feel it. But I need those files to jog my memory."

"I got a question for you. Do you recall any letters written in pen or marker on the bodies?"

"Letters? Like alphabet letters?" Dad hung his head and scratched his forehead. "Can you be more specific?"

"It appears the letter *S* was written on Adam's palm."

Dad's eyes widened and his eyebrows sprung skyward. "Holy shit. Yeah, yeah. But not a letter. Numbers. Each victim had a number written on the palm of their hand. One, two, three. I have a feeling that what you saw wasn't an *S*, Susan. It was a five."

"If this is victim number five, then it stands to reason there has to be a number four."

"You would think."

"Sally searched ViCAP, the Violent Criminal Apprehension Program database, and didn't come across a murder with a similar signature. She's still digging around the internet." I pursed my lips as I puzzled this out. "How public was this numbering thing?"

"That I don't know. I mean, initially we kept a lot of information from the public. But after Gardner committed suicide, I have no idea who was privy to what." He ran his hand through his thick mane of gray hair. "Susan, we gotta get our hands on those files."

When he sat back down, Moxie moseyed over to him.

Probably sensing Dad's frustration and anxiety, she snuggled her muzzle into his palm. Dad ran his hand across her back, then petted her head. "Such a good—" He stopped mid-sentence and turned to me. "She had a dog."

"Who had a dog?"

"Sam Blackstone's wife. Mac Gardner's third victim. Her name was Helen." He tilted his head. "Helen. I'm pretty sure it was Helen. They had three kids, school-aged twins and a baby—I can't believe I just remembered all this." Dad smiled at Moxie, then scratched his chin. "I might not remember the details, but I sure as heck remember interviewing the victim's widow the day after her husband's murder. My partner, Jimmy, pretty much saved her kid's life."

I hit record on my phone. "Tell me what you remember."

DETECTIVE WILL FORD

July 6, 1969

Helen Blackstone took the hankie I offered. She thanked me, then dabbed the tears escaping the corners of her eyes. She lowered the hankie to below her nose and held it there.

Her eyes remained mostly downcast, although she occasionally looked up at me and my partner, Jimmy. A hasty glance, then her gaze shot back down toward her knees. An unidentifiable mutt with wiry fur and a long snout lay at her feet, unfazed.

Jimmy and I took turns asking her the typical questions. Did her husband have any enemies? Was he involved in any illegal activity? Was he meeting up with someone? And because she didn't report him missing—did he usually spend the night out? The answer to the first three: "Not that I know of." As for the last question, she replied, "Yes." All her answers muffled by the hankie.

"Can you elaborate, Mrs. Blackstone?" Jimmy asked. "Knowing his night habits will help us. What he did, where he went, who he met up with. That kind of thing."

Helen sucked in her breath and held it for a few seconds before releasing the trapped air into the dangling hankie. "He works—" She paused, pursed her lips, then wiped away a runaway tear. "He worked three shifts, breakfast, lunch, and dinner. We have no family nearby, so it's been hard taking care of the twins and the baby. The baby has colic and cries like the dickens at night. So sometimes he'd crash in one of the staff rooms at the hotel to get a good night's sleep. Honestly, I didn't blame him."

"He worked at the Lakeview, right?"

"Yes." She wiped her nose with the hankie. "Is that where Sam was found?"

"He was found in one of the staff rooms there, yes," I replied.

Jimmy leaned forward. "We'll need you to come with us to identify your husband's body."

"So it's possible it's not Sam?"

"It's just standard procedure," Jimmy explained.

"Where are your children?" I asked.

"Camp." She dropped the hankie to her chin and smiled. "They're twins, seven years old." She sucked in her breath again and held it a bit longer. "And the baby is sleeping."

As if on cue, the sound of gentle crying drifted in from another room. "Elizabeth," she whispered. "She's not a very long napper." Helen balled up the hankie and stuffed it into her jeans pocket. "Excuse me," she said, rising. "I'll be right back." As she stood, the mangy dog rose and followed her.

I watched this willow of a woman shuffle across the room in a ratty old terrycloth bathrobe, the sash cinched tight around her waist. For a woman who recently gave birth, she was awfully thin. Even her face had a sunken quality about it. Her mousy brown hair, straight as a curtain, was draped down her back to the waistband of her jeans.

Helen reemerged moments later with a baby in her arms. She suddenly swooned.

Jimmy leaped up, stretched out his arms, and caught the baby as Helen melted to the floor.

How in the heck is this woman going to manage raising three kids by herself? *Probably best not to think about that.*

3

I TEXTED my mother to let her know I would be stopping by around noon. The trip to Kingston would have to wait until tomorrow—perhaps even the following day—depending on how soon we could wrap up the local interviews with members of the cast and crew. It was purely voluntary at this point, but everyone Sally contacted was willing to be questioned.

Jack and I chose a well-lit room in the basement of the theater to hold our interviews—a recreation room replete with a billiards table, Ping-Pong table, a couple of old couches, and a folding card table with four gunmetal chairs. Board games, books, and boxes of poker chips were stacked haphazardly on a rickety wood shelf along the back wall. The basement also housed five dressing rooms, two bathrooms, a prop room, and a storage room. All of these rooms had been thoroughly searched for Adam's clothes, as well as the weapon purportedly used to knock him out.

We walked away empty-handed on both fronts.

The strategy was to probe our subjects gently. Get everyone to relax and perhaps let slip some personal grievance . . . or rat out one of their castmates. Mainly, the key here was elimination. Narrow down the suspect pool. The specificity of the crime—how it was carried out—pointed to a person who had nothing to do with this theater troupe—a copycat killer with intimate knowledge of the 1969 murders. But, wouldn't a copycat killer have picked an easier location—such as a hotel room or someone's bedroom? Why go through all this trouble? This victim. This location. This was deliberate. This was meant to send a message.

According to multiple witnesses, Adam left the theater soon after tech rehearsal ended. He must have been lured back here. Which meant he might have known his killer.

With the exception of Shana Lowry, the entire cast and crew of *A Walk on the Moon: The Musical* were alibied out—all in Manhattan on the night of the murder. They were all due to arrive back tomorrow on their chartered bus to start rehearsals on their next and final show of the 2019 summer season, *Little Shop of Horrors*.

That left the cast and crew of *Murder on the Orient Express*. First up would be those who had keys to the theater. According to Malcolm, Ricky Saunders was the only other person besides himself with a full set of keys (front door, two side doors, back door), while each of the other key holders had a key to only the side door nearest the dormitory.

Eventually, all members of cast and crew would be interviewed, our main goal being to ascertain if anyone had a beef with Adam Kincaid—or knew someone who did. We would also have to dance around the question of what they knew about the 1969 serial murders. Perhaps find someone who was fascinated with true crime or had some kind of connection to this area or that earlier case.

Sally had gotten in touch with the folks we wanted to chat with first to let them know they would receive a text from me when it was their turn. We positioned the table and chairs so that Jack and I were seated on one side, facing the door, while whoever we were interviewing would be sitting across from us, back to the door.

Nathan Fowler, the show's production manager, was up first. Jean Cranmore called him a stickler for details. The murder scene was as detailed as you can get. Right down to the way the pillow was positioned. Nathan appeared at the doorway, hesitant, as though seeking permission to enter. He wore round wire-frame glasses that he kept touching and adjusting. Was this a run-of-the-mill nervous habit or guilt-ridden jitters?

"You can take a seat," Jack said to Nathan, pointing at the metal chair.

The guy was the definition of average—average build, average height, average looks. He wore a lightweight tan turtleneck shirt and navy-blue blazer, giving him an air of pretentiousness. He cleared his throat and sniffed at the air several times as he pulled out the chair and sat. "Very dusty in here," he said as he pulled a folded handkerchief from his pocket and dabbed at his nose.

I thought I'd start off with an easy question, get him settled and comfortable. "What exactly does a production manager do?" Besides, I was curious.

"I work with the management team, technical crew, and designers to make sure the technical elements of a show are completed safely, on time, and on budget," he said in a rehearsed manner. Seemingly satisfied that he had given a full description of his duties, he leaned back in his chair and crossed his arms over this chest.

"This is a preliminary interview, Mr. Fowler," Jack began. "A number of people had access to the theater, and we need to start eliminating suspects so we can move forward in the right direction. Your cooperation here today is crucial to the investigation. We'll ask you a few standard questions, and then you can be on your way." Jack smiled in an attempt to soften the edges of his perfunctory speech.

Nathan reciprocated with a faint smile. He then pressed his index finger to his lips and tapped a few times. "Well, I'm not sure what I can tell you. I left the theater after tech rehearsal wrapped and went directly to bed. I know that's not much of an alibi, but it's the truth." His voice was high-pitched and nasal, a tonality that grated on my nerves.

"We're trying to understand how the killer might've gotten into the theater," I said. "You have a key. Is it always in your possession?"

"Oh yes. Malcolm is a maniac when it comes to these keys." He pulled a keychain out of his pocket and placed it on the table. "Had special locks installed on each door. Read us the riot act about safeguarding the key. So, to answer your question, yes, this key is always in my possession." He scooped up the keychain and put it back in his pocket. He scoffed. "You'd think he was guarding Fort Knox."

"We understand from Malcolm that you were the one who recommended Adam to direct the play. Is that right?" Jack asked.

Nathan cocked his head to the side, then the other, releasing a crack. "Yes. I'd seen Adam's work and thought Malcolm would like to work with a brilliant up-and-coming director."

"How did Adam get on with the cast and crew?" I asked, then added, "In your opinion."

Nathan removed his glasses and pinched the top of his nose. "Adam was all business, if you know what I mean. Not one to hang out with the cast or crew. Kind of a loner. But man, he was good at what he did. Really creative." He gripped his left wrist with his right hand and rested his forearms on the table. "Got the best performances out of the actors. He was going places."

"And what about you? Did you get along with him?" Jack asked.

"Yeah. I mean we didn't pal around, but we got along just fine. If we got into an argument, it was related to the play." He shifted his gaze to Jack, then back to me, in a way that made me think he was assessing if we were buying what he was hawking. "Nothing personal."

"Did anyone have a personal beef with him?" I asked.

"With Adam?" Nathan tilted his head to the right. "Well, I don't know if 'beef' is the right word, but he had a few words with the one of the actresses last week. Leslie Brattle."

"Words?" I asked, remembering that it was Leslie Brattle's make-up slathered on Adam's face. She was not on the key list, but because of the makeup connection, she was a high-priority interview.

"He berated her performance in front of everyone. But she was having none of it and tore him a new one. Then he said to her, 'That's it, that's the fire I want to see.' He was trying to get a rise out of her to improve the scene. And she did give a great performance after that. But she stormed off the stage swearing under her breath and threatening to go to Malcolm if he ever did that again." He wiggled his glasses. "There was definitely a lot of tension between those two. But, would she kill him over it? I find that hard to believe." He leaned back with a smug look on his face, like he had aced a test. I also got the sense he was enjoying the attention. Probably something a producer doesn't get to experience when the actors always seem to be hogging the limelight.

"We would like to eliminate you as a suspect," Jack said. "To do that we need your fingerprints and a cheek swab."

"You're welcome to my fingerprints," he said, raising his arms and waving his fingers. "But I will not give you my DNA. I just . . . well, that just feels like an invasion of privacy."

He had every right to turn down our request. Unless he was under arrest, our hands were tied. Which reminded me . . .

"Do you have any ties to this area? Relatives who used to live around here?" I asked.

"Born and bred in Iowa. Why?"

"Just getting to know everyone, that's all," Jack said.

I held up my phone. "Do you recognize this necklace? Perhaps seen someone around here wearing it?"

Nathan leaned over and squinted. "No, and no."

"Is there anything else you can think of that might have a bearing on this case?" Jack asked.

Nathan drummed his fingers on his thigh, then abruptly stopped. "Not really. I mean, if you want my opinion, I don't think this has anything to do with us. For the most part, we are one big happy family with an occasional bout of dysfunction. But murder the director? That's just insane."

I SCANNED the list of key holders. All those entrusted with keys in the "musical" troupe had turned over their key to Malcolm upon boarding the charter bus to Manhattan. As for the "drama" troupe, the key holders were Adam Kincaid, our deceased director; Jean Cranmore, costume director; Nathan Fowler, production manager; and George Zettler, lead actor.

George Zettler was now in the hot seat. George played the role of Hercule Poirot. Typecast, for sure. He was short, rotund, and balding. No handlebar mustache though. That was applied prior to every performance.

"I was probably his only friend," George said before his butt landed on the chair. "Everyone thought he was an ass, but when you got to know him, he was an okay guy. Ambitious, for sure." He leaned forward and placed both hands, palms down, on the table. "He treated all the actors the same, didn't matter if you were Equity, non-Equity, an old pro, starting out—all he cared about was that you gave it your all every time you were on that stage." He leaned back and crossed his arms over his chest. "I guess some people had a problem with that."

"Tell us, Mr. Zettler—"

"George, please."

"George . . . we heard he made you do something that, well, I would find humiliating," I said.

"I'm not sure what you are referring to."

"Shana told us that you uttered the word *Mac* . . . um, The Scottish Play." I felt a bit silly swapping out the cursed word for the permissible one. But, maybe there was something to it. Besides, I didn't want to be sent outside to spin around and spit.

"Oh that." He laughed. "Adam was being a hard-ass and I yelled, 'For fuck sake, this isn't . . .' well, y'know. The minute the word came out of my mouth, I knew what I had to do. We all know the drill. I had no choice but to reverse the curse."

"Okay, let's assume you weren't holding a grudge for how you were treated and move on," Jack said, clearly not inclined to believe being forced to follow this ritual would be a motive for murder. "Can you please retrace for us your movements after tech rehearsal? We're trying to understand where everyone was that night."

"Sure. A few of us decided to hang around . . . kind of wired and not ready for bed; we thought we might run through a scene or two. I knew Ricky was waiting around for us to leave so he could lock up. So I went outside to look for him, figuring he was having a smoke. I found him puffing away near the entrance to the gift shop and told him he could leave and that I would lock up. Then I went back inside the theater. I think we were there for another forty-five minutes, one hour tops. When we were done, I, I . . . um . . . locked the side door, and we all retired to our rooms."

"When you say 'we,' who are you referring to?" I asked.

"Leslie Brattle and Grant Holcomb."

"So the three of you were the only ones in the theater after tech rehearsal?"

"There were some folks from the production crew striking the set, but they left before we did."

"Who turned on the ghost light when the three of you left?" I asked.

He quickly replied: "Grant."

"So the ghost light was on when you left the theater?"

"Yes, I'm sure of it. Grant joked about my slipup with The Scottish Play and made a big deal about turning on the ghost light. We're a superstitious lot, Detectives. That's why we say 'break a leg' instead of 'good luck.' And we never whistle in the theater."

"I always wondered about that," Jack said.

George chuckled. "That superstition started in the middle of the sixteen hundreds, when theatrical scenery began to fly. Sailors had extensive knowledge of ropes, rigging, and knots and were hired backstage as crew. Like on a ship, the sailors would communicate with each other through whistles to bring a backdrop in or out. So imagine if an actor onstage whistled! He could initiate a scene change or get knocked out by incoming scenery. Obviously, that's not a thing anymore. But old habits die hard."

"Well, you learn something new every day," I said flatly, hoping to put a lid on this superstition nonsense and move the interview along. I cleared my throat, and continued: "Did you see anyone outside the theater when you headed back to the dorm?"

"Not outside. But I did see Jean Cranmore, our costume director. She was sitting in the common area—sort of like a community living room on the second floor."

My head snapped to attention. Somebody was lying. George? Claiming he saw Jean? Or Jean? Claiming she went right to bed after tech rehearsal?

Jack glanced over at me, his eyebrows raised, probably also recalling Jean's insistence she called it a night. "What was she doing in there?"

George shrugged. "She was in a deep conversation with her niece—"

"Her niece?" I asked, trying to recall if Jean had mentioned having a relative in the play.

"Yeah, Samantha Cranmore," George said. "She's an apprentice with the lighting crew. Anyway, looked kinda private, so I didn't go in. I don't even think she saw me."

Why wouldn't Jean share this information? I wanted to wrap up this interview so we could have another go at Jean. I twirled my finger, hoping Jack would pick up on my signal of wanting to bring this interview to a close.

"Well, thank you for cooperation, George," Jack said. "Oh, and if you would be willing, your fingerprints and DNA will help us eliminate you from the suspect pool."

"Am I a suspect?"

"What Detective Tomelli means is that we expect to find your fingerprints, perhaps even your DNA around the theater, but need it to sort out whose fingerprints and DNA *shouldn't* be present."

"Um, okay. I have no problem with that."

"Appreciate that," I said. "Oh, and one more thing . . ." I held up my phone and turned it toward George. "Do you recognize this necklace? Perhaps seen someone around here wearing it?"

George leaned forward and shook his head. "Can't say that I have."

"Okay, then, if there's anything else you think might have a bearing on this case, please don't hesitate to get in touch. Any small detail that strikes you could be helpful."

"Of course. Of course." He hung his head. "Poor Jean. Finding Adam. That must have been awful. I hate to say it, but this production has been cursed, and I just hope it wasn't my fault."

ALTHOUGH WE didn't broach the subject, neither Nathan nor George voluntarily mentioned or even hinted at the Shana Lowry-Adam Kincaid affair rumor. I didn't want to be the one to bring it up—partly due to discretion, partly to see who would bring it up to us. So far, the only person to do so was Jean Cranmore. Jean, who lied to us about going directly to bed after tech rehearsal. Jean, who implicated Leslie Brattle. Jean, who just happened to find the body. Problem was,

Jean was maybe five foot three. She couldn't have weighed more than 115 pounds. If she'd had something to do with Adam's murder, she would have needed an accomplice.

But now we learned she had a niece on the crew. Something else she failed to mention.

Jack ran out to get coffee ahead of our interview with Ricky Saunders, the maintenance guy. I peeked at my phone and saw several texts from my daughter, Natalie. I started to tap out a response to let her know I would check out the "Wedding Ideas" Pinterest board she'd created, when a knock at the door diverted my attention. It was Ricky Saunders. He was ten minutes early.

"You can come in." I motioned to Ricky to take a seat.

Head down, shoulders slumped, Ricky shuffled in, barely lifting his feet off the floor. He took the seat across from me without saying a word.

My phone dinged with a message from Sally: *Interviewed Libby Wright, the prop mistress. The necklace was not a prop in any play. Nor does she recognize it.* I responded with a thumbs-up emoji, then slid my phone into my pocket.

"My partner will be right—"

Before I could finish the sentence, Jack burst into the room. He checked his watch. "Back in time, with seven to spare," he noted.

Ricky wiggled slightly in his chair, releasing stale cigarette smoke from his clothes. He looked to be in his mid to late fifties. Steel eyes, silver hair and goatee, ashen skin. Everything about this guy was gray. As he hunched over, his eyes flitted about the room. He bowed his head and picked at an inflamed cuticle on his right thumb, then he slowly looked up, although his eyes refused to meet ours. His aimed his gaze between our heads. I tried to discern if he was shy, nervous, or simply lacked social skills.

Jack cleared his throat. Ricky quickly looked his way, then shifted his attention back to his infected cuticle.

"Thank you for agreeing to chat with us," Jack began. "Detective Ford and I are interviewing the cast and crew in an effort to understand Adam Kincaid's movements the night he was murdered. Who saw what, that kind of thing. Help us build a time line."

Ricky nodded. "Mr. Slater wants everyone to cooperate."

Well, that explained everyone's acquiescence.

"When was the last time you saw Adam?" I asked.

"Thursday night. I watched a bit of the rehearsal from the back of the theater. Adam was sitting where the audience would sit to watch the show. He was by himself. Taking notes. When I seen enough, I went outside to have a smoke. One of the actors came out looking for me—the one with the fake mustache. Told me a few of them were going to hang around longer to rehearse and that he would lock up. So I took off. Went home."

"So, you're in charge of locking up, but Thursday night you did not?" I asked.

Ricky's leg jogged up and down. "Yeah, I'm supposed to lock up. But there have been times when rehearsal runs late and one of the other key holders offers to lock up for the night. Mr. Slater ain't keen on that. But yeah, sometimes it happens."

"And you headed home when Mr. Zettler told you he would lock up?"

Ricky knitted his brow. "Zettler?"

"George Zettler is the actor with the fake mustache," I clarified.

"Oh, okay. Yeah. He's the one who said he would lock up."

"And home is where?" Jack asked.

"Up the road a mile or so."

"You walked?"

"Motorcycle."

"Did you see anyone lurking about who would have no business being on the grounds that night?" I asked.

Ricky gnawed at his lower lip and gazed slightly upward. "No."

"You sure?" I asked, noting his hesitation.

"Yeah. I'm sure. I was just trying to remember, that's all."

Jack leaned back and smiled, signaling a softening of our questioning. Jack probably sensed, as I did, that accusing Ricky of not sticking around to lock up the theater might upend this inquiry. "What is it you do here? At the theater?"

Ricky's leg stopped shaking. "Mostly maintenance and repair. Some janitorial work. Some carpentry." He paused, scoping out the room. "The old church and rectory might look to be in great shape since the renovations, but it's got its issues . . . there's always something that needs fixing."

"So, you're around the property a lot?"

"Yeah. I guess so."

"Have you ever seen anyone having an argument with Adam?"

Ricky rocked slightly, then cracked his neck by tilting his head to the left, then the right. "Well, not *with* Adam. About Adam."

We waited for him to say more, but he merely stared ahead.

"Can you elaborate on that?" Jack said.

"Just something I overheard. Last Monday. It wasn't exactly an argument. One of the actors was talking with one of the actresses and they dropped Adam's name more than once. I didn't hear much, but I did hear the word *douchebag*." Ricky shrugged. "I mean, I didn't think anything of it. I still don't. I have a feeling many people thought that about Adam."

Jack leaned forward. "And you? Did you think that?"

"I have no feelings either way. They all come and go. I just have to put up with their shit for the summer."

"Which actress and actor called Adam a douchebag?" I asked.

He stroked his goatee and squinted. "The one with reddish hair. She has a big part in the play. And the tall Black guy. I don't know their names."

He'd just described Leslie Brattle and Grant Holcomb.

"How long you've been working here?" Jack asked.

"Since the beginning. Five, six years."

We gave him the same spiel about needing his fingerprints and DNA.

"I had nothing to do with this," he said emphatically.

"Malcolm would appreciate it if everyone cooperated to the fullest," I reminded him.

Ricky picked at his cuticle again. "Sure, okay."

"Have you ever seen this necklace around the theater? Or worn by someone?" I asked, holding up my phone.

"What is that? A peace sign? No, never seen that."

Jack slid his business card across the table. "In case you think of something."

Ricky pocketed the card. "Sure."

I WAS supposed to stop by my mother's house for lunch, but I had no intention of leaving the theater grounds without taking another crack at Jean. I texted Mom to let her know I would stop by closer to one o'clock. She didn't reply. But she rarely does.

Jean Cranmore picked up on the first ring and agreed to meet me and Jack by the picnic table nearest the gift shop. "Be right down," she said.

The sun was darting in and out of fluffy clouds. Jack planted himself on the edge of the bench seat. I paced around the area, hoping the movement would quell the growls emanating from my empty stomach. Five minutes turned into ten.

"Here she comes," Jack said.

I twisted around and spotted Jean exiting the dormitory. She waved with both hands, then broke into a fast walk and hurried toward us.

"Sorry," she said, slightly out of breath. "I had just gotten out of the shower when you called." She pointed at her wet hair as proof.

Jean and I sat down on the same side of the picnic table, facing Jack, making this tête-à-tête feel more likely a friendly chat than an interrogation. Intentionally engineered on my part.

I began, "We've been interviewing a few members of the cast and crew to help us understand where everyone was the night of the murder. Making sure we're getting accurate accounts. Details matter in a case like this." I noted her expression remained neutral—no alarm at possibly being caught in a lie. "Now, you told us you went straight to bed after leaving the theater Thursday night. Is that correct?"

She nodded, albeit hesitantly. "Yes." The sun slipped behind a huge cloud, and the temperature dropped a few degrees. Her shoulders collapsed inward and she shivered slightly as she wrapped her cardigan tightly around her torso.

"Someone saw you in the community room on the second floor with your niece at around two in the morning. So, perhaps you didn't go right to bed?" I said.

Jean drew her shoulders back and sat up a little straighter. "I did. I did go straight to bed. But, yes, I got up to meet Samantha in the community room. She rang me. She was upset. Wanted to talk to me." She blinked a few times, then cleared her throat. "It had nothing to do with Adam, if that's what you're thinking."

"After you had this chat with your niece, did the two of you go back to your rooms?" Jack asked.

"I did."

"And your niece? Did she go straight to bed?" I prodded.

Jean inhaled as she sucked in her lips. Then she slowly exhaled. "Samantha needed to clear her head. She often walks the grounds at night. She's on an antidepressant that causes insomnia." She shifted her gaze from me to Jack, then back to me. "I asked her if she saw something suspicious that night, and she said no."

"You do realize that not coming forward about this benefits no one," I said. "It only makes you and your niece look suspicious."

Jean ground the toe of her sandal into the dirt. "I know. I'm sorry. I was just trying to keep her out of it."

"You said Samantha was upset. What exactly was she upset about?"

Jean clapped her hand to her heart. "She had recently broken up with her boyfriend, and she still hasn't gotten over it. He was her first real boyfriend. Her first love. She just needed a sympathetic ear."

I was willing to accept that explanation, for now. "One final question: Is the key to the side door of the theater always in your possession?"

Just as Jean was about to answer, the sun emerged from behind a cloud. She shielded her eyes from the sudden bright light, and emphatically stated, "Always."

I wish I could've seen her face.

As she headed back to the dormitory, I turned to Jack. "I'll have Sally arrange a meeting with Samantha." I wasn't buying Jean's version of events.

I UNLOCKED Mom's front door and poked my head in. "Mom?" No answer.

Her car was in the driveway. I glanced at my watch: 1:05. Was she napping? Did she head out with a friend? I closed the door and bounded up the stairs. The door to my childhood bedroom was ajar. I peeked in. Empty.

Up until a few months ago it was occupied by Thomas Dillon, a student over at Sullivan County Community College who, in exchange for light housecleaning, got a roof over his head. Dad had cooked up this arrangement and it worked. Unfortunately (well, fortunately for Thomas), he graduated from the two-year program in May and moved to the city to finish his criminal justice degree at John Jay University. In his absence, I no longer had eyes and ears on Mom. Not that he spied for me, but at least I knew I could count on him if anything went awry. Mom had been sober eight months now. And it had done wonders for our relationship. Sure, we sniped at each other once in a while, but the underlying seething had abated. Now I was left wondering if the cruise was a good idea. Booze aplenty on those floating party barges. She swore up and down that she did not imbibe. But that's what alcoholics do. Lie. Deceive. Cover up.

I opened her bedroom door. Bed made. Thomas had showed her a YouTube clip of a Navy SEALs guy named Admiral William McRaven who'd given a speech called "Make Your Bed." A few days later the book arrived from Amazon. The gist, she had told me, was if you made your bed every morning, you will have accomplished the first task of the day, giving you a small sense of pride and encouraging you to do another task, and another, and another. There was another lesson from that speech she repeated whenever anyone complained: "Get over being a sugar cookie and keep moving forward." And when the recipient of that message raised an eyebrow in confusion, she'd follow up by explaining: "Life's not fair. Get over it."

I headed back downstairs. The house was tidy enough. Certainly not up to Thomas's standards, but Mom was trying. Something to be said for that. Felix the Cat slunk out from under the sofa and followed me as I went from room to room. I slipped into investigation mode, snooping around for evidence of drinking. Nothing outwardly obvious, but I wasn't in the mood to scrounge around in drawers and garbage pails.

Perhaps she was out on the back deck sucking a cigarette, a habit she claimed she would never abandon. One caveat: she promised not to smoke around her grandkids.

As I approached the kitchen entryway, I could see the gleam of the white subway tile that had replaced the decades-old flowered wallpaper. The mustard-colored oven, dishwasher, and refrigerator were gone, swapped out for stainless steel Frigidaire appliances. No kitchen table. A marble-look granite island in its place. Two barstools tucked under the overhang. A pile of envelopes and papers splayed out on the surface. I leafed through the opened mail and saw a few past-due bill notices.

I opened the refrigerator to see what might be lurking inside. Oddly, two bottles of milk, two cartons of eggs, two boxes of butter, two packages of swiss cheese, two packages of sliced turkey, and one loaf of bread.

No beer. No wine. No booze.

I peered over my shoulder at the glass slider. The vertical blinds were partially drawn, and I noticed that the lock was not engaged. I closed the refrigerator door and stepped out onto the deck. It took a moment for my eyes to adjust to the sunlight. Then I spotted her. Mom was in the shaded corner of the backyard kneeling near the edge of the fence, pulling out weeds.

"Mom!"

I must have startled her, because she pitched over slightly before catching and steadying herself. She reached for her cane and made use of it to get into a standing position.

"Jeez, Susan. You scared the bejesus out of me."

I hurried over to her. "Here, let me give you a hand." I hooked my arm around her arm to steady her on the uneven ground. My ulterior motive was to get close enough to smell her breath. Coffee and cigarettes, with a hint of peppermint. No detectable booze.

"I'm not an invalid, Susan," she said, wresting her arm away from me. "What brings you around?"

"I texted you. Thought we could grab a bite to eat. Or we can hang here. I can make us turkey-and-cheese sandwiches."

"Sure. Let's just sit out here for a bit." We settled on the deck chairs facing each other.

Mom reached into her windbreaker pocket and pulled out a pack of Marlboros. "Mind?"

I shrugged. Knew she would light up regardless of what I said. We sat quietly for a few minutes. "Can I ask you something, and you promise you won't get mad?"

Mom stitched her eyebrows together. She inhaled, waited a few beats, then blew out a line of smoke. "You're going to ask me if I'm drinking again."

"Can't put one past you." My attempt to say this jokingly landed a bit too harshly, prompting a sneer on Mom's face. I leaned forward in anticipation of her response. If she said no, would I believe her? If she said yes, how much sway did I really have in getting her back on the wagon? I wasn't even sure I could continue to be in her orbit if she chose to drink again.

I closed my eyes. I envisioned her answer as a torpedo headed my way. If the answer was *abstinence*, the torpedo safely veers away. If the answer was *drinking*, I feared I would suffer a direct hit. Our relationship obliterated.

"I don't see how my drinking is any of your business." Mom leaned back and waved the cigarette in circles. "But I haven't touched the stuff." Then added, with a smirk, "Scouts' honor."

I exhaled the breath I had been unconsciously holding. "Okay," I said somewhat tentatively. I wanted to believe her, and I had no evidence to the contrary. "So, what's with the past-due bills?"

"I misplaced my checkbook before I left on the cruise. I'll take care of it today."

"Why is there two of everything in the refrigerator?"

"Why do I feel like I'm being interrogated?" She pursed her lips, then let out a jaunty laugh. "It's actually a funny story. I went to the store to buy a loaf of bread, and when I got there, I reached into my pocket and pulled out a grocery list. Only that grocery list was from another time I shopped. So now I have two of everything. Well, except bread. Because that's the one thing I forgot to buy when I went shopping the first time around."

This story struck me as odd, not funny. Should I be amused? Concerned? Alarmed? Was this a sign of drinking? Of memory loss? The grocery-shopping snafu, the missed appointments, the misplaced checkbook, the overdue bills—what exactly was going on?

JACK WAS hunched over his desk when I returned from lunch.

"Eldridge wants a quick debrief," he said before my butt hit the chair.

"There isn't much to report," I countered. "A bunch of preliminary interviews with a handful of cast and crew? Everyone claims to have guarded their key as though their lives depended on it. No one liked the guy, but that's not enough to start handing out arrest warrants. There's a rumor of an affair gone sour. Two people called Adam a douchebag. We still have nothing on the connection to the 1969 murders, except the MO. I'm not throwing out theories. Not yet. We've got zero evidence right now that ties anyone associated with the theater to this murder." I stood up and walked over to our whiteboard. "All we know for sure is that Adam was knocked out, suffocated, and made to look like a drag queen sometime between two a.m. and nine a.m. Friday morning."

My phone rang. Caller unknown. I swiped to answer. "Detective Susan Ford."

When I hung up, I spun around to face Jack. "That was Jean's niece, Samantha. Turns out she did see something that night. Actually, someone." I paused, drawing out the punch line just enough to get a rise out of Jack.

"Are you going to tell me?"

I waited one beat longer, then said, "Shana. Shana Lowry."

Jack slammed his palm on his desk. "Now we're talkin'!" he yelled. "I think we got ourselves a prime suspect."

SAMANTHA CRANMORE had asked to meet us at the police station. Said she didn't want anyone from the theater knowing we talked with her. Which further piqued my interest in what she had to say. Now, an hour later, I led her into a room in the precinct that looked more like a den than an interrogation room. A less intimidating space to make witnesses feel more comfortable. The idea was to lull someone into thinking they were a cooperating witness, not a suspect.

Samantha tucked herself into the corner of one of the love seats. She was about my height, five seven, but bone thin. As Mom would say, a stiff wind would blow her over. She twirled a lock of her stick-straight blond hair, which was parted down the middle with exacting precision. Jack and I sat facing her, both of us on the edge of our love seat, leaning slightly forward. Jack's elbows rested on his knees, his hands clasped. I reached into my right jacket pocket for my pen and notepad, then flipped it open to a clean page.

"To start off, can you please repeat what you said to me earlier, on the phone?"

She smoothed out her knee-length skirt, tugging slightly to cover her knees. "You have to understand . . . I need this apprenticeship. I didn't want to get involved. If Malcolm finds out that I ratted out his girlfriend, I'll be fired. I didn't even tell my aunt what I saw. She doesn't know. I . . . I'm sorry. I just figured you would quickly find who did this and I could stay out of it." She bit down hard on her lower lip, enough so that I thought she would draw blood. When she released her lip, she rubbed the indented area gently with her fingertip. "I was planning to call you before I heard from the officer who told me you wanted to speak with me. It was my aunt who insisted I call you—she didn't want you to think that I had anything to do with this . . . seeing that I was walking around that night and someone may have seen me."

"Okay. Well, you're here now," Jack said. "So why don't you just tell us what you saw?"

"It was dark. Moonless dark. And misty. I saw a figure near the gift shop, but I couldn't make out who it was . . . at first. Then the person activated their phone and the light illuminated her face." She swiped her index finger in the air, mimicking the action. "Shana's face."

"Did she see you?" I asked.

"No. I hung back. I had no intention of going up to her. We're not friends."

"Did you wonder what she was doing there?" I pressed.

"Yeah. But I thought perhaps she had gone to the tech rehearsal and was waiting for a ride home . . . or . . ." She did that thing with her lip again. A little less intense this time. "There was a rumor going around that she was sleeping with Adam. I thought maybe . . ."

We sat silently for a few seconds.

"Then what happened?" Jack asked, his impatience front and center.

I preferred to let witnesses tell their stories at their own pace. They mull, they ponder, they analyze, then they carefully choose their words. There's a lot you can read into from those carefully chosen words. As well as the words they choose not to use. Jack's eagerness messed with my interrogation style, and I couldn't help but wonder if we'd ever get used to each other.

Samantha scrunched her face in a way that led me to believe she was trying to recall the next sequence of events. "I started to walk away, back to the dormitory. When I got to the front door, I glanced over my shoulder and saw that someone had joined her. And before you ask, I have no idea who it was. The person was taller than Shana, but that's all I could make out. I had no reason to snoop, and honestly, I didn't care, so I just went back to my room."

A myriad of questions hit me all at once. *Was Shana with Adam? With an accomplice? Or did she have an innocent explanation for hanging around the theater grounds in the middle of the night with another person?*

"And what time was that?" Jack asked. Really? That was the first question that popped into his head. I was pretty sure Samantha did care and had an opinion to share.

Samantha scraped her top teeth along her bottom lip, but this time did not bite down. "I was back in my room at two forty. I know because I checked my socials and noted the time."

Before Jack had a chance to ask another softball question, I wanted to circle back to what she alluded to earlier. Press her a bit harder, hoping she could elaborate on the rumored affair.

"You said earlier there was a rumored affair between Adam and Shana. Can you tell us about that?"

Samantha shrugged, then sighed. "I don't know for sure. I've seen them huddle together and talk in hushed voices. But have I ever seen them steal glances or sneak away? Nope."

"And you're sure it wasn't Adam with Shana that night?"

"I honestly have no idea who she was there with. And even if she did meet up with Adam, there is one thing I feel fairly certain about when it comes to Shana. She would never risk her career by murdering someone, especially someone who could help her career." She shook her head. "No way."

I pulled out my phone. "Ever see this necklace?" I asked.

"No. But it's kinda cool. As you can see, I'm into nineteen sixties styles," she said running her hands down the sleeves of her peasant blouse. "Does it have something to do with the case?"

"We're not at liberty to say," I replied.

We escorted Samantha back out to the parking lot. Before parting ways, she begged us not to let anyone know that she had come forward with this information. We told her we would keep things on the down-low for now (which was advantageous to us as well), but depending on how the investigation played out, there was a possibility she would be called upon as a witness. Her response to that was a slight involuntary tic at the edge of her eyelash.

Jack and I watched her drive away.

"Thoughts?" he asked.

I gazed out past the parking lot and rubbed small circles into my forehead. I turned back to Jack. "Let's get those reports written up for Eldridge. Might help us sort out what we know so far. As for Shana, we need to arrange an interview with her—formally—tomorrow. At the station, this time. She's going to lawyer up, so let's make sure we're prepared and on the same page."

"Are you suggesting we are not on the same page?"

I smirked. "It's just a figure of speech, Jack. Lighten up."

Jack started to walk away, then spun back toward me. "I get the sense you're not happy with our partnership. I'm racking my brains here trying to figure out what I did to piss you off." He held up his hands, palms skyward. "Whatever it is, I can't fix it unless you tell me."

My issues with Jack were petty, at best. He hadn't done anything truly egregious. So he made a snide comment about my sweaty palms. So he opened a door for me. So he wants to drive all the time. So we have a different interrogation style. And yeah, he's a bit impatient. My knee-jerk reflex was to immediately assume Jack was purposely trying to undermine me or push my buttons (thanks, Mom!). Maybe he's genuinely concerned about my sweaty-hand condition. Maybe his parents taught him to open doors for women. Maybe he feels safer driving his own car because he was once an accident victim in the passenger seat of someone else's. Maybe his style of interrogation works for him.

I stared out toward the parking lot. "You did and said a few things that got under my skin. Like that crack about my sweaty palms and holding a gun." I turned to face Jack and caught that befuddled expression of someone trying to recall what he had said. "There were other little things, but—" My phone rang. I glanced at it quickly and tapped Dismiss.

"Do you need to get that?"

I shook my head. "Just my dad."

"Look, I get it. New kid in town. Flexing my muscles. You don't know me. I don't know you. Probably said and did a few things that didn't sit right with you. How about a reset?"

"I could go for a reset," I said cautiously.

"If I do something that gets your goat, just tell me. I can handle a little criticism." He waited a beat, then added, "Emphasis on the word *little*."

"Tell you what: How about coming over to my house tomorrow evening? Beer. Wine. Or if you prefer, something harder. No cop talk. I'm sure Ray will be up for it."

"I can go for that. Can I bring a date?"

Did he see my eyebrows jack up? "Sure. The more the merrier."

DAD HAD left me a voice mail message—he remembered something, but I also got the sense he was fishing for an update on the case.

He picked up on the first ring. "What's up?"

"I'm returning your call, Dad."

"Oh, yeah. I figured until you find those old case files, I can feed you bits and pieces of things I remember. Maybe it'll be relevant."

"Sure. You never know what'll help."

"I've been digging into the recesses of my brain to recall any conversations we had with Joanna Gardner, Mac's wife. And you know what? I remember that first encounter with her. The one I told you about, when Jimmy and I met up at the diner and then went to see her." Dad paused, then said, "Maybe you can locate her. Maybe she remembers things about the case I don't . . . seeing that it was her husband that killed all those folks."

"Thanks Dad. I'll see what I can dig up on her." I sat down on the bench outside the precinct. "So, tell me about this encounter."

DETECTIVE WILL FORD

July 22, 1969

J oanna Gardner sat very still at the edge of a plaid sofa. *The room was dark, the curtains drawn. The air musty. I squinted to get my bearings. A small lamp with a dim bulb on a side table offered the only light. A toddler, clad only in a diaper, stood in a playpen making cooing noises. I couldn't tell if this cherubic child, with soft blond curls and big blue eyes, was a boy or a girl until I spied a pink blanket stuffed into one of the corners.*

Jimmy sat on the matching plaid chair across from Joanna.

"May I?" I asked, pointing to the vacant space on the sofa.

Joanna nodded and scooted over slightly.

I noted how petite and pale she was. The kind of pale that made you think she hadn't been outside in ages. She was twenty-four but could have easily been mistaken for someone in her midthirties. The dark bags beneath her brown eyes protruded like soft, puffy cocoons. Her pixie-cut hair was oily and stuck to the edges of her face. Faded pockmarks on her cheeks and forehead suggested a once-severe acne problem.

"We are going to need a formal statement," Jimmy began. "So we'll need you to come down to the station." He smiled gently, sensing her reluctance.

Joanna's gaze drifted to the toddler. "What about Shirley? I don't have anyone to watch her," she drawled in a Southern accent.

"You can bring her," Jimmy said.

"I didn't know," she whispered. "You're not goin' to arrest me, are you?"

Jimmy gave her his best reassuring smile. "No. No. We just need a statement. That's all."

I shifted my body slightly toward Joanna. "Where are you from?"

"Highlands, North Carolina."

I removed a pencil from my shirt pocket. "You're a long ways from home," I said, flipping open my palm-sized notepad. "Do you have family down there? Someone you can contact?"

"My folks are dead." She rubbed her fingers along her protruding collarbone. "I ain't got no sisters or brothers. I heard about this area from a friend of mine who said there were tons of jobs at the hotels."

"So you work at one of the hotels?" Jimmy asked.

"I did. The Reingold. That's where I met Mac." She started to weep. "Sorry."

"No need to apologize," Jimmy said.

"Are you sure it's Mac who done this?"

"We are," I replied.

"Did he ever hurt you?" Jimmy asked.

She lowered her chin and shook her head. "Nothin' like that. He'd come home from work, play with Shirley, never complain about my cookin'. He didn't drink or cuss. He'd just make himself comfortable on that chair you're sittin' on and watch some television."

Jimmy shifted on the chair.

"Will they take my baby away?"

"They?" Jimmy asked.

"The authorities."

"We have no reason to think that."

"Some lady came by the other day. Said she wanted to make sure my baby was okay. Told me she would be stoppin' by once in a while to look around. She said it was too dark in here for a baby to thrive." She sucked in the stale air. "But, well, the bright light bothers me."

I scanned the tiny living room and squinted, trying to make out the contours of the space. A small table, pushed up against the far corner of the room, caught my eye.

"My work area," Joanna said, noticing where my attention had landed.

"Work area?" I asked.

A slight smile lit up her face. "I carve peace signs out of wood to make necklaces. I drive around to the hotels and sell them to staff and guests."

I side-eyed Jimmy. Was she somehow involved, or did Mac help himself to her necklaces?

Jimmy nodded. "We'll need to take those materials."

"Why?"

I decided not to inform her that her necklaces hung around the necks of her husband's victims. "Might be evidence." With less reassurance, I added, "We'll make sure you'll get it all back."

A single tear rolled down Joanna's check. She swatted it away.

"We'll need you to come down to the station with us for a formal statement," I said, tucking my pad and pencil back into my shirt pocket. "Can you do that now?"

Without warning, the toddler let out a bloodcurdling scream.

I glanced over at Joanna, slouched in her chair, head down, ignoring her daughter's cries. Four broken families. Four families destroyed by a monster of a man. This woman's husband.

4

MONDAY | AUGUST 19, 2019

SHANA'S LAWYER could have starred in a Woody Allen biopic. A nebbishy-looking man, five six, maybe. Circa *Annie Hall* age, forty or so. Wispy hair, haphazardly combed over right to left: destined for baldness.

Jack and I took our seats across from Shana and "Woody."

He cleared his throat. "Dirk Benson," he said, then added, "Representing Shana Lowry."

The nasal Brooklyn accent nailed the comparison. But his name, which had more of a cowboy sensibility, didn't quite match the character before me. Shana sat statue still, her back ramrod straight, her shoulders back. Her fingers clasped and resting on the table. The only movement, an occasional blink. Dirk Benson, on the other hand, was quite fidgety. He kept rearranging the pen and paper on the table in front of him. His right leg jiggled under the table.

After formal introductions—names, date, time—we got down to business.

"We have a witness who places you on the grounds of the theater at two thirty a.m. the night of the murder," I said. "Care to explain?"

Dirk held up his hand. "Unless you are charging my client, she will exercise her right to remain silent. Are you charging my client?"

"Mr. Benson, Ms. Lowry," I began, shifting my head to each as I addressed them. "We are gathering information to solve a heinous crime. I am talking to you as a potential witness to this crime, as you were in the vicinity the night of the murder. You are here because there are rumors about your relationship with the deceased, which might have a bearing on this—"

"What? What rumors?" Shana said slowly.

Dirk held up his hand again. "Shana," he said sternly. "We agreed that—"

Shana cut him off. "What rumors?" This time the words came out sharp and clipped.

"Rumors of an affair," Jack replied.

"Between me and Adam?" she scoffed. "That's absurd."

Dirk's leg stopped shaking. "Shana!"

"I need to defend myself, Dirk. I wasn't having an affair with Adam, and I refuse to let that accusation cloud this investigation."

"We'll get to that in a minute," I interjected. "We know you were on the grounds of the theater at two thirty a.m. We are not accusing you of murder, Ms. Lowry." I wanted to add the word *yet* but thought better of it. "But you must admit, that's a bit strange, seeing you were not in that play and you were supposed to be in the city with your fellow castmates. We simply want to know what you were doing there and if you ran into anyone else on the grounds at that time. Perhaps you saw a car in the parking lot you didn't recognize. Or perhaps a stranger walking about."

Shana glanced sideways at Dirk.

Dirk rolled his eyes and shook his head. "Tell them exactly what you told me. Nothing more, nothing less. Got it?"

Shana nodded. "I've been having trouble sleeping lately. Adam's been prepping me for an audition. A Broadway show. Maybe that's why people thought we were having an affair. I didn't want anyone to know, not even Malcolm, because if I got the part, I'd have to leave before the summer season ended. So, yeah, we probably snuck around a bit. Anyway, like I said, I couldn't sleep. So I called Chase, and he—"

"Chase?" Jack asked.

Shana ran her tongue over her lips and flashed a flirty smile at Jack. "Chase Dunham. He's the manager of the gift shop."

I scribbled down that name. "Go on." Shana glared at me, the flirty smile gone.

"Chase is someone who people go to for, y'know—" She pressed her lips together. "Pharmaceuticals."

I jerked my head slightly at her admission, but managed to keep my expression neutral. In my experience, the less I reacted to unexpected revelations, the more people tended to spill. "So you needed, what? Sleeping pills?"

"Yes. The audition is in two days and if I don't get some solid nights of sleep it's going to affect my performance. Not to mention, worsen these bags under my eyes," she said, pointing to perfectly smooth skin.

Jack's right eyebrow shot up. "So you met this guy Chase in the middle of the night? This couldn't wait until the next day?"

Shana leaned forward toward Jack, wrapped her arms around herself, purposely creating more cleavage. "Chase was leaving the area for a few days. He was planning to visit his buddies on Nantucket. Some fishing excursion. Anyway, I knew he wouldn't be around after that night. He gets back on Wednesday."

"Why not just go to a doctor? Get a legal prescription?" Jack asked, doing his darndest to look anywhere but the space between her breasts.

"This is easier . . . and more discreet." She chortled. "Well, I thought it would be."

"Okay, so you went to meet Chase . . . in the middle of the night," I said. "Did you see anyone lurking about? Any cars in the lot you didn't recognize?"

Shana chewed on the question for a bit. Was she tapping her memory or coming up with a lie? There are those in law enforcement who claim they can discern when someone is lying. Usually by a tell. A nose scratch. An eye flicker. Slight muscle movements. But a skilled liar will keep their tells in check. In my experience, it's what's said or not said that is more telling. Liars tend to hold back. Or deceive by omission. But even my methodology is far from foolproof—some liars prefer to embellish, believing a barrage of details makes their stories more convincing.

Or harder to disprove. Throw in the fact that Shana is an actress, and by the sound of it, a good one, I was fairly sure my lie detection skills had met their match.

"No," she finally said. "You mentioned that someone saw me. But, honestly, I didn't see anyone. Not even the person who claims to have seen me." She tapped her perfectly manicured finger on the table. "And who would that—"

"I think we're done here!" Dirk interrupted.

Jack ignored Dirk's outburst and faced Shana. "Seeing that you had a good working relationship with Adam, is there anything he might have told you that, in hindsight, might be relevant to his murder?"

"You mean like did he mention being fearful of someone?"

"Yeah. Or anything related to a secret or indiscretion in his life that might have gotten him in trouble." Jack flashed his own flirty smile. He was clearly leveraging his good looks to get her to open up. And I was (surprisingly) all for it.

Shana cocked her head to the left and stroked her collarbone, scraping her red fingernails along the ridge. "As far as I know, no one ever threatened him. At least not that he mentioned to me. As far as secrets are concerned, the only thing I can think of is that he was doing some genealogy research. He wanted to find his birth parents, but he didn't want his adoptive parents to know. But he had just started the process. And I think he was hesitant. At one point, he wasn't going to go through with it. Y'know . . . cold feet."

"I'm curious, Shana, do you have any ties to this area?" I asked.

Shana crumpled her face. "Ties? Like did I grow up here or vacation here?"

"Or have relatives who live around here?" I added.

"Um, no." Shana ran her fingers through her hair, then flipped up the ends to inspect them. When my daughter, Natalie, was a teenager, she did this split ends check whenever she wasn't completely forthcoming. I tucked that away as a potential tell. "I grew up on Long Island."

"Shana," Jack said gently. "You've been very candid and we appreciate that. As we explained when we spoke earlier, we would like to eliminate you as a suspect, but in order to do that we need your DNA and fingerprints. Perhaps you've given it some more thought, and you'd like to help us out here."

"I'm innocent," Shana offered. She glanced at her lawyer, then let out a puff of air.

Dirk shrugged. "Up to you, Shana. You are not compelled to do so without a warrant."

She thought for a minute, then said, "Sure, fine. I have nothing to hide."

"One last question," I began. "Do you know if Adam was a customer of Chase's?"

"Absolutely not. In fact, Adam didn't like me taking sleeping pills. We had a bit of a tiff over that. His best friend died of a drug overdose, and he's like a preachy, in-your-face antidrug crusader. He can get pretty worked up when talking about the *evil* of drugs." She air quoted *evil*.

"Was Chase dealing to anyone else in the cast?"

"I have no idea. You'll have to ask him that yourself."

Oh, that was definitely in the cards.

DRUGS. WHEN it came to motives, *drugs* invariably bubbled to the surface.

"Maybe Adam was going to report Chase," Jack said to Eldridge, "and Chase got wind of that."

"But why go through all the trouble to imitate the 1969 murders?" I said. "I think we should go to Nantucket and question Chase."

"You're not going anywhere," Eldridge shot back. "Let's do some legwork on this. The fact that he's on an island somewhere off the coast of Massachusetts works in our favor, Ford. Do another sweep of the gift shop. Look for anything that ties Chase to the murder or his drug dealings. Find out if anyone else is involved in his little pharma side hustle."

"Because the gift shop is on the premises, it was part of the original search," Jack said. "Nothing was found that aroused suspicion."

Eldridge squinted hard at Jack. "Doesn't hurt to look again, now, does it? Especially in light of this new information."

We nodded like admonished children sitting in the principal's office.

He grunted. "And what about Shana Lowry? Has she been read the riot act if she attempts to contact him?"

"Yes, sir. She's cooperating now," I said.

"Good. Good. I know you're focusing on the folks who have keys, but what about the rest of the cast and crew?"

"Sally conducted the preliminary interviews. They all claim to have gone to bed after rehearsal. I'll"—I glanced at Jack "—we'll be following up on that."

"Luckily, the play has a smaller cast of characters than the book," Jack said. He shifted his head back and forth between me and Eldridge. "What? I've been reading up on the adaptation by the playwright, Ken Ludwig. Just doing my homework."

Eldridge grunted. "I understand the crime scene tape came down this morning. I realize you had a lot of pressure to wrap it up from the powers that be."

"If we needed more time at the crime scene, that tape would still be up, sir. This case was not compromised in any way."

"Glad to hear it, Ford." Eldridge leaned back in his chair. "What's happening with the play? Has it been canceled?"

"No sooner than we cleared the scene, Malcolm Slater announced the show would be opening tonight," Jack said. "Got a cleaning crew in there immediately after we gave him the all-clear signal."

"Well, at least that means everyone is sticking around." Eldridge slapped his palms on the desk. "Go find out everything about Chase Dunham. Dismissed."

We hustled out of Eldridge's office and back to our side-by-side desks.

I turned to Jack with a smirk on my face. "Homework?"

"Yeah, well, I was curious, so did a little research on the differences between the book, the movie, and the stage adaptation."

I laughed. "Or . . . you're trying to impress me."

"Yeah, or that." If he rolled his eyes any harder, his eyeballs would've gotten stuck inside his forehead.

MALCOLM SLATER was waiting for us in front of the gift shop. He unlocked the front door and stood aside as Jack and I entered.

"Let me know when you're done so I can lock up," Malcolm said before turning and heading back to the theater.

A bell tinkled above our heads when we closed the door. The forensics team had swept through here the morning we found Adam's body and then again on Saturday when the autopsy revealed that Adam was bludgeoned before being suffocated, prompting us to once again search the grounds and buildings for a potential weapon. Nothing was found on that second search. Jack and I walked the aisles of the gift shop, hunting for anything that would tie Chase to the murder.

"We're going to need a warrant to search Chase's house and to confiscate his computer and phone," Jack said as he lifted and examined touristy tchotchkes off the shelves. "We should be able to get that with Shana's statement about his drug dealing."

"Eldridge is working on that," I said, eyeing an unaligned panel behind the cash register. I removed my phone from my back pocket and snapped a couple of pictures, then put on my latex gloves. I ran my fingers along the side of the panel and pushed gently. Out it popped. "Jack!"

"Find something?" he yelled from across the store.

"Yeah. Get over—"

Jack leaned over the counter. "Holy shit."

I took a few more photographs at various angles and distances. I reached into my backpack and grabbed a plastic baggie from my kit. Then I carefully lifted the foot-long leather blackjack and deposited it into the bag and sealed it. "Maybe our perp is into martial arts?"

He shrugged off my hunch. "Perhaps, but anyone can buy one of those batons online."

When we stepped outside, I spotted a woman with a cane limping through the parking lot. What the heck? My mother slowly made her way around the picnic tables toward us.

"I was told you were here," Mom said, catching her breath. "I need to speak with you."

I held up my phone. "You could've called."

"I guess. But I was out and about anyway, so—" Mom shifted her gaze and smiled at Jack. "You must be um, um—"

"Jack," Jack said.

"Jack. Right. I'm Vera. Susan's mom. Will told me Susan got a new partner. Susan tends to keep mum about these things," she said as though I wasn't standing there.

"Well, it's lovely to meet you, Vera."

Did Mom just bat her lashes?

"What's so important that you had to track me down?"

"Oh, yeah. That. I thought it would be important for you to know that I have a tangential connection to your case." I didn't know what surprised me more—Mom's use of the word *tangential* or that she had a connection to the case.

"And what would that be?"

"I was good friends with Shana's grandmother, Phyllis Lowry. She was a free spirit, that one. A real hippie. She begged me to go to Woodstock with her, but you were sick and I was stuck at home."

I glanced at Jack, whose cinched eyebrows led me to believe he was thinking the same thing I was. That Shana just got through telling us she had no ties to the area.

"Does Phyllis still live around here?"

"No. She moved to Long Island with her husband in the midseventies to raise their son, Brian. Shana's father."

That might explain Shana's answer. It was plausible that Shana had no idea her grandmother hailed from these parts. Or, as I suspected with her hair-grooming gesture, she was hiding something. But what, exactly? Her knowledge of the 1969 murders? Her relationship with Adam? Or what actually happened during that rendezvous with Chase?

"Phyllis called me." Mom raised her cane slightly and shook it. "She told me you're harassing Shana."

"What?"

"Shana complained to her father, and I guess it got to Phyllis. You can't possibly think Shana has anything to do with a murder? Phyllis says she's destined for stardom."

I turned to Jack. "Can you excuse us, please?"

"Nice to have met you, Vera," he said, then walked toward his car.

"Isn't he a dish?"

I ignored her remark. "Mom, you can't talk to anyone about this case, let alone the relatives of a person of interest. And you certainly can't tell me how to do my job."

"Don't get snippy with me, Susan. I'm not telling you how to do your job. I'm telling you that Shana's grandmother is concerned about her granddaughter's well-being."

I tamped down my growing anger. It wasn't my mother's fault that Phyllis got in touch with her. "Mom, I can't have you meddling in this case," I said, in the calmest voice I could muster. "Or any case, for that matter," I added, to put a fine point on it.

"I'm not meddling," she huffed. "I'm doing you a . . . a favor."

I opened my mouth, then snapped it shut, deciding to abdicate the last word on this subject for one reason: thanks to Mom's meddling, Shana was back in the spotlight.

AFTER DELIVERING the blackjack to the lab, Jack and I made our way back to the Monticello Playhouse to have a word with Leslie Brattle, the actress whose makeup was slathered on the face of our victim (and who Sally referred to as cagey when she initially interviewed her).

"What are your thoughts on what we found in the gift shop?" Jack said as we headed up the walkway to the residence building.

"I'm not jumping to conclusions. You know as well as I that the blackjack could have been planted. You can even say it was too easy to find. And I looked at the photos that were taken during the initial search. The panel was squared up with the adjoining panels—so definitely placed there after we did the initial sweep. We'll need to find out who has the key to the gift shop. We already know Slater does. I'm sure Chase Dunham has one."

Leslie Brattle had informed us that the dormitory building's main entrance door was left unlocked during the day and to just knock on her apartment door when we arrived. As an Equity actress, she resided in a private one-bedroom apartment on the first floor. Jack tapped three times with his knuckle.

The door swung open. In front of us stood an impeccably dressed woman in an emerald-green sleeveless blouse paired with flared white linen pants and gold strappy heels. A gold belt cinched snugly around her hips accentuated her tiny waist. "Come in." Leslie stepped aside. "I just brewed some coffee. Any takers?"

Jack eyed me as though seeking permission. "Sure," he said. "Just a bit of milk."

"That would be nice. Black, please."

"Make yourself comfy," Leslie said, pointing to a love seat positioned under the window. She busied herself at the kitchenette in the corner of the room—a single counter with a small stainless-steel sink, a twenty-inch electric range, an under-the-cabinet mounted microwave, a small Keurig machine, and a coffeemaker. She hummed softly to herself as she removed three mugs from the white cabinet and poured the coffee. She removed a container of milk from the under-the-counter mini refrigerator.

Sally has razor-sharp instincts, but there was nothing in this woman's demeanor that suggested caginess. Quite the opposite, actually. She was relaxed (maybe too relaxed?), warm, and inviting. Granted, she was an actress. And a beautiful one at that. Green, almond-shaped eyes, wavy auburn hair, soaring cheekbones. She also fit the description given by Ricky Saunders as the woman who called Adam a douchebag.

Leslie carried a mug in each hand and placed them on coasters in front of us. She hurried back to the kitchenette and filled her own mug. She then sat on the wingback chair across from us. She took a careful sip of her coffee, then settled back in her chair, striking a regal pose. Shoulders back. Head high. "Malcolm's accommodations are the best in the business," she said, then blew gently on her coffee before taking another dainty sip. "I mean, it's nothing fancy, but it's light-years better than other regional theaters. Of course, I'm in a room reserved for Equity actors. The upstairs rooms are . . . how should I put this . . . more primitive. The one annoying thing is the spotty cell-phone service."

Perhaps it was because she was exceedingly relaxed, I felt oddly anxious. Did I find her a bit intimidating? Yes. And that too could've been throwing me off balance. So I decided to start off with an ice-breaker, some casual chitchat, so I could settle my nerves and find my groove. "I understand you play the role of Mary Debenham, the governess of the Armstrong family."

"Yes. A wonderful part. Have you seen the play?"

"I've read the book and seen the movie," I replied. "The one where your part was played by Vanessa Redgrave."

"Why, yes." She smiled, then took a sip of her coffee. "I've been told I look like her."

I eyed her heart-shaped, diamond-encrusted pendant dangling from a delicate gold chain. "Beautiful necklace." I pulled out my phone and turned it toward Leslie. "By any chance, do you recognize this necklace?"

"If you're asking if that's mine, it is not."

"Have you seen it worn by someone else?"

"No, and to be honest, I'm not really sure how I can be of help." She waved her hand through the air. "I really don't know anything."

It's been my experience that when people say they don't know *anything*, they know *something*. "We're just trying to get a handle on everyone's whereabouts and movements on the night of the murder, after tech rehearsal," I said. "So, let's start there."

"Of course. George Zettler, the actor who plays Hercule Poirot, wanted to run through a scene that wasn't quite working well during rehearsal, so George, Grant, and I continued to rehearse after Adam called it a wrap."

"Grant Holcomb, the actor who plays Colonel Arbuthnot?" Jack asked. I knew Jack knew this, so I wondered if he was just showing off his newfound knowledge of the play.

Leslie nodded. "Yes. We rehearsed for just a little while longer and left together. There was no one in the theater. Well, no one I saw."

"And George locked the door?" I asked.

"He is one of the key holders. But, honestly, I can't remember if he locked the door behind us. I mean, I'm sure he did. But if you're asking me if I absolutely remember him doing so, that I can't recall." She brought her finger to her lip. "Come to think of it, Grant and I were walking and talking when we exited the theater. I guess I wasn't really paying attention to what George was doing."

"Did you see anyone lurking around the grounds when you headed back to your rooms?" Jack asked.

She tapped her chin. "No."

"We understand that you and Adam Kincaid didn't always see eye to eye." I said.

She snorted. "That's putting it mildly. I hate to speak ill of the dead, but he was psycho. Everyone will sing his praises as God's gift to the theater, but *please*, there are plenty of directors who are creative and exacting without being dickheads. There was something off and off-putting about him. He was definitely the kind of guy who could rub someone the wrong way."

"So you think Adam may have been targeted?" Jack asked.

"Lord, I hope so. I mean, I hope this isn't some random killing that puts the rest of us in danger. Maybe we each get offed like that other Agatha Christie story . . . *And Then There Were None*." Leslie took a sip of her coffee, then pulled a face. "Seems to have gotten lukewarm while I was talking." She plunked the mug on the coffee table; a little bit of coffee sloshed over the rim. "Anyway, the only person he treated with respect was Shana Lowry. But that was probably because of her relationship to Malcolm."

"We heard Shana and Adam got along quite well," Jack said.

Leslie rolled her eyes and leaned toward us. "I've heard the rumors, but that's all they were, gossip and innuendo."

"Well, we'll soon get to the bottom of that when we finish mining Adam's computer and phone," Jack said.

Leslie's shoulders caved in slightly as she shifted her gaze from Jack to her hands clasped on her thighs, then to me.

"So, have you found anything on Adam's computer that sheds light on his murder?"

"Not yet," I replied.

"I see." She adjusted her gold belt, which had shifted sideways.

"We have another matter we need to discuss with you," I said. "Your makeup case."

"Oh yes, that. I was meaning to talk to you about that. I don't want to accuse anyone associated with the theater, it's just, well, my very expensive makeup case seems to have gone missing." She lowered her voice to a whisper. "I believe it was stolen. "

Jack and I glanced at each other.

"When was the last time you recall seeing the case?" I asked.

"A few hours before tech rehearsal, around four o'clock. That's when I applied my stage makeup. Then, after rehearsal, I went to my dressing room to grab my jacket and the case and couldn't locate it. I was tired and figured I forgot that I brought it back here, but as you can see," she said, extending her arm and sweeping it to the side, "It's not here either."

"We have your makeup case," I said casually.

Leslie smiled broadly and clapped her hands together. "Oh good!" Her expression quickly morphed from delight to confusion. And unless she was the greatest actress of all time, she definitely looked baffled. "Why?"

"It's evidence. We found it near Adam's body. We've had to dust the case and its items for fingerprints."

"Oh dear. But why would—" she paused. "Y'know what's interesting?" She paused again, bringing her finger to her lip as though she was letting us in on a secret. "I mean it's crazy to think this, but if the makeup was applied to his face, it would've been just like that weird murder case in 1969."

Jack and I exchanged glances again.

"You know about that case?" I asked.

"Wait a sec. I'll show you." Leslie stood and crossed the room to a waist-high bookcase. She crouched down and sifted through some papers on the bottom shelf. "Here it is." She walked back holding a flimsy newspaper and flipped it over to show me the back page. "The back page of this town newspaper features local stories that appeared in print fifty years ago, and there's a story about two detectives from Monticello who arrested a serial killer who put makeup on his victims' faces and smothered them with a pillow." She handed the newspaper to me. "So, anyone who reads this paper would know about that case." Leslie tilted her head to the side, puzzling out the implication of what she just told us. "Wait. Is . . . is that what happened? Was my makeup applied to Adam's face?"

Clearly we wouldn't be able to keep this under wraps any longer.

GRANT HOLCOMB was not a key holder, but he was in the theater the night of the murder, rehearsing with Leslie and George. Maybe he wedged one of the doors open, paving the way for access later on. Or perhaps he lured Adam, who did possess a key, back to the theater on some pretense.

Grant's apartment was two doors down from Leslie's. She had texted Grant to let him know we would be stopping by. Even so, he hesitantly opened the door with the latch in place.

"Oh," he said, shutting the door. I could hear the metal button slide along its track before the door swung open. "No peephole. And well, y'know. Just being cautious these days." He stepped aside to let us into his apartment, an exact replica of Leslie's—same layout, furniture, and wall art.

When he thrust his enormous hand toward me, I felt oddly compelled to shake it. He had an intensely vibrant, charismatic presence. And he wasn't bad to look at. Broad shoulders. Bulging biceps. His tight T-shirt accentuated his washboard stomach. I had seen his headshot in the program, but the black-and-white photo did not do this man justice. His skin tone was darker in real life. His brown eyes sparkled with flecks of green. I think I finally understood the swooning effect some men have over women. *For goodness' sake, Susan, get ahold of yourself.*

"Just a few questions and we'll get out of your hair," I said, gazing at his close-cropped afro peppered with light gray strands.

Jack and Grant sat on the sofa and I took the seat opposite them. Grant settled against the back cushion and crossed his slender legs. Jack leaned forward, trapping his hands between his knees. I removed my notepad and pencil from my backpack.

"It's imperative we understand where everyone was and what everyone saw in the early hours of Friday morning." I fished my phone out of my pocket and showed him the photograph of the stained glass peace sign necklace "But before I dive into that, do you recognize this necklace?"

Grant leaned over to get a closer look at my phone. The scent of earthy aftershave wafted over the coffee table. He smiled broadly as he examined the photograph. I could have sworn I saw a gleam of light bounce off one of his incisors.

"It's quite lovely, but no, it doesn't look familiar. As for my where-abouts that night . . ." He rubbed his square jawline. "George, Leslie, and I decided to stay on after tech rehearsal to go over a scene that Adam wasn't one hundred percent pleased with. We ran the scene a few times, tweaked it here and there, and when we felt satisfied, we headed toward the exit."

"So you were the only ones in the theater?"

"As far as I know, yes."

"By any chance, did you see Leslie's makeup case, either on the stage or in her dressing room?" I asked.

"Her makeup case?" He leaned forward on his elbow, flexing his well-defined bicep. "I see it all the time. She's quite possessive of it. But if you're asking me if I specifically saw it that night, I'm afraid I don't have an answer. I don't think I saw it, but I can't be positive."

"What time did you leave the theater?" Jack asked.

"Around two o'clock."

"And who turned on the ghost light when you left? I asked.

"I did," Grant replied, which lined up with the answer George had given us.

Jack and I ticked off our other standard questions. Did he go straight to bed? *Yes.* Did Adam have enemies? *No idea.* What, if any, ties did he have to this area? *None.* Did he see anyone lurking about? *No.*

Actors were a tricky lot to interview. Every answer sounded convincing, persuasive. But that's what they were trained to do. Make me believe whatever came out of their mouths was the gospel truth. Exude the appropriate emotion—shock, fear, sadness, surprise.

"Did you notice if George locked the side door?" Jack asked.

"Hmm. I was chatting with Leslie as we exited. George hung back by the door. I assumed he locked it. But again, if you're asking me if I actually saw him locking the door, unfortunately I cannot say one way or another." He scratched the back of his neck. "Although . . . he did say something when he turned to lock the door."

"And that would be what?" I asked.

"'You two go on ahead, I'll catch up.'"

RAY POKED at the sizzling hamburgers and hot dogs on the grill with a spatula, testing their doneness. "Line up!" he yelled.

Jack was first in line—with his "date." Turns out his plus-one was a fluffy white dog named Sophie, with a pink bow on its head. Moxie was none too happy to have this yappy creature on her turf and trotted off to her dog bed to wait out her departure. Sophie dutifully stood beside Jack's leg as he waited to be served.

"Cheeseburger or hot dog?" Ray inquired.

"I'll take one of each," Jack replied.

With the spatula in one hand and tongs in the other, Ray scooped up a cheeseburger and slid it on an open hamburger bun. He then snatched a hot dog and laid it inside a hot dog roll. "Potato salad, coleslaw, chips, and fixings are over there." Using the tongs, Ray directed Jack to a small table near the porch. "Beer in the cooler over that away."

Dad was up next—he requested a single hamburger while announcing that cheese was not agreeing with him these days. Usually, I'd throw caution to the wind and go for the double cheeseburger, but with a slinky wedding dress to squeeze into, I nixed that notion and settled for a single cheeseburger.

"So, you're the new kid in town," Dad said to Jack once we were all seated. "Settling in all right?"

Jack smiled at me. "Yeah. Couldn't have asked for a better partner." He toasted me with his hot dog, then took a bite. Then he pinched off a piece and fed it to Sophie, who was curled up at his feet like a wad of cotton.

"How's the case coming along?" Ray asked. When none of us answered immediately, he grunted. "C'mon guys, I know it's a bit hush-hush, but there must be something you can tell me."

With two theater people knowing about the makeup—Jean Cranmore, who saw Adam's face, and Leslie Brattle, who put two and two together—we knew our hush-hush days were numbered. Both women swore up and down they would keep it to themselves, but I've been around long enough to know how that plays out—just like in that 1980s Prell shampoo commercial—tell two friends, and they tell two friends, and so on and so on and so on.

I looked at Jack and Dad, and they both nodded.

Dad told Ray about his case from 1969, then, Jack and I took turns telling Ray about the current case: the autopsy report, the actors and crew we had interviewed thus far, and the recovery of the blackjack, possibly the weapon that knocked Adam out cold.

"It was hidden behind a paneled wall in the gift shop," I said.

Ray's eyebrows shot up. "What did the gift store manager have to say about that?"

"Nothing yet. The guy's on Nantucket. We'll grab him when he gets back on Wednesday. He doesn't know what we know, so we think he thinks he's safe."

"Is he a local?" Dad asked.

"Don't know. We were planning on digging into his background tomorrow. His name is Chase Dunham. Ring any bells?"

Dad shook his head. "Chase is not a common name, so I think if I knew him I'd remember. But I'm an old geezer, so my memory ain't what it used to be."

Ray abruptly stood up. "Be right back."

"Were you able to get fingerprints and DNA from the folks in the play?" Dad asked.

"Mixed bag," Jack replied. He lifted his hand and ticked off his fingers. "Malcolm Slater, Shana Lowry, Ricky Saunders, and George Zettler gave us both. Nathan Fowler and Samantha Cranmore would only provide their fingerprints. And Leslie Brattle, Grant Holcomb, and Jean Cranmore refused to provide either. I get that. I'm not sure I would just voluntarily hand over my fingerprints and DNA to the authorities." Jack shrugged, then leaned over to feed Sophie a scrap of burger. "It helps to have it, for sure, but not a must-have at this point."

"So, what kind of dog is this?" Dad asked peering down between his legs to the dog under the table.

"A Havanese. My . . . my wife adopted her ten years ago."

"You're married?" I blurted out.

Jack lowered his head for a moment. When he looked back up he cleared his throat. "She died two years ago in a car acci—"

The back door slammed, diverting our attention.

Ray stood on the porch holding up a notepad. "Found it!" He bounced down the stairs and joined us. "What's with all the serious faces?"

Jack looked up at Ray. "Sorry. I was just telling Susan and Will about how my wife died in a car accident a couple of years ago. I didn't mean to spring it on you here."

"Man, you have nothing to be sorry about." Ray said. "That's some heavy shit. Believe me, I know. My parents were killed when a drunk driver slammed into their car."

"Similar. Whitney was driving. I was in the passenger seat. Drunk driver broadsided us. I walked away. She hung on for a couple of days. In a coma. She never regained consciousness, so I never got to say goodbye." Jack brought his fist to his mouth and held it there for a few seconds. Then cleared his throat. "The drunk driver is doing time. He lost an eye when his airbag exploded." A faint smile slid across Jack's face, perhaps glad for some measure of karma.

It just occurred to me that this might very well be the reason why Jack insisted on driving. Not so much a machismo flex, but more like a subconscious response born out of tragedy. Although he could have easily been the victim of that accident if the car was coming at them from the other side. I had a feeling there was more to the story, but now was not the time and place to probe.

Jack glanced at me, then changed the subject deftly. "But as you were saying, Ray, you found something?"

"Um, yeah. As you probably know, I'm working on the Brandy Johnson murder."

"The community college student who was found buried in the woods behind one of the bungalow colonies?" Jack asked.

"Yeah, that's the case." Ray opened up the notebook. "Yesterday, I finally got to talk to Brandy's girlfriend who had just returned from Europe. She told me that Brandy was hanging around with a guy named Chase who sold pharmaceuticals to students—Adderall, Xanax, Ambien."

Jack's head swiveled to face me, his mouth open, his eyes wide.

Holy shit, I mouthed.

"She couldn't remember his last name, but thought it was Drummond or Drummer."

"Dunham is damn close," Dad said.

Ray tapped his notepad. "What's the chance that there are two guys named Chase cosplaying pharmacist?"

"I'd say they are one and the same," Dad replied, then turned to me. "How long has Chase been managing that gift shop?"

"Not that long," I said. "I know the woman who used to manage it—she's the sister of a friend of mine. Retired at the end of last summer—"

Dad slammed his hands on the table. "Sister!" His eyes narrowed. "I just thought of something. When Jimmy and I went to see Mac Gardner in prison to press him about why he did what he did, he mentioned he had a sister. Not sure if it's relevant, but just throwing it out there if you want to chase her down. We talked to her but got a whole lotta nothin'."

"Her name?"

Dad sighed. "I'm drawing a blank. We only spoke to her once. With the case closed, we were told our work was done and we moved on to the next case." He shook his head. "But I'll tell you, that trip to the prison to speak to Mac Gardner—that was something else."

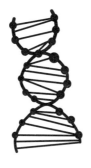

DETECTIVE WILL FORD

July 30, 1969

*S*hackled at the wrists and ankles, Mac Gardner stared straight ahead, purposely avoiding eye contact with me or Jimmy. His steel-blue eyes bore into the wall behind us. He seldom blinked. But when he did, his eyes would water slightly, making his pupils shine. But not in a good way.

I found it deeply unsettling. That and how his hunter-green prison uniform hung loosely on his slender frame like an army jacket on a POW.

"So, you have something you want to say to me," Jimmy began.

Mac Gardner did not turn his head toward Jimmy. He continued to stare straight ahead. But he did shift slightly in his chair.

The only sound was the rattle of the air vent attempting to blow cool air into the stuffy room.

The silence dragged on.

"You gonna tell us why you asked to see us?" Jimmy finally said, firmer this time.

Mac Gardner's lips curled up at the edges. Then quickly collapsed into a straight line. "Just wanted to see if I could get you to do my bidding." He turned his head toward Jimmy. "And I did." He snickered. The shackles clinked.

Jimmy banged his palms on the table, then stood. I pushed back my chair. The metal legs screeched on the concrete floor.

Mac Gardner smacked his lips. "Tell you what. I'm gonna tell you why I'm not gonna tell you anything."

Jimmy remained standing. I looked over my shoulder at Jimmy.

"You're going to tell me that you're not going to tell me anything. What the fuck?" Jimmy bellowed. "Will, let's go."

Mac Gardner turned toward me. "You wanna know, don't you?"

I hesitated, unsure if I should follow Jimmy's lead or stick this out.

"I'm not going to tell you anything because there is nothing to tell. I'm just a sick motherfucker." Mac raised his hands and clapped slowly three times. The metal clang of the shackles echoed around the room. "Congratulations, by the way. I figured I had at least three more kills in me before I got caught. Six is my lucky number. Oh well."

No sooner than I stood, Jimmy stormed out the door.

I leaned over the table. "You can rot in hell."

Mac Gardner lowered his head. When he looked back up, his icy eyes were practically glowing. Spit lodged in the outer edges of his lips made me think of a rabid animal. He growled, "I did this for my sister."

"What? You did what for your sister?" I demanded.

Mac Gardner squeezed his lips and narrowed his glistening eyes. A whisper of a smile appeared, then quickly disappeared. He leaned back and fixed his stare to a spot on the wall to the left of my head.

I waited a few more beats for an answer, but when none came, I turned and walked out of the room.

5

TUESDAY | AUGUST 20, 2019

RAY LINGERED by the coffeepot. I knew what he was doing: weighing the pros and cons of pouring himself a third cup.

I cleared my throat.

He spun around. "Hey," he said, placing his empty mug on the counter. "Didn't hear you come in."

"I'm stealthy that way."

I reached around Ray and grabbed a mug.

Ray snagged my arm and pulled me toward him. "Everything all right? You seem a bit stressed." He wrapped his arms around my waist and gave a tight squeeze. "Things good with Jack now?"

"I guess."

"Well, from where I was sitting last night, it looked like you two buried the hatchet. You guys seemed pretty chummy at dinner."

"You jealous?" I laughed, pulling away and slapping him playfully on the arm.

"Me? Jealous? Of that hunk?"

"I'm happily engaged," I said, holding up my left hand. "Not to mention, I'm a tad too old for a whirlwind romance with a guy who is about the same age as my daughter." I poured coffee from the carafe, then leaned against the counter. "Jack and I had a little heart-to-heart the other day, cleared the air a bit. We'll see if it holds."

Ray grabbed the carafe and poured that third cup. "So . . . is it . . . the wedding that's got you stressed?" he stammered, concentrating on filling the mug and deliberately avoiding eye contact.

"Surprisingly, no," I replied, the words caught between a laugh and a choke. "Besides, Natalie is doing all the heavy lifting. She's having fun planning it. She says it's the one thing she'd miss out on because she doesn't have daughters, so she's pretty gung ho about being in charge— all I have to do is show up. She even set up a Pinterest board."

"A what?"

"I'll explain later." I blew out a puff of air. "But, you're right, I am worried about something. Have you noticed anything, um, off, with my mom?"

Ray frowned as he mulled my question. "You think she's drinking again?"

I shrugged. "I have no evidence to suggest that, but . . ." I tried to sort out what came after the "but," but couldn't quite come up with what that nagging feeling was exactly. "I'm sure it's nothing. I'm probably reading too much into my mother's quirky habits."

"Susan, you should trust your instincts. If you think something is out of whack with her, there's a good chance you're onto something. Ever since your mom stopped drinking back in January, your relationship with her has improved immensely. Talk to her." Ray kissed me on the forehead. "Do what you do best: getting people to open up to you."

Ray downed the rest of his coffee, then scurried upstairs to use the bathroom. As I was deciding between pouring myself a bowl of Cheerios or attempting something more ambitious, like scrambling an egg, my phone rang. *Sally McIver* illuminated the screen. I swiped. "Hey."

"I found something. Are you sitting down?"

I stood in front of the cabinet I had just opened. "Yeah."

"In September 2012, in North Adams, Massachusetts, a female, forty-three years old, was found dead, partially naked in her bed with her hands and feet bound, makeup caked all over her face."

"Holy shit."

"That's not the holy shit part." I pictured Sally smiling on the other end of the line. "Her name is—was—Shirley Gardner. Mac Gardner's daughter."

WITH THE news that Shirley Gardner had been found murdered in a similar fashion, I contacted the North Adams police. That murder remained unsolved. I also learned that the detectives assigned to that case never connected Shirley's murder to the 1969 killings. Not sure if we would have either, if Dad hadn't been part of the original investigation.

None of the 1969 cases were listed in ViCAP, the Violent Criminal Apprehension Program database. And it's not beyond the realm of possibility that Shirley never told anyone about her family history, and therefore the detectives would never have learned she was the daughter of a serial killer.

Brian Carew was the lead detective on the Shirley Gardner murder case and agreed to meet with me and Jack at ten o'clock. It would be our first stop on our two-stop road trip. On our way home, we planned to swing through Kingston to look for the missing 1969 files.

I hadn't seen Jack since last night and had yet to say anything to him after he told us about what happened to his wife.

"I'm sorry about your wife," I said, thinking it heartless to not address this at all.

He nodded, his eyes never leaving the road.

"Sorry for springing that on everyone at your barbecue. I thought you knew. I guess Eldridge never told you."

"Is that why you moved here?"

"It was one of many reasons. I was hoping for a reprieve from the murder and mayhem. Figured small-town policing would offer a change of pace." He clicked his teeth with his tongue. "But bad things happen everywhere."

"That they do." This conversation felt like an opening, an opportunity to expand our partnership beyond the professional. Now seemed as good a time as any to share some tidbits of my life. "I moved to the city after graduating from college. Never in a million years did I think I'd end up moving back here. But, when Dad had a heart attack—"

"Shit. Is he okay?"

"Oh, yeah. That was in 1999. Fit as a fiddle now. Diet. Exercise. Quit smoking." I smirked. "Girlfriends."

"Ha. I have no doubt he's a ladies' man."

I hesitated, but then let it spill: "I also wanted to fix my relationship with my mother." I paused to gauge his reaction. He was listening intently. "She's a recovering alcoholic. But that's a story for another day."

"I sensed there was something going on between you two."

"Yeah?"

"There was a bit of tension between you and your mom when she showed up on the theater grounds to talk to us about Shana's grandmother."

"Well, these days, I'm more worried about her than angry with her. I guess that's a good thing. Besides, there's enough anger in the world these days without me contributing to it."

"It was my fault," Jack said.

His comment felt like a non sequitur. What was his fault? That people were angrier?

"My wife," he continued. "Her death was my fault. I had too much to drink, so she insisted on driving that night. It shouldn't have been her." He pressed his lips together and sucked in his breath. "She'd be alive if I was driving my own damn car." He smacked the heel of his hand on the wheel. Not hard. But enough to release some of the tension in his rigid body. "Sorry."

"No need to be sorry, Jack."

He glanced at me and offered a tight-lipped smile. "Do you mind if we talk about something else?"

"Sure."

"Something's been bugging me about our interview with Leslie Brattle yesterday. Did you find it odd that she asked if we found anything enlightening on Adam's computer? I kind of got the sense she was fishing."

I thought back to Leslie's inquiry about Adam's computer, asking if we found anything incriminating on it. "Now that you mention it, I see how it could be construed that way."

"When we get back to the station, we should look for email correspondence between those two."

"Good catch," I said to Jack, before silently berating myself: *Susan, how in the world did you miss that?*

AFTER BUZZING us into the North Adams police station, Detective Carew ushered us into a small conference room, where his partner, Detective Melody Walters, was waiting. They appeared to be around the same age, midforties.

They resembled each other in the way that siblings sometimes do. Both had prominent foreheads with a widow's peak, dark brown eyes set close together over cute upturned noses, pronounced cheekbones, and pointy chins.

Melody caught me staring, "We're cousins. Our mothers are identical twins," she said flatly, as if it was the thousandth time she explained this.

"Ah, I thought you two might be related."

"You're not the first." She frowned. "I doubt you'll be the last." She moved to the far side of the long oak table and sat in one of six gray swivel chairs.

Brian joined Melody on the far side of the table, while Jack took the seat opposite Melody. I parked myself in the chair next to Jack.

Jack proceeded to fill them in on our case and its similarities to the 1969 serial killings. They listened attentively. Although they looked alike, their mannerisms and expressions were vastly different—one could even say polar opposites. When Brian raised his eyebrows, Melody would furrow hers. When Melody squinted, Brian's eyes would open wide. And while Brian's leg shook under the table, Melody sat stock-still. However, they both tugged at their right ear when Jack said something surprising. When Jack was done, he said, "We're hoping you can tell us about your case."

Brian opened the folder in front of him. "Before I get into details, these are the autopsy photos from our case." He removed a photo and tapped on it. "You had asked to see a photograph of the victim's palm. As you can see, there's nothing there."

"The 1969 victims had a number written on their palms with an ink pen—in order of their murders." Jack reached into his soft-leather briefcase and pulled out a manila folder. He leafed through our autopsy photos, pulled out the one he was looking for, and placed it in front of Brian and Melody. "Ours had the number five." He tapped on Adam's palm. "So, our perp must have known there was a fourth victim."

"Perhaps Shirley's killer didn't know about the numbering system," Melody said. "Which means we are probably looking at two perps."

"Or, it's the same killer and he, or she, forgot to write the number four on Shirley's palm," I countered.

"It's also possible our killer became aware of this particular detail after murdering Shirley," Jack threw out.

"We spun our wheels on this case," Brian said. "According to the victim's boyfriend, Shirley's parents were deceased, she had no siblings, no known relatives. Because of the strange MO, we ran her case through ViCAP but came up empty. It didn't even occur to us to dig back fifty years."

"No one mentioned her father was a serial killer," Melody said. "Obviously, she kept it a secret. Wouldn't you?"

"I suppose," I replied, although wondered if I truly could keep such a thing to myself. At the very least, I think I would've told Ray. "You said on the phone that Shirley Gardner had a boyfriend. Was he ever considered a suspect?"

"No. He had a solid alibi. He was a drummer and had a gig over in Springfield that night. His buddy dropped him home the next morning and that's when he found Ms. Gardner."

"Do you know how we can get in touch with him?" I asked.

"Not unless you know how to speak to the dead," Melody replied. "Ms. Gardner's boyfriend died of cancer two years ago."

"There was another person of interest. But we couldn't get a bead on him." Brian shuffled through the papers and pulled out a sheet. He scanned it, then said, "According to Ms. Gardner's boyfriend, she talked about a guy she met at Blinkers, a local bar around here where she bartended. He wasn't one hundred percent sure of this guy's name. Thought it was Derek or Darren. Said they grew up in the same area, so they reminisced. According to Shirley's boyfriend, they shared 'war stories' about their tumultuous childhoods. We sought him out, but he was dust in the wind. He always paid cash. And no one seemed to know him. All we got was a description." He flipped the sheet around and slid it across the table.

I glanced at the drawing. Caucasian male, long stringy hair. His features indistinct.

"The bartender who gave us this description said he wore a trucker's cap that obscured his face," Brian explained, perhaps sensing my disappointment with the sketch. "Guessed he was in his forties."

I scanned the report. "Here's something interesting. The bartender saw this guy's phone light up with the name *Elizabeth*."

"Oh, yeah!" Brian exclaimed as the memory hit him. "We asked around for an Elizabeth, but that was a dead end."

"Any DNA evidence collected at the scene?" Jack asked.

"There was DNA that wasn't Shirley's on one edge of the pillowcase. We never found a match. It's also possible the pillow might've been handled by someone who had nothing to do with this. I can get that analysis over to you. Might take a few days."

I held my phone over the vague sketch of Derek/Darren and snapped a picture. Might come in handy somewhere down the line.

"Do you think this guy was the doer?" I asked.

"I do. Brian doesn't." Melody smiled, finally. "Call it woman's intuition."

DETECTIVE HANK Webb, who had taken possession of the Mac Gardner evidence boxes, was dead; as luck would have it, his daughter, Hope, was alive and living in the family home. She was pretty sure the boxes were still in the attic but claimed she hadn't been up there in years and had no plans to check it out. "I had enough with murder and mayhem when my dad was alive, so not about to rifle through his things now that he's gone," she said when we asked if she knew if all the files were still intact.

For a good chunk of the two-hour drive between North Adams, Massachusetts and Kingston, New York, Jack and I bantered about the case. We were about ten minutes from Kingston, when Jack spotted a Starbucks and pulled into the parking lot.

With coffee in hand, all I wanted to do was listen to some guitar-heavy rock 'n' roll—clear the noggin a bit before hunting for those old evidence files. I rolled down the window, then fidgeted with the radio.

"So, tell me, Jack, what kind of music floats your boat?" I asked as I tuned in the classic rock station on his Sirius XM console. The Doors launched into "Riders on the Storm." I took a sip of coffee.

"Well, definitely not this old-timey music."

Coffee sprayed from my lips onto the dashboard. "Old-timey? This is circa 1970s, not 1920s. So what are you into? Techno? Hip-hop?"

He glared at the dashboard, then pointed to a napkin tucked in the cupholder between us. "As a matter of fact, yeah. Well, I'm more hip-hop than techno. I grew up listening to Nas, Dr. Dre, Eminem, Jay-Z. These days I listen to Kendrick Lamar, Travis Scott, Little Uzi." Jack turned to face me. "I can tell from your expression you don't even know who these artists are."

"I know some of them," I said, sopping up the spit take. "Well, I know Eminem. I saw *Eight Mile*."

Jack laughed. "Maybe I should school you on hip-hop."

I held up my palm. "I think my music tastes are pretty much set in stone. So, your parents never exposed you to classic rock?"

"My dad is a Dead Head. All he listens to is the Grateful Dead. Although he also likes a guy named Steely Dan—"

"That's a band. Not a guy. It's also . . . never mind."

He raised an eyebrow, registering my correction, then continued: "My mom was into Broadway show tunes and liked easy-listening stuff, like Barry Manilow. If your name was Mandy, we'd really have a problem." He chuckled at his lame joke. "In high school, I had a Walkman and pretty much drowned out whatever they were playing in the car or on the radio at home."

I noted that he referred to his dad in the present tense and his mom in the past tense. A get-to-know-you discussion for another day. "Well, you're missing out."

"Well, to each his own," he retorted as he pulled up in front of Hope's light blue three-story colonial with white shutters. "So, you spoke to this guy's daughter, right?"

"Yeah. Hope." I released my buckle. "In 1985, Hank got shot while apprehending a murder suspect. He was pretty much sidelined after that but held a part-time training role within his department. With time on his hands, he was itching to write a true crime book. He was a patrol officer at the time of the 1969 murders, so he was aware of the case, and it intrigued him. His plan was to hunt down both the victims' relatives and Mac Gardner's relatives and interview them, hoping to gain more insight into the motivation behind these killings."

"Did he get anywhere with it?"

"Seems not. Soon after he collected these boxes, his health started to decline further. Liver failure and transplant. Needed dialysis, that kinda thing. So he never really got to tackle this."

"Too bad. If he had made some headway, it might have helped us out," Jack said, opening the driver's side door.

An uneven brick pathway led us to the house, which was situated about fifteen yards from the street. A dog in the adjacent yard barked at us.

Hope opened the door before we knocked. "The neighbor's dog always warns me people are approaching," she explained with a gentle laugh.

She stepped aside and let us into her sparsely furnished home. And by sparsely, I mean no living room or dining room furniture.

"Moving?" I asked.

"Redecorating. Out with the old, in with the new," she said with a hand flourish. "The carpet will be torn out tomorrow. There's beautiful hardwood underneath. Dad loved carpet. The plusher, the better.

Wouldn't let my mom rip it out." She ran her sneaker along the carpet. "She died four months ago, and I inherited the house."

Hope led us up the well-worn carpeted center staircase to the second landing. The doors to the bedrooms were closed. We took a hairpin turn and followed her down the hallway to the door that led to the attic. She stood in front of the door, staring at the handle for a few seconds before opening it.

"Dad finished the attic himself and used it as a private office-slash-hideaway. Feel free to open a window if it's too hot up there." She paused for a moment, then said, "Well, I'll leave you two to carry on. If you need anything, holler." And with that directive, she turned and headed back to the ground level of the house.

The staircase to the attic was narrower and steeper than the main staircase. I counted twelve stairs as I ascended. With the windows shut tight, the air was stuffy and warm but not suffocating. Jack hurried to the window on the side-facing wall and flung it open. A bumblebee flew in.

"Shit. No screen." He glanced over to where I was standing on the other side of the attic. "Does that one have a screen?"

I inspected the window. "Yup." As I opened my window, he closed his.

I glanced around the room and eyeballed a stack of three cardboard boxes to the right of Hank's oak desk. Instantly, I recognized the case file number scrawled on the side of the top box, 1682-1. *Bingo!*

Each box had a different case file number scrawled on its side. Which made sense, seeing that Hank collected them from three different jurisdictions. The box we found in the warehouse was numbered 1682-2. Our hunch that someone had consolidated the Monticello files into a single box explained the one box here and the other box, with the lone newspaper clipping, back at the warehouse.

Jack grinned as he lifted the lid off the top box. "I think we hit the mother lode." He sifted through the contents, whistling.

I'm not a big fan of the whistle-while-you-work din. Humming I could handle. Whistling was downright annoying. But I held my tongue. Jack and I had cleared the air and were moving in a positive direction, and if I complained about this irritating (bordering on odious) habit, I was afraid it would set us back. Instead, I cleared my throat.

He stopped whistling momentarily. Then started up again. Obviously, he didn't get my subtle hint.

He lifted the top box from the stack and placed it on the desk. I scooted in next to him to inspect the contents of the middle box. Then I moved that box to the floor and lifted the lid from the bottom box.

"Looks like each box is specific to each jurisdiction," I said. "But these are just the paper files. I was hoping we would find clothes so we can run some DNA tests."

"All the victims were naked, so maybe there wasn't anything to collect."

"There were the ropes. The pillowcases. The peace sign necklaces."

"Good point," Jack conceded. "Hopefully, there are photographs."

"Let's get these boxes down to the car."

Jack stacked two boxes and headed toward the staircase, while I grabbed the one on the floor.

I heard it before I saw it. Jack's sightline was blocked by the boxes and he must have misjudged the steepness of the stairs. About halfway down he tripped. In his instinct to grab the banister, he released his grip on the boxes. The two boxes tumbled down the stairs, the contents scattered on the plush carpet.

"Shit!" Jack exclaimed, as he surveyed the jumble of folders and papers.

Hope must have heard the commotion and materialized at the foot of the stairs. She looked down at the papers and photographs strewn all over the floor. Staring up at her was Sam Blackstone, naked, tied up, and caked in makeup. She glared down at the photograph. "Excuse me, I think I'm going to be sick." As she hurried away, she mumbled, "And this is why I never went through Dad's things."

BACK AT the station, Jack and I spent time double-checking the contents of the boxes to make sure we had put all the displaced documents and photographs back in their rightful places. Now they sat stacked on the floor next to my desk, ready to be moved into a conference room, where we would review every scrap of paper in them. With all this paperwork to mine, we decided to hold off on looking for any email correspondence between Leslie and Adam until the next day. Besides, I wasn't as convinced as Jack was that her question about Adam's computer was nefarious.

Dad was hunched over in Sally's chair, his elbows on his knees, his hands clasped, staring at the boxes. He had the look of a predator eyeing his prey. Waiting impatiently for the chance to dig in and feast.

I gave him the rundown of what we learned on our field trips to North Adams and Kingston.

"Could be a coincidence," Dad began. "But Sam Blackstone's daughter's name is Elizabeth."

"Yeah, I remember you told me. That crossed my mind when Detective Carew told us that the bartender had seen the name *Elizabeth* appear on the phone display of the person chatting it up with Shirley Gardner." I lifted the Kingston box. "Ready?"

Jack grabbed the Ellenville box and Dad picked up the Monticello box. They followed me to the small conference room, where we placed our boxes on the oak table.

Dad scrolled through his phone. "Do you mind?" he asked, as he held his phone up. Without waiting for an answer, he tapped the arrow and the Allman Brothers blasted from his Apple Music app. "It's like a transistor radio, but with every song in the universe at your fingertips. Man, ya gotta love technology. You like classic rock, Jack?"

"Don't answer that," I said to Jack. "Dad likes you, let's keep it that way."

At first, Dad looked perplexed, but then chuckled when it dawned on him that Jack and I probably had gone down that road. "To each his own," Dad said.

"So how do you want to proceed?" Jack asked over Greg Allman's guitar licks.

Before I could answer, Sally and Ron poked their heads in the door. "Eldridge said you might need some assistance."

"The more the merrier," Jack said, waving them in.

I handed Sally a piece of paper with the names of the three 1969 victims. "I'd like you to find the victims' wives. If they're alive, they might be able to tell us how much they were privy to at the time and if they divulged anything about the case to anyone. That might give us insight as to who knows what about these cases and has enough information to reenact them."

"Can do," Sally replied, scanning the list.

"And Ron, I need you to chase down Elizabeth Blackstone, Sam Blackstone's daughter. She was a newborn in 1969, so she would be fifty now. Once you establish her whereabouts, we'll take it from there."

"Gotcha," Ron said.

"Dad, I just want you to reacquaint yourself with the case. Come at it with a fresh eye. See if anything pops out that didn't occur to you back when you were a rookie detective."

Dad went right to work. He sat down in front of a pile of folders, opened the one on top, and dug in.

"And what's my job, boss?" Jack asked with a smirk.

"Let's you and I focus on the current case. Namely, Chase Dunham." I glanced at my watch. "Pull what you can on Chase—let's be armed to the teeth when we haul his ass in here tomorrow."

"Holy crap!" Dad exclaimed.

All heads turned toward him.

"I can't believe I forgot this." He held up what appeared to be a transcript. "Remember I told you that Jimmy and I went to see Mac Gardner in prison. He claimed he had something to tell us. But he was just jerking us around, playing mind games."

"Yeah, you mentioned a sister we should track down because he blamed her for his actions," I said.

"That's right. Mac had said, 'I did this for my sister.' Well, stapled to this transcript from that prison visit is a note I wrote after meeting with him. Jeez, I can't believe I forgot this." He sighed.

"Dad?"

"His sister's name was Barbara." He ripped off the note and handed it to me. "Her married name was Zettler."

"So?" Jack said.

"Hercule Poirot," Dad and I said in unison.

Jack snapped his fingers. "George freaking Zettler."

"Zettler is not a common name." I scanned Dad's handwritten note. "I bet they're related."

"Oh, they are," Dad said, cradling his forehead in his hands. "I met her." He sighed, then lifted his head to look at me. "And I'm pretty damn sure she had a son named George."

DETECTIVE WILL FORD

August 13, 1969

Jimmy and I climbed the three rickety steps of the front porch, which was in dire need of repair. A fresh coat of paint wouldn't hurt either. I politely nodded at the woman sitting on the porch. Barbara Zettler was short, plump, and guarded.

Her eyes narrowed as we neared. She stopped peeling the apple cupped in her hand and tossed it into a basket. She slid the peeler into her pocket, rose from her wicker chair, then wiped her hands on her apron. "I know why you're here. And I've got nothing to say," she said curtly.

Jimmy flashed a smile. "Just a few minutes of your time, ma'am, is all we ask." He glanced over her shoulder at the bassinet, positioned in the shade. He could hear a baby cooing. "You making apple pie?"

"Yeah. My husband took in some boarders looking for a place to stay during the Woodstock festival." She jutted her chin out toward the road that led down to the festival site on Max Yasgur's farm. "They arrive tomorrow."

A toddler pushed open the screen door and waddled out. Her blond hair was plastered to her flushed cheeks.

"I'm hot, Mommy," she said, tucking herself into her mother's apron folds.

"Mac was supposed to fix the air conditioner." She scoffed, pointing at the unit sticking out of the window.

"I can take a look at it," Jimmy offered.

"Sure. But it don't mean I'm having a conversation with you."

I leaned against the porch post, thinking how best to phrase my question without raising her ire. If Mac, as he claimed, 'did this for her,' she would probably know what he was referring to, but then again, it would also lay the blame at her feet. "We spoke to Mac and he mentioned you. Said you might be able to shed some light on why he did what he did."

Her eyes shimmered as she blinked away impending tears. Blue, like Mac's but warmer, less glacial. "Please, leave me be. I can't . . ." The toddler peeled away from Barbara and stomped back into the house. "If you want to try and fix the air conditioner, be my guest." She walked back to her wicker chair and sat, removed the peeler from her apron pocket, lifted an apple from the basket at her feet, and started to peel.

Jimmy shrugged, then opened the screen door. "I'll see what I can do."

The baby started to fuss. Barbara reached into the bassinet and lifted him out. "Shh, George," she repeated a couple of times, tapping his back.

When the baby settled, Barbara laid him back down.

I tried again. "Mac said he did what he did for *you. Do you know what he meant by that?"*

Barbara pursed her lips and stopped peeling. "You got a family, Detective?"

"I do."

"You would do anything to protect your family? Right?"

"That's correct."

"Well, that's what I'm doing. My brother ain't right in the head, doing what he did. But that doesn't give you—or anyone—the right to poke and pry and ruin our lives. Leave me be. You caught him." She shook the half-peeled apple. "No one else will die."

6

GEORGE ZETTLER ran his hand across his nearly bald head, disturbing the comb-over. He must have seen me glance at the top of his head, because he quickly smoothed the errant hair back into place.

"Do I need a lawyer?" he asked, as we stood in the foyer of his apartment.

"Now, why would you say that?" Jack asked.

George shrugged. "Well, for one thing, you're back to ask me more questions. That tends to make me wary."

"Just standard follow-up," I said. "We've heard from several people now, so just making sure we got everyone's story straight." I was feeling claustrophobic in the small entryway. "May we come in?"

George stepped aside. "Sure," he said with a hand flourish.

The layout of George's apartment was slightly different from that of his fellow actors, Leslie Brattle and Grant Holcomb. The living room was smaller, but it had a galley kitchen. Crusty dishes lay in the sink. The door to his bedroom was open and clothes were strewn around the floor and on the bed, as if a suitcase had exploded. As we passed it, he grabbed the handle and pulled it shut.

He sat on the one wingback chair, so Jack and I sat to the right of him on the love seat.

He wedged his hands between his knees and rocked his body back and forth a couple of times.

"I know this question is going to sound strange," Jack began. "But is your mother Barbara Zettler?"

"Um, yes, Barbara. She died eight years ago. What has that got to do with—" George's blue eyes fluttered.

Jack and I simultaneously leaned to our left in anticipation of how that sentence might end when he figured out why we were asking.

But he remained silent.

"Can you venture to guess why we're asking?" I asked.

He mussed with his comb-over again. "I'm not my uncle, if this is where this is going. Are you suggesting that I inherited a killer gene?" He air quoted the last part of that sentence. "Now I need to ask you to leave," he said standing abruptly.

"It's here or the station," Jack said, sounding like a bad TV script.

George sat back down.

"Look, we're not here to accuse you of killing Adam Kincaid. However, you might be able to help us."

"I don't see how I can possibly be of any help. I mean, just because my uncle killed people, doesn't make me an expert."

"Perhaps, but it makes you privy to information that was not public at the time," I said.

"Huh? What information?"

"Like for instance, did your mother ever describe the murder scenes to you?"

"Jeez, what? No. I was a baby at the time. I was born in 1969, when those murders took place."

"So you have no idea what your uncle did?"

"I know he killed three people, but beyond that, no! I don't!" he exclaimed. He seemed stunned by his own outburst and relaxed into his chair. "I don't understand why you're even bringing this up unless—"

I raised my eyebrows, prompting him to continue his line of thinking.

"Are you saying there are similarities?" He cupped his forehead in his palms. When he dropped his hands, he said, "This is crazy."

"So you're telling us that you have no insight into your Uncle Mac's murders?" Jack asked, incredulously. "That you were never curious to ask your mom what happened?"

"I asked her. Once. When I was a teenager. She told me to never bring it up again. And I didn't." His voice was steady. He maintained eye contact. He seemed to be telling the truth. But I reminded myself he was the lead actor of the play.

"The detective on the case at that time was my father. He interviewed your uncle soon after he was arrested." I paused to watch his expression. Wide-eyed, mouth forming a small O. "Your Uncle Mac said, and I quote, 'I did this for my sister.'"

George didn't move a muscle. His eyes still wide. His lips still slightly parted. After a few seconds, he finally blinked. "He said that?"

"Yeah. Any idea what he meant?"

He narrowed his eyes in that way people do when they are trying to remember something. "I know my mom had a rough childhood. They both did. Their mother was quite abusive, which might explain a few things. But it was my mom who took the brunt of her mother's abuse, not Mac. She was older than Mac, and from the few tidbits I managed to coax out of her, she did her darndest to protect him."

"Is there anything specific you remember? Anything that would explain what Mac said?"

He slowly shook his head. "Like what? I told you she never talked about it."

Jack touched my forearm. "Can I talk to you for a sec?" he said, tilting his head toward the front door.

We excused ourselves and stepped outside his apartment into the hallway. I wasn't exactly fuming, but he'd better have a good reason for interrupting the flow of that interview with this sidebar.

"I think we should give him details about the crime scene and the condition of the victim," Jack said. "See if he can make some connections he might be unaware of." He had a point. A good one. And I appreciated that he conferred with me before questioning George.

"Good idea. The cat's pretty much out of the bag anyway. Leslie Brattle put two and two together from that town newspaper article. I get the feeling the whole cast and crew will be yakking about this soon enough."

When we reentered the living room, George was nowhere to be seen.

"Well, he couldn't have escaped through the front door," I said.

George emerged from the bedroom holding a photo album. "Oh, you're back," he said, a bit flustered. "I had recently done one of those online DNA tests, so I brought this old photo album up here, should I get any hits from relatives. My dad left my mom soon after I was born and died when I was four, so I don't really know that side of my family. Figured maybe I could find them through DNA." He sighed and frowned. "Anyway, I thought you might want to see pictures of my mom and Mac, and their mother." He handed the album to me.

"Okay." Not sure how helpful this would be, but I sure was curious. I could tell Jack was as well.

George joined me on the oatmeal love seat. Jack sat on the matching wingback chair. I opened the album.

"It's in chronological order. There are some real early photos of my grandparents and great-grandparents that I found in my mother's belongings after she died. The earliest photo I could find of my mother is this one here," he said, pointing to a toddler leaning into a voluptuous woman. "I would say that was taken in the late thirties, before Mac was born." He cleared his throat. "They were three years apart."

"Is this your grandmother?" I said, pointing to the voluptuous woman.

"Yes. I think she's pregnant in that photo because if you turn the page, you'll see her with my mom and Mac, and she is . . . well, she isn't as big. Just Jane Russell-like curvy."

Sullen faces greeted me as I leafed slowly through the album. I know people didn't "smile for the camera" back then, but these faces were downright dour. I continued to turn the pages until one picture stopped me in my tracks. Although black-and-white, it was clear that George's grandmother was wearing heavy makeup. I turned the album around and showed the picture to Jack. He scrunched his eyebrows.

I spun the album back toward me and turned the pages, getting to the late 1940s, when Barbara appeared to be ten and Mac seven. More pictures of Mac and Barbara's mother wearing an excessive amount of makeup. Could this be why Mac smeared makeup on his victims? Yet, his victims were male, not exactly stand-ins for his abusive mother. Did that matter? Was it the makeup and something else about his chosen victims?

"And your grandfather, your mother's father. What can you tell us about him?"

George shrugged. "Not much. He left my grandmother after Mac was born. Rumor had it that he was gay. Ran off with another man. A farmer. Which back then, did not go over well in the community. She was pretty much shunned."

"Can you tell us about your grandmother?" I asked.

"You ever see the movie *Sunset Boulevard*? About a washed-up actress named Norma Desmond?"

I nodded and said, "Yeah," while Jack shook his head, and said, "No."

"That's who she looked like. Crazy eyes. Tons of makeup. Mean as the day is long. She would come over when I was young, and she and my mother would always get in some kind of dustup. She died when I was a kid, so not much more I can tell you."

"You said your mom took the brunt of your grandmother's abuse. What do you mean by that?" Jack asked.

George squeezed his eyes shut and rubbed his temples. When his eyes popped open, he said, "When my mother got the news that her mother died, she broke down crying. Which, as a kid, I thought was odd because clearly my mother was not a fan of my grandmother. When I asked her if she was sad, she said she was relieved, that her tears were from years of abuse at the hands of a warped woman. That's what she said: warped. That kinda stuck with me. But I was a kid, and I didn't exactly press for details." He paused and scratched the back of his neck. "However, there was this one time—"

My phone rang. I glanced down at the caller ID and hit decline. Mom would have to wait. "Sorry about that. As you were saying . . ."

"One night I came home after a date and found my mother three sheets to the wind. Every year, on the anniversary of her mother's death, she would get shitfaced. Usually, I would just get her up to her bedroom and she would spend the next day sleeping it off, but this one time she was belligerent, screaming at me as though I was her husband, my dad. She kept repeating, 'I'm not a whore. My mother made me do it. Please come back, Tom.' I eventually got her to calm down and it never happened again."

"And you never asked her about that outburst?" Jack asked.

"No. I didn't. It felt personal and weird to me at the time. I let it go."

Was it possible Barbara's mother was pimping her out? Did young Mac know? Did he seek revenge in some psycho way, avenging his sister's abuse by going after young men who fit the profile of those who raped her? Applying makeup on their faces to signal who was really to blame for his actions—his mother.

"You had a sister, right?" I asked, recalling Dad's story about a toddler at the house when he visited Barbara.

"Yeah. She died ten years ago. Ovarian cancer." George cleared his throat. "Can you please tell me why you are dredging all this up?"

I nodded in Jack's direction.

Jack laid out what we knew about Mac's murders. If there was a pause in the story, it was filled by the birds chirping outside. George merely nodded, his lips pursed tight. Jack glanced in my direction, and I picked up the thread.

"Like your uncle's victims, Adam Kincaid was found in similar fashion: hands and feet bound by rope, naked, face caked with make-up, asphyxiated by a pillow."

"Oh my God." George's mouth hung open a few seconds, then he repeated, "Oh my God."

"We need to ask you something else, George," Jack said. "You claimed to have locked the side door to the theater, but no one actually saw you do that. So, I'll ask you again, did you lock that door?"

George lowered his head, took a deep breath in, then blew it out. He then slowly lifted his head. "I . . . I was going to tell you. I swear. I just . . . Malcolm and his whole crazy key thing." He rocked back and forth a couple of times. "I have ADHD. I'm terribly disorganized and forgetful. I'm constantly losing things, misplacing things. Anyway, I left my key in this apartment. I realized it when the three of us started to pack up and leave. So I made them go on ahead and pretended to lock up."

"How much time passed between the time you left the theater and went back to lock up?"

He let out a breath and rubbed the top of his head, once again dislodging the strands. "We left the theater at around two. The minute I got back here, I grabbed the key and went back to the theater and locked up. All in all, I would say fifteen minutes passed from the time I left the theater with Leslie and Grant and got back here after locking up."

"Why didn't you tell us this?" Jack asked. "You realize this means anyone could have snuck into the theater."

"Someone would have had to assume the door wasn't locked. And it's *always* locked. It has to be someone who already knew they could gain access—someone who had a key." He coughed and sputtered. "Someone besides me."

He had a point. A plan this elaborate would mean the perp had to be certain they could enter the theater. If so, there were only two possibilities: it was either someone Adam planned to meet and he let the murderer in, or it was someone who had a key and lured Adam to his death.

"One last question," I said. "Did you see anyone outside when you went to lock up?"

George vigorously shook his head. "No one. Not a soul."

ADAM'S CLONED documents and apps from his laptop and phone had been uploaded to my desktop by one of our techies. With our trips to North Adams and Kingston, not to mention a whole myriad of other priorities that needed our attention, I had put this off long enough. I opened up Adam's email account and plugged in the search term *Leslie Brattle*. About twenty emails populated the page. But it was the one with the subject line "funding my new project" that caught my attention. I clicked it open. I twisted around in my chair searching for Jack, and spotted him near the bubbler outside Eldridge's office filling his water bottle.

"Oh Jack!" I yelled over my shoulder. "Got something to show you."

Jack grabbed his chair and rolled it over to my desk.

I pointed toward the screen. "I think Leslie has some explaining to do."

JACK AND I had some time to kill before Chase Dunham's flight touched down, so we headed back to the theater grounds to have another chat with Leslie Brattle.

I had printed out the email exchanges between Leslie and Adam, and now she sat on her wingback chair quietly reading the pages. Her fingers trembled slightly. When she was done, she folded the papers in half and handed them back to me.

"I know what you're thinking, but I didn't kill Adam," Leslie began.

"How did he even know all this about you?" I asked.

"After *Mousetrap* wrapped, Malcolm arranged for the cast and crew to go to the city to celebrate. Just like he did for the cast of *A Walk on the Moon*." She sighed, heavily. "It was there that I introduced Adam to my husband, Chet Rockwell."

"*The* Chet Rockwell," Jack asked, seemingly impressed.

Leslie nodded.

Jack turned to me. "Überwealthy guy. Old money."

Leslie ignored Jack's fiscal assessment of her husband and continued: "Unfortunately, the next morning, Adam saw another man emerge from my hotel room. He must have done a little sleuthing, or maybe he hired a private investigator, but he found out I had a prenup. If Chet divorces me, I get nothing. Adam then approached me and asked me to fund a play he wanted to direct. Although, *asked* is not really the right word. He demanded I pay up or he would tell Chet."

This might have explained why Sally reported to us that Leslie seemed edgy and cagy during her initial interview—she was afraid her affair would go public if we discovered her email correspondence with Adam. Then again, her edginess could also be an indicator that she was, indeed, our murderer.

"I am not a murderer!" Leslie exclaimed, as though reading my mind. She raised a perfectly penciled-in eyebrow, then oddly added, "Besides, I could think of a whole host of other ways to kill Adam more efficiently than imitating some old murder that I read about in a town newspaper." She leaned forward. "Is this going to become public?" she demanded, seemingly more concerned about her affair being outed than being a suspect for a murder.

"I suggest you hire a good lawyer, Ms. Brattle," I said, holding up the folded emails. "As for this getting out, I suggest you have a heart-to-heart with your husband sooner rather than later so he hears this from you, not the *New York Post*."

SALLY AND Ron greeted Chase Dunham at Westchester County Airport when he deplaned. Surprisingly, he willingly went with them. Unfortunately, he requested a lawyer.

"Wish you could've seen the look on his face when he saw us standing at the gate," Sally said to me when she got back to the station.

While Chase was fishing with his buddies on Nantucket, we had obtained a search warrant, which we hoped would lead to an arrest warrant for illegal possession and distribution of Schedule IV narcotics. Chase's landlord obligingly gave us access to his apartment, but the search yielded nothing. Unfortunately, Brandy Johnson's friend wasn't 100 percent sure that Dunham was the last name she heard, and she wasn't willing to point fingers. On top of that, the judge was wary of Shana Lowry's statement. He pushed back, arguing that Shana could be lying to save her own ass. And with my mother's revelation that Shana did indeed have ties to the area, the judge might be onto something.

So, no arrest warrant, but at least we had Chase sweating it out in an interrogation room.

I watched Chase from the two-way mirror. He looked good for a man about to turn fifty. Tan from his couple of days on a boat. He wore a short-sleeved shirt that not only showed off his well-defined biceps but also revealed that he was quite pale on the upper part of his arms and on one wrist where I noticed the outline of a watch. He slouched on the hard wooden chair, every so often checking out his fingernails and picking at a cuticle. He refused to speak until his lawyer showed up, due any minute.

Sally led a man with a briefcase into the room.

The lawyer glanced up at the mounted camera, then took a seat beside Chase. They were the same height, but Chase had the slender body of a basketball player, while the lawyer could have easily played defensive tackle on a football team.

The lawyer pulled a leather-bound notepad out of his briefcase. He removed a pen from his jacket pocket. They conferred for a few minutes.

Jack and I entered the room.

The lawyer stood, extended his hand to Jack, and said, "Reggie Callahan, Chase's attorney."

I took my seat and lowered my hands to my lap before Reggie could thrust his beefy palm in my direction.

"Let's get started, shall we?" I said, pressing record. I introduced everyone who was present, the date, time, and the reason we'd brought Chase in for questioning. "Alleged possession and distribution of a Schedule IV drug, Ambien, which, by the way, is a Class D felony in the State of New York."

Chase opened his mouth to speak before getting cut off by his lawyer.

"From what I understand," Reggie began in a thick Brooklyn accent, "is that a woman accused, falsely I might add, my client of selling her a sleeping aid." He paused, then added, "I think we are pretty much done here."

I ignored Reggie's opening salvo. "Chase, where were you the in the early-morning hours of August sixteenth? Between two a.m. and nine a.m., to be exact?"

"Is that the night this woman claimed to buy a couple of sleeping pills?" Reggie answered.

"It's the night Adam Kincaid was murdered. It's the night a witness placed your client on the grounds of the Monticello Playhouse." I shifted my gaze toward Chase, who was actually looking quite surprised at this turn of accusation.

"What are you talking about?" Chase shouted.

"Hold on one minute here." Reggie jumped in. "Are you accusing my client of murder?"

"Actually, two murders," Jack said. "Does the name Brandy Johnson ring a bell?"

Red blotches erupted on Chase's neck. *Did we hit a nerve?*

Reggie slammed his hands on the table. His pen rolled to the floor. "My client came willingly to clear his name of a trumped-up allegation that he was selling drugs. What's this about? Where's the evidence for these accusations, or are you just shooting from the hip here?"

Sally walked into the room with the blackjack sealed in a plastic evidence bag and handed it to me. Jack opened up the folder in front of him and removed several photographs. The photographs taken at the gift shop, showing where we had found the hidden blackjack. He laid them on the table like he was dealing a game of Texas Hold'em. I then placed the blackjack on the table.

"I have no idea how that got there," Chase said.

Reggie's head whipped sideways. "Quiet!" He turned back to me. "Explain this," he said, sweeping his hand across the table, mere inches above the photos and baton.

Jack cleared his throat, then said, "With news that Chase was on the grounds of the Monticello Playhouse in the early-morning hours of August sixteenth, we decided to do another sweep of the gift shop.

And lo and behold, we found the weapon that was used to knock Adam Kincaid out cold. Blood and hair DNA on the top edge of the blackjack confirmed it. We'd like a sample of your DNA to clear you as a suspect." Jack pointed to the swab kit on the table.

"This is insane," Chase said. "Can they do that?"

"I said be quiet," his lawyer chastised. "I do all the talking. You just sit there. Capiche?"

Chase nodded obediently.

Reggie examined the photographs. "So let me get this straight. You searched the gift shop high and low on the first day of the investigation, and you came up with bupkis. You get a dubious tip that my client was selling a couple of sleeping pills to someone, prompting you to do another search. And voilà! You find the weapon used in the murder. In an obvious location. Easy to spot. I might not be a detective, Detectives, but it is clear to me that my client is being framed. Perhaps by the person who set up this wild-goose chase." He grinned, quite satisfied with his monologue. He leaned forward. "And what's this about another murder? Does this also include planted evidence?"

"We'll get to that. Let's concentrate on one murder at a time," I said. "Tell us about the night you met with Shana Lowry."

Chase whispered in Reggie's ear. Reggie nodded.

"Shana Lowry called Chase in the middle of the night and asked him if he had any sleep aids. They agreed to meet halfway between their homes, which just happens to be the Playhouse. Chase has a legal prescription for Ambien. His friend was in need and he was simply helping her out. Shana offered to give Chase money for his trouble, and he accepted it. He handed her the pills, then went straight home."

"Why did she call *you*?" I asked Chase.

Reggie raised his eyebrows slightly, tacitly giving Chase permission to finally speak.

"Because we once commiserated over the fact that we both need a little help falling asleep." He air quoted *help*. "I told her I took Ambien once in a while and that it really helped. She must have remembered I had some."

"So you just rolled out of bed to meet with her in the middle of the night?" I snorted, making sure the sarcasm was loud and clear.

"I was up. It was no biggie." He removed a tissue from his front pocket and blew his nose forcefully. "This fucking sinus infection has been keeping me up at night."

Chase was one cool cucumber. Nothing in his affect made me think he was bullshitting me about his interaction with Shana. So I changed tack. Perhaps treating him like a witness would be more productive. "Let's just assume for a moment that this story you've spun is true. Did you see anyone else hanging around when the two of you were swapping drugs for money?" I asked.

"No!"

"They were not swapping drugs for money," Reggie chimed in.

I leaned forward. "You say tom-*a*-to, I say tom-*ah*-to." I leaned back.

"I *say* you got nothing on my client. A bogus drug charge. An obvious frame-up." The pitch in his voice escalating. "I expect you to drop this inquiry immediately, to save you and this department any further embarrassment!"

"Did you leave the theater grounds together?" I asked Chase, ignoring his lawyer's outburst.

"No. Before we got back into our cars, she said she left something on the picnic table and she went back for it."

"So you didn't wait for her?"

"Nope. I was tired and had an early-morning flight to Nantucket."

"There you have it. Chase helped out a friend and quickly left, leaving him no time to murder anyone," Reggie sneered.

"Let's move on to the second murder," I said, tuning out his snarky remark. Ray thought it best that I conduct the preliminary interrogation, while he observed behind the two-way mirror. He figured once

I got into a rhythm with Chase, established a rapport, I might stand a better chance of extracting information. I was of the mind that Ray and Marty should take over, that the changeover would rattle Chase. But Eldridge preferred Ray's strategy. "Do you know Brandy Johnson?" I removed a photograph of Brandy from a manila folder in front of me and spun it so it was facing Chase.

Reggie leaned toward Chase and whispered in his ear.

Chase nodded. Then, he turned to me and said, "Yes." A slight tic in his eye caught my attention. "I tutored her in math. I used to be a math teacher, and these days I tutor as a side hustle. We would meet in the library." He rubbed the back of his neck. "I heard what happened to her and I swear to you I didn't kill her."

"Did you ever sell drugs to her?"

Chase leaned forward and opened his mouth. Again, those red blotches appeared just below his jawline.

Reggie touched Chase's upper arm and gently pulled him back. "As I told you, Detective, my client does not deal drugs."

"According to a friend of Brandy's, a man named Chase, with the last name starting with the letter *D*, sold pharmaceuticals to students. I don't know about where you're from, but up here, the name Chase is pretty rare. And it just so happens that your last name starts with the letter *D*."

"Well, where I'm from, you can't arrest a person based on their first name and last initial without evidence that that person was involved in a crime. You searched Chase's apartment. Did you find anything?" Reggie paused. "I thought not."

A knock at the door prompted us to shift our attention. Eldridge poked his head in. "Detectives, may I have a moment?"

I stopped the recording, then Jack and I left the room.

Eldridge pinched the top of his nose with his right hand, then rubbed his eyelid. Clearly exasperated from the line of questioning. "From what I've seen so far, we have nothing solid. The DA is not going to be happy with the lack of hard evidence—seems all we've got is circumstantial evidence and hearsay. Finish your line of questioning, then let him go."

"But—" I started.

Eldridge held up his hands to interrupt my dissent. "I don't trust Shana Lowry—from what I've seen, she is quite the manipulator. And, I hate to say this, but the lawyer's theory of a frame-up with the blackjack is not far-fetched." Eldridge grunted. "Just give him the don't-skip-town warning and keep digging."

Jack and I nodded, then reentered the interrogation room. I started up the recording device and picked up from where we left off.

"Chase, besides yourself, who has the key to the gift shop?" I asked.

Chase glanced at Reggie, who nodded. "Malcolm is insane when it comes to keys—who has them, who doesn't. As far as I know, Malcolm and I are the only ones with the key to the gift shop. I keep mine on me at all times." He reached into his pocket and dangled them off his index finger, then put them back. "Although . . ." He coughed. "There was this one time when I saw Shana in the gift shop, and when I asked her what she was doing there, she said Malcolm had given her a key. Said she wanted to give a show-related tchotchke to her grandmother. So, I guess Malcolm is not as duty bound as the rest of us with his stupid rule."

It took a fair amount of willpower not to turn my head toward Jack and make any expressions. I held my face still, although I had a sneaking suspicion that a "what-the-fuck" look was bleeding through. Shana pointed a finger at Chase.

Chase was pointing a finger at Shana. Was it just a diversionary tactic to keep us off their individual trails? Or were they somehow in cahoots, muddying the water?

Reggie returned his leather-bound notepad to his briefcase, then clicked his pen and placed it back in his shirt pocket. "We're done here, Detectives."

"One last question," I said, defeated. I pulled out my phone and held it up. "Recognize this?"

Chase squinted, then turned to Reggie and whispered in his ear.

"No. My client has never seen that necklace."

Jack collected the photos, stacked them, and placed them in his folder. He then pulled out the DNA swab kit.

"You can put that away," Reggie said. "I suggest you find the real culprit to take a swab from."

"YOU WATCH?" I asked Sally.

"Sure did. Something occurred to me when Chase talked about the keys and the gift shop."

"Yeah?"

"Remember when you went to talk to Malcolm at the crime scene and I deposited the costume lady in the gift shop?"

"Jean Cranmore. Yeah."

"She was in there—by herself—for some time until you went to interview her."

"Are you saying she might have had the blackjack on her at the time and hid it there?"

"Think about it. We had already cleared the gift shop before planting her in there to wait for you. She knew that. Maybe she had the blackjack hidden under her jacket."

"Come to think of it, she was wearing a zipped-up windbreaker."

"I mean, it's not implausible. Too bad you didn't get any fingerprints off it."

"Whoever held it was probably wearing gloves." I pursed my lips, thinking this through. "Jean is a very small woman. Can she even wield a blackjack with enough force to knock out a guy of Adam's stature?"

"Maybe not. But, as you mentioned earlier, this could be the work of two people," Sally said. "I know you're not keen on the 'they all did it' theory, but—"

I held up my hands. "Don't you start with that nonsense."

"Just sayin' don't rule anything out." Sally leaned against the side of my desk. "I saw your dad in the conference room poring over the old case files."

"Yeah, he's—"

Sally spun her head around as my father walked into the bullpen. "Speak of the devil."

"There you are!" Dad shouted as he neared my desk, waving a blue folder. "Found another tidbit I forgot about." He rolled a nearby chair over to my desk. "I was looking to see if there was something that tied the three victims together. Perhaps help us understand why Adam Kincaid was chosen by our perp." He removed a few sheets of paper from the folder. "I came across these statements from friends of the victims."

I leaned over, elbows on my knees. "Were you able to determine if they were opportunistic targets or specifically targeted?"

"Hard to say. But the one thing they had in common was that they were all planning to go to Woodstock. According to these statements, all the victims bought their tickets from someone who made food deliveries to the hotels where they worked. And, as I already told you, Mac Gardner was a truck driver for a commercial bakery." Without skipping a beat, Dad handed me two of the statements. "And get this— two of the friends said that the guy who sold our victims the tickets also gave them a peace sign necklace. Mac must have taken them from his wife Joanna's collection." Dad grinned as he spoke, clearly thrilled to be piecing this together. "So, it seems they all crossed paths with Mac."

"Which means he assessed his prey before taking them down. Perhaps they fit some sort of criteria. If he chatted them up, he might have learned enough about each of them to lay his trap."

Sally looked over my shoulder at the statements. "Perhaps Mac Gardner gifted the victims the peace sign necklace to gain their trust. So, it wasn't really part of the staged MO. The victims just happened to be wearing the necklaces when he killed them."

Dad nodded. "Only Mac would know that. So, our new killer probably thought it was part of Mac's signature."

"Anything else I should know?"

Dad held up three fingers. "All three were waiters at three different hotels—the other common thread that I had forgotten. Maybe Mac learned that these guys crashed in the staff rooms once in a while. If they trusted Mac, well, that gave him access to their rooms."

"This still doesn't help us understand why our killer chose Adam Kincaid. Shirley Gardner's murder may have been a warped revenge killing—paying for the sins of her father. But Adam? What's his connection to this?"

Dad scratched his chin. "Can we even be sure that Shirley's killer and Adam's killer are one and the same? I'm thinking two different perps."

"That's what the detective in North Adams said. But like I said to her, our killer had to know that there was a fourth victim because he, or she, wrote five on Adam's palm. As for Shirley's murder, maybe the killer got interrupted or simply forgot or learned about this numbering detail later."

Dad shook his head, admonishing me. "I just like to keep an open mind, that's all. Tunnel vision is a detective's worst enemy."

"I'm keeping an open mind, Dad, but logic tells me whoever killed Shirley killed Adam."

"Logic. That and a dollar will get you—"

My phone rang. Thank God. I really didn't want to hear what a dollar and logic would get me. "Gotta take this. It's Jack." I swiped. "Hey."

"Hey. I just got a call from Hope Webb. After we left, her son Brandon came over to visit her and she told him that we had stopped by to pick up the old case files. Turns out Brandon was visiting Grandpa seven years ago, when two people came to the house inquiring about those files."

"Interesting. Maybe Brandon can describe these two or tell us what they were doing there. How old was he at the time?"

"He's twenty now. So, thirteen. I remember jack shit when I was thirteen, but maybe this guy has a better memory than I do."

"I remember a lot of things that happened when I was thirteen." *Nineteen seventy-eight . . . Dad left Mom, my grandfather died, my best friend dumped me, my mom dumped vodka in her morning coffee. It's hard to forget the shittiest year of your life.* "Maybe he will too."

"According to Hope, he works in the city. I'll reach out, see if he's willing to swing by here so we can get a face-to-face."

After hanging up, I filled Dad and Sally in on this development.

"If someone looked through those files, they would know an awful lot about the original crime scenes," Dad said.

"Two people," Sally chimed in. "The 'maybe it's more than one person theory' is not that far-fetched after all."

WHEN I finally returned Mom's call, she invited me over for dinner. Normally, I would have come up with some lame excuse to say no, but I was feeling a bit sorry for her these days. Ever since she returned from the cruise, she hadn't seemed herself.

She seemed lonelier. Needier.

"I know you need to get back to work," Mom said, spooning perfectly browned meatballs into a pot of tomato sauce. On the adjacent burner, a pot of spaghetti boiled vigorously. "Would you mind setting the table?"

I took her invitation to set the table as an opportunity to open cabinets and sneak a peek in the trash, trying my darndest to be nonchalant in my quest to find either full or empty bottles of booze. No bottles. Not even a nip. "You look nice, Mom," I said as I pulled plates from one of the cupboards and set them on the island. "I see you had your hair colored."

She patted her hair. "Almost didn't make it to my appointment in time. Couldn't get the map thingy to work and ended up on the wrong street. I called my hairdresser and turns out I was just around the corner from the salon. Imagine that." Mom dumped the spaghetti in the colander, the steam rising and fogging her glasses. "Go ahead. Serve yourself. I'll get the grated cheese out of the fridge."

In this moment, Mom seemed herself. Puttering around the kitchen, in command of cooking and serving. Maybe I shouldn't be worried. Perhaps I was right about the jet lag.

She patted my forearm as she sat down next to me. "Oh, I meant to tell you something. My old friend Phyllis called me. She told me you're harassing her granddaughter, Shana. Accusing her of murder, or some such nonsense."

I put my fork down. "Mom, besides the fact that I asked you not to interfere in my case, we've already had this conversation."

"We did? When?"

"Two days ago. Monday."

Mom drew her eyebrows together. "You sure?"

I sucked in my breath. "Mom . . . are you drinking again?"

"For the love of God, Susan, no I'm not drinking again," she said forcefully. Perhaps a little too forcefully, which made me think of The Scottish Play.

Only this time, it wasn't Macbeth who came to mind, it was his wife, Lady Macbeth. The one who doth protest too much.

If I wanted to get through this dinner without a fight, I had to push my doubts aside. Well, until I had evidence to prove otherwise. I held up my hands in surrender. "I'm asking out of concern, that's all. I'm worried about you."

"Well, don't be. I'm fine. Maybe a little tired. I ain't no spring chicken anymore." She put her hand around my fist. "But, I swear, I haven't touched the stuff since January."

I looked Mom dead in the eye, wanting to believe her. "I believe you, Mom."

She smiled. "Now finish up so you can go back to your case and your sexy new partner, Phil."

"Jack."

"Phil. Jack. Whatever."

JACK AND I were hoping to tie up a few loose ends before calling it quits for the night. Another chat with Jean Cranmore—the one person who was in the gift shop after the initial search—was high on that list. Granted, it would have been pretty daring of her to have snuck that blackjack into the gift shop with all the police milling about that day. And she didn't strike me as the daring type. I wasn't keen on accusing her of planting the weapon without proof—a fingerprint, a video, a witness, something—to give us justification for such an allegation. It would be so easy for Jean to deny it.

Unfortunately, Jean was busy getting the actors dressed for the show and unavailable until the next morning. However, Shana agreed to meet with us this evening—but couldn't leave the grounds because she was helping out backstage. We asked her to meet us at the picnic table area, which had become our go-to spot for informal interrogations. Neither of us spoke on the way to the theater. Jack seemed lost in thought. I was thinking things through as well. There were two gift shop key holders: Chase Dunham and Malcolm Slater. Chase left for Nantucket the morning of the seventeenth, so he couldn't possibly have put the blackjack in the paneled wall *after* the initial sweep. Unless CSI missed it on that first go-around. Except, the initial search photos and my later search photos showed a definite change in the panel alignment. Malcolm had the only other key, but Shana had once finagled the gift shop key from him. Maybe she did it again. Or instead of asking for it, she just helped herself to it.

With the sun setting, the air temperature was dropping precipitously, like a hot-air balloon running out of propane gas. Typical weather for mid-August in the Catskills. Warm days. Chilly nights.

"Quite the day," Jack said as we strolled toward the picnic tables.

"Understatement of the century." I jutted my chin out toward Shana, who was leaning against one of the picnic tables, scrolling through her phone. "And it ain't over."

Shana looked our way, waved, and slipped her phone into the pocket of her denim jacket.

Jack and I slid onto the same bench seat, while Shana slid in across from us.

She tugged her jacket around her, shivered, then quickly glanced over her shoulder toward the theater. "I've got a few minutes until I'm needed backstage."

"I thought you weren't in this show," I said.

"I'm not. But I'm helping out the stage manager tonight."

"This won't take long," Jack said.

"We spoke with Chase," I began, then stopped to gauge her reaction. Neutral. Of course she knew we would be talking to him, but I thought the news of the interrogation would trigger some sort of facial expression. "Just want to clear up a few details, that's all."

She nodded, her facial muscles remaining relaxed.

"Chase admitted to meeting you that night, but he claimed he was going to give you the sleeping pills for free, but you insisted on paying for them."

She scrunched her face, then followed it up with an eye roll. "He said that?" She gnawed on her lower lip, smearing the red lipstick. "And you believed him?"

"Look, we don't care what the two of you were doing out here, as long as it didn't involve murdering someone," Jack said, tapping his index finger on the wood table. "He claims he left before you did. Which means you were on the grounds, alone. Perhaps Adam saw what you were up to. You said he was an antidrug crusader because of what happened to his friend. Maybe Adam threatened to tell Malcolm. And you couldn't let that happen."

She opened her mouth, a genuine surprised look on her face, then let out a raucous laugh. "Oh my. You guys are really something. I'm the one who left first. He hung back, said he had to take a leak in the woods."

I glanced at Jack, who, like me, was definitely not expecting to be dealing with this "he said, she said" bullshit.

Shana squinted and leaned forward. "You're going to believe a drug dealer over me?" She slid off the bench.

Just as I was about to answer her, the theater door flew open and Ricky Saunders trotted down the steps, lighting a cigarette. Shana turned to watch him, then looked back at us with a scowl on her face. "Weird dude."

"Yeah? Why do you say that?" I asked.

"I don't know. I find him creepy. He doesn't talk to anyone. Just lurks around. But Malcolm likes him, and Malcom's the boss." She glanced back over her shoulder at Ricky and shuddered. Was she afraid of him?

Or was she simply bothered by his reticent nature?

"Do you think he is capable of killing someone?"

She chortled. "Well, he does fit the bill of the antisocial loner who ends up the villain in every serial murder case." She tapped her Apple watch. "Gotta go."

Shana started to walk away.

"Hold on. One more thing," I said.

She stopped and turned toward me. "What now?" she said tersely.

"The other day I asked if you had any ties to this area and you said you didn't. I've since come to learn that your grandmother grew up in Liberty."

"So?"

"That's considered a tie," I said.

"My grandmother moved to Long Island before I was born. All I knew is that she came from Upstate New York." Shana air quoted *Upstate*. "I didn't exactly know where. Jeez. Why do I get the feeling you're trying to pin Adam's murder on me? Are we done here?"

Before I could answer yes or no, she spun around and swiftly walked away. I let her go.

"Who do you believe? Her or Chase?" Jack asked me when Shana was out of earshot, storming back toward the theater.

"I can't believe I'm saying this, but I'm more inclined to believe Shana. Maybe Chase had plans to sell drugs to someone else in the troupe, but he couldn't exactly tell us he hung around knowing that would put him right in the middle of our murder investigation. Which by the way, makes Chase look less guilty. If he was planning on killing Adam, I think he would have made a big show of leaving the grounds so that Shana could attest to that. I also find it hard to believe that he would meet with Shana on the night he planned to kill someone. Unless he's an idiot."

Jack nodded. "It was Shana who called him in the middle of the night. If he was planning to carry out this murder, the last thing he would want is to be seen on the theater grounds." Jack slid off the bench. "It sounds like we're talking ourselves out of Chase as the possible perp."

I shrugged, feeling somewhat noncommittal on that assessment.

"What about Shana?" Jack asked.

"I don't see her wielding a blackjack, or doing something that would ruin her career, like murdering the director who was supposedly helping her land a Broadway role. But . . . we can't rule her out.

She easily could have gotten ahold of Malcolm's keys, for both the gift shop and the side door of the theater." There was something about her I didn't trust. Or maybe it was just that Shana was the type of person who drew my ire. Taking shortcuts to succeed. Playing by her own rules.

RAY RUBBED my shoulders. My head drooped forward, my chin less than an inch from my collarbone. I splayed my palms out on the dining room table.

"This good?"

"Mmmmm."

"I'll take that as a yes."

His thumbs worked downward along my trapezius muscle. "You've got quite a few knots."

"Mmmmm."

He laughed. "Let's go upstairs. I'll work them out."

My phone rang. The word *Dad* lit up the screen.

Ray stopped massaging my neck. "Su*san*," he said. He didn't have to say more, because with the inflection on the second syllable, I clearly understood the part he didn't say out loud: *Don't you dare answer that phone.*

I glanced up at Ray and pursed my lips. I hit decline. Then thought about the case I worked earlier this summer. A woman named Madison Garcia called me one night and I didn't answer my phone. The next morning she was dead. I picked up my phone and looked up at Ray. "I promise this will take a minute. You go upstairs. I'm right behind you."

Ray shook his head. "Do what you gotta do, Susan."

I hit *Dad* in the Recents list. He picked up on the first ring.

"Sorry for the late call," Dad said. "I was reading through the old files and didn't realize what time it was. This could wait until morning."

I glanced up at the clock. It was almost nine. "Well, you have my attention now. What's up?"

"Remember I told you about Jimmy and I going to Helen Blackstone's house to break the news about her husband's murder and her baby, Elizabeth, was there, but the older kids were in camp at the time."

"Yeah, I remember."

"So get this, I just found my notes from when we went back to her house to tell her that Mac committed suicide." He paused. "This time all her kids were home and I jotted down the names of the older ones. Ready?"

"Yeah Dad, ready."

"Derek and Thomas."

"The bartender in North Adams mentioned that a Darren or Derek was seen chatting it up with Shirley Gardner. And that this guy got a call from someone named Elizabeth. Are you thinking what I'm thinking?"

"I sure am."

We just got ourselves three solid suspects. Now we just had to find them.

This might just be a case of multiple perps after all.

DETECTIVE WILL FORD

August 14, 1969

A back door squeaked open and then slammed shut. Two boys—
one blond and fair skinned, the other brown-haired with an olive
complexion—raced past me and Jimmy, then clomped up the stairs.

"Sorry about that," Helen said. She planted herself at the bottom of
the stairs and cupped her hands around her mouth, fashioning a mega-
phone. "Derek! Thomas! Get down here this minute! No muddy sneakers in the house!"

I scratched the kids' names in my notebook. "No worries, Mrs.
Blackstone. Got a young one at home myself. You said they were twins?"

"Yeah. Fraternal, though—they don't look alike. Very different per-
sonalities too."

"How are they holding up?" Jimmy asked.

Before she could answer, the two boys descended the staircase,
sneakers dangling from their fingertips. "Sorry, Mom," they said in unison. They deposited their sneakers near the front door, then ran back up
the stairs.

"Boys'll be growing up without a dad." Helen shook her head. "They're already acting out. Derek especially."

I nodded, unsure of what advice I should impart, if any.

"I'm sure it will all work out fine," Jimmy said. The tenor of his voice betrayed the sentiment.

I cleared my throat, then said, "We have news about Mac Gardner."

"I heard."

"You heard?"

"My cousin works at the prison." Helen bowed her head and privately wiped away tears. After a few seconds, she lifted her head. "So no trial?"

"He was a coward, Mrs. Blackstone," Jimmy said. "He took the easy way out."

We stood in awkward silence for a few minutes.

"I was thinking of getting in touch with Joanna Gardner," Helen said. "See if she'll tell me why he did this. Wife-to-wife. Maybe something she didn't want to tell the cops."

"That's really not a good idea," I said. I knew from experience these well-intentioned meetings between families of the victim and families of the perp brought more heartache than relief. More questions than answers. More despair than repair.

A loud crash outside diverted our attention. The boys raced down the stairs. I scrambled toward the front door and flung it open. A car had plowed into a tree. Four teenagers were in various stages of crawling out of the wreckage. Only the driver remained in the car, head slumped over.

"Call for an ambulance," I shouted at Helen, as I watched the driver gain consciousness and push open his door.

"Woodstock," Jimmy grumbled as we dashed toward the car. "And it's only Thursday."

7

THURSDAY | AUGUST 22, 2019

A PICNIC table on the theater grounds was once again our rendez-vous spot. This time with Jean Cranmore. Jack and I arrived first, at ten o'clock. I settled on a bench, while Jack paced off to the side.

"It's five after. Should I call?" Jack asked, tapping his watch.

As I was about to suggest we hang tight a tad longer, a woman emerged from the residence building.

"I think that's her," I said, tipping my head sideways in the direction of the figure advancing toward us.

Jean waved both her hands high above her head as she walked along the stone path, a slight limp discernible from this distance. Jack waved back.

As she slowly made her way toward us, Jack asked, "What's Ray up to now that he's got a lead on the Brandy Johnson murder?"

"Him and Marty are out canvassing neighbors at Brandy's apartment building today, looking for anyone who might have seen Chase hanging around."

Jack nodded, then turned slightly as Jean gained momentum and neared us.

"So, how can I help you?" she said as she gently lowered herself to the bench across from me. "My sciatica is flaring up today. I need to sit."

Sciatica or lifting dead bodies? I glanced at Jack to see if his mind went to the same place mine did, but he just smiled and sat down next to me.

"Hunched over a sewing machine all these years hasn't done wonders for my back," she said, not so much as a complaint, just a fact.

"And it just flared up out of nowhere?" I asked, trying to sound more curious than accusatory.

"Stress can set it off. And, suffice it to say, these last few days have been rather stressful."

Couldn't argue with her about that. "We just need to ask you a few questions. We're trying to get clarity on some new developments."

She nodded.

"How long have you worked at this theater?" I asked.

"I've been here since the beginning. Why?"

"In all that time, do you recall a Derek, Thomas, or Elizabeth working here? Either part of the cast or crew? Their last names might've been Blackstone."

She shook her head. "I don't think so. But, you should ask Malcolm."

"We did. Earlier this morning. He didn't know them either."

"Oh. Okay." She began to stand. "Is that it?"

"Afraid not. On the morning of the murder, I asked you to wait for me in the gift shop. Do you recall seeing anything out of place? Something that didn't seem right?"

She raised her hand, palm down, above her eyes as the sun rose higher in the sky. She pivoted her head slightly, away from the bright sun's glare as she spoke, which made it look as though she was talking to an imaginary, invisible person sitting next to her. Or perhaps she was avoiding eye contact. "Out of place? I don't go in there often enough to know whether things were in their place or not." When the sun snuck behind a cloud, she lowered her hand and faced us. "Can you be more specific?"

Jack cleared his throat. "Did you notice if the panel behind the cash register was . . . askew?"

"Askew?"

"Out of whack with its adjoining panels," I explained.

"Not that I noticed. Why?"

"We found something behind the panel that wasn't there when CSI swept it, which was before Sally placed you in—"

"Are you suggesting that I hid something in the gift shop?"

I sat still. I hoped Jack wouldn't say anything. Let her answer her own question.

She swiveled her head from Jack to me and back. "Are you accusing me of something?" She pursed her lips tightly before loosening them with a sigh. "I didn't touch anything in that shop. I didn't call anyone. Or text anyone. Or do anything to interfere with your investigation." Her hand trembled. Tears flowed to the edge of her chin before she wiped them away.

"Jean, you were the only person in the gift shop between August sixteenth and August nineteenth, the day the . . . this object was found. We are simply seeking to understand how that object got into the shop."

She swallowed hard, regained her composure. "I don't know anything about that."

"Do you know if anyone has access to the gift shop, besides Chase and Malcolm?"

She clasped her hands, then cracked her knuckles. "Arthritis." She dropped her hands to her lap. "As far as I know, they are the only ones with a key. Although . . . there's an old root cellar under the gift shop.

I guess someone could've entered that way." She swung her legs over the bench seat and stood. "I'll show you."

Jean led the way. As we turned the corner from the side of the building to the back, the only thing I could make out was an overgrown bush snaking along the back wall. As we trudged further along, I spotted it. Weathered wood doors about four feet across lay almost flush against the ground, angled slightly upward where it attached to the shop. A rusty padlock looped through metal handles held the doors together.

"Chief is going to have our heads on a platter for missing this," I said to Jack.

"I'll take the blame. I was supposed to scout behind the buildings. I came this way, and peeked around, but it was a muddy mess and pouring rain and I didn't notice the doors." Jack bent over the lock, inspecting it closely, then snapped a few pictures. "It's not locked," he said, as he stepped away from the doors.

I bent over the lock. Upon closer inspection, I too noticed that the U-shaped bar was not fully nested in the square metal body. I rummaged around in my backpack and pulled out a pair of latex gloves and an evidence bag. After slipping on the gloves, I grabbed the padlock and pulled it downward. The rusted metal loop disengaged fully from the bottom half. I slid it off, then deposited the padlock into the plastic bag.

"Have you ever been down there?" Jack asked Jean.

"No. But there's a little door in the floor at the rear of the shop that leads down to it. It's covered by a rug, so I would imagine that most people don't even know it's there."

"How did you know this was here? Is it common knowledge?" Jack asked, eyeing the cellar doors.

"For those of us on the crew, I would say it's fairly common knowledge. Unlike the actors who come for a single season, many of us have been coming here for years."

Two scenarios crossed my mind. If this is the way the perp gained entry to the gift shop, either that person did not fully engage the lock when he or she emerged from the cellar after planting the blackjack. Or the rust in the holes rendered the lock useless and impossible to lock, making the cellar accessible to anyone. "Who has the key to the padlock?" I asked.

Jean shrugged. "You'll have to ask Malcolm or Chase. Or Ricky, I suppose. I can't imagine that anyone else has one. There's no reason for anyone to go down there." Jean kneaded her lower back with the tips of her fingers. "Am I free to go?"

I nodded. "Once again, we ask for your discretion about what we discovered in the gift shop."

"Of course." She turned heel and slowly walked away.

Jack and I stood on either side of the wood doors.

I touched the door with the toe of my shoe. "Ready to root around a root cellar?"

"It'll have to wait until later," Jack replied, wincing at my pun. "We got a lunch date with Hope's son at that diner in Ellenville, and we're already running late."

"Shit. Okay. I'll get Sally or Ron down here to secure crime scene tape on these doors and stand guard."

BRANDON RESEMBLED his mother, Hope—dark brown eyes, curly brown hair, wide nose, recessed chin. As we settled onto the red plastic-covered booth seats, his phone buzzed, but instead of looking at the screen, he picked it up and slid it into his pocket.

"Sorry about that. You have my full attention."

"We're hoping you can tell us about the day you were at your grandfather's house when someone came around asking about your grandfather's files," Jack said.

"Yeah. My mom told me you retrieved the Mac Gardner files from my grandfather's attic. That's when I reminded her about those people who came around years ago wanting to read them."

"Really just looking for a name or description of the folks who visited your grandfather. Maybe you remember why they were interested in the case files?"

"What I remember is that two people, a man and a woman, came to the house one day, and I'm pretty sure it was Easter weekend. My grandmother was decorating eggs and wanted me to help and I thought it was babyish and refused." Brandon chuckled. "Funny, the things we remember. Anyway, these visitors asked my grandfather if they could take a peek at the files. I assumed they were true crime fanatics like Gramps."

"Can you describe them?"

He closed one eye as if that would make the memory sharper. "Been a while, but yeah." He motioned to the waitress, then turned to us. "Do you mind? Haven't had a bite to eat today."

The waitress sauntered over. "Decided, hon?"

"Yeah. Turkey club and a Coke."

"Pepsi okay, hon?"

"Sure."

"And your friends here?"

"I'm all set," I said.

"Iced coffee with milk," Jack said.

"Turkey club, Pepsi, and an iced coffee. Sure I can't get you anything, dear?"

Never one for being the odd one out, I caved. "I'll have an iced coffee. A little bit of milk."

"As you were saying," Jack said to Brandon as the waitress drifted away.

"So, I thought they were old. But I was thirteen, so everyone over thirty looked old to me."

"Your best guess," I said.

"Hmm." Brandon picked up a fork and examined it, then put it down. "I'm thinking the man was in his forties, but I couldn't tell you if he was on the low side or high side of forty. The woman was younger than the man, so she might have been in her thirties."

"Can you describe them?"

"The guy had long black hair tied back in a ponytail, graying at the temples. He was beefy. Wore a Harley jacket, which I remember because I thought it was kinda cool."

"And the woman?"

Brandon raised his index finger to his lower lip and rubbed it gently. "Skinny. Anorexic skinny, if you know what I mean."

"Tall? Short?"

Brandon shrugged. "I was a short preteen, so everyone was tall to me. But she was definitely way shorter than the guy."

"Did they introduce themselves to your grandfather?"

"If they did, I don't remember."

"And did your grandfather show them the files?"

"He did. They were up there for the entire morning."

"Do you recall hearing the names Derek or Elizabeth?"

"Elizabeth," Brandon said slowly. His eyes widened. "Yeah. At one point, the woman came down to use the bathroom and the guy called down to her and yelled, 'Hey, Liz, get up here.'"

The waitress delivered Brandon's turkey club and his Pepsi. "Be right back."

"What were you doing while they were up there?" I asked.

"Playing video games in the den." Brandon pointed to his sandwich. "Do you mind?" Without waiting for a response, he took a small bite, then said, "Which is why I wasn't paying much attention. The one time I did eavesdrop, they were talking about baseball. Gramps had some cool baseball memorabilia up there—especially Mets stuff from 1969, the year they won the World Series. The Harley guy said he loved watching the run-up to the World Series on TV when he was a kid. Gramps even let him look through his baseball card collection, which kinda pissed me off because that stuff was off-limits to me."

The waitress returned with our iced coffees. "If you want anything else, just holler."

"Anything else you can think of?" I asked.

He shook his head as he adjusted the straw and took a long sip. "Well, not about them. But I do remember Gramps telling me a bit about the case. Pretty gruesome stuff. My thirteen-year-old self was fascinated by it." He took another bite of his sandwich.

"Did you go through the boxes?"

He stopped mid-chew. "My mom wouldn't let me anywhere near those boxes. She said it would give me nightmares. Besides, I would have been grounded for life if I disobeyed. I was a pretty toe-the-line kind of kid." He put down the sandwich and picked up a potato chip. "So, why the renewed interest?"

As Brandon ate, Jack superficially told him about the current case and its possible connection to the murder of Shirley Gardner, seven years ago, and the 1969 cases. Brandon bobbed his head as Jack shared the few details he was willing to relinquish.

I zoned in and out during Jack's monologue as I thought about the new piece that just got added to the puzzle . . . the high probability that "Liz" was Elizabeth and "Harley guy" was either Derek or Thomas.

SALLY AND Ron were standing right where we left them—in front of the wooden doors leading down to the gift shop cellar. With them stood a teenager, who started pacing as we neared. The boy was gangly, with the hunched frame of a preteen in the throes of puberty who wasn't quite sure how to walk in his new body. Twelve or thirteen, I guessed.

As we neared, Ron exclaimed, "Hey! This is my son, Tyler. He biked over here from camp to keep me company. Hope you don't mind. Tyler, this is Detective Susan Ford and Detective Jack Tomelli."

Tyler gave a small wave. "Hi," he mumbled.

"Nice to meet you," I said.

"Enjoying camp?" Jack asked.

"Guess so," Tyler said, before noting his dad's disappointed frown. He recalibrated his answer. "Yeah, it's great."

"Well, Tyler's got to get home, and I gotta head back to the station. Y'all good here without me?"

"We're good," Jack said. He turned to me. "Ready?"

Jack and I slipped on a pair of latex gloves, covered our shoes with paper booties, and headed down into the cellar.

Jack led the way.

As we descended the rickety stairs, we switched on our palm-sized flashlights. The air was noticeably cooler down here. I breathed in the dank, musky smell of earth and fieldstone as I flicked my light from one corner of the underground space to another. Jack pointed his light at the overhead bulb and pulled the string.

The dim wattage barely illuminated the space, so we kept our flashlights on. Before stepping onto the floor, we swept our flashlights along the ground in the hopes of finding footprints. The dirt floor appeared to have been raked, with thin lines running through the dirt. When I shone my flashlight to my right, I spotted a rake leaning against the stairs.

It would have been easy for someone to rake away footprints as they made their way to the stairs and then stand on the last step and erase any remaining footstep.

If this is how the killer gained entry, we were dealing with someone smart and meticulous.

We made our way to the pull-down ladder that led to the little door in the floor above. Jack gave a tug and the ladder unfolded.

He turned to me over his shoulder. "Our blackjack wielder probably wore gloves, but we should get someone down here to dust for fingerprints. Starting with that rake handle."

"Hey down there," Sally yelled. "Find anything?"

I walked back to the steps and peered up. Sally was in a crouched position leaning over the cellar entrance. "Nothing so far. Can you call Eldridge and have him send a couple of CSIs down here for fingerprints and whatnot?"

Sally flashed a thumbs-up, and I headed back to where Jack was standing. He was pointing his flashlight at the floor, illuminating the edge of ladder.

I crouched down, then pulled my phone from my back pocket and snapped a couple of pictures of a watch. A Timex with a toffee leather band and a slightly scratched surface.

I carefully picked up the watch to inspect it more closely. "Looks like a man's watch. The buckle is broken. The doohickey that fits into the holes is missing. Might explain how it slipped off someone's wrist." I turned the watch around. "There's an inscription on the back, but it's scratched over—or worn out. I can't make out what it says." I laid it back down on the ground for CSI to recover.

Jack lowered his hand and the room darkened. "My thinking is that our perp wanted to hide the blackjack but do so in a manner that implicates someone else. I mean, if it was me, I'd just chuck it in Sackett Lake. This feels like a deliberate ploy to get us off his, or her, trail."

"Or them. We haven't ruled out a duo." I paused. "The Blackstone kids, Derek and Elizabeth."

"Or Chase and Shana," Jack countered. "Maybe their whole 'he said, she said' routine is meant to sow confusion."

I scrunched my face. Although in the darkness, I doubt he saw my dubious expression.

"You're the one who noticed that Chase had a tan outline of a watch on his wrist," he reminded me.

"Yeah, but he works in the gift shop. If this is his watch, there could be a perfectly innocent reason why we found it here in the cellar. Besides, his lawyer put the kibosh on getting his fingerprints or DNA, so the only way to find out if this is his watch is to ask him." I swept the cellar with my flashlight as I walked over to the metal shelves against the wall. "Whoa."

"Found something?"

I snapped a picture of the neatly folded clothes—a pair of jeans, a white T-shirt, and a pair of black underwear. On top, a pair of loafers with socks balled up inside. "Yeah. I think I just found Adam's clothes. I'll have CSI bag it."

My phone pinged with a text message. It was Ron asking if I was almost done, that he had a bit of news to impart. I headed back up the cellar steps to respond, blinking furiously as my eyes adjusted to the bright sunshine.

"We found an old Timex watch and—" I started to tell Sally, then turned slightly, surprised to see Nathan Fowler and Leslie Brattle standing there.

"We were passing by and wondered what was going on here," Nathan said. "Just curious. Sorry, we'll leave you be."

"While I have you two here, did you know about this cellar?" I asked.

Nathan peered down the opening. "Actually, I had no idea this existed, which is why I wondered what you were doing back here."

"Hadn't a clue," Leslie said. "Carry on." They turned and headed back toward the theater.

I waited until they were out of earshot before dialing Ron's number. "Hey, what's up?"

"Y'know how you wanted me to try and find Elizabeth and Derek?"

"You found them?"

"Uh, no. But I did find Derek's twin brother, Thomas. Well, sort of. He's six feet under, unfortunately. The coroner's report says suicide. Seven years ago, January. I called over to the funeral home that handled the service, wanted to see who made the funeral arrangements as it might've been a way to track down his siblings."

"And?"

"He said the funeral was arranged by Thomas's husband. If you want to get in touch with him, he lives in the city. Do you want the deets?"

"Sure, hold on." I walked over to my backpack and pulled out my notepad. "Go ahead."

"First name Simon. Last name Pierce. Phone number is 212-555-5560."

I looked up and watched Jack emerge from the cellar. I waved him over. "Thanks for this," I said to Ron and hung up.

"Seems Thomas Blackstone is dead. Suicide. Seven years ago. Coincidence?" I snorted. "Seven years ago two people go snooping around the case files. Seven years ago Shirley Gardner is murdered. And seven years ago Thomas Blackstone commits suicide."

"In what order?" Jack asked.

"Thomas committed suicide in January. Ponytail man and his companion, Liz—possibly Thomas's siblings, Derek and Elizabeth—read the case files that spring. Shirley is murdered in the fall."

"Perhaps avenging not only their father's killer but their brother's death. If they believe Mac Gardner was the curse upon their family, Derek and Elizabeth directed their anger to his one living daughter, Shirley. An eye for an eye."

"I like your theory," I said. "But what the hell is the connection to Adam Kincaid?"

RAY ROLLED back his chair, then spun it to face me. "I heard you had one hell of a day."

"Yeah. I'll fill you in later. How did the canvassing go?"

"Neighbor who lives a couple of doors down from Brandy Johnson has one of those Ring doorbells and gave us permission to review the footage. She works at the theater." Ray rolled back his desk and shuffled some papers. "Libby Wright. She's the prop mistress there. Whatever that means."

"Well, for one thing, it means she knows what Chase looks like. Did she ever see him coming or going?"

"No. She said the only place she's seen him is in the gift shop. But if Chase went to see Brandy, he would've had to have passed by Libby's door. I'm just hoping we can connect Chase to Brandy and haul his ass in here again." Ray started to roll back to his desk, hesitated, then asked, "Have you interviewed Libby regarding your case?"

"Yes, but not me personally. Sally spoke to her the morning of the murder. She was sick the night of the murder, some kind of stomach bug, which was confirmed by her roommate. Someone else handled her prop duties during tech rehearsal."

"I didn't realize Malcolm hired locals."

"He doesn't. According to Sally, she's a friend of Ricky's and he finagled a job for her three years ago."

"Interesting."

"Yeah? How's that interesting?"

"Not that. About the roommate." Ray hesitated, then said, "When I asked Libby if she had a roommate—hoping there would be someone else who might have seen Chase—she said her roommate packed up and left a few days ago. Weird timing, huh?"

JACK AND I made our way to the conference room and huddled with Dad, Sally, and Ron to review what we had learned so far and lay out next steps. I pulled Sally aside to ask her about Libby's roommate. "Do you recall your interview with Libby's roommate?"

"Yeah. I wanted to confirm Libby's whereabouts the night of the murder. She told me Libby was sick and in bed all night with some kind of stomach bug. Why?"

"What was the roommate's name?" I asked.

"Grace. Grace Sinclair. Why?"

"She left town. Just wondering if her sudden departure is connected to all this," I said, waving my arm over the papers and photographs stacked on the conference-room table.

"Hmm. Well if you want, I'll get in touch with Grace. Make sure her departure is not to avoid the law." Sally held up her iPad. "Ready to get down to business?"

Sally brought us up to speed on her assignment—tracking down the spouses and children or grandchildren of the 1969 victims. She powered up her iPad, scanned the screen, then looked up at us. "The first victim, Kenneth Waterman, was not married, so no wife to track down. The second victim, Robert Sherman, was married to a woman named Leah but had no children. Sadly, Leah Sherman died forty years ago, a drug overdose."

"Whatever became of Sam Blackstone's wife, Helen?" I asked.

"She remarried a few years after Sam was murdered." Sally bowed her head and scrolled though her iPad. "To an Owen Riggs. Police were called to their home often to break up domestic disputes."

"Owen Riggs?" Dad snapped his fingers. "I remember him. There was this incident—" He rubbed his forehead for a few seconds. "It'll come to me."

"Is he alive? This Owen Riggs?" I asked.

Sally glanced down at her iPad. "Sure is. Lives in Woodbourne."

I turned to Sally. "Anything—"

"Got it!" Dad exclaimed. "The incident with Owen Riggs went down in the summer of sixty-nine, so years before Helen hitched her wagon to his. But, man, I knew I should have hauled his ass into jail and thrown away the key when I had the chance."

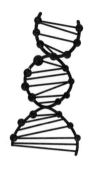

DETECTIVE WILL FORD

August 15, 1969

Owen Riggs stood outside his small shack of a house, his hands behind his back, handcuffed.

His wavy blond hair fell over his eyes, and without access to his fingers, he kept rolling his head back and to the side to shake the bangs off his forehead.

"Hey man, this ain't fair," Owen said.

"Life ain't fair," I retorted, then backed up a few inches to escape his stale beer-and-onion breath.

Jimmy waved me over to the front door of the house.

"Don't move," I commanded as I hustled toward Jimmy.

"Where am I gonna go with my hands cuffed behind my back?" Owen twisted his torso and lifted his arms slightly. "And I ain't got no shoes on, man," he shouted.

"His girlfriend doesn't wanna press charges," Jimmy whispered. "Said things just got a little out of hand and the neighbor who called it in is making a big fuss over nothing."

"*That bright red mark on her right cheekbone don't look like nothing,*" I countered.

I walked over to the woman standing in the doorway. "Laura, right?" She nodded. "Laura, we can help you if you let us," I said, rubbing my right cheekbone.

She brought her finger up to her bruise. "It's nothing. Not Owen's fault. Really, I yelled at him about drinking too much, that's all. He has a right to do whatever he wants after work."

"He doesn't have a right to hit you."

Laura peered over my shoulder at Owen, who was chipping away at the dirt with his toe. "Um, he didn't hit me. Clumsy me, I just walked into the door." She smiled faintly. "We were supposed to go to Woodstock, but I told him I wasn't up for it, and he got all mad because he bought the tickets and—"

"Hey!" Owen yelled.

"Shut the hell up!" Jimmy yelled back at him.

"How old are you?" I asked.

"Twenty-two."

"You sure you don't want to press charges?"

She blinked away a couple of tears and shook her head.

Jimmy walked over to Owen and unclasped the handcuffs.

"Fuck, man. You had those on too tight."

"If we come around here again, we're hauling your ass to jail. And a nice-lookin' guy like you will get quite the welcome in there, if you get my drift," Jimmy said.

"I didn't do nothin'. Ask her," Owen mumbled, cocking his head in his girlfriend's direction.

I reached into my wallet, pulled out a card, then whispered to Laura, "Here. If you need anything. Wanna talk." I glanced over my shoulder. "Or if things get out of hand."

8

FRIDAY | AUGUST 23, 2019

"THAT STORY your father told us yesterday was something else," Jack said, hovering over my desk. "And to think that guy Owen ended up marrying Helen Blackstone."

"Right, crazy? If he abused that woman Laura, I'm willing to bet he abused Helen. Maybe even her kids. It's like a shitty game of dominoes. A lifetime of bad things stemming from that initial push of the first tile—like there's no escaping it."

"Deep."

"There's a name for it."

"Yeah?"

"Intergenerational trauma. My daughter, Natalie—she's a psychologist—explained it to me. A ripple effect from one generation to the next, stemming from a traumatic event such as a violent death of a parent and its effect on the survivors—in our case, the mother and kids. Natalie said sometimes, if the fallout from the trauma is not resolved, there is an overwhelming desire to blame someone and exact some kind of satisfying justice. Could explain why the son or daughter of Sam Blackstone would seek revenge."

"Interesting. Would love to pick her brain some time."

"Good idea. Meanwhile, let's do something productive now," I offered. "Up for a ride to meet Owen? He might just know where his stepkids—Derek and Elizabeth—are and what they've been up to."

As I settled in the passenger seat of Jack's Volvo, it dawned on me that I could get used to riding shotgun—these cushy leather seats certainly swaying me. He fiddled with the GPS on his phone, connected it to Apple CarPlay, and put the car in gear.

"My turn to choose the music," he said, tuning in to a hip-hop station.

I tried to follow the lyrics, but found myself straining to hear them against a deep bass. I'd take Bruce Springsteen over this any day.

Jack pulled into a narrow dirt driveway and parked behind a beat-up Chevy Impala. I gave it the once-over when I exited the Volvo: dents and dings on all four doors, the hood, and the rear bumper. Hanging from the rearview mirror, an air freshener shaped like the silhouette of a well-endowed stripper. The windows were down, and the breeze carried the sour smell of stale cigarettes. So much for that air freshener.

Jack closed his fist and hammered gently on the front door of Owen's mobile home. *Mobile* was a misnomer. The vehicle no longer had wheels and was mounted on concrete blocks. The door opened immediately. His expression neither quizzical nor surprised at our appearance on his doorstep, as if he was expecting us.

He hitched up his jeans, which were having a hard time staying put on his buck-fifty frame. "How can I help you . . ." he began, then squinted at the badges secured to our belt buckles. "Detectives."

"We think you can help us with a case we're working on," I said.

"Yeah? I doubt it." He pointed to four lawn chairs near the edge of his trailer. "But sure." He led us to the upright chairs.

The torn, crosshatched nylon provided little faith that these chairs would accommodate our rear ends. I carefully lowered myself onto one of them and watched Jack take the same precaution. Owen, confident in his chair's durability, plopped down. It gave slightly.

"Nice day," he said, waving his hand in the air. "Gotta love the Catskills in August."

I glanced at Jack and got the impression he was thinking the same thing I was: *Was this guy really doing weather small talk?*

Jack leaned forward, placing his elbows on his knees. "Owen, we're looking for two people you know—"

"I know a lotta people," he blurted out.

Jack nodded. "Specifically, your stepkids, Derek and Elizabeth."

As Jack spoke those names, Owen leaped from his chair. "Those fuckwads." His expression and body language shifted instantly from "friendly guy shooting the shit" to "get the hell off my property." He ran his hand through his gray hair and started pacing. "I haven't seen those two psychos or their faggot brother in years." He seemed awfully worked up for not seeing them in years.

"When was the last time you saw them?" I asked.

He sat back down on the edge of his lawn chair. "Mind?" he said, pulling a pack of Marlboros from his shorts pocket. He didn't wait for an answer before lighting up. "Why do you want to find 'em?"

"Tell you what," Jack began. "We'll ask the questions here. And trust me, it'll be easier here than down at the station."

"Well, I haven't seen 'em since I left their mother in the nineties. The two of 'em robbed me blind. My dad left me a little dough and they scammed me out of it. Haven't seen 'em since." Owen took a quick drag on his cigarette. "Don't think I didn't try and track 'em down. I even hired me a private detective. He thinks they changed their identities. I'd get a tip every now and again, but after six years of chasing 'em, I gave up. Heard their homo brother Tommy-boy offed himself." He stubbed the cigarette out on the metal arm of the lawn chair. "If you find those two, I'd like to have a word with 'em." He snickered.

Jack stood up. "Lots of domestic calls out to your property back then. Reports of you abusing Helen and her kids. Their dad was killed. Their lives turned upside down," he said, picking up steam. "And you treated them like shit. So, you know what? Maybe they deserved that money. Karma, you know."

Well, well, well. That was a side of Jack I hadn't seen yet. And I liked it.

SIMON PIERCE, Thomas Blackstone's widower, was nursing a broken ankle—the result of tripping over a tennis ball that fell from his pocket while serving. When Ron reached out to him to set up a meeting, Simon asked if we could conduct the interview over Zoom, as mobility was an issue. I didn't mind. It beat spending four hours in the car driving to Manhattan and back for a thirty-minute (if that) meeting. We hoped Simon could shed some light on the whereabouts of Derek and Elizabeth. Perhaps even provide some background on what they'd been up to these past fifty years.

Jack and I sat side by side in the small interrogation room waiting for Simon to log on.

Jack shook his wrist, then glanced at his watch. "I hate Zoom."

At 10:03, Simon's forehead appeared on the bottom edge of our screen. He shifted forward to adjust his laptop and when his face was centered, he leaned back. He said a few words, but we didn't hear because he was muted.

He took note of my hand motion—pointing to my ear and shaking my head—and he brushed his fingers along the keyboard to unmute himself. "There, that should be working now," he said softly. "Now, how can I help you?"

Jack and I took turns telling Simon as much as we could. He bobbed his head as he listened attentively. We positioned the narrative as though Derek and Elizabeth were persons of interest. That we weren't even sure they were the Derek and Elizabeth we were looking for. Although how many *other* Dereks and Elizabeths would have interest in the Mac Gardner evidence files?

"So, are they in some sort of trouble?"

"That's hard to say at this point in our investigation," I said. "But we do think they have information that can help us."

Simon rubbed the top of his bald head, then crossed his arms in front of his chest. A defensive posture that he held for several seconds. "They were all dealt a nasty hand. The three of them were deeply traumatized. Especially Derek. And Elizabeth was under Derek's spell. She was too young to remember her father's death and might've gotten over it. But Derek spun her up and it gave her an angry edge. And their stepdad, Owen. Jeez. He was the icing on the cake. I always thought Thomas had come to some kind of peace with what happened, that he managed to escape the toll of the trauma." He blinked in slow motion. "Obviously not."

"When was the last time you saw them?" Jack asked.

"It's been ages. Probably a year or so before Thomas, uh, died." He let out a long breath.

"They didn't go to the funeral?"

"No. They were afraid their stepfather would be looking for them there."

"So you knew what they had done to Owen?"

"Yeah." He smiled. "Bilked him out of a hundred thousand dollars, give or take a few grand."

Jack let out a low whistle. "Didn't realize it was that much."

"It ain't chump change. But it's not enough to set you up for life. I think they got more pleasure in taking it than living off of it."

"So you have no clue as to where they might be?" I asked.

"Well, I'm sure that money ran out years ago. I imagine they have jobs somewhere. Maybe they're on the government dole."

I heard a knock, then a muffled voice. "Simon? You in there?" Then a figure appeared in his doorway.

Simon muted his microphone and turned to his right. He spoke for a couple of minutes before turning back to us and unmuting himself. "Sorry about that."

"Mr. Pierce—"

"Simon, please."

"Simon. Do you have a photograph of Derek and Elizabeth?" I asked.

"If I have any pictures, it would be from their youth. Nothing current, I'm afraid."

"If you can send a couple to us, we'd appreciate it. There is technology that can age a face. It might help."

"Can I think about that? I mean, obviously those two don't want to be found. Maybe if you told me they've done something illegal, but if they are law-abiding citizens, well . . . I feel funny, that's all."

"I get that," Jack said sympathetically. "But they did rob their stepdad. Justified or not, that is illegal." Jack cleared his throat. "But we don't care about that. We met Owen. What we really need to do is get in touch with Derek or Elizabeth so we can sort out what they might know. One or both of them might even want to help us put a lid on this case." Jack paused. "And with their cooperation, hopefully, justice will be served.

He nodded, his eyebrows pinched together. Definitely a sign of mulling. We let him mull.

"Let me see what I can find," he finally said.

Sometimes people just need a bit of persuasion, and Jack's little speech landed just right.

"Did Thomas ever talk to you about what happened to his father?" I asked.

"No. Thomas didn't tell me much, only that his father was murdered in a hotel room. In-depth discussions on that matter were off-limits. He refused to talk about it. And I didn't press. From the little he did divulge, I could understand why."

The minute we logged off Zoom, my phone rang.

"Detective Susan Ford here."

"Detective Ford, George Zettler here."

Hercule Poirot, I mouthed to Jack while switching to speaker mode. "I have Detective Jack Tomelli on the line. We're listening."

"If you recall . . . last spoke, I . . . waiting . . . DNA results from one . . . online genealogy websites. Well . . . got them."

"You're breaking up, George," Jack yelled into the phone, as though shouting would fix the problem. Then I remembered Leslie Brattle mentioning the spotty cell-phone service at the dorms.

"Some . . . wasn't expecting. A cous . . . of mine on my mother's side . . . searching for relatives. And it's . . . caid."

"George, we're only catching every other word," I said.

"Hold on a . . ." A few seconds passed. "How's this? I'm outside now."

"Yes, we can hear you better now. Repeat what you said."

"I just got my genealogy results along with some matches. Adam Kincaid must have been in the system because he showed up as a relative of mine, on my mother's side. A cousin. He told a few of us he was adopted—I guess he went looking for relatives. Jesus. I need to go. I need to process this." He abruptly hung up.

I stared at the phone in a stupor before disengaging on our end.

This was it. This was the connection.

Adam was specifically targeted because someone knew he was Mac Gardner's grandson. Which meant twenty-eight years ago Shirley—Mac Gardner's daughter—had a son . . . a son she gave up for adoption to the Kincaids.

The bigger question was, who else knew?

DAD WAS pretty much in the same position I'd left him in that morning—hunched over a set of old crime scene photos. When he looked up, I told him what I had just learned.

"Wait. Let me get this straight," Dad began. "Adam did that online DNA thing before he died and set it so that anyone who had a familial match could contact him. And George Zettler was a match?"

"Right. And get this, it was a close cousin match."

"Close cousin?"

"Yeah. George sent over the DNA results for us to analyze. George and Adam share eight percent of their DNA, which Ancestry pegs as first cousins once removed," I said.

"Dang. That's precise."

"And we know that George's mother, Barbara, had only one brother, Mac, who had only one daughter, Shirley."

Dad wrinkled his forehead. "I'm still not following."

I continued to explain, "George and Shirley are first cousins, making George and Adam first cousins once removed.

Dad nodded and grinned. "Got it."

"Y'know what I wanna know? How did the killer know that Adam was Shirley's son? Adam's father told us it was a closed adoption." I chewed on my own question a bit, then added, "It's possible that Shirley told Derek about having a son during one of their bar chats in North Adams. Which means it's looking more and more like Derek is knocking off Mac's offspring."

"Except you're forgetting one thing, Susan. The numbers on the palm. Only one of the two recent victims had them. And, look here," Dad said, laying out three photos on the table. "Mac was in the navy. Knew his way around nautical ropes. Used fancy knot ties on his victims. This is a photo from Shirley's murder. Not a fancy knot. Here's Adam's photo," he said shuffling the photographs. "Fancy knot. Oh, and one more thing: Shirley was found with her bra and underwear on. The others were buck naked." He smirked condescendingly, as though my theory was hogwash. "Still think it's just one person who did both jobs?"

"So, a few details are off."

"C'mon Susan. Why get every other detail right but not write a number on Shirley's palm or tie fancy knots around her wrists and ankles?" Dad coughed into his fist as he got worked up over his theory. "I'll tell you why. Whoever killed Shirley just wanted to get it right *enough*, copy just enough of the original to satisfy whatever was getting his goat. But the person who killed Adam was fastidious, detailed-oriented—probably took pleasure in it being exact."

"Or . . . maybe Shirley being a woman influenced the manner in which he left her body. Maybe the killer had to leave Shirley's crime scene quickly and didn't get the chance to go full-on copycat. Maybe the killer acquired more information about the crime scene between the two murders." I blew out a breath of air. "Look, I'm not dismissing outright that two different people did this, it just seems highly improbable to me. That's all."

Dad opened his mouth to debate this further but was interrupted by my ringing phone.

"Gotta take this," I said, leaving him hanging.

JACK AND I settled into a booth at Miss Monticello Diner. You didn't have to be a detective to deduce that he had taken a shine to Kelly, a waitress who recently moved to the area to pursue her passion—painting. Jack twisted around in his seat looking for her, but Kelly was not working this afternoon.

Ray and his partner, Marty, came blasting through the front door and beelined it to where we were sitting.

"Scooch over," Ray said, edging his butt toward the middle of the seat, hip-checking me.

Marty sat next to Jack. Jack obligingly slid over toward the wall.

"Hope we're not interrupting anything . . . like a date." Marty smirked and winked.

I lifted my left hand. "I'm happily engaged."

Marty motioned to a waitress who appeared with a carafe in one hand and two mugs hooked to her fingers in the other. She poured quickly and fled. She'd been around long enough to recognize a police huddle.

"What's up?" I asked.

"We reviewed Libby Wright's Ring footage," Ray said, tipping the small metal pitcher of milk into his mug. "Guess who we saw passing by Libby's apartment?"

"Well, since you've gone out of your way to hunt us down at this diner, I am going to guess that it was Chase Dunham," I said.

"You have guessed correctly," Marty said, grinning.

Ray sipped his coffee. "Problem is we can't arrest him for walking down the hallway. We're still in circumstantial territory, here. But the timing is interesting." Ray reached across my body to extract a sugar substitute packet from the rack. He ripped open the pink packet and tapped the powdery contents into his coffee.

"I heard that stuff is crap for your body," Jack said, pointing to the now depleted packet.

"Okay, Mom. I'll take that under advisement," Ray retorted. "So, anyway, the timing. On August sixth at around eleven fifteen, Brandy passes by Libby's door in the direction of her apartment. About an hour later, Chase makes an appearance, walking rather quickly past Libby's door. About ten minutes go by, and Chase walks by Libby's apartment toward the elevator. Definitely steaming. Hands clenched. Scowl on his face. Then, about five minutes after Chase exits, Brandy runs past Libby's door."

"And that's the last time she's seen," Marty adds. "There are no CCTV cameras in the parking area of the apartment building, so the trail goes cold."

I touched Ray's arm to get his attention. "Sally is trying to locate Libby's roommate, Grace Sinclair. She taught at the college, and Brandy was her student. Maybe she knows something."

"From your lips to God's ears," Marty said. An expression I always found cringey. "Speaking of lips and ears, how's your case going?"

"There's a possibility that someone related to Mac Gardner's victims is snuffing out Mac's descendants." I drummed my fingers on the table. "But I'm not ruling out that Adam's murder could be tied to some drug-dealing shenanigans involving your suspect, Chase."

"There's also the Leslie Brattle extortion business—if her husband got wind of her affair and divorced her, well, she would no longer be living the lifestyle she has come to enjoy," Jack said. "She certainly has motive."

"I think this case would even give Hercule Poirot, Jane Marple, and Tommy and Tuppence a run for their money." Three confused faces stared at me. "You guys really need to read more."

I FOUND Dad in the conference room where we had deposited the case files. Head down over folded arms.

"Dad," I whispered, gently shaking his shoulder.

He lifted his head and stretched his arms over his head. "Must have dozed off there," he groaned.

"You need a lift home?"

"Yeah. If you don't mind. Kinda late to call Harry to pick me up." Dad picked up the folder his head was lying on and pulled out a sheet of paper. "I was going through the files from the Ellenville murder and a name popped out at me, as did a memory." He stood, adjusted his cheaters, and pointed to the sheet of notepaper in front of him. "Here, Madeline Klein. She was the first victim's girlfriend."

"Sally mentioned that Kenneth Waterman wasn't married. But she didn't say anything about a girlfriend."

"Maybe she didn't think it was relevant." Dad cocked his head. His eyebrows gamely arched. "Well, there's something you should know about her."

DETECTIVE WILL FORD

August 16, 1969

My right foot sank in the muck. *"Jesus H. Christ,"* I mumbled as I lifted my foot out of the swampy pasture and removed my shoe. *"These are my best loafers."* I shook the clump of mud off the soles, then placed my hand on Patrol Officer Marvin Kooplehaus's shoulder for balance as I slipped the soggy shoe back on.

Koop and I stood at the edge of Max Yasgur's dairy farm—near the half-constructed ticket booth. We had heard that the late change in venue—from Woodstock, New York to Bethel, New York—gave the festival organizers little time to prepare. When fifty thousand people un-expectedly showed up Wednesday morning (a whole two days before the first band was due to play) the organizers were forced to choose between completing construction of the stage or completing construction of the fencing and ticket booth. The stage was built. The ticket booth and fenc-ing were not.

And they kept coming and coming.

Ticket, or no ticket, they got in.

I surveyed the sea of hippies sloping down from the stage. Tie-dye swirls for as far as the eye could see.

"What the heck are we supposed to be doing here?"

I held up my index and middle finger. "Keeping the peace, man."

"I still can't believe the New York City police commissioner withdrew three hundred cops at the last minute." Koop removed his hat and wiped his brow. "I guess we're the cavalry."

"Supposedly there are a couple hundred volunteer NYPD guys here. I was told they're wearing red T-shirts with the word peace across the front." I pointed down into the field. "I think I can make out a few."

Koop squinted. "Two hundred cops to handle half a million teenagers?"

I spotted a bus about fifty yards away. The words Poughkeepsie Sheriff Department were painted on its side. "Hey Koop, maybe we should park our motorcycles over there," I said, gesturing toward the bus.

We remounted our motorcycles and slowly traversed a narrow dirt-and-grass path until we got to the makeshift parking area, where a handful of Poughkeepsie cops were milling around.

A patrol officer waved us over.

"Patrol Officer Frank Miller," he said, hand extended.

"Patrol Officer Marvin Kooplehaus, Monticello Police. Just call me Koop."

"Detective Will Ford."

"They sent a detective down?"

"I got a motorcycle." I tilted my head toward my Triumph. "So I volunteered."

"You got radios or walkie-talkies?"

I shook my head. "Nope. We were sent in to help with traffic on Seventeen B at Hurd Road, but one of your guys told us you need some assistance down here."

"That was hours ago. Seventeen-year-old kid got run over by a tractor this morning. Right now we are responding to overdoses and the other medical issues."

"Jeez." I gazed skyward as a helicopter made its way closer to the festival grounds.

"Food, water, medical transport . . . and to get the performers in and out," Frank said, as though reading my mind.

"I'm surprised no one is playing," Koop remarked.

"Next act goes on at two o'clock. According to the schedule, it's a band called Santana, but they haven't been sticking to the schedule." Frank shrugged. "I'm not too familiar with these bands. I'm more of a Johnny Mathis kind of guy."

"Any arrests?" I asked. "Nearly got a contact high from all the marijuana wafting up from the field."

"Our guys are just concerning themselves with the hard stuff. Everyone is pretty cool and we'd like to keep it that way. Word handed down from the chief of security is that we're to be helpers, not enforcers. And some guy named Wavy Gravy claims to have a "Please Force" made up of hog farmers from New Mexico."

With the helicopter blades whirring above us, I could have sworn he said please. "Please?"

"Yeah. As in 'please don't do that, please do this instead.' He's been making announcements on stage for the past two days and it seems to be working." Frank looked around. "There ain't too many of us, so not inclined to stir the pot. We're essentially making it up as we go."

"I heard NYPD were here."

Frank scoffed. "Yeah. Their commish got into some kind of dustup with the festival organizers and pulled the plug on an official presence. So, the festival organizers offered fifty bucks a day and free food to any NYPD cop who would volunteer his time here. They got like two hundred or three hundred takers. Wes Pomeroy—the guy heading up security—dubbed them the Peace Force. No guns. No clubs. Us local law enforcement were told to direct traffic and stay along the perimeter."

"The Peace Force and the Please Force. Hell of an operation they got going here." Koop snickered. "How long you been here?"

"Our bus rolled in Thursday morning and we knew right away the organizers misjudged the size of the crowd. Now we got ourselves a nine-mile backup on Seventeen B from here to Monticello. And, we're all working long shifts. Last night's set ended at three forty-five, or there-abouts. Good singer though. Joan something."

"Joan Baez," I said. "She's an anti-war folk singer."

"Yeah? I guess I didn't catch the lyrics." Frank squinted. "You in Vietnam?

"Nope, wife and kid."

"Hmm. And you?" Frank asked, turning to Koop.

"Still waiting to be called up."

"I take it you were there?" I jutted my chin to the left thinking I was somehow pointing it toward Vietnam.

"Yeah," Frank replied. We stood in awkward silence for a few seconds. "I get it. I know some folks don't want to go." Frank removed his hat and ran his hand along his buzz cut. "Tell you the truth, I came here with a bunch of misconceptions about these hippies. But every single young person I've come across has been polite, cooperative, willing to help. We just come from two different worlds, that's all."

"Johnny Mathis versus Santana," Koop said.

"Yeah. Something like that. I was taught to respect authority, follow the rules, not make waves." He shrugged. "But like I said, these kids are doing a great job of self-policing. Gotta admire what they're doing here. I don't agree with their stance on the war, but—"

Thump-thump-thump.

We turned our heads toward the landing helicopter and watched as a couple of gurneys were unloaded.

"Well, we'll be heading back to our traffic duty now," Koop said, holding out his hand. "Thank you for your service."

As Koop and I headed back to our motorcycles, we heard Frank call out to us. When we turned around, he was administering help to a woman who seemed to have fainted. A pregnant woman. We ran back to assist. *A tall man, wearing a red T-shirt with the word Peace emblazoned across the front, emerged from the crowd below and kneeled beside the woman.*

As the woman came to, the man said, "Miss, miss, can you tell me your name?

She batted her lashes. "Madeline." She lifted her torso slightly and took a sip of water. "Madeline Klein."

9

IF MADELINE Klein was visibly pregnant on August 16, 1969, she was most likely carrying Kenneth Waterman's baby.

There was no mention of her pregnancy in the Ellenville police report, which made sense if the detectives did not think it had a bearing on the case.

Besides, she probably wasn't showing at the time of her boyfriend's murder in early May 1969—it's quite possible she didn't even know. Yet she was clearly far enough along to be showing by the time Woodstock rolled around.

I asked Sally if she could do a little sleuthing on this front and try to locate Madeline Klein, or a friend or relative of hers who might know the whereabouts of her child.

The Ellenville files had some information about her, including an address and phone number. Sally would start there. I would have done it myself, but Jack and I had an early-morning appointment with a psychologist.

NATALIE CROSSED her legs, then leaned into the cushions of the sofa. Just eighteen years younger than me, she could pass for my sister. That is, if I bothered to style my hair and put on some makeup. We shared the same cornflower-blue eyes, almond-shaped, set below long, thick eyelashes and naturally arched brows. We were both five seven with the same boob size (34C), and we could still both squeeze into size 6 jeans (well, I squeezed).

Where we diverged was our hair. While mine was unruly curly, hers was more of a wavy curl, and depending on the weather (and the application of expensive hair products) she could wear it either curly or straight—and both ways suited her. Today, she wore it curly, scooped up in a high, loose bun with a few strategically positioned tendrils spiraling to her chin.

"So you want the skinny on intergenerational trauma?" Natalie asked in her soothing therapist voice.

"We think it might be relevant to our case," Jack began. "A glimpse into the psyche to get a handle on what might be going on here."

"So let me begin by saying that there are two types of generational trauma: intergenerational and transgenerational. The former refers to the impact of the trauma on the offspring of the victim. In the latter, the trauma is experienced by the offspring of the offspring. In other words, someone who was not even present for the initial trauma, but experiences the by-product of said trauma. There are those in my field who reference the Holocaust and Black slavery in the US as examples of transgenerational trauma."

Natalie's choice of words and authoritative vocal affect amused me somewhat—it sounded like she was a guest on an afternoon daytime talk show or playing the role of an expert witness on a legal drama.

"Let's use your case as an example," she continued, perhaps taking note of our perplexed expressions. "Bear in mind, without having spoken to the parties involved, I'm merely giving you a possible scenario of how intergenerational trauma might have played out in this family." Natalie leaned forward and clasped her hands on her thighs. "Helen Blackstone's husband, Sam, is brutally murdered. She is asked to ID the body, she is told what happened to him. The likelihood she went for counseling back then, let alone family counseling, is slim to none. She suffers silently, she experiences high levels of maternal stress dealing with a baby and seven-year-old twins. Boys old enough to feel the loss and who might be—or feel—neglected by a distraught mother. The family unit is no longer fully functional, which can manifest itself in strained communications and lack of parental warmth and involvement. That can affect the kids in two ways. The first is internal: feelings of depression, anxiety, and guilt. The second, equally insidious, is outward behavioral issues, such as misbehaving in school or at home, stemming from anger." Natalie paused to make sure we were following the narrative. Once satisfied we were, she plowed on: "Sometimes there is an overwhelming desire to blame someone for what happened—and make them pay. Usually, it's directed to the person who set the trauma in motion, and in your case, that would be Mac Gardner. But with Mac Gardner dead, that ire could be aimed at his offspring. If obsessed, anyone could find his—or her—way to the logic of revenge."

"Susan told me you said it was like a game of dominoes. Once the first tile falls, the consequences are set in motion. That Mac Gardner's victims' families were doomed as soon as the first domino fell."

"Well, that's not exactly what I said." Natalie reprimanded me with her cinched eyebrows. "Picture a single domino as a single life event, whereby each life event is connected to something before and something that will happen in the future. But, in life, like in dominoes, there are certainly ways to interrupt the flow. People do have the capacity to rise above their circumstances—whether on their own or with professional help—and course correct the trajectory of their future. Unfortunately, in your case, Helen's next moves certainly did not help their situations."

"Because she married an abusive man?" Jack asked.

Natalie nodded. "Fuel on the fire. Unstable living environment leads to compromised parenting, diminished attachment, chronic stress. Kids are resilient, to a point. Those kids endured quite a bit."

"What about Mac Gardner's family? How might that play out?" I asked.

"Well, from what you told me, Mac and his sister Barbara were abused by their mother. And for all we know, their mother was abused by one or both of her parents. So, it's possible that intergenerational trauma and transgenerational trauma exist in this family as well. Take Mac Gardner's daughter Shirley, for example. With the lack of good parental role models, perhaps she gave up her child because she believed she couldn't have been a caring parent. She might have also believed she had an evil gene." Natalie air quoted *evil gene*. "Which some people believe, even in my profession. The MAOA gene or warrior gene, which has been linked to aggressive behavior. We'll never know because she can't tell us, but she might have felt that a more nurturing environment than what she could offer would break the cycle."

"Perhaps. But Shirley was unwed at the time. So it could be as simple as that," Jack said.

Natalie nodded. "Absolutely. I'm just giving you possible psychological reasons for her decision. But, without speaking to these folks, all of this is conjecture." Natalie rolled back her shoulders and sat up a little straighter. "Well, educated conjecture." She relaxed her posture. "So, how's the wedding planning going?"

"Would love to stay and chat about that," I said as Jack glimpsed at his watch and tapped it. "But Jack arranged a meeting with a potential witness, so I'll have to take a rain check." I was about to stand but changed my mind. The witness could wait. "Jack, would you give me a sec? I need to talk to Natalie."

Jack stood. "Sure thing. I'll wait in the car."

"I want to talk to you about something else—your grandmother. Have you seen her lately?"

"Grandma? No. Why?"

"I can't quite put my finger on it, but she's been acting a bit odd lately."

"Do you think she's drinking again?"

"The thought crossed my mind. But it feels like something different."

"You're going to have to be more specific."

I ran down a list of recent oddities. The missed appointments, the lost checkbook and unpaid bills, the grocery-shopping snafu. "She swears she hasn't touched a drink. And I saw no evidence of her drinking around her house."

"Look, I'm not a geriatric specialist, but I do work with patients who are taking care of their elderly parents and have told me similar stories. What you're describing to me sounds like mild cognitive impairment."

"You mean Alzheimer's?"

"No. I mean, maybe. But that's for her doctor to sort out. I would suggest she get the Montreal Cognitive Assessment, and then take it from there."

"It could be jet lag," I offered unconvincingly.

"Could be. But I don't think you'd be bringing this up to me if you really thought that."

As I made my way across the parking lot, I watched Jack at the wheel scrolling through his phone. I slow-walked it to his car so that I could process Natalie's take on the situation. While concern for my mother bubbled to the surface, below it was a modicum of resentment at the thought of having to become her caregiver. It would fall to me, no doubt, as her only daughter. Could I see past our past and take on the role with unconditional love and kindness? Or would this sever our already-strained relationship and serve as a reminder that our mother-daughter bond was frayed by years of warring? And then there was the dilemma of convincing her to see a doctor. I knew my mother. She would be suspicious.

Accuse me of gaslighting.

I finally made it to Jack's car. As I stood outside the passenger door, I clenched my fists and squeezed my eyes tight. After a few seconds, I shook my hands and blinked back the tears. When I slipped inside, I flashed a quick smile. "Ready whenever you are," I squeaked out.

"You okay?"

No. "Yes."

"THANK YOU for seeing us on short notice," Jack said to Libby Wright as we stepped into her apartment. We had several reasons for wanting to visit the play's prop mistress, but first and foremost was to see if she was privy to any backstage secrets.

Libby bent her head down slightly and murmured, "I was here, so . . ." She shrugged and led us into the living room, where she motioned us toward a worn brown leather couch. She sat on the edge of a La-Z-Boy recliner. "I'm sorry . . . would you like something to drink?" she said, starting to stand.

Jack threw up his hands, palms outward. "We're all set. But thank you."

Libby settled back in her chair. I pegged her for early forties, but her childlike stature made it hard to discern her age. She was so petite, she was practically swallowed up by the recliner. An image of Lily Tomlin's Edith Ann character sitting on an enormous rocking chair flashed through my mind. Libby's grayish doe eyes and pixie haircut accentuated her childlike demeanor.

"Is this about Brandy? I already spoke to another detective. Um, Ray Gorman."

"Actually, this is about Adam Kincaid," I said.

I waited for her to say something, but instead she just fidgeted with the hem of her T-shirt.

"We've been interviewing the cast and crew, and well, we're finally getting to you." Her eyes widened, although hard to tell whether from curiosity or apprehension, so I added, "This is all standard procedure."

Libby circled her index finger around her thin, chapped lips. "Okay."

"We understand that you were home sick the night Adam was murdered," I said. "Is that correct?"

She nodded. "I think it was a stomach bug. Or food poisoning." She cleared her throat. "I told this to an Officer Sally McIver the day Adam was found. My ex-roommate was interviewed as well."

"Grace Sinclair, right?" I asked.

She licked her parched lips and nodded. "Do you have any leads?"

"We're pursuing several leads." Jack replied. "But it's important that we try and get a handle on who he was. How well did you know Adam?"

"I really didn't know him at all. I'm just the prop mistress. If he even knew my name I would be surprised."

"Do you know if anyone held a grudge against Adam?" I asked. "Maybe you overheard something?"

Libby chewed on that question for a minute or so. "Not specifically. But I did get the feeling he wasn't well-liked. Respected, yes. But liked, no." She narrowed her eyes and leaned forward. "Grace saw the other play Adam directed earlier this summer and went up to him afterward to tell him how much she liked the show and he was very rude to her."

"We're trying to get in touch with Grace, but our calls go straight to voice mail. Did she tell you where she was going?"

"We weren't friends. She was just someone who needed a room and I had a room to spare. We're both introverts. Great for watching TV together but lousy at conversation. But she mentioned she was starting a new teaching gig. In the Midwest. That's really all I know."

"So you haven't heard from her?" Jack asked.

"No." Libby brought her hand to her throat. "You don't think—I mean, I saw her pack. And yes, she was in a hurry. Are you saying she's missing?"

"We just can't reach her, that's all," I said, hoping to quell the alarm bells Jack might've set off with his question. "Do you mind if we look around her bedroom?"

Libby edged to the lip of the recliner and planted her feet on the floor. She launched up suddenly, in that spry way wiry people are able to do. "Follow me."

We fell in line behind Libby, following her through a narrow hallway. I squeezed past a mahogany table with a jade Buddha sitting on a small riser. To the Buddha's left sat a small brass container filled with incense sticks, to its right were tea light candle holders. In front, seven miniature silver bowls. Floating shelves mounted behind the table held small jade statues.

We ended up in a ten by fifteen-foot bedroom with a queen-sized bed and matching oak dresser. A narrow beige rug ran from the side of the bed to a small pink-tiled bathroom. Jack opened the closet and was greeted by empty wire hangers. The mirror affixed to the back of the door had a crack running down the center—Jack's reflected body was jaggedly dissected in half. On the floor was a plastic four-tier shoe rack, sans shoes. Dust bunnies congregated in all four corners. While Jack was checking out the closet, I opened and closed the dresser drawers. A light coating of dust kicked up as I worked my way through the drawers. All empty. As was the nightstand drawer.

"I haven't had a chance to clean yet," Libby said apologetically, staring at the airborne dust particles. "New roommate won't be here until September first. So I told Grace not to worry about cleaning, that I'd get to it later this month."

I stepped inside the bathroom and glanced around. I looked at the toilet, lid down, and saw what looked like a prescription bottle on its side, sticking out from behind the porcelain pedestal. I donned the pair of latex gloves I had shoved into my back pocket, then squatted to reach behind the toilet. I grabbed the bottle, then stood to the sound of my cracking knees. A prescription for Bactrim, typically prescribed for a urinary tract infection. The prescribing doctor was Mitchell Sinclair. *A relative?* She must have aimed for the wastebasket—which was filled with rumpled tissues, makeup removal pads, and dental floss—and missed. I wrapped the bottle in a tissue and pocketed it.

The medicine cabinet was ajar. It squeaked as I pulled it open. "Oh."

Jack stepped into the bathroom. He stared at the empty glass shelves. "Oh what?"

I pulled the cabinet door open wider and pointed to the envelope taped to the MDF behind the medicine cabinet mirror. Written in neat cursive was the name *Libby*. "Libby," I shouted.

Her head appeared in the doorway.

Jack turned to her. "You got mail." He stepped behind me, allowing her to enter the cramped space.

"Did you know this was here?" I peeled the letter from the plywood.

She shook her head. "You can read it. It's probably just a thank-you note that she expected me to eventually find."

The envelope was sealed with a single piece of tape, making it easy to open without tearing. Inside the envelope was a folded piece of paper and a smaller envelope. I pulled out the folded note and read out loud, "Hi Libby, hoping I am long gone by the time you find this. You said you weren't planning to clean for a few days, so I took my chances. I need to disappear for a while. I'm fine. Just need a fresh start. Please give the enclosed envelope to Chase when you see him at the theater. Best, Grace." I handed the note to Jack and pinched the smaller envelope out of the larger envelope. The name Chase was scribbled on it. This envelope was sealed. "Libby, do you have a letter opener or knife?"

"Are you allowed to read that? I mean, don't you need a search warrant or something?"

"Not if you give us permission to read it," Jack said. "It might be addressed to Chase, but it's in your apartment. Therefore, the Fourth Amendment doesn't apply to Chase here . . . there is no expectation of privacy on his part. If his name was on the lease, well, that's when we would need a search warrant."

Libby clenched her fists tightly, seemingly trying to control her anger. "If he did something wrong, he should be held accountable." She unclenched. "I'll get you a small knife."

When she returned, I carefully slit the envelope open. This time I read the note to myself.

Libby raised her eyebrows in anticipation of its contents.

"Sorry," I said. "This needs to stay confidential as it's pursuant to our investigation."

Libby nodded. "Sure. I get it. Should I be worried about Grace?"

WHEN JACK and I rolled into the police station parking lot, I eyed Ray leaning against the driver' side door of his Jeep scrolling through his phone. His partner, Marty, was pacing alongside the bumper, smoking a cigarette.

Ray looked up momentarily, nodded in my direction, then dove back into whatever he was reading on his phone.

Gripping the baggie that contained the envelope, I sidled up next to Ray. "Got something for you." I turned toward Marty. "Hey, put that out, you're going to want to hear this." He sucked the cigarette down to the nub, dropped it, then stubbed it out.

"I hope you're not planning on leaving that there," Jack said, pointing to the butt.

"You the litterbug police?" Marty said, his tone falling somewhere between joking and pissed.

"Just pick it up, Marty," I said. "The receptacle is ten feet away."

Marty bent over and picked up the butt. We waited until he rejoined our little circle, a scowl planted firmly on his face.

I briefed them on our conversation with Libby, then held up the baggie containing the envelope addressed to Chase.

"So you went there to confirm Libby's whereabouts on the night of Adam's murder and to get her take on the situation, but instead got me some intel on Chase," Ray said. "Impressive."

"Yeah." I smirked. "You owe me one."

"I'm marrying you. Does that count?" he deadpanned as he opened the rear door of the Jeep and retrieved a pair of latex gloves from a duffel. "Okay, hand it over." He opened the envelope addressed to Chase and removed the folded note.

He cleared his throat. "This arrangement is over. We're done. In fact, I'd like to pretend it never happened. Don't bother trying to find me—because you won't. I'm very good at disappearing." Ray folded the note, slipped it into the envelope and placed it back in the baggie. "Why leave this for her roommate, Libby, to find and deliver? Why not just mail it to Chase?"

"Give her some time to thoroughly disappear," I surmised. "Grace knew that Libby wouldn't come across the envelope for a while."

"Seems risky," Ray said. "But I guess better than revealing her route or final destination with a postmark from somewhere."

"What do you think she means by 'arrangement'?" Jack asked. "It makes it sound like they were in cahoots. Which means she might know something about the drug dealing, or Brandy's murder."

"Or Adam's murder," Ray said. "Is there a connection between Grace and Adam?"

"Libby told us that Adam was rude to Grace," I replied. "But who murders someone for being rude to them? Especially in such a dramatic way. And she would've had to have known all the details of the 1969 murders."

"Could Grace Sinclair be an alias?" Ray asked. "She said she knows how to disappear. Perhaps reinvent herself. Could she be Elizabeth Blackstone?"

"Nope. Too young. Elizabeth would be fifty now." I pulled up a picture of Grace Sinclair that Sally had texted to me and handed my phone to Ray. "Sally interviewed Grace and pegged her for midthirties. Women can certainly make themselves look younger, but going from fifty to midthirties—that would be hard to pull off."

"Yeah. No way she's fifty," Ray said after gazing at the photograph.

"I'm of the mind that this has something to do with Brandy, not Adam, therefore you and Marty should haul Chase in for questioning this time," I said.

I took my phone back from Ray and pocketed it. "And if it turns out the two of them killed Adam, well, we'll be close by to swoop in during your interrogation."

SALLY HURRIED into the break room. "There you are," she exclaimed, a bit out of breath. "I've been running all over looking for you." She glanced at Jack. "You too."

"You found us," I said, spilling what was left of my late-morning coffee into the sink. "What's up?"

"First the bad news: Madeline Klein, the pregnant girlfriend of Kenneth Waterman, is dead. Died in 2011 of breast cancer."

"Shoot. That might make it harder to find her child. How did you find that out?"

"That's the good news: I located an old friend of hers." Sally pulled out her notebook. "The guy who bought Madeline's house still had her forwarding address. He kept it for decades in a utility drawer. Madeline moved to Roscoe and a neighbor of hers told me Madeline was close friends with a woman named Rebecca Crowley. Rebecca was easy to locate because she still lives in Roscoe."

"Nice going," Jack said.

"Just following the breadcrumbs," Sally replied with a sly smile. "Rebecca said she would be happy to speak with you about Madeline. She said you're welcome to swing by today." Sally tore out a piece of paper. "Here's her address."

Jack slapped his palms on his thighs, then stood. "Who's up for a road trip?" he exclaimed. Before I could answer, he was out the door.

At 12:05, Jack pulled into the driveway of a farmhouse-style home about one mile from the center of town. White clapboard siding with black shutters. An American flag, mounted on the right beam of the farmer's porch, flapped in the breeze. Brown wicker chairs and frosted-glass tables were arranged like a living room set on the left side of the immense porch. A pair of white rocking chairs were situated to the right. Before our feet hit the gravel of the driveway, a young woman stepped out on the porch. Although hard to see her facial features from this distance, I could make out thick blond hair tied in a loose French braid tapering down to the center of her back. As we approached, a golden retriever nosed its way through a flap in the door and stood obediently next to the young woman, panting and wagging its tail in anticipation of our ascension up the steps.

After introductions, she led us into the kitchen, where an older woman was peering inside the bowl of a stand mixer. "Hey Grandma, two detectives here to see you. What did you do now?" She grinned mischievously.

Rebecca Crowley wiped her floured hands on her apron. "Never you mind. Now scoot." As her twentysomething granddaughter turned to leave, Rebecca picked up a red plastic spatula and waved it toward two barstools tucked under the granite counter.

"Thank you for agreeing to speak with us on such short notice," Jack said.

"I hope you don't mind if I bake and talk. Gotta get this cake done for a housewarming later."

"Go right ahead," I said.

She scooped the batter from the bowl to a cake pan. "Your colleague told me you had questions about Madeline and her boyfriend, Kenneth—" She laid down the spatula and wiped her hand across her brow, leaving a floury smudge mark. "And that Kenneth's murder might be connected to one you're currently working on."

"So you know about the 1969 murders?" Jack asked.

"Yes. I think Madeline told a few people about what happened to her boyfriend that summer." She pulled open the oven door and inserted the pan. "Her life was pretty messed up because of it."

"Messed up how?" I asked.

Rebecca picked up a timer and set it for fifteen minutes. "After Kenneth's death, she went looking for Mr. Right and met Mr. Couldn't Be More Wrong. Her first husband was pretty abusive. And even after he died, she ended up in another abusive relationship. That one ended in divorce. My sense is that she never really got over the murder. After what happened to Kenneth, Madeline decided she didn't want to be with someone she cared about because she didn't want to go through losing a loved one again. So she hooked up with men she didn't give a shit about, but who could put a roof over her and her son's head." She paused, the ticking of the cooking timer the only sound in the room. "And these men weren't exactly father figures."

This tale was eerily similar to Helen Blackstone's life after her husband's murder.

The dominoes falling without getting the support to stop or divert them.

"I met Madeline in 1992. By then, she had found a modicum of peace. Maybe her meeting with Joanna Gardner the year before was a turning point for her."

That took me by a bit of surprise. "Madeline went to see Mac Gardner's wife?"

"Yeah, crazy, huh? She thought if she met with Joanna, she could get closure on the whole sorry ordeal. Madeline wanted to know why Mac Gardner killed her boyfriend—she said not knowing the *why* hung around her neck like an albatross. Weighed on her soul, is how she put it." Rebecca frowned. "That's when she learned that Mac and Joanna had a daughter. She was there."

"Madeline met Shirley Gardner?" Jack said.

Rebecca leaned against the counter and gave the question some thought. "Yeah. Shirley. That was the daughter's name."

"And what year was that again?" I asked.

"Nineteen ninety-one. Madeline saw that Shirley was pregnant, and persuaded Shirley to give the baby to her sister and brother-in-law. Her sister wanted a baby so badly. A couple of adoption attempts didn't pan out. They were devastated." She paused. "Madeline convinced Shirley it was the ultimate act of contrition for her father's sins. Madeline also told me that Shirley was quick to acquiesce, that she was considering giving the baby up for adoption anyway."

A few dots started lining up when Rebecca mentioned "adoption" and "sister." *But could it be possible?* I side-eyed Jack to see if he suspected what I suspected, but saw nothing in his expression that led me to believe he did. I turned back to Rebecca. "Do you know Madeline's sister?"

"I never met her, but I know her name. Lynn."

Jack blinked a few times, clearly puzzling out the implication. "Lynn Kincaid?" he said slowly.

"Why, yes. Do you know her?"

"As a matter of fact, we've spoken to Lynn Kincaid. She never mentioned having a sister."

"I got the sense they weren't really close. Come to think of it, Madeline never really talked about her family. What does this have to do with—"

"Who else knew about this adoption?" Jack asked, cutting off Rebecca's line of questioning.

"Madeline told me I was the only person she ever told. So, as far as I know, just me." Rebecca lowered her gaze suddenly. When she looked back up her eyelashes were moist. "She confided in me because I had told her that my mother was brutally murdered by our neighbor. His reason: he didn't like her perfume lingering in the elevator. Turns out my mom was not his first victim. A few other women assaulted his olfactory senses. I was eleven." She picked up the red plastic spatula and wiped off the bits of remaining cake batter with a dish towel.

"I'm sorry for your loss," Jack said.

I nodded, surprised by the lump in my throat. Perhaps because I was trying to mend the relationship with my own mom, and grateful for the opportunity to do so, it was hard to hear stories from those whose familial ties were cut short for no other reason than being in the wrong place at the wrong time.

"Madeline didn't like to use the word *victim* to describe our circumstances. She said we were both casualties of crime. Collateral damage. Not directly assaulted, but in the impact zone." Rebecca swung the spatula through the air in what felt like an attempt to swat away the memory. "I was raised by my aunt—my mother's sister—and her husband, and they warmly welcomed me into their home. I got therapy. I had a support system. Madeline, on the other hand, had no one to guide her through the grieving process. Her mother died when she was young. Her father remarried, and well, you know how that sometimes goes. She was consumed with guilt and what-ifs. She—" Rebecca abruptly stopped. She cocked her head to the side. "I just remembered something. There is someone else who knows about the adoption. Her son. Kenny. Madeline told me he went with her when she visited Joanna and Shirley.

"He was born in 1969, so he must have been"—I paused to do the math—"twenty-two at the time," I said.

Jack glanced at me, then shifted his attention back to Rebecca. "So Madeline's son, Kenny, knows that Shirley Gardner had a son . . . and that the baby ended up with the Kincaids?" Jack asked.

Rebecca nodded. "What does this have to do with the case you're working on?"

"What can you tell us about Kenny?" I asked, ignoring her question.

"Hmm. Taciturn. I think that's the right word. Quiet. Never said much. I remember he was kind of a neat freak. Everything had to be just so."

"And physically? What did he look like?" Jack asked.

"Hmm. Medium height, like five ten, I guess. Medium build. Brown hair. brown eyes. Bulbous nose. Thick eyebrows."

"Do you know where we can find him?" I asked.

"He's dead. Died in the 9/11 attack." Rebecca sighed. "What's really sad is that Madeline and Kenny were estranged at the time. She never got to set things right with him. He blamed her for his crappy childhood. And, on some level he was right. Like I said, she deliberately sought out less than desirable mates. Me, I would rather love again and be hurt again than live the life she chose." She eyed the timer. "And then she died of breast cancer eight years ago. She was only sixty-two." She shook her head, then glanced at the timer again. "A life of lemons."

Ding.

JACK AND I sat on the sofa waiting for Lynn Kincaid to join us. She was in the kitchen, putting a roast in the oven. Jason Kincaid sat with us, flashing a smile every so often and occasionally wringing his clasped hands. Nothing in the room had changed since the last time we were here. The crocheted throws in the same position on the sofa and recliner. The glass trinkets atop doilies on the end tables were in the exact spots they were eight days ago.

"Sorry about that," Lynn demurred as she took a seat next to her husband. "Needed to get that going. It takes several hours to cook."

"No worries," Jack said.

"So you have news for us? Did you find out who did this?" Jason's eyes widened in anticipation of our answer.

"We've made a lot of progress," I began. "But no, no arrests have been made. As for motive, *why* Adam was targeted, well, for that we have a theory." I waited a beat, then added, "And we believe you can help us out with that."

Jason and Lynn glanced at each other, inscrutable expressions on their faces. Although I got the sense they knew where this was going.

"We think he was targeted because someone knew who his grandfather was." Jack quickly added, "Adam's *birth mother's* father."

Neither of them moved a muscle.

"We're just trying to figure out why you didn't tell us the truth about Adam's adoption," I said.

Jason grasped his knees and leaned forward. "What does that have to do with anything?"

Lynn started to cry. Softly at first, but the restrained weeping quickly gave way to heaving sobs. "We didn't do anything wrong," she managed to say between gasps. "We were desperate." She stood abruptly and fled the room. A few seconds later we heard the tap running in the bathroom.

"Excuse me, but I'm a little confused here. Yes, we handled the adoption privately. Perhaps not through a normal channel. Lynn's stepsister, Madeline, knew a pregnant woman who didn't want to keep her child, and so she contacted us."

I held up my hand, palm out. "Step?"

"Yes. Madeline's father married Lynn's mother when they were teenagers."

"Okay. Go on."

"We hired a lawyer, an intermediary, who drew up the papers, and everyone was happy." Jason eyed the bathroom door. "As for Adam's grandfather, well, I have no idea who he was." Lynn's soft cries continued to emanate from behind the bathroom door. "I need to tend to my wife. I think you should leave—"

"So, you're telling us that you know nothing about Adam's birth family?" I asked, more brusquely than intended. But, if they truly didn't already know, they needed to know the truth. There was no way I was going to leave without telling them.

"The intermediary was hired so that both sides could remain anonymous. The birth mother insisted, and we agreed." His eyes darted around the room, eventually landing on the wall of family portraits. "In fact, Lynn preferred it that way. It really was no different from a closed adoption . . . except we didn't use an adoption agency."

The click of a door prompted the three of us to swivel our heads toward the bathroom.

Lynn cleared her throat as she weaved her way around the furniture and rejoined her husband on the sofa.

"I'm okay." She glanced at her husband. "I suppose Jason just told you about the adoption."

Jack and I nodded.

"There's something Jason doesn't know." Lynn bowed her head. When she looked up, she wiped away a tear. "Madeline and I were never close, but soon after the adoption, I tried to find a way forward with her. I invited her over for drinks and well, she overdid it and in her inebriated state inadvertently told me the birth mother's first name: Shirley. But we never learned her last name. The only one who knew was Madeline, and she's . . . she's no longer with us."

I took a deep breath and released it slowly. "How much do you know about Kenneth Waterman's murder?"

Jason and Lynn glanced at each other, confused, clearly not expecting that question.

"Madeline's boyfriend?" Lynn asked.

I nodded.

"I know he was murdered by a serial killer named Mac Gardner in 1969," Lynn said. "I wasn't told much about the case. I was fifteen at the time. I think everyone shielded me from the details."

"Did you know Mac Gardner had a daughter?" I asked.

They shook their heads. Jason reached out and grabbed Lynn's hand, perhaps anticipating the shocking news I was about to impart.

I laid out what we had uncovered.

The genuine shock on their faces, the tremors and twitching of their facial muscles, made it clear that they were hearing, for the first time, that Adam was the grandson of Mac Gardner and that his birth mother, Shirley, was killed in the same manner in which Mac killed his victims.

Lynn was the first to speak. Her voice raspy, her delivery tentative. "So you think Adam was killed by someone trying to end the Gardner bloodline?"

"Well, that's one theory."

Jason raised his hand. "Just wondering out loud here, but if Adam's killer was motivated by a desire to end Mac Gardner's bloodline or exact revenge on his offspring, are there other children or grandchildren at risk?"

Shit. George Zettler.

Mac Gardner's nephew. *Was he a sitting duck?*

THE CHASE Dunham interrogation was scheduled for later that afternoon, affording us just enough time to swing by George's apartment and give him a heads-up—and to try and do so without scaring him.

George leaped from the couch and began to pace the confined space between the living room and kitchen. "So you're telling me I'm a target?"

"Us telling you is just a precaution—" I started to say.

He stopped pacing. "A precaution?" He started gesticulating wildly like a deranged orchestra conductor. "What am I supposed to do? Quit the show? Go into hiding? Buy a gun?" A bluish vein bulged from the right edge of his temple.

"Look, even if Adam's killer is someone seeking revenge against Mac's living relatives, how would the killer know that you're related to the Gardners?" Jack offered.

"You've got to be kidding me. You guys figured it out. I've made my DNA public. Who's to say someone else can't figure this out?" George sat down and cradled his head in his hands.

"I suggest you keep your kinship with Adam to yourself," I said. "In the meantime, we'll do everything in our power to protect you."

George lowered his hands and tilted his head toward us. "So, do you have any suspects?"

Jack and I glanced at each other.

"We're pursuing a few leads," Jack said to assuage him. "Adam's murder may have nothing to do with his bloodline."

"God, I hope not," George said.

Unfortunately, for George, I was fairly confident that Adam's murder had everything to do with his bloodline. And if that was the case, George needed to keep his wits about him.

JACK AND I arrived back at the station just in time to watch Ray and Marty make Chase sweat, if not crack. They were eager to confront him with both the Ring footage and the note left for him by Grace Sinclair. Neither proved anything, so our hope was that he would cave under the pressure of questioning. Jack and I stood behind the two-way mirror as Ray and Marty settled in the metal chairs facing Chase and his lawyer, Reggie. Reggie scribbled something on a pad of paper, then turned the pad toward Chase. Chase leaned over, read it, and nodded.

"So, Detectives, Chase tells me you've discovered some so-called evidence to, once again, browbeat him."

Ray decided to start with the Ring footage, since he believed the note was more damning. Get him squirming, then go for the jugular. Ray fired up the doorbell camera video and directed everyone's attention to the monitor resting on the table.

Chase and Reggie watched the monitor. Ray and Marty watched Chase's expressions. Chase pulled his lips inward as the action unfolded, possibly trying to thwart any sound he might inadvertently produce.

Ray hit the pause button. "Chase, you told my colleagues the other day that you only met with Brandy Johnson at the library. Yet here you are headed to her apartment. Care to explain?"

"I'd like to confer with my client," Reggie said, flatly.

"You've got five minutes," Marty said.

Six minutes later, everyone was back in their seats, the cameras rolling.

Chase cleared his throat. "As I told you, I was Brandy's math tutor. I totally forgot about this, but, yeah, I went to her apartment to pick up cash for services rendered. It's my preferred method of payment."

"Did you get into a fight with Brandy? Because you seem kinda steamed," Ray said.

"Do I? Well, I wasn't."

"Let's take a look, shall we?" Ray rewound the footage to where Chase stormed by Libby and Grace's door camera. He hit pause. "You look pretty angry to me."

Chase waited a few beats, then said, "I was angry about a phone call I had just received. Had nothing to do with Brandy."

"Do you have any idea where she was going after she left her apartment? Which, by the way, was only five minutes after you left," Ray said. "Because if you didn't kill her, you are most likely the last person to have seen her alive."

Chase leaned forward, his jaw clenched. "I did not kill her!" He unclenched slightly, and added, "And no, I don't know where she went."

"Moving along," Ray said. "What can you tell us about this note?" Ray slid Grace's note across the table.

Chase read it first, then slid it to Reggie. Reggie started to speak, but Chase held up his palm. "Well, that's a kick in the pants. Sounds like she's breaking up with me. I wondered where she ran off to. And things were going so well." He shrugged. "Well, at least I thought they were."

Marty grunted. "So, you're telling us this is a Dear John letter?"

"What do you think it is?" Reggie directed his question to Ray and Marty.

"'This arrangement is over' does not sound like a breakup line. It sounds like the two of you were partners, possibly in some illegal enterprise, and she wanted out."

"That's your interpretation," Reggie said. "So, let's recap what you've got. Chase collecting payment for his tutoring services. Chase walking by a door slightly miffed after receiving a disturbing phone call. Chase getting a terse Dear John letter from someone he dated." Reggie picked up his notepad and placed it back in his briefcase. "I think we're done here."

I FOUND Dad by the pickleball court—which up until a few weeks ago had been a badminton court. ("Pickleball is all the rage these days,"

Dad explained when I asked him why the switch.) Seems the residents raised hell to the Horizon Meadows' board of directors to allocate a portion of the recreation budget to convert the rarely used badminton court into a pickleball court, and to eventually build at least two more. According to Dad, there had been some heated words over the scheduling of play, with some residents accusing other residents of mismanaging the sign-up sheet. Clearly, one court was not enough. ("If someone is murdered here, pickleball scheduling might just be the motive," Dad had half joked when I asked about the conversion.)

Dad and Harry were sitting on a bench, waiting for the arrival of their opponents, Max and Maxine, a married couple who had led the charge for the creation of the pickleball court. Four women were currently playing, and for a bunch of old biddies, they were quite nimble.

"These gals are something else," Dad said, as he stood to greet me. He tilted his head toward the right side of the net and pointed. "Gail and Irene smoked Harry and me the other day." He spun the paddle in his right hand. "Here to watch?"

"Another time. Just wanted to bring you up to speed on the case."

Dad turned to Harry and said, "I'll be right back." He turned to me. "We got fifteen minutes until our turn. What's up?"

I filled Dad in on our conversations with Madeline's friend, Rebecca Crowley, and the Kincaids about the private adoption, which elicited a whole lotta gentle swearing. I thought about mentioning my conversation with Natalie regarding Mom, but didn't want to distract him before his match. Besides, I had better news to impart. "Oh, and one more thing: Ray has two tickets to the Mets game tomorrow, against Atlanta. Wants to know if you want to join him."

Dad eyes lit up as he twirled the racket in his hand. "The Braves are in first place. Should be a good—" He tilted his head and lowered the racket to his side. "Oh shit. The Mets. I just remembered something." He turned to Harry. "Gimme five minutes!" he yelled, then turned back to me.

DETECTIVE WILL FORD

August 21, 1969

Helen lowered the flame under the percolator when the gurgling reached a fever pitch and the whistle began to blow. Thankfully, the rich aroma of freshly brewed coffee overpowered the lingering odor of what I suspected was fried onions from last night's dinner. I crossed the brick-patterned linoleum to join Jimmy at the Formica table. The floor felt sticky, which I imagined hadn't been cleaned since her husband was killed. The least of her worries, I thought.

For a minute my attention drifted to the sound of the TV blaring from the living room, where Derek and Thomas were watching the New York Mets, who were on a bit of a comeback streak and gaining on the Chicago Cubs. I still thought it would take a freaking miracle for them to sail past the Cubs to take first place in the National League East, let alone win the World Series.

"Would you like a cup of coffee?" Helen asked.

"That would be lovely," Jimmy said. "Black for me."

"I take mine with a bit of milk."

I took a seat at the table, then rested my clasped hands on the floral-patterned plastic placemat, which felt greasy to the touch. After a few seconds, I lifted my hands and put them down by my side.

Helen pulled a carton of milk from the fridge and placed it on the table. She then set three coffee mugs in front of us and filled them to the brim. "Have you learned anything new? Is that why you're here?"

I opened the carton and caught a whiff of rancid milk. I quickly closed the lid, opting for black. "We wanted you to hear from us that the case is formally closing. With Mac Gardner's confession and other evidence, we know we had our guy. And now that he's dead, there's no trial to prep for. Our work is done," I explained.

"So no finding out why he did this or why he went after Sam and those other two men?"

"I'm afraid not," I replied. "We—"

I paused. Our heads simultaneously turned to the rising voices of the two boys in the other room.

"Those boys are having a rough time," Helen lamented. "Fighting with each other over the littlest thing. Mind you, they fought before, but this is on a whole other level. The camp director says Thomas has become withdrawn and Derek is bullying other kids. Between the baby and the boys, I'm just . . . I'm just tired." She stared down into her coffee, then blew on it and took a sip, wincing at its bitterness.

Crash! Helen's head jolted up and she dashed out of the kitchen toward the sound of the clatter. Jimmy and I followed on her heels. By the time we joined her in the living room, Helen was already squatting down, picking up the large pottery shards of a lamp base.

"He did it," the blond-haired boy snapped. "He threw a pillow at me and missed."

Helen turned toward the dark-haired boy. "Ricky, you go to your room right now." As he stomped off, Helen fell to the floor in a heap and cradled her head in her hands.

The blond-haired boy joined her on the floor and hugged her.

"Sorry Mom."

Helen lifted her head. "That's okay, Tommy."

I turned toward the TV just in time to see Tommie Agie hit a home run. They just might go all the way. I swiveled my head back and surveyed the sad scene in front of me, killing the joy I had felt mere seconds earlier.

10

SUNDAY | AUGUST 25, 2019

CHIEF ELDRIDGE knitted his brow, his expression somewhere between skeptical and amused.

"So you think Ricky Saunders, the theater maintenance guy, might be Derek Blackstone because your dad remembered that Derek's mother called him by the nickname *Ricky*? And your invitation to a Mets game triggered this memory?"

"Yeah. Look, I know it's a long shot, but the age maps out. Ricky looks to be about fifty-seven. He rides a motorcycle."

Eldridge peered over his cheaters. "What does that have to do with anything?"

"Brandon, the grandson of the ex-cop who hoarded the investigation files, told us that the man who came to his grandfather's house wore a Harley jacket. Usually people who wear those jackets ride motorcycles," Jack explained. "If we show Brandon a picture of Ricky, he might be able to confirm our suspicion."

"We can ask Simon Pierce if he's got an old toothbrush or hair-brush of Thomas's," I said. "We've got Ricky Saunders's DNA, so if they're brothers, we'll get a sibling match."

Eldridge nodded. "Good idea." Then he tilted his head toward the door, signaling our dismissal.

"The plan?" Jack asked as we neared our desks.

"I'll get in touch with Simon Pierce and see if he's saved anything that might contain Thomas's DNA. Meanwhile, you reach out to Brandon and show him a picture of Ricky."

Jack shot me a thumbs-up, then planted himself at his desk. "I'll also check in with the lab. See where they're at with the DNA they got off the pillowcase from the Shirley Gardner murder. If we're lucky, we might just get a match to one of our persons of interest." Jack insisted on calling them persons of interest, not suspects, seeing that we were still light on motive and evidence.

Just as I was about to call Simon Pierce, Ray slammed his desk, diverting my attention (and everyone else's in the bullpen).

"Yes!" Ray exclaimed, then turned to me. "Grace Sinclair was just picked up in the Bronx. She'll be escorted back here this afternoon." He rubbed his palms together, clearly anticipating grilling her.

I spun away from Ray and tapped in Simon Pierce's number. He picked up on the second ring. When I inquired about obtaining something of Thomas's that would contain his DNA, he said there was nothing, as he'd moved to a new apartment and discarded Thomas's personal items years ago.

He also told me he was unable to find any photos of Thomas, Der-ek, and Elizabeth when they were kids. True or not, it meant another dead end. I turned to face Jack, who was wrapping up his phone call with someone at the lab.

Jack twisted around in his seat. "Caroline Deaver said we'll have the DNA report shortly. Apologized for the delay, yada, yada, yada." Then he punched in Brandon's phone number, eager to show him the photograph of Ricky Saunders. After a few seconds, he shook his head and left a voice mail message.

I DRUMMED my fingers on my desk, then quickly glanced at the clock on the wall. Five after ten. Grace Sinclair was on her way. Brandon had yet to call back. And still no email from the lab.

When I refreshed my email (yet again), there it was (finally). "Hey, Jack!"

My phone rang. The display read *Deaver*. "Hey Caroline, just got the report. Jack's here. Let me put you on speaker."

"Thought you should hear it from the horse's mouth. I think you're going to love the results." Caroline paused. "Ready?"

"Lay it on us," I said.

"The DNA found on the edge of the pillowcase that asphyxiated Shirley Gardner is a sibling match to one of the theater folks you collected DNA from."

"Let me guess. Ricky Saunders."

"How in the world? That's right."

Jack let out a low whistle. "So, Ricky's sister, Elizabeth Blackstone, killed Shirley Gardner?"

"Well, that I can't say for certain. But her DNA was on the pillowcase."

I looked up at Jack. "Let's pick up Ricky—or should I say Derek?"

"NO FUCKING way she had anything to do with Adam's murder." Ricky slammed his palms on the wood table, knocking over the glass of water in front of him. Thankfully, only about two inches remained.

"Where is she?" Jack asked, ignoring the spill.

Ricky pursed his lips, then lowered his head.

"Look at me!" Jack leaned forward.

"I don't know."

"I don't believe you," Jack countered.

Ricky held Jack's stare. "I'm telling you man, she wouldn't hurt a fly."

"Okay, well, if that's true, why don't you just let us know where she is? If she's innocent, then she has nothing to worry about."

"Ha! That's rich coming from a pair of cops these days. Innocent people go to jail every day. In fact, guilty people sometimes get away with their crimes and commit more crimes. Or they're not held accountable."

"Are you referring to Mac Gardner?" Jack asked.

Ricky started to blink rapidly. He crossed his arms over his chest and shuddered slightly.

"Why didn't you tell us that you were Helen Blackstone's son?"

"Well, first of all, what in the hell does that have to do with anything?"

"You know very well why that would be relevant. It didn't strike you as odd that Adam's murder was eerily similar to what happened to your dad?"

"Was it? I only heard dribs and drabs of what happened to Adam. I didn't make the connection."

"Come on," Jack countered. "You expect us to believe that?"

Ricky snorted. "Believe what you want."

"What's with the name charade, Ricky?" I said. "Or should I call you Derek?"

"I changed my name a few years ago when obsessive true crime fanatics came looking for me for interviews and whatnot. Derek Blackstone no longer exists."

"And Elizabeth Blackstone? Did she change her name?"

"I told you, she wouldn't hurt a fly."

"Then perhaps you can explain what her DNA was doing at the Shirley Gardner crime scene?"

He started to blink rapidly again.

"Do you understand what an obstruction-of-justice offense is?" Jack asked. "Or for that matter, aiding and abetting a suspect in a murder case?"

I bent forward. "What Jack here is trying to say is that providing false or misleading information to law enforcement or impeding an investigation or helping a suspect avoid arrest will end very badly for you." I leaned back. I didn't want to come across as a bully—I got the sense he would respond better if he felt one of us was on his side. "Detective Tomelli and I are going to step out now. Give you a chance to think about this a bit. Okay? Meanwhile, would you like me to refresh your glass?" I said, setting the glass upright.

Ricky said nothing, just stared straight ahead.

"Whaddya think?" Jack said, as the door to the interrogation room closed behind us.

"If he's smart, he'll ask for a lawyer."

Jack took out his phone and glanced at the screen. He held it up, then swiped it to show me a missed call. "Brandon."

I PLACED a full glass of water on the table in front of Ricky and took the seat opposite him. Jack folded his hands on his lap and leaned back in his chair.

Ricky took a long sip, wiped his forearm across his lips, then slumped back in his chair.

Jack placed his iPhone on the table. "I just got a call from Hank Webb's grandson. You remember Hank?"

Beads of sweat were now visible on Ricky's forehead. "I . . . I . . . that name is not ringing bells. No."

"Well, it seems Hank's grandson remembers you." Jack went on to explain what we knew about the two folks who paid Hank a visit seven years ago to read through the Mac Gardner murder files. "Hank's grandson was in the house at the time. I sent him that picture of you we took during our first chitchat at the theater and guess what? He recognized you as the guy who came to the house looking to learn more about the 1969 murders. He said you looked exactly the same, minus the ponytail."

I turned to Jack. "I bet if we asked that bartender in North Adams if Ricky here is the guy he saw hanging out with Shirley Gardner, we'd get another positive ID." I shifted my gaze to Ricky.

Ricky rubbed his forehead in an attempt to sop up the moisture. But otherwise, his expression remained stoic.

"Here's what I think," I said. "After your brother Thomas died, you and your sister sought revenge, perhaps justice, for how your lives turned out. Mac was never held accountable, but someone had to pay. Somehow you found out that Hank Webb kept the old Mac Gardner files at his house. My guess is that you called around to the various police precincts, pretending to be a reporter or podcaster covering true crime, and someone gave you the tip. Then, when you learned that Mac had a daughter, you made her your target. An offspring for an offspring. You tracked down Shirley, got her to trust you by reminiscing about your lousy childhoods. You learn that her boyfriend would be out of town one night, so you and your sister, Elizabeth, murdered Shirley in a way that was eerily similar to the way your father was murdered. Which, by the way, is creepy."

He swallowed. Hard. "My sister had nothing to do with that. She tried to stop me. That's why her DNA is there. She showed up and grabbed the pillow." Ricky clenched his fists and jaw. His shoulders rose to his ears. "But it was too late. I did what I had to do." He blew out a puff of air, then lowered his shoulders. His jaw relaxed as he unclenched his fists. "But I didn't kill Adam," he mumbled. "Why would I? I don't even know the guy, or for that matter, give a flying fuck about him."

"Well, we'll get to that in a minute, Ricky," Jack said. "But I'm gonna ask you one more time. Where is your sister?"

Ricky had nothing to lose at this point by not telling us. He'd just confessed to first-degree murder. An additional charge of aiding and abetting a suspect was not going to make his prospects any worse.

Ricky shrugged and shook his head. "Go ahead, arrest me for Shirley's murder. I knew sooner or later it would catch up with me."

"So you killed Shirley, but you didn't kill Adam. Is that what you're telling us?" Jack spat.

"Man, I just said that."

"Maybe your sister killed Adam," I tossed out. "The both of you were familiar with the MO."

Ricky slammed his palm on the table. "No way. I'm telling you. There. Is. No. Way."

"How did you find out the truth about Adam?" Jack asked.

"Find out what? I told you, I don't know the guy. You think because he was killed in the same way as my dad and Shirley that I had something to do with this? How about other people who might've seen Hank's files? I'm probably not the only one."

"Like your sister, perhaps."

"For fuck's sake. It's not my sister. I told you already, she tried to stop me from killing Shirley. She doesn't have a mean bone in her body. She's a big believer in karma—that the universe will eventually set things right. She found religion. She found peace." Ricky bowed his head.

And something clicked in mine.

Jack leaned in. "So you're telling us that some other person got it into his head to murder Adam exactly like they killed your father when they found out that Adam was Mac Gardner's grandson."

Ricky's head snapped up so quickly I heard his neck crack. "What?"

"MAY WE come in?" I asked.

She opened the door the rest of the way. "Are you here with news about Grace?"

I peered down the hallway at the Buddha shrine. My mind drifted to the minute the puzzle pieces fell into place. It was Ricky's mention of his sister's belief in karma and religion. A lightbulb-slash-eureka moment. The Buddha shrine in Libby's apartment. Their matching gray eyes. The cleft chin, although hers was less pronounced. Like Derek/Ricky, she used a derivation of the name Elizabeth. We never compelled Libby's DNA—as she had a solid alibi for the night of Adam's murder and was not considered a person of interest. But there was no denying that the woman standing before me was Elizabeth Blackstone. And Elizabeth Blackstone, like her brother, had motive. Payback for their father's murder and their brother's suicide. Or, as Natalie had pointed out, a twisted justification for ending the Gardner bloodline.

"We're here to get a few answers from you, Libby . . . or should I call you by your given name, Elizabeth?

AT NOON, Jack escorted Libby to the interrogation room, the one in which her brother had been questioned two hours earlier. He was now in custody for the murder of Shirley Gardner.

Libby nibbled at her cuticles as we recorded the formal introductions. She stopped chewing momentarily when Jack recited her full name, Elizabeth Blackstone Wright. Wright being her married name, although she was no longer married.

"So, Libby. Why the charade?" Jack began. "Your brother confessed to killing Shirley Gardner. Maybe he did it. Maybe he's protecting you." He shrugged. "Either way, Shirley Gardner was killed in the same manner in which Adam Kincaid was murdered. Not a stretch for us to conclude that your brother was involved. Or you, for that matter."

Her lip quivered. "Am . . . am I under arrest?"

"The likelihood that the North Adams police will obtain an arrest warrant is fairly high," Jack replied. "Your brother voluntarily gave us his DNA, and the DNA found on the pillowcase that suffocated Shirley is that of a sibling, a female sibling. Just because your brother says you weren't involved won't cut it as a get-out-of-jail-free card."

"As for Adam's murder, Detective Tomelli and I are building a case against you and your brother, and it doesn't look good for either of you." I folded my arms across my chest and leaned back. Then I raised my finger to my lips and eyeballed Jack, hoping he would infer my signal to keep quiet. In that uncomfortable silence, someone was bound to speak, and I wanted to hear what Libby had to say at this point.

But she remained silent.

Her gaze darted between me and Jack.

Thirty long seconds ticked by.

Then she cleared her throat.

"I tried to stop him," she said softly. "He had called me earlier that night to tell me he planned to go through with it. When I tried to call him back, he ignored my calls . . . and texts. I drove four hours to get there. But I was too late."

"Are you referring to Shirley or Adam?" I asked.

She wrinkled her forehead. "Shirley."

"And when you heard that Adam was killed exactly like your dad and Shirley, it didn't occur to you to bring your insight to our attention?" Jack asked.

A single tear made its way from the corner of her left eye to her chin before she swatted it away. "I know what it looks like. I asked my brother if he did this, and he told me he didn't. And I believe him."

She sniffled. "He has no reason to lie to me. But we also knew that if you knew who we were, you would pin this on him. He has no alibi, he had access to the theater, he had done it before." She inhaled and exhaled. "I even told him to leave the area, but he said he had nothing to worry about 'cause he didn't do this." Libby pursed her lips, giving the impression she was done speaking. But then she scooched forward and said, "My brother killed Shirley because he was distraught over Thomas's death. He thought killing Shirley would set his mind and the universe right. Balance the scales, so to speak. He wouldn't kill some random guy."

That last sentence was offered so convincingly, it was hard not to believe that she truly had no idea that Adam was Shirley's son. Before revealing to her who Adam was, and to keep this interrogation on an even keel, I changed tack, hoping to better understand the depths of her involvement and complicity.

"Were you the woman who accompanied Ricky to Hank Webb's house?" I asked.

Libby cocked her head. "Is that the guy who had the Mac Gardner files?"

"Yes."

She closed her eyes, inhaled deeply, then slowly exhaled. Her eyes popped open. "Yeah. Ricky was always obsessed with the case. Wanted to know why Mac Gardner did what he did. Why he chose Dad. Why murder him the way he did? When he got in touch with the Kingston police, someone told him that all the case files ended up with Hank Webb. That the guy was writing a book or something. Ricky asked me to call Hank . . . He thought a woman would stand a better chance of convincing Hank to give us a peek. We told him we were true crime podcasters, and he was more than happy to share the files." She waited a beat, then continued: "Look, I know this doesn't look good for me. I should've up and left town when Adam was murdered. But Ricky begged me to stay, said we had nothing to worry about. That no one would make the connection." A tight-lipped smile left as quickly as it came. "Kudos to you, Detectives."

"I want to come back to motive," I said. "Why Adam? You said he was just some random guy, therefore Ricky would have no reason to murder him. But what if Ricky, or you for that matter, learned something about Adam that didn't make him just a random guy?"

Libby scrunched her nose as though a bad smell had wafted into the room. "You're going to have to be more forthcoming, Detective Ford. I almost feel like you're trying to trick me into saying something. Only I can't quite figure out what you're getting at." She relaxed her facial muscles. "Are you telling me that Adam is connected to the Mac Gardner cases?" A hint of nervous laughter infiltrated the tail end of the question. "That's insane. I told you, we both just met Adam."

I watched her expression for any whiff of deception. But she seemed genuinely baffled by this line of questioning. "Shirley Gardner had a son."

Libby blinked rapidly, clearly processing this bit of information, working out the significance of my statement. "Adam? You mean Adam? Is that what you're telling me?"

I slowly nodded, giving the revelation time to sink in.

Libby's bony fingers traced the bump of her collarbone. "Adam is . . . was Shirley's son?"

"So what if your brother knew this?" I asked rhetorically, then continued: "Only this time he didn't tell you. Perhaps he was afraid you'd talk him out of it. Or that you would warn Adam."

Jack leaned forward. "Or maybe you already knew who he was and you're giving us the performance of a lifetime."

She swallowed hard. A sputtering cough followed as though she had choked on her spit. Her eyes were glassy now from the coughing fit. "I didn't know." She paused, then added, "Ricky didn't know." Her voice croaked out the words.

"How can you be so sure he didn't know?" Jack asked.

Libby pursed her lips so tightly, a thin line replaced her mouth. She remained in that position for ten seconds. As her eyes narrowed, I sensed she was trying to remember if Ricky might have said or done something that belied what he had told her. She gently shook her head. "I would know if he knew," she finally said, although the conviction in her voice had diminished slightly from her earlier forceful defense of him.

But I too wasn't convinced that Ricky knew. He seemed genuinely surprised when we told him that Adam Kincaid was Shirley Gardner's son. The way he jerked his head up and the shocked expression on his face suggested he was hearing the news for the first time.

BY THE time Jack and I finished up with Libby, the warrant for her extradition to Massachusetts had come through. Detectives Brian Carew and Melody Walters had dispatched a couple of North Adams police officers to pick her up. Libby had requested a lawyer, and was told a public defender would be at the station when she arrived.

"You believe her?" Eldridge asked after we briefed him.

"I believe the evidence," I replied. "And right now the evidence is neither confirming nor denying her guilt in Shirley's murder. The evidence tells me she was there. But her story is plausible . . . Maybe she did try to stop her brother. As for Adam's murder, we know for a fact—from Ring cameras in her building—that she entered her apartment on August fifteenth at six o'clock in the evening and didn't leave until the next afternoon."

"Could she have left her building through a window?" Eldridge asked.

"Her apartment is on the fifth floor, so highly doubtful." I liked Libby. I hoped I was right about her.

JACK AND I made ourselves comfortable in the observation room, where a two-way mirror provided a view into the interrogation room where Grace Sinclair sat with her lawyer, Graham Walden. Grace sat primly with her hands folded on the table, her back straight. She was mousy-looking, with rounded cheeks and sharp features. Her eyes bulged slightly, magnified behind large-framed glasses pushed high on her pointed nose.

Her lawyer glanced at the two-way mirror; probably because he was told Jack and I would be on the other side. Graham and I had attended Monticello High School together. Class of 1983. We weren't friends, ran in different circles. I was far from popular. But he was even further down, on a lower rung of the ladder. I believe he went off to college somewhere in the Midwest. After law school, he moved back here with a wife and hung out a shingle proclaiming his solo law practice. Word was he met his wife while in college, but she was not keen on this area and left with their five-year old daughter in 1996. I'd seen him around the courthouse, occasionally at the local bars, and had glimpsed him at the ShopRite.

If we ran into each other at any of those places, we'd nod and smile. That was the extent of our relationship. I watched him now as he conferred with Grace. His salt-and-pepper head bowed toward hers. When he touched the back of her hand with his index finger, she recoiled, pulling her hand down to her lap.

Ray and Marty entered the interrogation room and promptly took their seats. Ray took the chair facing Grace, while Marty planted his butt in the chair across from the lawyer.

Jack rubbed his palms together. "Let's get this party started!" he exclaimed as Ray started the proceedings in the adjoining room.

After formal introductions, Ray laid the note Grace wrote to Chase on the table.

She leaned forward slightly. Her mouth moved silently as she read the note. I recited it in my head: *This arrangement is over. We're done. In fact, I'd like to pretend it never happened. Don't bother trying to find me—because you won't. I'm very good at disappearing.*

"Care to explain this?" Ray said, leaning across the table.

She pinched her lips together. From where I stood behind the glass, it was hard to tell if it was in defiance or to stave off tears. When she relaxed her lips, she brought her right hand up to her eyelid and swiped away tears.

Marty put the empty prescription bottle of Bactrim on the table. "Your father's name is the prescribing physician. Only thing is, he's been out of the game for a while," Marty said sternly. "Is this how you were supplying Chase?"

Grace glanced at Graham. He nodded for her to answer. "It was all Chase's idea. I needed money to pay for my father's caretaker. I didn't want to put Dad in a nursing home and couldn't afford top-quality care. My dad is still a registered pharmacist and I have his script pads. Chase convinced me we weren't hurting anyone. College kids wanted Adderall and Ambien, and if it wasn't us supplying, they would find it elsewhere. But he got greedy. He found another source to supply him drugs like Molly and oxy, because there was no way I was getting kids hooked on that shit."

"What about your neighbor, Brandy Johnson? She seems to have been chummy with Chase. Where does she fit into this drug scheme?" Ray asked.

"She spread the word to students, and he gave her a kickback." Her eyes widened. "You don't think her murder has something to do with this? That's crazy. I mean, Chase is an asshole, but he's not a killer."

"So it's not possible that Brandy was going to rat him out?" Marty waited a beat, then added, "Perhaps rat you out? And the two of you put the kibosh on that?"

She shook her head so hard I thought her glasses would fly off her head. "What? No? Oh my goodness. Oh, no. What are you saying? Are you accusing—"

"Hold on one minute here," Graham interjected. "How did we go from drug dealing to murder? Do you have any evidence to back up that accusation?"

Ray narrowed his eyes and directed his indignation toward Graham. "This is an interrogation. We don't need evidence to ask your client questions. Grace just admitted she was writing illegal scripts for Chase. Chase was using Brandy Johnson to find customers. So far, your client has been very cooperative, which will bode well for her . . ." Ray shifted his gaze to Grace. "We will find out if you had a hand in Brandy's murder, Ms. Sinclair. Your best bet is to either come clean here and now, or—"

"Or what?' Graham bellowed. "Grace is a cooperating witness to help you build a case against Chase. She was strong-armed and threatened herself by Chase. She's willing to pay her penance for her role. Feels a little bait and switch, if you ask me. Haul her in here for one thing, and then lay a trap to accuse her of murder. Again, unless you have evidence that ties Grace to Brandy Johnson's murder, I suggest your line of questioning sticks to the drug charge."

Ray clenched his fists. His shoulders rose slightly.

Shake it off, Ray, I thought, hoping that a bit of mental telepathy would penetrate the two-way mirror.

He unclenched his fists, then relaxed his shoulders. "Where did Chase get the oxy and Molly?"

"I don't know." Her eyes darted from Ray to Marty and back to Ray. "I swear, I don't know. But it might have been someone from the theater. He started dealing that stuff soon after he started working there."

"Are you aware of a relationship between Chase and the theater's director, Adam Kincaid?" Ray asked.

"Are you asking if they were boyfriends?"

"Boyfriends, chums, drug partners?" Marty said. "Interacted in some way or form."

Grace leaned back in her chair and tapped her index finger on her chin. "I'm not sure if Chase knew Adam, but Adam sure did know Brandy." She leaned forward. "I'm pretty sure those two were dating, or, as they say these days, hooking up."

RAY, MARTY, Jack, and I rendezvoused in the conference room.

"Who here thinks Adam's murder and Brandy's murder are related?" Ray asked.

"I don't know what to think," Jack replied. "If Brandy and Adam were dating, you would think there would be correspondence between those two on email or texts. What did they do? Send smoke signals?"

"Well, they both had Snapchat on their phones," I said. "They could've been communicating through that app. Unfortunately, those messages disappear ten seconds after viewing. You didn't Snapchat, Jack?"

"I was in my early thirties when that app hit the scene. So, no."

A hard knock at the door interrupted our conversation. The door swung open and Eldridge stepped into the room.

"Sally and Ron just got back from Chase's apartment. He's cleared out. According to the landlord, he even had a cleaning crew come in and wipe away any vestige of him. Probably heard we picked up Grace and figured the walls were closing in."

IT HAD been four days since I last visited Mom. With Chase in the wind and nothing new to track down, I decided to check in on her. It felt strange to feel the pull of her these days. When she was drinking, I would go out of my way to avoid her, our interactions few and far between. I wanted to believe she was still on the wagon. And perhaps popping in—unannounced—would put my mind at ease (or confirm my suspicions).

I let myself in and found her sleeping upright on the couch with a book across her stomach. I sat next to her and gently touched her arm. "Mom?" I whispered. She made a sputtering noise and blinked as she drifted back to a waking state. "Have you eaten dinner?"

She glanced up at the clock on the mantel. "Shit. I must've fallen asleep." Only that last word came out as *ah-shleep*.

"Do you want me to make you something?"

She turned to face me and half smiled. No, that wasn't it. The left side of her face was drooping.

"Mom, is your left arm or left leg numb?"

She started to ball up her left fist and stopped. "My arm feels funny," she slurred.

"We're going to the hospital, Mom." Her face contorted into a confused scowl and I wondered if she was going to argue with me or acquiesce. "Right now!"

She attempted to launch out of the sofa but wobbled. I grabbed her upper arm and got her upright.

"Lean on me," I said as we hurried to the car.

"Susan, slow down. My knee."

I felt like saying *fuck your knee*, but getting into a dustup now with Mom seemed totally inappropriate and counterproductive.

After securing the seat belt around her waist, I said as calmly as possible, "I think you're having a stroke."

She leaned her head against the headrest and closed her eyes.

I patted her leg to reassure her, then hit the gas knowing minutes mattered. Once we were on the road, I called Dad and told him to meet me at the hospital.

"Shit. My head's banging."

"Hang on, Mom, we're almost there." I grabbed her hand and squeezed gently. I held on to her the rest of the way.

I threw the car in park in front of the emergency-room entrance, then dashed out and into the lobby area to flag down an ER attendant. With the words, "I think my mother is having a stroke," two people dressed in scrubs followed me outside with a wheelchair, then whisked her away. I stood there, alone, catching my breath.

After conferring with a nurse, I called Dad again. "Take your time," I said. "It'll be a couple of hours until we know anything. They're running tests now."

Twenty minutes later, Dad was sitting with me in the waiting room, nursing a cup of vending-machine coffee.

"YOUR MOTHER experienced a TIA—a transient ischemic attack—or in layman's terms, a pre-stroke," Dr. Renard explained. "An MRI confirmed the diagnosis." He must have recognized the alarmed expression on my face, and quickly added, "The prognosis is good. Minutes matter, and getting here as quickly as you did should be commended. We were able to restore blood flow to the brain with an Alteplase IV."

I finally let myself breathe.

Dad wrapped his arm around my shoulders. "You done good, Susan."

"But there's something else you should know." Dr. Renard glanced at his clipboard. "The MRI revealed some gray matter atrophy. So, we administered what's called a Montreal Cognitive Assessment."

I nodded, recalling Natalie's advice to have Mom take that test.

"It's a test that helps us measure cognitive impairment. She scored a twenty-two, which is borderline between mild cognitive impairment and mild dementia."

"Alzheimer's?" Dad asked, incredulously.

"It's too early to make that call. And just so you know, Alzheimer's is only one form of dementia."

Dad rubbed his face. "Jeez."

"Is she okay to be living by herself?" I asked.

"I can refer her to a geriatric specialist who can help her with those decisions. In the meantime, you might want to consider part-time help. Not necessarily a nurse, but someone who could help with shopping and chores. And if you haven't already, I would suggest setting up a power of attorney to have oversight of her finances, because this is where a lot of patients manage to get themselves into a whole heap of trouble." He sighed. "At this stage, most of the issues she'll face revolve around forgotten conversations, appointments, plans, and organizational skills, like paying bills on time or grocery shopping. Technology also gets tricky."

Well, that explained her inability to program her GPS. "Can she drive?" I asked.

"After a ministroke, it's protocol she not drive for one month. As for whether she should drive in general, that's a conversation to have with the geriatric specialist, who can better assess her capabilities." Dr. Renard blew out a puff of air. "When my dad was first diagnosed with mild cognitive impairment, he was able to drive to places he was familiar with. What got him in trouble was driving to places he was unfamiliar with, like the airport, or a new restaurant."

"When can we see her?" Dad asked.

"If you wait here, I'll have a nurse come get you. Shouldn't be long." The doctor checked his watch. "Another fifteen to twenty minutes."

Dad and I settled back in the upholstered chairs.

It was a relief to learn that Mom was not hitting the bottle. But on the other hand, this diagnosis and its inevitable march toward oblivion seemed a million times worse.

A soft moan escaped Dad's lips, then he said. "We'll figure this out, Susan."

I nodded and managed a smile. A conversation for another day. So I opted for what is always a safe subject for us: shop talk. "Have you given any more thought to the case?"

"Actually, now that you mention it, I was looking for you at the station earlier. There was something bugging me about that Woodstock story I told you. About Madeline Klein. So I called Koop, the cop who was there with me. He remembered something else that's worth looking into." He leaned back in his chair and began: "The festival was supposed to wrap up Sunday, August seventeenth, but because of the delays caused by the rain and traffic jams, it rolled into Monday morning. And there was an artist I really wanted to see."

DETECTIVE WILL FORD

August 18, 1969

T he heavy rain had subsided, and Monday dawned with partly cloudy skies. The festival was supposed to draw to a close Sunday night, so I was surprised to see a substantial throng of bodies still milling around the large meadow. It was eight thirty in the morning, with one final artist set to take the stage. Jimi Hendrix. I had caught Jimi Hendrix at the Scene, a basement club in Midtown Manhattan, two years earlier. I was itching to see him again, and cajoled Koop into joining me back at the festival grounds, this time as spectators.

We made our way to the center of the field, stepping over deflated tents, crushed water bottles, empty food tins, and varied detritus and debris. Koop lifted his new Nikon camera to his eye and snapped a few photos.

A tall man wearing a red T-shirt approached us. "Hey, weren't you the guys who helped that pregnant woman the other day?" He jutted his chin toward the stream where the festival-goers skinny-dipped and bathed. "Up over there."

"That was us. You with the . . . um, the Peace Force?" Koop said, pointing at the man's shirt.

The tall man chuckled. "Yeah. Sal Valero," he said, holding out his hand. Will spotted a tattoo on his upper arm—101ST AIRBORNE PARATROOPER was etched into his skin. "NYPD Tenth Precinct."

"You guys did a bang-up job of keeping the peace," I said. "Heard nothing really bad went down."

"Yeah, gotta hand it to Wes Pomeroy, the head of security. He got up onstage that first night and introduced us as the 'red peace force.' Once the booing subsided, he laid down three rules. One, 'Don't hurt anyone.' Two, 'Don't steal from anyone.' And three, 'If you see someone who needs help, help them or find one of us red shirts.' Everyone, pretty much, stuck to these rules. A few fights here and there. Some stealing. But in the scheme of things, and considering what a clusterfuck this could've been, it was a pretty chill four days."

"Yeah, well we're off duty today. Just here to see Jimi Hendrix."

"Me too. Just met him backstage. He recognized my tattoo." Sal pulled up his sleeve and twisted his arm. "Turns out Hendrix was also a one hundred first Airborne Division paratrooper. He served two years before me."

"Holy shit. Didn't know that."

"I don't think too many folks do. Well, gotta head over—"

"Hey! Hey!" a young man shouted in our direction as he made his way through the loose crowd. A woman followed close behind him.

When the young man got within earshot, Sal asked if they needed assistance.

"No man. You were the guys who helped my stepsister out two days ago. We just wanted to say thanks."

His stepsister emerged from behind him. "Hi," she said, bowing her head shyly. She held out her hand. "I guess we should formally meet. I'm Madeline. And this is my stepbrother, Dan."

"I think this calls for a picture," said Koop, raising his camera to his eye as the foursome formed a jagged line. "Say cheese!"

11

MONDAY | AUGUST 26, 2019

IT DIDN'T take much sleuthing to find Madeline's stepbrother. We simply asked Lynn. Lynn hadn't spoken to her brother Dan for years, but she knew where he was: behind bars at Woodbourne Correctional, a medium-security men's prison just a couple of towns over. He had spent his youth working the hotel circuit as either a bellhop, waiter, or security guard. After the last of the storied hotels closed, he drove a taxi. When the income from that didn't quite feed his heroin addiction, he decided to rob a bank.

"At least we can strike him off our suspect list," Jack said on our way over to the prison.

"I wouldn't jump the gun on that. It's possible Dan set this up. Perhaps found someone on the outside willing to do his dirty work."

"Chase is still my number one." Jack turned into the visitor's parking lot. "On the property the night of the murder. Blackjack found in his gift shop. We know he owned a watch, one that wasn't on his wrist the first day we interviewed him. Dealing drugs with Adam's girlfriend, Brandy. And for all we know, he has a connection to this area we haven't quite figured out yet." When he killed the ignition, he turned to me. "You seem a bit distracted. You all right?"

I filled him in on Mom's stroke. I left out the dementia diagnosis. He listened quietly and not once did he peek at his watch.

Not sure why I felt the need to open up, but it did feel cathartic to talk to someone who was not privy to the past machinations between me and my mother, like Ray or Natalie, or even Dad—all of whom would offer advice from an insider's perspective. So I continued: "My mom and I have had a tumultuous relationship since I was around thirteen. We finally got on even footing earlier this year when she quit drinking. And now this." I exhaled. "I'm not sure we've had enough time to heal for me to be thrust into the role of caregiver."

"Shit, Susan, that's some heavy personal baggage."

"Well, you did ask me if I was all right."

He laughed. "I have no business offering up advice, but since you shared a personal story, my turn. Maybe it'll help."

This time, I glanced at my watch. "Do we have time?"

"Yeah. It's a short story."

"Let it rip."

"When I was twelve years old, my mother got pregnant. Not planned. Anyway, my sister, Lucy, was born with cerebral palsy. She required a lot of care, but my parents were totally up for the task."

"I see where this is going, Jack."

"No, you don't. This story has nothing to do with my parents. It's about me. When I was sixteen, my parents told me that I would be babysitting Lucy every Friday night so that they could play bridge, which is something they did before Lucy was born. Only Friday night was the night I played basketball with my friends. I was pissed, to put it mildly. I was like, 'I did not sign up for this.' But I had no choice. My parents didn't have the money to pay an experienced caregiver, and I knew all of Lucy's routines and could communicate with her."

He must have caught my surprised expression, because he then said, "Yeah, I sign." He smiled. "The first month, I was an ass. I went through the motions because all I could think about was missing my basketball game." He paused. "Do you now see where this is going?"

"Yeah. You embraced your role as caregiver and loved it."

"Well, I loved Lucy. The caregiving, not so much. But it gave me an opportunity to really get to know her in a way I didn't before. There's real joy in that." He sneaked a peek at his watch. "It's one of the reasons I moved here. My dad found an adult home for her in Liberty— he's nearing seventy, so it's become harder for him to care for Lucy twenty-four seven."

"So, you're not really into small-town policing?" I asked sarcastically.

"It's growing on me."

DAN LIMPED into the windowless room, favoring his right leg. He winced slightly as he lowered himself onto the metal chair across from us. Once seated, he grinned broadly—a chipped front tooth ruined a row of perfectly squared-off teeth. His eyes were clear and bright, a copper brown with flecks of green. The coppery hue of his eyes matched what was left of his hair, which was tied back into a ponytail.

"To what do I owe the pleasure of your visit?" Dan said, in a deep, resonant baritone—radio disc jockey territory.

"We'd like to ask you a few questions about your stepsister, Madeline," I said.

"Madeline? Okay, wasn't expecting that. Quite the curveball. I thought you were here to tell me you found Elmore."

"Elmore?" Jack asked.

"Yeah. The dude who actually robbed the bank. He tricked me. Told me he was going in to make a deposit. I got set up as the getaway driver." He pouted, then cocked his head to the side. "Maybe you can look into that for me."

Jack side-eyed me, then shifted his attention back to Dan. "We'll see what we can do."

"Okay, yeah," Dan said, his gaze darting between me and Jack. "That would be great. You do me a solid. I'll do you a solid."

I cleared my throat. "Twenty-eight years ago, Madeline arranged a private adoption for your sister, Lynn Kincaid. Know anything about that?"

Dan's eyes widened. "I don't know anything about that." He must have clocked our skepticism, and quickly added, "I wasn't that close with either of them. Madeline and I drifted apart in the mid-seventies, when I started getting into trouble with drugs and the law. And don't get me started on Lynn. Putting on airs, always acting so high and mighty, like she was better than me."

"So you never heard anything about this from Madeline's son, Kenny?" Jack asked.

"Jeez. Again, no. No one told me. Not Madeline. Not Lynn. And not Kenny. Why don't you go ask him yourself?"

"I hate to be the bearer of bad news, but your nephew Kenny died in the 9/11 attacks," I said.

Dan choked out a laugh. "Oh, man. He ain't dead."

"What?" Jack and I exclaimed in unison.

"Like, I said, he ain't dead. I mean, maybe he's dead. But he didn't die on September eleventh. He's like a jack-in-the-box. Goes into hiding, then pops back up outta nowhere. For a while, I too thought he was dead, but then he contacted me about five years ago. I guess he knew I was still living in the area and he wanted me to do a little sleuthing for him."

"So he what? Called you? Came to see you in person?" I asked.

"Called."

"So what did he ask you to do exactly?"

"He told me that there was this ex-cop in Kingston who had all the files pertaining to the serial killer who murdered his father. He wanted me to get in touch with this cop and see what I could find out about the killer's family. Any of his relatives that might have been interviewed. Or any living children or grandchildren." Dan knitted his brows. "Why are you asking about this?"

"We're not at liberty to say," Jack said. "But before we were told that your nephew—"

"*Step*-nephew," Dan corrected.

"Before we were told that your *step*-nephew was dead, we were searching for him. He's a person of interest in a case we are currently working."

"Ha! A person of interest. That's what they called me, and now look where I am." He swung his arm around like a game-show hostess unveiling the grand prize behind door number one. "Although I did get clean in here. So there's that. Not happy about my tooth though. I had a perfect set of choppers when I got here." He grinned.

"Back to your story," I said, aiming to regain control of the interview. "Were you able to get Kenny the info he wanted?"

"Yeah. Kenny gave me the ex-cop's contact info and the guy was eager to share. Kenny specifically wanted photos of the crime scenes. Which, by the way, made my toes curl. He said he was planning on writing a memoir and he would pay me royalties once published. So I took photos of the photos and emailed them to him." He hesitated, then added, "I kinda remember taking photos of the statements of the victims' spouses and people who knew the killer, but I'm a bit fuzzy on that."

"You remember Kenny's email address?" Jack asked.

"Man, I was doing heroin at the time, so the answer to that would be negative-oh." He yawned. "Anything else?"

"When's the last time you actually saw Kenny?"

"That would be the summer of 2001. He was working as a courier for a company that had an office in the World Trade Center." Out of the corner of my eye, I saw Jack flinch. "The insurance company in the North Tower that took a direct hit."

"Marsh and McLennan," Jack whispered.

Dan's head pumped up and down. "Yeah, that one. Never heard from him after that happened, so we figured he got killed in the attack. But then he called me out of the blue five years ago. Which, I'll tell you, was like something out of *The Twilight Zone*. I kept pressing him about why he didn't let us know he was alive or where he'd been, but he refused to tell me. Said something like 'here, there, and everywhere.'"

Jack blew out of a puff of air. "So you never got confirmation that he was actually among the dead?"

"No. In fact, I convinced Madeline to submit her DNA in the hopes they could find a match among the remains."

"*Her* DNA?" I asked.

Jack let out a heavy sigh, then said, "Scientists figured out how to extract genetic information from poor-quality DNA, and they set up what's called the World Trade Center Kinship and Data Analysis Panel. Relatives could either submit *their* DNA for an indirect test or provide an original sample of the victim's DNA, like from a toothbrush or razor for a direct test."

"That's exactly how they explained it to us," Dan said. "We didn't have anything of Kenny's to give to the authorities, so she gave them her DNA."

"And you didn't find it odd that there was never a match?" I asked.

Dan was about to answer when Jack coughed, then cleared his throat. "If Kenny was in the Marsh and McLennan offices when that first plane hit, the chance of DNA recovery is nearly impossible. To this day, eleven hundred victims aren't accounted for. And the majority of them were working in the plane impact zone between the ninety-third and ninety-ninth floors. The so-called 'hot zone,' where the fuel exploded."

I wanted to ask Jack how he knew all this, but felt like this was neither the time nor place. Instead, I turned toward Dan: "So it sounds like Kenny took advantage of the fact that people assumed he was dead, and what? Disappeared?"

"Why are you asking me? I don't know. And besides, what does this have to do with the stuff Kenny asked me to dig up five years ago?"

I decided to divulge more information. At this point, we needed all the insight we could get on this, and Dan was the closest connection we had to Kenny right now. "Did you hear about the murder over at the Monticello Playhouse?" I asked.

"No. I don't pay attention to the news. It's all doom and gloom these days. A bunch of crazy people running for president. Global warming. Riots in the streets." He leaned over the table and whispered: "Police brutality." Then winked.

Jack's jaw tightened. He edged out of his chair but just as quickly restored his butt to his seat. His jaw slackened slightly.

I glimpsed at Jack, then turned my attention to Dan, who was still grinning over his provocative barb. "How well do you know Lynn's son, Adam?" I asked.

The grin vanished from Dan's face. "Haven't seen him since he was five. Like I told you, me and Lynn have nothing to do with each other. And that's on her. Not me." He scratched at a pimple on his chin. "Are we done here?"

"Lynn's son Adam was murdered at the Monticello Playhouse and there are quite a few similarities between the way in which Kenny's father was murdered and the way Adam was murdered." He abruptly stopped picking his pimple. I had his full attention now. "Whoever killed Adam Kincaid knew quite a bit about the original murders."

"You mean someone killed Adam using the makeup, the pillow, and the ropes?"

"You catch on fast," Jack said tersely, his jaw still rigid.

Dan jerked his head back. "So you think Kenny has something to do with this?"

"We are trying to locate anyone who has intimate knowledge of the earlier murders. Find out who they might've told."

Dan let out of low whistle. "Well, it wasn't me. I was in here."

"And you never shared those photos with anyone else?"

"Nope. I don't get off on that kind of thing. I don't even think I looked at them after sending them to Kenny. I was so high all the time, probably didn't even remember I had them. Besides, I dropped that phone in the toilet. It didn't survive. All the rice in China couldn't bring that thing back to life."

"Did you save your photos in the cloud?"

Dan looked up. "The cloud?"

"Were your photos backed up on an external drive? Could someone have accessed them?"

His perplexed expression gave us our answer. "I have no friggin' idea what you just said. Clouds? Drives? Do you think I'm some kind of technology expert?"

"Do you have any pictures of Kenny?"

"I'm sure I did at one time. Have no idea where they ended up. I moved around a lot."

"You said the last time you saw him was in the summer of 2001. What was that about?" I asked.

He scratched his chin. "He asked me for money. I barely had two nickels to rub together, so that was a hard no. I told him to ask Madeline. That she would help. But he was adamant that he wanted nothing to do with her."

"So, let me get this straight," Jack said. "Kenny contacts you out of the blue in the summer of 2001 to ask for money. And then you don't hear from him again until 2014, when he asks you to go to the cop's house in Kingston to dig up the old Mac Gardner files? And you haven't heard from him since. Do I have that right?"

"That about sums it up." He smiled and ran his finger along his jagged tooth. "Don't forget. Elmore. The dude who jacked me up."

"Yeah. We'll get right on that," Jack quipped, obviously still pissed at Dan's comment about police brutality. Although this whole interview had Jack on edge well beyond a snide remark.

"We'll see what we can do," I said earnestly, partly because Jack's response was a bit out of line, and partly because Dan might know more than he was letting on or might remember something after we leave—and being on his good side was where I'd rather be.

"You seem to know an awful lot about that 9/11 DNA project," I said to Jack when we reached his car.

"A friend of mine works in that lab. They're still at it, y'know, trying to identify remains." He sighed, then added, "My uncle was a firefighter with the FDNY."

He opened the car door. Got in. Buckled up. Started the engine. Backed up and turned onto the main road.

In silence.

I got the message loud and clear.

"WHERE ARE we?" Chief Eldridge asked as we crossed the threshold into his office. But before I could speak, he softened his tone and said, "Will told me about Vera. If you need to step away from the case, I understand."

"Thank you, Chief, but I'm good." One of his eyebrows twitched upward. "I can manage the case *and* look after my mother," I declared with enough conviction to convince even myself.

I filled Eldridge in on our chat with Dan, that Kenny Klein was alive, in hiding, possibly living under an alias, and knew everything there was to know about the 1969 murders. All of this met with several grunts and a lot of head shaking.

"What about that actor, the one with the mustache. George Zettler? Are we still keeping an eye on him? 'Cause the last thing we need is another dead actor."

I was going to correct Eldridge that our first victim was a director, but thought better of it. "I got a surveillance team parked on the theater grounds," I replied.

"This murderer has eluded us thus far. No disrespect for our team's surveillance skills, but if this killer is hell-bent on doing to George what he did to Adam, we need to catch him before he has a chance to get his hands on another goddamn pillow."

Jack and I let the chief vent. Everyone was breathing down his neck. He had every right to breathe down ours.

"I know he's a possible target, but we can't completely rule out George Zettler as the killer," Jack chimed in. "Not only did he have access to the theater, he was Mac Gardner's nephew—and it's possible he knows more about the MO than he lets on. He admitted going back to the theater by himself to lock up . . . but honestly, that guy is so freaked out over this, he's my least likely."

"I have to agree with Jack on that. He doesn't quite fit the profile of someone meticulous and exacting. Well, unless his demeanor is all an act. He is, after all, an actor."

Eldridge leaned over his desk. "And what about your other suspect, Chase?"

"MIA. And right now, the only evidence tying him to Adam is the blackjack found in the gift shop." I paused. "Although there also seems to be a connection between Chase, Adam, and Brandy Johnson. While Brandy was drumming up customers for Chase's pharma biz, she was also hooking up with Adam."

Eldridge pulled a face. "Hooking up?"

"Y'know, friends with benefits."

"I don't know—" Eldridge paused, letting it sink in. "Okay, I think I know."

"It's possible that Adam was going to report Chase and, well, Chase silenced him," Jack said. "Shana told us that Adam was a bit of an antidrug crusader after his best friend died of an overdose."

"Problem is, the MO seems a bit over the top for someone simply trying to silence a rat." I cleared my throat. "However, it's possible that Chase killed Adam because he knew he was Mac Gardner's grandson. We're still trying to find the connection."

"Let's not forget Leslie Brattle," Jack said. "Adam was extorting her. And it was her makeup case found at the scene of the crime."

Eldridge tapped his fingers on his desk. "And last but certainly not least, the dynamic duo of Ricky and Libby a.k.a. Derek and Elizabeth. Ricky confessed to killing Shirley, but it was Libby's DNA that was found at the Shirley Gardner crime scene."

"Lots of motive. But no hard evidence tying any of them to Adam's murder."

I heaved a sigh so loud, I was sure it was heard on the other side of the building.

"HOW YA feeling?" I asked, employing my best upbeat voice. I stood beside Mom's hospital bed and patted her left shin.

"I could use a cigarette." She waited a beat than said, "Just kidding. Well, kinda."

"I see you haven't lost your sense of humor."

She smiled weakly. "I'm tired, that's all. They say I can get outta here tomorrow."

"Mom, did the doctor talk to you about, uh, the memory test you took?"

She rolled her eyes. "What a bunch of hogwash. So, I forgot a few things. Everyone forgets things once in a while. Doesn't mean I'm losing my marbles."

"How about we save this conversation for when you're feeling better?"

Mom fussed with the covers, then folded her arms across her chest. "The doctor told me I have to quit smoking. He's putting me on blood thinners." She grunted. "Oh, and I have to lower my cholesterol."

"Think of it as a lifestyle makeover. No drinking. No smoking—"

"No cheeseburgers." Mom tutted. "I can really go for a big, juicy steak and fries right about now."

"I'm glad you can joke, Mom, but this is serious. I do hope you are going to take this seriously."

"It's my life, Susan. I can't just stop this and that. I've stopped drinking. I'll quit smoking, okay? But not eat the things I love, that's a bridge too far. Next you'll be telling me to exercise or join a pickleball league or some other such nonsense."

"I'm simply trying to help," I said, regretting the words as soon as they tumbled out.

"I don't need your help. I don't need anyone's help. Now if you'll let me be, I want to take a nap."

I wanted to scream, *You do need my help!* Did she really believe that everything was A-OK? Or was she just throwing up walls, like she'd always done? Was every future interaction with her going to be an argument? Because she could easily wear me down to the point where I wouldn't want to help her. I stooped down and picked up my backpack. When I stood and shifted around, Mom's head was turned away. But there was no mistaking what she was doing: wiping away tears.

Before closing the door behind me, I looked over my shoulder. "I love you, Mom. I'll pick you up tomorrow."

SOON AFTER I got back to the precinct, Dad strode into the bullpen, rubbing his eyes. He looked spent. I knew he wasn't working the case like he would have in his prime—up early, then burning the midnight oil. But still, I could tell it was taking its toll. He was an old goat, not a spring chicken. He scratched at the stubble on his chin. In my estimation, he had read the case files at least ten times now. I had to hand it to him—he was handing us some solid leads to chase. Those memories were still in the recesses of his brain and the old files were helping him tap them.

He grabbed an empty chair and rolled it to my desk. I filled him in on our morning conversation with Dan.

"Man. So, Kenny's seen the Mac Gardner crime scene photos?"

I nodded. "Problem is, he's in the wind. And for all we know he might be dead—really dead this time—and have nothing to do with any of this."

"He used 9/11 to fake his death, so he could be operating under a stolen identity. Which means you're looking for a needle in a haystack." Dad's gaze shifted to my computer. "Do you think Adam's and Brandy's murders are related? Perhaps the same killer?"

I let the question hang in the air for a minute. My knee-jerk reaction was no. The MOs were wildly different, for one. Brandy's murder seemed spur-of-the-moment, not particularly well thought out. Disorganized. Adam's murder was meticulously planned, down to the formation of the knots and the placement of the pillow. "I'm not jumping to any conclusions."

Jack's phone rang loudly and the three of us jumped at the sound. Jack swiped to answer. "Detective Jack Tomelli." He listened and nodded, then said, "Hold on a moment, let me put you on speaker." Jack mouthed *Hope Webb* as he switched to speaker mode.

"You there?" A woman's voice rang out.

"Yes, Hope. Can you repeat what you just told me?"

We all leaned our heads closer to the phone.

"Um, yes. I was cleaning out my dad's attic office and came across a file that seems related to those boxes you took. In 1999, my dad interviewed a guy named Michael Mercer, who said he was a victim of Mac Gardner's. But he managed to escape."

Our heads shot up simultaneously. Equally stunned expressions all around.

"It looks like Michael Mercer kept his carbon copy of the police report and my dad made a copy of it."

"When did this occur?" I asked.

"July third—"

"That would be two days before Sam Blackstone was killed," Dad interrupted.

"Not exactly." Hope cleared her throat. "The date on the report is July third, 1968."

"1968? Are you sure?" I asked.

"Well, that's what's written here." She paused, then added, "I also think Mercer did some legwork on the case for my dad when he wasn't able to get around. At least that's what I recall. Anyway, I can scan and email the police report to you."

"Hope, does the police report say where this incident with Michael Mercer took place?" I asked.

"Yes. Monticello. The report was written up by a police officer named . . . hold on." She sighed. "Ah, here it is. I can't make out the first name . . . it looks like the carbon copy got smudged. But the last name is Ford. Maybe you can find him and ask if he remembers anything about it."

"DAD?" I said, drawing out the word, the inflection in my voice rising as I hit the second half. "Do you know what she's talking about?"

"Give me a minute. Let me think."

We all stood around silently waiting for Dad to provide an explanation. Well, until Jack could no longer hold his tongue. "Do you recall this guy Michael Mercer coming to you a whole year before the other murders and reporting a similar attack?

Dad looked up at Jack, a scowl on his face. "I said, give me a minute."

Jack backed away.

"I was still a patrol officer in July 1968. I mean, it's possible I was in the precinct when this guy came in and reported it. I'm just drawing a blank." Dad tapped on his head. "The old gray matter ain't what it used to be."

"Dad, don't be so hard on yourself. We're talking half a century ago. Hey, I can't even remember what I had for lunch yesterday."

"You had a turkey sandwich," Dad said, cracking a quick smile. "We should locate Mercer. If he's still alive we can verify all this. And if he did some legwork for Hank Webb, he might have additional intel."

"Good idea," Jack exclaimed, clearly trying to boost Dad's spirits.

"Did Hope send the email yet?" I asked Jack.

Jack jiggered his mouse, activating his screen. He refreshed his email. "Nope. Not yet."

"I need some fresh air. Text me when the email comes through," Dad said as he marched toward the door.

"Wait!" Jack shouted. "It just came in. I'll print it out."

Dad took long strides to the printer, which was up against the wall on the far corner of the room. He snatched it off the machine and immediately started reading. "Wait one goddamn minute here. This report wasn't written up by me. There was an officer named Murray Ford who overlapped with me for a year before retiring. He was an old goat back then—doubt he's still alive."

"Let me see," I said.

Dad passed me the paper. After I read it, I passed it to Jack, who was hunched over his computer searching for Michael Mercer.

Dad shook his head. "The MO is the same. Right down to the number one written on his hand. Man, if his roommate didn't walk in on this, this guy would've been toast."

"Found him!" Jack yelled out. "Got an address and a phone number."

Dad picked up the police report and scanned it again. He hovered behind Jack. "Any chance you got a photo of Michael Mercer? His name does sound a little familiar."

"Yeah." Jack rolled away from his desk to give Dad a clear view of his computer screen.

Dad put his readers on the edge of his nose and leaned forward. "Shit. I know him. He was a social worker at the local women's shelter, helped abused women start new lives." Dad snapped his fingers. "I crossed paths with Mercer that summer of 1969. Remember I told you about that young gal, the one shacked up with Owen Riggs."

Jack and I nodded like bobblehead dolls, eager to know where Dad's story was headed.

"I asked Michael if he could talk to that woman, try and convince her to leave that shithead. He actually helped her break free from Owen Riggs. Michael was a legend around these parts."

"What's the phone number," I said to Jack.

I tapped as Jack ticked off the numbers. Michael picked up on the third ring. I flashed a thumbs-up as I spoke. When I hung up, I smiled. "He can see us tomorrow morning."

Dad pumped his fist in the air. "Man, I hope he can shed some light on this." Dad's phone pinged. He checked the message, then exclaimed, "Cool!"

"What's cool?" I asked.

"Remember I told you about my buddy Koop and our little adventure to Woodstock. Well, he just texted me a couple of photos he took when we were there. Wanna see your dad in his prime?" he said, handing me his phone.

I tapped on the attachment. "Holy shit."

"Right? I was a good-looking dude."

"No. I mean, yeah, you were, I guess. But that's not it."

"What is it?" Jack pressed.

I reverse-pinched the photo, enlarging it slightly, then turned the screen toward Jack.

"Holy shit," Jack said, grabbing my wrist and bringing the phone closer to his face.

"Will someone please tell me what the hell you're looking at?" Dad huffed.

I pulled my hand from Jack's grip and repositioned the phone in front of Dad.

"So? It's a picture of me, Sal Valero, that NYPD cop I told you about, Madeline, and Dan."

"Look closer at Madeline, Dad."

He took off his glasses, breathed on the lenses, wiped them with the edge of his shirt, then put them back on. "Holy shit. The necklace."

The fucking stained glass necklace.

UPON LEARNING that the necklace belonged to Madeline, we high-tailed it back to Woodbourne Correctional to have another chat with Dan. Jack and I were kicking ourselves that we didn't think to ask Dan about the necklace when we were there earlier. But with all the revelations Dan threw our way, it just slipped my mind. Jack's too, for that matter.

"Missed me?" Dan said with a smirk as he was led into the room.

When he settled in the metal chair, I held up my phone. "Recognize this necklace?"

"Yeah. That's Madeline's necklace," Dan blurted out without hesitation. "She bought it from some artist selling his wares at Woodstock." He smiled wistfully. "There were all these little artisan tables lined up along the edge of the farm."

"Do you know what happened to the necklace after she died?"

His smile dissipated. "How the fuck would I know? Like I told you, I wasn't close to Madeline."

"Is it possible she gave it to Kenny?" I asked.

"It's possible. Look, I don't even know if Kenny is still alive. Like I said, haven't heard from him in five years."

Sure, he could be dead. But deep down, I sensed Kenny was still walking this earth and was quite possibly hiding in plain sight.

12

TUESDAY | AUGUST 27, 2019

JACK AND I rolled up to Michael Mercer's ranch house, which was set back about fifteen yards from the road. On one side of the house, a white wooden ramp sloped from the front door to the driveway. Along the other half, well-trimmed rhododendron bushes skirted a bay window.

Michael lived just thirty miles south of us, in Middletown, New York. A quick shot down Route 17. He said it would be easier for us to come to him than vice versa, seeing that he was confined to a wheelchair due to a spinal injury sustained in a motorcycle accident ten years ago.

A slight woman with gray hair matted to her head and dressed in jogging attire answered the door and stepped aside to let us in. She led us into the living room.

"Michael will be in momentarily. If you'll excuse me, I'll be jumping in the shower—"

"She's training for a marathon!"

We turned our attention toward the booming voice. Michael deftly maneuvered his wheelchair through the doorway and came to a stop near the sofa. "New York City marathon is in two months. It'll be Rosie's tenth go at it. She's tried to convince me to join the wheelchair race, but I'm more of a wheelchair basketball kind of guy." Michael pantomimed a free throw. "Well, glad you could come. So you think you got a Mac Gardner copycat? Wish I knew you were digging around this case sooner, could've been of assistance." He motioned toward the sofa and we sat. "So, you're Detective Will Ford's daughter. Nice guy, from what I recall."

I didn't think we would be pulling teeth with this guy. He certainly had a gift for gab.

Jack placed his elbows on his knees and leaned forward. "So what exactly happened to you?"

"With Mac Gardner?"

"Yeah."

"Oh boy. I had just gotten to my apartment about eleven o'clock at night. Before I could reach the light switch, I got whacked from behind. Out cold. Next thing I know I'm in my bed, ropes around my wrists and ankles, with my roommate standing over me, smacking my cheeks, trying to bring me out of unconsciousness. Turns out my roommate interrupted what was going on. And Mac ran off. Only I didn't know it was Mac at the time."

"According to the police report, you reported this the following morning," I said. "Why did you wait?"

He rubbed the back of his neck. "Honestly, I don't know. I think my roommate tried to convince me to go to the police that night, but I was a bit of a wreck. I thought maybe this was one of my clients' abusers. I wanted to tread carefully. My roommate documented the incident. He took Polaroid pictures of the ropes, my face, the bruise on the back of my neck, and the inked number one on my palm." He held out his hand to show us as though it was still there.

"Polaroid cameras were around back then?" Jack asked.

"Yeah, the peel-apart kind. Not the kind that you waved in the air to dry. That came later. Seventies, I think."

"Didn't know that."

"Learn something new every day. That's what I always say."

"You still have them?" I asked. "The Polaroids?"

H shook his head. "I brought them with me to the police station, and I'm fairly sure I left them with the officer I spoke to—not your dad, the other Ford."

"So, Mac Gardner put makeup on your face?" I asked.

"Yeah. Lipstick. He was applying the eye shadow when my roommate came home. Only one eye was done." He closed his left eye and touched his lid. "This one."

"What can you tell us about the ropes?" Jack asked.

"He used what's called a double-column tie on my wrists and a handcuff knot on my ankles.

"Same as his 1969 victims," Jack said. "And Adam."

"Did he hang a peace sign necklace around your neck?" I asked.

"No. But like I said, he barely got the makeup on me." Michael rubbed his chest where the necklace would have hung to. "When you called yesterday, you said there were two copycat murders. One seven years ago and one earlier this month. Is the MO the same on those two?"

"Not exactly," I replied. "But before we get into that, perhaps you can tell us what you were doing with Hank Webb?"

"Oh boy. Great story. Where to begin? The beginning, huh." He winked. "We met in 1998. Still had use of my legs. I think I told you on the phone, motorcycle accident. Guy crossed the centerline and bam! Turns out the driver was having a heart attack. So, hard to blame him. He survived. Comes around every so often. Nice guy." He tapped on the wheelchair's armrest. "So where was I? Oh, yeah. Hank. I was living in Kingston at the time. Sitting at a bar, minding my own business, when Hank sits down next to me. We start chatting it up. Two strangers at a bar, commiserating about this, that, and the other thing. He told me he was ex-law-enforcement. I was still working with abused women. So we had a lot in common. It's then that he mentioned the Mac Gardner case, that he was thinking about writing a book from the victims' families' point of view—sort of a where-are-they-now story—but health issues got in his way. I told him about my encounter with Mac. That I knew it had to be him who attacked me because the MO matched up. I'd say he was pretty floored. I guess you can call it kismet. Then Hank asked if I could do some legwork for him and find the victims' spouses or girlfriends."

"And did you? I asked.

"The only one who would speak to me was Kenneth Waterman's girlfriend, Madeline Klein. Robert Sherman's wife, Leah, died from a drug overdose in 1979. And Sam Blackstone's wife, Helen, refused to meet me. Crazy thing is she married a notorious abuser named Owen Riggs a couple of years after her husband was murdered. Lord only *knows* how that might've fucked up the kids." He sighed.

I knew. Jack also flinched at Michael's prescient words.

"My dad told me about you helping him out with a girlfriend of Owen's."

"Yeah. That was in 1969. Your dad asked me to talk to a woman Owen was shacking up with. Funny thing is, I feel somewhat responsible for what happened to Helen Blackstone. If I hadn't convinced that woman to leave Owen, Helen would have never gotten together with him."

Those pesky dominoes came to mind. Another one falling, making it harder for Helen to stop the chain of events that might have led to Shirley's or Adam's murders.

"Anyway," Michael continued, "This woman was real nervous about leaving Owen, afraid he would come after her, so I helped her disappear." He air quoted *disappear*.

"Disappear?" Jack asked.

"Back then, I helped women start fresh under a new name in a new place."

"You mean Witness Protection?" I asked.

"No, nothing like that. That's the jurisdiction of the U.S. Marshals Service Witness Security Program. But I called it WITSEC lite." He laughed. "Really just cosmetic changes—slight name change, new hairdo, residency in a different state. Usually that was enough to deter their abusers. They would just find someone else to terrorize. Lamont House, the shelter where I worked, held fundraisers, collected donations, which we used to help set up new lives for these women. We even had an education fund, if a woman wanted to get her GED or enroll in a community college." He tilted his head and narrowed his eyes. "When I told Madeline Klein's son what I did for a living, he—"

"Whoa." I held up my hand. "You met Madeline's son?"

"I did. He was there with Madeline when I visited her. Kenny, I think. Yeah, Kenny. As I was saying, he was super intrigued by the work I did."

"Intrigued in what way?" I asked.

"Well, for starters, he asked a boatload of questions about how to assume a new identity, like how to get his hands on someone else's birth certificate and social security number, that kinda stuff. Which is not actually *assuming* a new identity—that's more in the realm of *stealing* someone else's identity."

I shot a look at Jack, then turned to Michael. "And what did you tell him?"

"Well, I told him that's *not* what I did for these women, and what he was talking about was illegal." He grinned mischievously, then added, "But I did tell him there is a way to do it. You wanna know?"

"Yeah, I want to know exactly what you told him," Jack said. "Because it just so happens that we're looking for him, and this might be how he's eluding us."

"Oh boy. Okay. Well, here's how I explained it to him. First, you find the name of a dead person who died in a state he was not born in. Because death certificates are not filed in the same state as birth certificates, it is more difficult to cross-reference a birth and death. This person should be approximately your age and have no close relatives. And it gets trickier . . . You have to know a few things about this dead person in order to request a birth certificate—date of birth, place of birth, parents' names, and the mother's maiden name. It's also important to know that this person was not providing alimony or child support to anyone. Or that upon their death, someone would be collecting social security benefits or some kind of inheritance."

"Seems impossible to pull off," I said.

"If you're determined, patient, and good at research, you can find the right, um, candidate."

"So what's the next step, once you've determined whose identity you want to assume?" Jack asked.

"Obtain this person's birth certificate. These days you can use an online form, but you can also write a letter to the state's Bureau of Vital Statistics and, to give it an air of authenticity, type up your request on business letterhead that has the name of the person whose identity you are stealing. Following, so far?"

"Yeah," Jack said.

"Okay. Next, with birth certificate in hand, head on over to the DMV for a driver's license. But here's where it gets tricky. The DMV also requires you to show proof of residence, namely a bill mailed to your address with your name on it. There are several ways to go about doing this . . . but suffice it to say, it can be done. Just have to get creative. Now, with all this identification, the next step is to get a replacement social security card. You don't need to know the social security number—not everyone has it memorized—you just need to prove that you are who you say you are. And with a birth certificate and a driver's license, well, voilà." Michael snapped his fingers. "Oh, and for good measure I told him it doesn't hurt to change your appearance. Perhaps a nose or chin job or colored contact lenses. This way not only do you assume a new identity, you metaphorically erase the old one." He must have noticed our stunned expressions, and quickly added, "I also told him that he could spend a very long time in prison for doing what I just explained."

"And you chatted with Kenny about this in 1999?"

"Yeah. That's the summer I was helping Hank out with his project of interviewing the victims' relatives."

"Can you describe Kenny?" Jack asked.

Michael squinted. "Well, you can change your appearance, but you can't change your height, right? Medium build, my height, five ten. I would say he weighed about one-ninety, give or take five pounds in either direction. Not skinny, not fat. Effeminate. I think that would be hard for him to change. Perhaps with practice." He touched the tip of his nose. "Oh, and he had a rather large schnoz."

"Any unique distinguishing features?"

He gave that some thought, then ran his finger along his thigh. "He was wearing shorts, and I noticed a burn mark running vertically along his thigh."

Jack grimaced. "A burn mark?"

"Yeah. When he saw me staring at it, he told me that Madeline's first husband heated up a fireplace poker and ran it along the side of his leg."

"Jeez," Jack moaned.

Michael tapped on the armrest of his wheelchair. "So what can you tell me about these copycat murders? Maybe I can help."

We told him more than what we had shared publicly. My feeling was that he probably had a unique perspective, seeing he was the "victim that got away." And, he'd dealt with damaged people—knew their mindset. Having done some legwork for Hank Webb, he was already familiar with the earlier cases, and I wanted his take on whether he thought Shirley and Adam's killer were one and the same. Plus, the icing on this weird cake: he'd crossed paths with Kenny Klein and given the guy a roadmap to identity fraud.

Michael listened as we laid out what we knew so far, nodding rhythmically to a beat in his head.

"I think you're looking at two different killers," Michael said. "But I think both have a connection to the Mac Gardner murders."

"What makes you say that?" Jack asked.

"The ropes, mainly. You said that Derek, Elizabeth, and Kenny all saw the original crime photographs. Yet that aspect of the signature was strikingly different. The first murder—Shirley's—was a sloppy reproduction. The second murder was the work of a master forger."

"So, one a clumsy facsimile and the other an homage," I said. "Derek told us that he was in a bad mental state at the time—his brother had just committed suicide—and he was just seeking revenge. He said the details didn't really matter, and he just wanted to get it done as fast as possible."

"On the other hand, in Adam's case, you see meticulous handiwork," Michael said. "From the application of the makeup to the manner in which the ropes were tied, to the placement of the pillow, to the number on the hand."

"Something else you should know." I powered up my phone and showed Michael the photograph of the stained glass necklace. "Madeline's necklace was placed on Adam's chest."

He let out a low whistle. "I remember that necklace. Only when I chatted with them, it was Kenny who was wearing it. Madeline must have given it to him."

Jack turned toward me, his eyes bulging, his mouth hanging open. I'm sure my expression was no less extreme. If Kenny was still in possession of that necklace, then it stood to reason he was our perp—that is, unless he passed it along to someone else.

"You met Kenny. Do you think he's capable of this?" I asked.

"I met him that one time." Michael rubbed his palms along the rubber wheels of his wheelchair. "Perhaps that's a better question for Madeline's stepbrother. Dan, I think you said."

"Yeah, Dan," Jack responded. "He told us Kenny was a loner type, kept to himself, bullied in school, bullied by Madeline's husbands. Definitely the profile of someone who's at risk for doing something, well, terrible."

"If Kenny did assume a new identity, it's possible he's nothing like his old self," Michael said. "There's a kind of freedom in reinventing yourself. He could have shed the loner persona, and for all you know he's the most popular guy in the room. I know a few women who transformed more than their looks when they got a fresh start." He probably saw me raise my eyebrows, and added, "As a practicing sociologist, I can tell you we aren't old dogs. We can learn new tricks."

I SAT in the living room, alone, nursing a scotch. Not my typical go-to drink, which was usually a glass of wine, but after today's interview with Michael Mercer and getting Mom settled back at her house, I needed something stiffer. Something warm and tingly to relax my body and settle my mind. Ray and Dad were on their way here, and these few minutes of peace and quiet were just what the doctor ordered. I could already feel a comfortably numb sensation taking hold.

And then, as usual, the case seeped into my brain. The haze of alcohol dissipated just enough for me to start perseverating on where we were.

We had two days before the cast of *Murder on the Orient Express* packed up and went their separate ways. Chase was in the wind. Only Nathan Fowler and Jean Cranmore were hanging around, as they straddled responsibilities for both troupes. Chief Eldridge was getting antsy. The sheriff was breathing down his neck, which meant he was breathing down ours. The press was having a field day. Amateur crime sleuths claimed they would solve this before the professionals did. And every crackpot in Sullivan and Ulster counties crawled out of the woodwork to confess.

There was no fucking way someone was going to get away with this. And if another victim fell prey to the killer, guess who people will blame. Me! *Think, Susan. You've got a mere two days to solve this case. What are you missing? Think. Think*, my brain sputtered.

When I heard the key in the latch, I downed what was left of my Dewar's and settled back onto the cushions. "In here!" I yelled.

Ray hustled into the kitchen to grab a couple of beers.

Dad took a seat on the couch next to me and squeezed my knee. "Hey there, kiddo." He pointed to my empty glass. "Looks like you can use a refresh."

I held up both palms. "One and done. I'm good." I rubbed my eyes, then yawned. Growing up with an alcoholic mom, the phrase *one and done* was my go-to drinking mantra.

Ray handed an IPA to Dad and settled onto the recliner. "Cheers." He tipped his bottle.

"I know you're stuck," Dad said, sensing my frustration. "You'll get unstuck."

"We should be getting an analysis on the watch we found in the gift shop cellar any day now. There were no discernible prints, so they're testing for traces of DNA."

"You gotta have hope, Susan." Dad took a long swig. He belched quietly, and brought his fist to his chest. "It's been a tough few weeks for sure, but I've been having a bit of fun taking this trip down memory lane. Sure, the crime was gruesome, but that year was something. In 1969, change was in the air. Progress. The freaking moon walk. The Mets playing in the World Series had all of New York glued to their sets. Public opinion on the Vietnam war shifted after the Mỹ Lai massacre in 1968, although Nixon did a bang-up job of dragging his feet to end the war."

"There was also the civil rights movement," Ray offered. "Although I think the expansion of the Civil Rights Act got passed in 1968, not 1969." He searched for the answer on his phone. "Yup, 1968. It was called the Fair Housing Act. Gotta love Wikipedia."

"Yeah. In the olden days we just guessed at shit and never bothered to get our facts straight." Dad smirked.

"Hate to burst your bubble, Dad, but people now look up shit on the internet and believe whatever is there. The facts be damned."

"Yeah, sure, but it beats looking up everything in a fifty-volume encyclopedia." Dad took a swig from his bottle. "Ah, the good ol' days."

13

WEDNESDAY | AUGUST 28, 2019

DAD SAT to my left. Ray to my right. With the case at a standstill, we decided to play hooky and catch the matinee of *Murder on the Orient Express.* There were only two performances left after this one, that night and the next afternoon, before the switch to *Little Shop of Horrors,* which I already bought tickets for. Ever since I found out that show was scheduled, I couldn't get the song "Suddenly Seymour" out of my head.

As the applause died down, Dad leaned over and whispered in my ear, "Man, that was pretty good. Clever ending." He had told me earlier that afternoon that he'd never read the novel or seen the movie, and I'd better not spoil it for him.

"Yeah, Agatha Christie was the queen of messing with your head," Ray said, leaning over me. "Gotta hand it to the actor who played Hercule Poirot, he was fantastic." Ray completely butchered the Belgium sleuth's name.

"George Zettler," I said. "And it's pronounced *Air-cule Pwa-row.*"

"If you say so," he shot back, swatting me with his folded Playbill.

We stood in unison, then crab-walked out of our row to the center aisle, joining the throngs of theater goers slowly making their way out of the auditorium and into the lobby—like a school of fish in a narrow estuary heading toward the vast sea.

"Hey! Susan! Ray!" I heard from behind me. I turned to see Officer Ron Wallace coming toward me with his son, the one we had met in front of the gift shop cellar door. "Can we talk? Outside? It's about the case."

We left Dad chatting with someone from Horizon Meadows and followed Ron down the stairs to the picnic table area. I was surprised his son was tagging along.

We stood around in awkward silence for a few seconds.

"You remember my son, Tyler," Ron said.

"Hi, Tyler," I said.

Ron gently touched his son's shoulder and said, "Go on. Tell them what you told me."

Tyler twisted the rolled-up Playbill in his hands. "Um, well, I was fishing on Sackett Lake last month, and I heard some people arguing a ways down the bank. So I snuck over to get a closer look." He shifted his weight from one foot to the other. "Um, I saw a man push a woman to the ground. I stepped on a twig and the man must have heard it and turned toward me, so I ran off." Tyler unrolled the Playbill and opened it to the page with an In Memoriam tribute to Adam Kincaid. "Um, it was this guy."

"You sure?" Ray asked.

"One hundred percent positive."

"Can you describe the woman?"

He cocked his head as I waited for him to describe someone from either cast or crew.

"Um, young. Black. Pretty. Um, he also said, 'F you, Brandy.' But he, um, used the whole word."

I glanced at Ray, who blew out a puff of air while raking his hand through his hair.

"Why didn't you report this to your dad?" I asked.

He sheepishly glanced at his dad. "I was supposed to be at camp, not down by the lake by myself."

"So you didn't see what happened after you ran off?"

He shook his head and kicked at the dirt. "Maybe the other guy he was with could tell you what happened."

"What other guy?" I said slowly.

"The guy who runs the gift shop."

I glanced at Ray, just in time to see his eyebrows catapult upward.

"Tyler, how do you know the gift shop guy?" I asked. "He's not here today."

"Um, Dad took me to see the other show three weeks ago. It was called Moon Walk or something like that. We went to the gift shop to buy something afterward. I'm sorry I didn't say anything." He teared up a little and walked over to an empty picnic table and sat down. He turned away from us as he ran his arm under his nose.

"Shit," Ron said. "Sorry guys. I've always told my son 'see something, say something.'"

"He's a kid," Ray said. "I probably would've kept that incident to myself if I thought I would get in trouble."

"He's thirteen." Ron scoffed. "Almost fourteen."

Ray gazed over his shoulder at Tyler. "Well, he can help us out now."

TYLER LED the way to his fishing spot.

An hour earlier I had called Jack while Ray texted Marty. Now the four us trailed behind Ron and Tyler on a pilgrimage to where Brandy's murder might have taken place.

"Um, so I was there." He pointed toward the lake. "And when I heard those people arguing, I kinda snuck around this way," he said, jutting his chin out toward the wooded area. "Follow me."

We followed him to an outcropping of boulders. As we trudged along the muddy path, I tried to keep my anticipation in check.

"I hid behind these rocks, but I had a clear view. I could see them, but they couldn't see me."

"Okay. So show me exactly where they were standing," Ray said, as we all donned our blue plastic booties.

Ray gave a pair to Tyler, who readily accepted them, exclaiming, "Cool."

Once again we followed Tyler. He stopped and said, "The dead guy from the Playbill was standing here." He then took a giant step to his right. "And the woman was standing here, facing him."

"And the gift shop guy?" I asked.

Tyler took six steps to his left. "Here."

Ray walked over to where Tyler said Adam was standing. I took up position where Brandy was standing. We faced each other.

I turned to face Tyler. "So, Adam and Brandy stood here, like this?"

Tyler glanced at his dad, then back toward me. "Yes."

"And you're sure it wasn't Chase and Brandy facing each other."

Tyler hesitated, then looked at his dad again.

"Take your time, son. If you're not sure, that's okay."

Without any hesitation this time, he said, "I'm one hundred percent positive it was the guy in the Playbill who pushed the lady, not the gift store guy."

I twisted my neck to look over my right shoulder and spotted a triangular shaped rock jutting out of the dirt. I spun around, then crouched to get a closer look. There was a reddish-brown squiggle on one side of the stone. I'm no forensics expert, but I was damn sure I was looking at dried blood. "Call CSI! I think we just found the primary crime scene." I scanned the surrounding area, hoping something else would jump out at me that would connect this murder to Adam's murder. Nothing but undisturbed leaves and sticks.

Ray clapped Tyler's shoulder. "You just helped us solve a murder."

I don't think that kid's grin could've gotten any wider.

WE STUCK around while CSI collected evidence. Our theory was that Adam accidentally killed Brandy when he pushed her onto the sharp rock. Then, Adam and Chase carried her to the woods behind the bungalow colony and tried to bury the body. The thing is, people suck at burying bodies. Probably doubly true for a persnickety stage director and a middle-aged gift shop manager. The question was what were the three of them up to? Unfortunately, only Chase knew the answer to that. And there was still no sign of him.

My phone lit up with a text message from Dad asking me for an update. I ignored it. Not because I didn't think he should know. But because I wanted to see his face when I told him.

But that would have to wait. I needed to retrieve Mom and get her settled in the guest room at my house. After some hemming and hawing on her part ("I don't need a babysitter," she snapped), she finally relented, realizing it best she stay with me and Ray out of an abundance of caution. Just one week. Long enough to make sure she was functioning well. Short enough to not get on each other's nerves. Well, we'd see about that part.

DAD WAS waiting for me at the station, his butt in my chair, shooting the shit with Sally.

"Ahem," I grunted.

Dad rose and sought out a chair from another desk.

After giving Dad a blow-by-blow account of what went down at Sackett Lake (his expressions well worth the wait of telling him in person), I settled into my chair to type up the report.

"Could you do me a favor?" I asked Dad.

"Name it."

"Would you stop by my house on your way back to Horizon Meadows and check on Mom?"

My ask was met with silence and a scowl.

Dad pursed his lips, then said rather testily, "Hmm. I thought you were going to ask me to help with the case."

I was somewhat taken aback by his gruffness and annoyed at his terse response. He knew my plate was full—with this case, with my wedding plans, and now with figuring out what do with Mom.

Dad threw up his hands. "And there's no one else who can swing by? Ray? One of her friends perhaps?"

I stuffed down my anger. "If you don't want to, I understand. I mean, you're not married to her. I get it. I just need some help for the short term. Natalie's going to pitch in, but she's in the city today—she has some psych conference—"

He inhaled and exhaled slowly. "Susan, I'm happy to help you out here and there, but quite honestly, I don't think she'd be on board with me checking in on her and making her feel incompetent."

He had a point there. Mom was insisting she was perfectly fine and didn't need our help. That we were being overdramatic. Any assistance offered by Dad would not be met with gratitude. It would more likely be met with anger and resentment.

"If you want my opinion, I think she should consider moving to a senior community." He paused. "Not Horizon Meadows," he deadpanned.

"I'm sure she's on the same page with you on that," I acknowledged, knowing full well how awkward that would be. "Look, she's in a bit of denial. Which the doctor said is common. Mom doesn't realize how forgetful she has become. She even accused me of lying to her when I told her about a conversation we had yesterday that she couldn't recall."

Dad grunted. "I'll go and check on her. But Susan, we need to come up with a plan."

At least he said "we," not "you," giving me some hope that he would be part of the solution.

I leaned back in my chair and closed my eyes. Maybe the chief was right. Could I handle the case and my mom? I'd give this case another month. If we hadn't solved it by then, I'd consider a leave of absence. Just long enough to set up a long-term solution for Mom.

"Got it!" Jack yelled across the bullpen, waving a large white envelope and pulling me out of my reverie. "Got the report on the watch we recovered in the gift shop cellar," he added to clarify what it was he was all worked up about.

I rubbed my moist palms together. "This better be the smoking gun."

Jack unsealed the envelope. There were three reports enclosed. The first was a DNA analysis of the sweat on the leather watchband compared to the handful of theater folks who provided their DNA. No matches. But there was a note indicating that the DNA was from a single source—so if we found matching DNA we could be 99.99 percent positive that that person was the sole wearer of the watch. The second was a DNA analysis of the folded clothes. A positive match to Adam, meaning the killer was definitely in that cellar. The third report sent both our jaws to the floor.

Chemical etching, the technique used to restore serial numbers on stolen guns and car engines, revealed what had been engraved on the back of the watch: *To Kenny.*

"What the . . . what?" Jack exclaimed.

"Okay, let's just chill a sec and think this through."

"Here's what I think," Jack said quickly, clearly not thinking it through. "Kenny has an accomplice working at the theater. Perhaps someone else who has a connection to Mac Gardner and agreed to give Kenny access to the theater, as well as lure Adam there. Ricky fits the bill. Perhaps Libby?"

"Ricky, yeah. But Libby didn't have a set of keys, and we already established she was home sick that night. George?"

"Thing is, if it was George, I don't think he would have told us he was related to Adam."

I mulled over Jack's take on George and came to the same conclusion. No one puts themselves in the middle of the frame. "Jean, Nathan, and Malcolm have keys. But as far as we know, none of them have ties to this area, or for that matter, Kenny." Our background checks on those three matched what they told us about where they grew up. Jean, in the suburbs of Philadelphia; Nathan, some rural community on the outskirts of Des Moines; and Malcolm, a coastal town south of Boston.

"Shana has ties to the area," Jack reminded me.

"Leslie had a reason to do Adam in. She doesn't have a key, but she might've lured Adam back to the theater on some pretext related to the extortion. She knew about the makeup murders from the town paper. Maybe she knew Kenny."

"I also want to throw in here that with so many people having motive and opportunity, it's possible—"

"Don't even go there," I said sternly. Although even I had to admit it was quite possible that all the folks who wanted to exact revenge on Adam could have banded together. "I have another theory. And I know this is going to sound crazy, but hear me out."

"Hey, I'm open to any and all possibilities."

"What if Chase is Kenny?" I suggested. "If you recall, when we interrogated him about his rendezvous with Shana, he was missing a watch. There was an outline of it on his tanned skin. He's the right age. He's average weight and height, which is how people who knew

Kenny described him. The eye color is wrong, but he could be wearing colored contacts. He's got a large nose. And he fishes, so he probably knows a thing or two about nautical knots."

"Hmm, it's plausible."

"I even think there's a way to prove that Chase *is* Kenny. But you're going to have to call in a few favors." I laid out my plan.

Jack nodded, then said, "I'll see what I can do."

14

TUESDAY | SEPTEMBER 3, 2019

IT SUCKS when you can't solve a case.

It had been nearly a week since Chase did his disappearing act. The actors from *Murder on the Orient Express* had scattered like mice—off to their next theatrical adventures. Shana broke up with Malcolm the second she got the leading role in a Broadway play. Her understudy took over the role of Audrey in *Little Shop of Horrors*.

I was twirling around in my desk chair, when I spotted Jack barreling through the doors.

"Ready?" he said, slyly.

"Ready for what?"

"You know that favor you wanted me to cash in? Well, cashed and delivered."

"I'm impressed, Tomelli."

He blew on his fingers and polished them on his imaginary lapel. "My friend is going to call us in ten minutes with the information you requested."

I gnawed at my fingernail, trying to soften a jagged edge.

"Need a nail file?" Jack asked.

"You got one?"

Jack reached into his front jeans pocket and pulled out a Swiss Army Knife. He tossed it at me. "Good catch. There's a nail file in that thing."

Jack's phone rang. He immediately switched it to speaker mode. "Hey Jack, I got Detective Susan Ford on the line with me."

"Jack?" I mouthed, sliding the Swiss Army Knife into my blazer pocket. My nail would have to wait.

He smiled and nodded.

"Hello, Susan. Jack. Okay, you want me to bottom line it?" Jack's friend Jack said.

"Yeah," Jack replied.

"Okay. I ran the DNA from the wristwatch band you sent me against the World Trade Center Kinship and Data Analysis Panel and it's a biological match to the sample provided by Madeline Klein. The markers don't lie. You're looking at a parent-child relationship. The watch was definitely worn by Madeline's son."

"His name is Kenny," Jack said to Jack before turning to me. "Shit. You called that one, Susan."

"So, do you have this person in custody?" the other Jack asked.

"We think he's living his life under a stolen identity," Jack said. "But we've got an APB out on the guy we think it is. Thanks for doing this."

"No prob, my friend. Anytime."

"Ford! Tomelli!" Chief Eldridge bellowed from his office as Jack disengaged the line.

Before we even had a chance to take a step, Eldridge emerged from his office and hightailed it toward us. "Your lucky day—we found Chase. On a boat off Nantucket. You can thank Ray. He had a hunch Chase might be hiding out with one of this fishing buddies and got in touch with the local police there. Didn't take long for one of them to crack under questioning. Seems he's been living belowdecks this past week. He should be back here around one o'clock this afternoon."

THE FIRST thing I noticed when I walked into the interrogation room was a watch on Chase's wrist. Expensive-looking, with a gold link band.

"Nice watch," I said, taking a seat. "New?"

He glanced at it and tersely said, "No. I've had it awhile."

Reggie, his lawyer, brought his finger to his lips, clearly signaling Chase to keep quiet. Because Chase was an alleged accomplice in Brandy's murder and the alleged killer in Adam's murder, we decided that Ray and I would question Chase while Jack and Marty observed behind the two-way mirror.

"Let's cut right to the chase," Ray said after formal introductions, leaning in on the word *chase*. "We have a witness who will testify to your illegal drug distribution business. We have another witness who puts you at the scene of Brandy Johnson's murder, which makes you an accomplice. And once we get your DNA, we'll be able to prove you killed Adam Kincaid."

I was hoping that last statement would get a rise out of him. And it did. Chase dug his nails into the table.

"I didn't kill Adam!"

"Be quiet!" Reggie made a zipper motion across his lips, then turned to us. "My client will be pleading not guilty to all these charges. And every question you ask will be met with his Fifth Amendment rights." He lowered his head and peered over the top of his glasses at Chase, admonishing him.

This was the smart move. All we had was a witness placing Chase at the scene where Adam pushed Brandy. For all we knew, Chase could've walked away unaware that Brandy was fatally injured. That he had no hand in burying Brandy. Hard to believe, but a good lawyer could argue that. As for Adam's murder, at least we had an ace in our pocket.

I opened the folder in front of me and pulled out a photograph of the Timex watch. "Recognize this?"

Chase shook his head before Reggie had a chance to lay his hand on Chase's forearm.

"We found this watch on the floor next to the cellar ladder under the gift shop."

"What's your point, Detective Ford?" Reggie leaned forward to get a better view of the watch. "He already told you he doesn't recognize it."

I stared coolly at Chase. "Your DNA will give us our answer. It can't take the Fifth."

Tears welled in Chase's eyes. Which, I have to say, surprised me.

"HOW SOON until we get Chase's DNA results?" Jack asked when I got off the phone with the lab.

"It's on priority. But that can still mean two or three days." Which meant two or three more days of Eldridge breathing down our necks to wrap this up, so the DA had the hard evidence to ensure a slam dunk trial. We had our guy, but we still had to wrap a bow around this lousy present.

"Three more days of waiting to confirm what we already know." Jack stood and paced. "At least we got the arrest warrant this time on two of the three charges. He's not going anywhere awaiting arraignment. The judge turned down Reggie's lowball bail request."

"I can't wait to see Chase's face when we expose his charade."

"Yeah. That'll make this whole waiting game worth it."

I glanced at my watch, all of a sudden remembering I had told Malcolm I would meet him at the theater at three thirty to update him on the case. It would be quiet in the theater as there was no practicing troupe. As for the remaining actors and crew, I heard napping was the activity of choice in the afternoons. "I'm heading down to the playhouse to speak with Malcolm." I could tell Jack was only half listening as he continued to pace off his edginess.

WHEN I arrived at the theater, it was raining. Hard. The front door was unlocked—Malcolm said he had to run a quick errand, but would leave it open should I arrive before he got back. Which I did. It was three o'clock. I had thirty minutes to cool my heels. I wandered over to the wall of photographs I had scanned quickly on the day of the murder. Having spent endless hours interrogating and interviewing members of the cast and crew, I now knew all the faces in the photo. Standing far left was Leslie Brattle, preening for the camera. I slid my eyes across the group, landing on Nathan Fowler, the production manager, on the far right, expressionless.

Then I noticed it.

"Ahem. May I ask what you're doing here?"

I spun around and came face-to-face with Nathan. Without thinking, I glanced at his wrist. He followed my gaze, then he looked up at the photograph. A punch to the jaw was the last thing I remembered as my head slammed against the glass of the photograph, knocking both it and me to the hard marble floor.

WHEN I came to, Nathan Fowler was leaning over me, holding my gun. I attempted to rub my chin where Nathan's fist made contact with the side of my face, but quickly realized my wrists were bound behind my back with what felt like strips of cloth. As were my ankles. I spied a ripped costume on the floor and surmised that pieces of it were fashioned into ligatures.

My back was against a wall. Literally and figuratively. I tested my jaw, but when I opened my mouth the pain shot up my cheekbone into my temple, and I quickly shut it. I think I moaned but couldn't be sure. As my vision cleared, I realized where I was—in the storage room in the basement of the theater, lying on my side on a cot along the back wall.

"Well, hello there," Nathan mused. He placed my gun on a nearby table but made sure it was within his reach.

I tried out my jaw again. "Nathan," I gingerly mouthed. The pain was excruciating, but I did not think my jaw was broken. With a bit more force, I said, "You won't get away with this." It came out as a tight whisper.

He laughed. "I've already gotten away with it. And by the time someone finds you, I'll be long gone." Nathan held up my phone. "Malcolm texted you. But don't worry. I texted him back apologizing for not showing up. Don't you just love face-recognition technology? I held your phone up to your face, and voilà. By the way, he seemed a bit miffed." Nathan pocketed my phone. "I removed the cast photograph and cleaned up the glass in the lobby. It'll be a while before anyone notices." He crouched down next to me. "I actually haven't decided what to do with you yet. Sure, I can kill you, but I do pride myself on not murdering random people. I am not an evil person, Detective Ford. In fact, you can say I am someone who rids this earth of evil." He stood and started pacing, then stopped abruptly. "However, since you are the only one who has connected me to that watch you found in the cellar, I really have no choice . . . do I?"

"Trust me, Nathan. Someone else will make the connection." My head was banging, but I needed to think up a plan. And fast. If I disclosed to him what Jack and I had discovered—that Kenny Klein's DNA was on the watch—would it improve my chances of talking him out of killing me? Or at the very least, buy me time. I decided it was worth mentioning. "We found DNA on the watchband."

"So what?" he sniffed. "You'll need mine to make a match, and, like I just said, I'll be long gone before anyone can get a swab."

"The DNA on the watch revealed who you *really* are, *Kenny*."

His eyelashes fluttered as he processed what I just said, followed by a sly smile.

"Then you, more than anyone, should know I'm very skilled at disappearing and reinventing myself." Nathan stroked his chin. "I'll simply leave a message for Malcolm that I had an emergency to tend to and had to take off."

I was making progress on loosening the cloth ties. I needed to keep this conversation going long enough to wiggle my way out of them. There was no doubt Nathan was a narcissist, and egomaniacs, believing they are superior to the rest of us, would want to know how they tripped up.

Narcissists crave attention. When ignored, when their words aren't taken into account, they are compelled to rebuild their imaginary pedestal. I set the trap: "Right now, you are only facing one count of first-degree murder. Sure, you can end up with a life sentence, but there's also a chance for the minimum sentence of fifteen to forty years, maybe even end up in a cushy mental hospital. Kill me, and you will face life imprisonment without parole." I took a deep breath and said the words I hoped would keep him in engaged. "My partner will connect you to the watch. And when he does, he will hunt you down."

Nathan smiled. And not in a warm way. He walked to a corner of the room and grabbed a metal folding chair. He dragged it across the concrete floor, opened it, then swatted away some dust before sitting. "So, tell me, Detective, I am awfully curious, how did you come to learn that the watch belonged to good ol' Kenny Klein?"

Perfect. Baited him. I proceeded to tell him about the revived etching on the back of the watch, the 9/11 DNA project, and his mother's contribution to the database. My jaw was aching every which way from Sunday, but I had to keep him talking. Narcissists need to pump up their self-esteem, so I nourished him with admiration. "So, I'm curious, *Kenny*, how did you brilliantly fake your death and assume Nathan's identity?"

Nathan tapped his fingertips together, then steepled them. "I guess I owe you an explanation, seeing how clever you were." I was damn sure he really just wanted to tell me how clever *he* was.

"I appreciate that," I said, as I wormed my right index finger under the strip of fabric around my left wrist.

My hands were sweaty—more than usual—making this unknotting that much harder.

But I was getting married, and this dipshit wasn't going to prevent me from walking down the aisle.

Nathan placed his elbows on his thighs, clasped his hands, and leaned slightly forward. "My mother went to see Shirley Gardner and dragged me along with her. She didn't want to face her alone, or some such crap. She was masterful, my mom—convincing Shirley to give her baby to my aunt Lynn." He ran his thumb along his right thigh. "Too bad she wasn't masterful at being a mother herself. I'm not saying she would win Worst Mother of the Year Award, but probably place third." He snickered, then cleared his throat. His expression morphed from amused to sober in a hot second. "That's when the idea originally came to me, at that meeting twenty-eight years ago—to murder Shirley while she was pregnant. Kill two birds with one stone, so to speak." He snapped his fingers. "End the Gardner bloodline once and for all. But that thought was fleeting. I brushed it off as vengeful fantasy."

"I'm guessing it was not fleeting."

Nathan smiled thinly.

"By the time I hit my late twenties, I was in a dark place. I hated myself. I even contemplated suicide. I was made to feel like I didn't deserve happiness."

"Did it ever occur to you to seek professional help?"

He snorted. "As a matter of fact, I toyed with that idea. But then I met a guy who knew all the tricks of the trade to changing one's identity. That sounded way more appealing than seeing a shrink. An experiment of sorts. Start a brand-new life! Shed the old Kenny! Step into someone else's shoes. Someone else's life. My plan was to scour the obituaries to look for a dead person whose identity I could assume."

"I'm guessing that person was Nathan Fowler from Iowa."

"Actually, Nathan Fowler was alive when we met."

"So you killed him?"

"No, I didn't kill him, Detective. I bumped into Nathan Fowler at a coffee shop on the Lower East Side—he was hanging a notice on the coffee shop's bulletin board looking for a roommate. I told him I was looking for a room."

I was making headway with the knot, so I nodded with keen interest.

Nathan continued: "Over the course of the year I got to know the guy. I was working as a courier for an insurance company and he was a production assistant. We would chat about our jobs, our messed-up childhoods. We got along great. I even shelved my getting-a-new-identity scheme."

"So where is he?" My fingers were growing numb as I wrestled with the knot. I bit down on my lip to direct the pain away from my hands.

"Let's just say luck stepped in. Well, lucky for me. On the morning of September eleventh, I was sick as a dog. But one of the partners needed a package picked up that morning. Nathan, God bless his soul, volunteered to retrieve the package and deliver it to where it needed to go. We had similar physical traits, so when he presented my access badge to the receptionist at the security desk, he was buzzed through to the elevators in the North Tower. The receptionist survived and confirmed to the authorities that Kenny Klein did indeed head up to the 93rd floor on that fateful day."

"Goodbye, Kenny Klein. Hello, Nathan Fowler. Pretty brilliant!" I exclaimed, hoping to feed his ego so he would keep on talking.

He smiled broadly. "Yes, wasn't it? The perfect candidate, you could say. A guy around my age, similar physical traits, with no family, and just a handful of we-don't-keep-in-touch high-school friends from some podunk town in Iowa. In other words, someone who, if they fell off the face of the earth, no one would notice."

"And no one did."

"Not a soul. So I obtained his birth certificate, social security number, and driver's license. I moved out of that apartment and started to look for work in the theater. Turns out, I was a better Nathan Fowler than Nathan Fowler. I had a knack for production management. Got plenty of gigs. I was actually enjoying my new life. In fact, I had forgotten all about Shirley Gardner. Then, about six years ago, I was invited by a colleague to see a student play directed by an up-and-coming director: Adam Kincaid."

"How did you know he was Shirley's son?" I asked, shifting slightly to alleviate the numbness that had migrated to my arms.

"Adam was called onstage to take a bow. Those icy blue eyes. That light-blond hair. My mother told me that her stepsister, Lynn, named him Adam. How many twenty-two-year-old Adam Kincaids who had Mac Gardner's eyes could there be in the world?" He shook his head. "That vengeful fantasy reemerged."

"Only this time, you decided to act on it." I took a break from trying to unknot the fabric and wiggled my fingers in an attempt get the blood back flowing into them.

"Not at first. I decided to pay Shirley a visit—I thought maybe if I saw her, the feeling would go away. Only she was already dead. Her boyfriend was living in her house. He told me she was murdered the year before, in 2012. And when he told me how she was killed—in the same way my dad was murdered—well, you could have knocked me over with a feather. How genius, I thought. How diabolically genius." He sneered. "Someone beat me to the punch."

"Ricky. Sam Blackstone's son."

"Yeah, that was a kick in the head. But then I couldn't get Adam out of my mind. The Gardner bloodline existed in that man. Would Adam eventually pass along an evil gene to his offspring?" Nathan glared at me. "I couldn't let that happen. I fantasized about killing Adam in the same way that my dad was murdered, just like Ricky must have fantasized about killing Shirley in the same way. I just needed the details."

How much longer could I keep this up? At what point was he going to say "enough is enough" and put an end to this? To me. How could I keep him talking? *Think, Susan.* Then it dawned on me: goad him into telling me about how he found out the details of the 1969 murders.

"I would imagine the North Adams police were pretty tight-lipped about Shirley Gardner's case," I said. "I know I would be if someone came sniffing around. You probably thought you'd have more luck with the 1969 cases."

"Bingo. Remember I told you about the guy who schooled me in identity theft? We had met because he was doing research on the Mac Gardner cases for an ex-cop in Kingston. But I thought it was too risky to meet with this ex-cop." He rubbed his chin. "Hank Webb. That was the cop's name. So, I called my Uncle Dan. Gave him some bullshit story about how I was writing a memoir, and he took the bait. Got me all the information I needed to stage the murder."

"According to Dan, you reached out to him five years ago. Why wait five years?"

"I could be patient. Adam was young, unmarried, so as long as he didn't get a girl pregnant, I could bide my time. There were even stretches when I gave up on the idea. I guess I was waiting for a sign. Then, this past spring, Malcolm told me he was looking for a director for a play up here in the area where my father was murdered. That felt like fate, so I recommended Adam and set my plan in motion."

I thought back to what Natalie told me the day Jack and I went to see her to discuss the killer's mindset: *anyone can find his way to the logic of revenge.*

Nathan yawned and stretched. He stood and walked over to the far side of the room, then turned to examine the mishmash of props on the shelf. He pulled a hanky from his pocket and started to dust them. "A shame no one tends to these," he muttered.

With one last tug, I finally managed to slip my left wrist out of the cloth ligature. With his head still turned toward the props, I dug into the pocket of my blazer. I palmed the Swiss Army Knife Jack had given me to file my jagged nail and returned my hands behind my back. With as little motion as possible, I unfolded the larger of the two blades. But with my ankles bound, I wasn't confident that I could successfully overpower him. I needed Nathan to come close to me. My options were limited. I'd have to target a part of his body that would neutralize him immediately.

Nathan eyed me from across the room, then quickly returned and sat down, but not before grabbing my gun off the table. He leaned back in the chair. I really needed him to lean forward.

With the gun firmly in his grip, I was running out of time. But I also sensed he was enjoying this. Reveling in the ruse he'd pulled off. Eager to tell someone his story. I had to keep him talking.

"Your Aunt Lynn gave us photographs of you, taken when you were a teenager. You've changed quite a bit."

He pointed to his nose. "Nose job, along with some other cosmetic changes. Contacts. Brow waxing. Even reprogrammed my mannerisms. I spent a year with Nathan and knew how he walked, spoke, ate—and emulated him." He smirked. "Like acting, I suppose."

"How did you lure Adam to the theater in the middle of the night?"

"He had an unrequited thing for Shana, so I told him she was passed out in the theater. Plus, he loves to play the hero. He couldn't come fast enough. And because Adam demanded everyone text him via Snapchat—like we were all teenagers—I knew the message would vanish after he read it."

"How did you get into the gift shop cellar?"

"I'm observant. I noticed the rusty old lock was broken weeks before I killed Adam. Thought I could easily pin this on that moronic gift shop manager."

"Why did you hang around here after the murder? Seems a bit . . . risky."

"That was my downfall. Hubris. I won't lie; I enjoyed watching you blame others in the cast." He glanced at his barren wrist. "That goddamn watch. My mother gave me that watch. And that peace necklace, like it was some kind of family heirloom." He shrugged. "The necklace came in handy though. Helped complete the scene." He snickered, then rubbed his left wrist. "I actually didn't know what happened to my watch. I had no idea where I had lost it—well, until you let it slip when you emerged from the root cellar under the gift shop. I should've tossed that watch in the trash back in 2001." His lips curled into a snarl. "Maybe I'm sentimental, after all."

"Why kill Adam in the theater? Why go to all the trouble?"

Nathan smiled coyly. "I guess I have a flair for the dramatic." His smile flattened as he shifted slightly in his chair. "No one gave a shit about my father's case. No one bothered to find out why Mac Gardner killed my dad. I wanted to make sure this was very public. Force the police to make the connections, and perhaps get some answers about why Mac did what he did."

"The case was dropped fifty years ago because Mac committed suicide. Not because of incompetence or ambivalence," I said defensively. "Mac killed your father for the same reason you killed Adam.

A lousy childhood filled with abuse." I wasn't about to tell him that we had learned Mac's mother wore a lot of makeup, which most likely explained the MO, and that she pimped out his sister, which explained his male targets. But I was willing to give him something. "In a very warped way of thinking, Mac was avenging the abuse of his sister at the hands of their mother."

"But why *my* dad?"

"Opportunity. Dumb luck. He was in the wrong place at the wrong time," I replied. "You're looking for answers that don't exist."

"Doesn't matter. The thought of Adam living a carefree life, while my dad suffered at the hands of his grandfather, festered in me like an infected wound." Nathan rubbed his thigh with my gun. "And it wasn't just the fact that he killed my father. No, he destroyed my mother's life and in turn, made mine a living hell." He abruptly stood up, unzipped, and dropped trou. "See this?" he seethed, leaning toward me. "A gift from my stepdad. If Mac Gardner hadn't killed my father, my mother would never have shacked up with him. Mac ruined so many lives. So many lives."

This was my moment. I swept my legs around, knocking him off balance. My gun flew from his grip and skittered across the floor, disappearing deep under the shelving. I lunged at Nathan and plunged the blade of the Swiss Army Knife into his left triceps, then yanked it out. Not exactly my target, but it did buy me a few seconds. I toppled to the floor and swiped the blade across the cloth tied around my ankles while he pulled up his pants. I crawled toward the door. He picked up a brass candlestick, charged at me, and swung. I lifted my arm, my forearm taking the brunt of the hit. He raised the candlestick again. As he swung, I rolled to my left and under the cot into a fetal position.

"I still have the knife," I said, panting. "Come at me, and I will stab you."

Nathan crouched down and peered at me. "Yeah? Well, I got something better." He stood and walked over to a cabinet, then came back and laid down on his belly. He pointed a 9mm at me. "I had hidden it down here in case I ever needed it. Guess I need it. Goodbye, Detective Ford."

The door burst open. Jack rushed in. Sally and Ron came up behind him. Guns drawn.

"Drop the gun!" Jack yelled. "Now!"

Nathan did not heed the warning. He spun around with his finger still on the trigger.

Jack aimed at Nathan's right shoulder and fired.

Nathan's gun clattered to the concrete floor.

Jack stepped forward and kicked it away. Then he lunged toward Nathan, knocking him to the ground. Jack pinned Nathan's back to the floor, then deftly spun him around as he slapped handcuffs around his wrists.

Nathan yelped in pain. Jack rolled him back over, then pulled him up into a sitting position. Jack examined the gunshot wound. "A through and through. He'll live."

I rolled out from under the cot and crouched next to Nathan. "Did killing Adam change anything for you?"

He shrugged, then winced. "It gave me peace of mind, if that's what you mean. No more Gardners in this world."

I could've told him about George Zettler, but this was neither the time nor place. I'll drop that bombshell on him when he is solidly behind bars.

Ron and Sally came forward and hooked their hands under Nathan's armpits. They lifted him from the floor and escorted him out of the room to a waiting ambulance.

Jack helped me to a standing position. I was wobbly but managed to not fall down. I squeezed my hands into fists to control the shaking, then realized I was still palming the knife.

"Here's your Swiss Army Knife," I said, dropping it into Jack's hand. I wiped my sweaty palm on my dust-covered pants.

"I was wondering where that disappeared to," Jack said, pocketing it. "I see it came in handy." He glanced down at my still shaking hands. "You okay?"

My heart was beating like a jackhammer, but I felt oddly euphoric. "I'm better than okay. Really." I gave Jack the once-over. He was still trying to catch his breath. His clothes were rumpled. His hair mussed. A smear of blood on his shirt. "But you sure look like you need a drink."

Jack stared at the blood on the floor where Nathan went down. When he gazed back up, his eyes were glassy. "So do you."

I wrapped my arms around my chest, and shuddered. "So, how'd you find me?"

"When I couldn't reach you, I stopped by Malcolm's house. You told me you were meeting with him, but I couldn't remember if you said at his house or the playhouse. He told me you were supposed to meet at the theater but you stood him up, so I figured you had to see your mom or something. Anyway, I was standing in Malcolm's foyer, in front of those cast pictures he's got hanging on the wall, and spotted that damn watch on Nathan Fowler's wrist. I actually came to the theater looking for Nathan, not you. That's when I saw the photograph missing from the wall and heard the crunching sound of broken glass under my shoe, so I called for backup." He exhaled mightily, as though he'd been holding his breath since he burst into this room. "Figured you also figured it out. Obviously, there must have been some sort of scuffle when you confronted him."

"Well, it was more like I let my guard down and he got the better of me."

Jack removed his jacket and hung it around my shoulders. "I went into the theater first, to the stage, thinking he took you where he took Adam. Ron and Sally got here quickly and we headed down to the basement. We were just about to enter the recreation room when we heard the noises in this room." He smiled. "Guess you can call me your knight in shining armor."

I punched Jack gently on his shoulder. "Or just doing your job."
He playfully punched me back. "Yeah, that too."

MY ARMS felt like concrete. My jaw throbbed. An Advil and hot
bath were in my not-to-distant future. Key in hand, I stood outside
my front door contemplating my future. It was time for "The Talk."
No, not that talk, although it would be a talk between a mother and
her daughter. My mother. Parenting experts say you should love your
children without ifs, ands, and buts. Unconditional love. From my experience—being on the receiving end of her taunts and jabs—I was
pretty sure Mom wasn't completely onboard with that concept. The
liquor didn't help. I get that now. But what happens when the role of
parent and child flip-flops, when a parent is in need of care? What's
my obligation here? Sure, Mom and I had been getting along swim-
mingly since the start of this year, when she started going to AA meetings and collecting her tokens. She'd owned up to her dereliction of
unconditional love.

I must admit, Jack's story about his sister Lucy made a dent in my
thinking. Giving up basketball might not sound like a huge sacrifice,
but in the scheme of his life at that time, it was. And he rose to the
occasion. Maybe not at first. But after getting over the anger of this
role being foisted upon him, he eventually found joy in the task of
caring for his sister. He said it brought them together in a way that
might not have happened if his parents decided not to go out on Friday nights or had hired a babysitter. If there was ever a time to get
to know my mother better, and she me, this was the time. How long
would it be until she no longer recognized me, Dad, Ray, Natalie, her
great-grandsons? A year? Five years? Ten years? That's the awful thing
about dementia—there's no set timetable. There's no telling how long
I'd have with her. But I did know one thing: I could do this. And not

just because it was an obligation. Not just because it was the right thing to do. But because there was the possibility it could bring joy to both of us.

I unlocked my door and stepped inside. As I closed the door behind me, I stared at the Woodstock Music and Art Fair poster (still hanging askew) in my foyer.

"Susan, is that you?" Mom yelled from the living room.

Epilogue

THE WEDDING invitations were stacked on the dining room table. The television was on in the living room, just loud enough to make out Lester Holt's voice reciting the evening news. Dad had a habit of not turning it off when he left a room.

Dad sat down across from Ray. Mom was already seated across from me. Natalie, who had orchestrated my entire wedding, sat at the head of the table. A small pile of stamps and a stack of five moist sponges were in front of her, ready for doling out to her worker bees. Us.

"You're going to make a lovely bride," Mom said, patting my hand. Which felt like something one would say to a twentysomething, not a woman staring down her midfifties.

"Thanks, Mom. Maybe when we have some alone time you can tell me about the birds and the bees."

"Oh, stop it," Mom said, swatting my forearm. "Did I ever tell you how my mother explained the birds and bees to me?"

"Only a hundred times," Dad replied.

Mom made a sourpuss face at him.

Dad laughed.

"You like it over at Lochmore Manor?" Ray asked Mom.

"Well, it's only been a week, but yeah." She glanced my way. "I'm glad you guys twisted my arm. It would've been nice to use that brand-spanking-new kitchen, but at least it made the house more sellable." She picked up an invitation and ran a finger across the embossed letters. "I made a new friend already. Hmm, can't think of her name, but she has two birds."

It felt like a lifetime ago, but it was only four months since Mom had her stroke. Between her dementia diagnosis and the Adam Kincaid case, I was eager to put the summer of 2019 in the rearview mirror. We wrapped up the case by the end of September. Chase was serving time for a whole host of drug-related crimes and accessory to murder. It was his summer cold that did him in. A tissue found in the shallow grave he and Adam had dug matched his DNA. Hoping for a lighter sentence, he ratted out one of the musicians as the source for his harder drugs. Chase also gave us the skinny on what went down at the lake. Seems Adam got wind that Brandy, his hookup pal, was dealing for Chase and was none too happy. As Shana had explained to us, Adam was on an antidrug crusade because his friend had overdosed. Ironically, Brandy didn't die from drugs but at the hands of the guy trying to keep her away from them. Chase told us that Adam waited outside Brandy's apartment on that fateful day and followed her to the lake, where she had planned to rendezvous with Chase after he picked up the drugs from his drug-dealing musician buddy. Adam confronted them. After accidentally killing Brandy, he coerced Chase to help bury her. Chase's fishing days on Nantucket were pretty much over.

Derek Blackstone, a.k.a. Ricky Saunders, was convicted of murdering Shirley Gardner.

The one piece of bright news in all this was that Elizabeth Blackstone, a.k.a. Libby Wright, was exonerated. Detectives Brian Carew and Melody Walters tracked down the roommate she was living with in 2012 who bore witness to the fact that Libby was as distraught as hell on the phone trying to stop her brother from doing something, pleading with him, "Don't do this! Don't do this!" before jumping in her car. She said Libby came home despondent, refusing to tell her what had happened, but Libby had conveyed she was too late to stop her brother. Libby later told us that her anger abated when she started practicing Buddhism, and she only wished her brothers found a modicum of peace.

Kenny Klein, a.k.a. Nathan Fowler, was awaiting trial for killing Adam. Even with his full-throated confession, his lawyer convinced him to plead not guilty. Maybe they would use the insanity defense. If the prosecution does its job, he'll be facing life in prison without parole.

Ray leaned toward the living room trying to catch what the reporter was saying. "You hear that? Some virus spreading in China."

"I guess we'll scratch Shanghai off our honeymoon short list," I said sarcastically, knowing full well Ray wanted to go camping in the Pacific Northwest, like his parents did, and had somehow convinced me that it would be our own little summer of love. But after tracking down a murderer this past summer, the first thing that came to my mind when Ray suggested it was the Pacific Northwest's most notorious serial killer, Gary Ridgway, the Green River Killer.

"Do you think we should be worried?" Mom asked. At first, I thought she was alluding to our choice of honeymoon location, but quickly realized she was referring to the virus.

"Worried about what?" Dad replied. "A virus on the other side of the world? Besides, even if it did manage to get here, how bad could it be?"

Mom tutted. "I just don't want to get sick, that's all, with the wedding next week."

"The wedding is in . . ." I was going to correct her, remind her it wasn't until next June, but managed to hold my tongue. I got the feeling that, for Mom, memory was something that constantly needed to be untangled, like knotted-up earbud cords. Or those cloth strips Nathan Fowler tied tight around my wrists. Events, past and future, becoming crossed, obscured, and twisted. With every passing day, the knots getting tighter, harder to untangle.

"Oh, before I forget," Ray exclaimed, jumping up out of his chair and, thankfully, pulling me out of my head trip.

As he strode out of the room, everyone stared at me, waiting for some kind of explanation. I shrugged. I was equally in the dark.

A few minutes later he returned with a rectangular box.

I locked eyes with Ray. He smiled, then turned away from me and held out the box. "Vera, for you."

Mom took the box from Ray and lifted the lid. She peeled back the white tissue paper and pulled out a photo album. She pushed the invitations to the side, then slowly opened the album to the first page. "Ooooh," she intoned.

I squeezed Ray's hand and mouthed, *You're the best.* I turned back to watch Mom as she leafed through the album filled with pictures of me, Dad, Natalie, her great-grandkids—smiling, staring, shaking her head, then laughing at a memory.

❀ **THE END** ❀

ACKNOWLEDGMENTS

IT'S BEEN nearly a year and a half since my last novel came out. A lot has happened in those seventeen months (see Author's Note), but the one constant has been the loving support and encouragement from my family . . . my husband, Lew, my parents, Larry and Shelly Strickler, my sisters, Karyn Anastasio and Sari Breuer, and my daughters and stepdaughters, Hayley, Taylor, Molly, and Hannah.

The wonderful folks at CamCat Books have supported my writing career since September 2020 when they acquired *The Disappearance of Trudy Solomon*. For that, I am ever grateful. Thank you Sue Arroyo, Laura Wooffitt, Abigail Miles, Meredith Lyons, Bill Lehto, Gabe Schier, Abby Conlon, Ellen Leach, and Maxine Higginbotham. Maryann Appel designed the outrageously groovy cover. Editor extraordinaire, Helga Schier, once again, made me a better storyteller.

Detective Susan Ford comes to life through the vocal talent of Rachel Fulginiti, who won a Society of Vocal Arts and Sciences (SOVAS) Award for her stellar narration of *The Murder of Madison*

Garcia. And for the first time in the Ford Family Mystery series, Will got his very own narrator. Thank you Stephen Bowlby for bringing Will to life.

They say write what you know. But what's the fun in that? I enjoy going to the theater, but I know nothing about the operations of a regional or summer stock theater. Thank you to my very dear and super talented friend, Janet Metz (who has graced the stages of Broadway, Off-Broadway, and Regional Theaters), for schooling me on who does what in the theater. Bear in mind, I'm writing fiction, and I have taken a few liberties. All inaccuracies are mine. I'm familiar with the bands that played Woodstock and have even visited the site of the festival a few times, but hadn't a clue as to how law enforcement operated at the event. Then fate stepped in. At Bouchercon Minneapolis I was chatting with fellow author Greg Renz about this book and how I was hoping to find someone who had firsthand experience with security and policing at Woodstock. Well, he knew someone. Greg introduced me to Nick Chiarkas, an ex-NYPD police officer who volunteered to "keep the peace" at Woodstock. Nick not only provided the skinny on what went down at Woodstock, he also regaled me with personal anecdotes that snuck their way into the story.

Thank you to librarians and bookstore owners who have added my books to their shelves, bookstagrammers and BookTokkers who have creatively shared my books with their followers, and readers who bought or borrowed this book. Once again, a scrumptious thank-you to Stephanie Hockersmith (@pielady) for the beautiful piecrust depicting the novel's cover.

My debut novel, *The Disappearance of Trudy Solomon*, was released during Covid (September 2021), delaying the opportunity to meet authors and fans at the various conferences that bring together mystery/thriller writers and readers. I took full advantage of going to as many conferences as I could in 2023 and 2024, and enjoyed forging friendships and making connections. It is an incredibly supportive community, and I am grateful for all the ways in which authors have supported me, from inviting me onto a podcast to blurbing my novels to sharing social media posts to showing up at my book events. A special thank you to Edwin Hill, Sarah DiVello, Hank Phillippi Ryan, Joanna Schauffhausen, Nina Wachsman, Lori Robbins, and Edith Maxwell for joining me at my various book events. Your participation meant the world to me.

AUTHOR'S NOTE

I STARTED writing this novel in January 2022 and submitted it to my publisher in November 2022. In the original version of *The Summer of Love and Death*, my story did not include Vera Ford. I sent her off on a cruise and instead created a subplot focused on a contentious relationship between Detective Susan Ford and her new partner, Detective Jack Tomelli. The response from my publisher: "revise and resubmit" (the dreaded R&R). After all, this was the Ford *Family* Mystery Series, and Vera was part of the family. Also, the feuding between Susan and Jack wasn't exactly working. It felt contrived and unoriginal.

As I thought about how to incorporate Vera back into the story, specifically in a way that had bearing on Susan's character arc, I was dealing with my own family crisis: my husband had been diagnosed with dementia in July 2022. Hints of something "off" caught my attention in the fall of 2021, which we both dismissed as "senior moments." Some behaviors were funny (constantly buying jars of jam), others quite frightening (like when he threw the car into neutral while driving because he used to drive a stick shift). But by the spring of 2022, the memory snafus were piling up, and the alarm bells were ringing loud and clear. I started keeping a journal in order to document the unusual behaviors and memory lapses—or as I referred to them: "glitches in the matrix"—for discussion with the doctor.

I think many people are familiar with what the latter stages of dementia look like, as it's what we typically see depicted in movies and books (including my novel, *The Disappearance of Trudy Solomon*). But I get the sense that most people are not attuned to what the early symptoms of the disease look like, which are easy to write off as "senior moments." If I had to venture a guess as to why, I would blame denial, fear, and stigma. A natural inclination to dismiss, or downplay, or hide what's going on because the behaviors can sometimes be embarrassing. Even the word "dementia" sucks, sounding like "demented" (defined as crazy, insane) or demeaning (defined as causing someone to lose their dignity and the respect of others). The term has its origin in Latin, and is formed from the prefix "de," which means a deprivation or loss; root "ment," which means mind; and suffix "ia," which indicates a state. In short, dementia refers to "a state out of mind." Dementia is a thief. And it will eventually rob you of everything—your livelihood, your essence, and, of course, your memories.

The confluence of these two things—the directive to write Vera back into the book and coming to terms with my husband's diagnosis—steered me in the direction of the new subplot. That journal I kept reminded me of how baffling the early symptoms were, and I thought about how the already-strained relationship between Susan and her mother, Vera (a recovering alcoholic), might play out if Vera began to exhibit signs of cognitive impairment and Susan was thrust into the role of caregiver. At first I was hesitant to go there, but in the end I found it cathartic.

Luckily I have the support of my stepdaughters, my daughters, my sisters, my parents, my friends, my caregiver group, and my husband's friends. There are many caregivers who do not have a support system in place. So if it comes to your attention that someone you know is caring for someone with dementia, think about how you might be able to help. A grocery shop. An errand. A casserole. A shoulder. An ear.

ABOUT THE AUTHOR

MARCY McCREARY is the author of *The Disappearance of Trudy Solomon,* a Killer Nashville Silver Falchion 2022 Finalist in the Best Investigator category, and *The Murder of Madison Garcia.* After graduating from George Washington University with a BA in American literature and political science, she pursued a career in the marketing field, holding executive positions in marketing communications and sales at various magazine publishing companies and content marketing agencies. She has two daughters and two stepdaughters who live in Brooklyn, New York, Nashville, Tennessee, Madison, Wisconsin, and Seattle, Washington. Marcy lives in Hull, Massachusetts, with her husband, Lew.

CHAPTER ONE

THERE IT WAS—smoking meat, the sweet stench of my childhood. Hickory, molasses, tomato, brown sugar. Kansas City's love letter to everyone but me. Darnell, my best friend from our early rehab days, drove us into the parking lot of Rocky's BBQ Smokehouse, and I gagged on the meat-laced air. *Don't toss your waffles, Tori.* The giant statue of Rocky the Pig—"Rocky the Cannibal"—smiled down at me in his chef hat and apron, holding a platter of ribs like he enjoyed making my stomach angry.

Darnell parked his truck with a displeased grunt. "Seriously, Tor," he said, wiping the sweat from his bald head. "I said I'd help you move, not run a stakeout in a hundred degrees."

"Don't worry." I took a gulp of Topo Chico to help settle my queasy gut. "My target should be here soon. Then you can help me move into my aunt's place." I twisted the zoom lens onto my digital camera and aimed it at a family tottering out of the restaurant with sauce-splattered shirts.

"Fine, then I'm running in for some brisket," Darnell said. "At least, assuming they've got any, with the meat drought they've been—"

"Hold up," I cut him off and nodded at a green sedan rolling into the lot. "That's her." I pointed my lens at the driver's door, getting ready to fire away. When a woman stepped out with crutches, I groaned.

"Guess she wasn't lying." Darnell shifted the car out of park. "The brisket will have to—"

"Wait."

Darnell hit the brakes, jerking us forward. "Now what?"

"I want to see if she uses them inside. It would be hard in a buffet line."

"You're kidding, right?" He raised his brows at me. "If you go in there with that huge camera, there's no way she's ditching her crutches."

"That wasn't what I was thinking. I only knew to come here because my target's sister posted this online." I pulled out my phone to show Darnell the selfie post of Sasha Wolf with the caption, "Waiting for @GinnyWolf. #RockysBBQ #SisterLove."

"Okay," Darnell said. "Am I supposed to be seeing something here?"

I tapped on Sasha's photo, zooming in on her sunlit head. "See that sunlight shining on her ponytail?"

"Yeah, and?"

"She's under an atrium, which means I'd have a great shot from the roof."

"The roof? You're not seriously thinking of climbing Rocky's, are you?"

"Why not?" I said, tying my blond curls into a fist of a ponytail. "You've seen me scale walls and trees before. I'm a nimble little freak."

"I meant about trespassing." Darnell pointed to his police badge like he might arrest me.

"You know us private eyes don't have to follow your rules." I gave him a reassuring smile. "Just have a smoke, and I'll be back before you've even put your butt out."

"One cig, Tor," Darnell warned, tapping a pack of Marlboro Lights on the face of his watch. "Otherwise, have fun moving by yourself."

For a recovering addict, Darnell was a horrible liar. I knew he'd never abandon me, not for anything. Hanging my camera around my neck, I hopped out of the truck into the afternoon sun, where I already felt like I was sucking meat-flavored steam through a cocktail straw. I'd just have to deal with the nausea. I hustled toward the black-and-orange pavilion, noting its unclimbable plastic siding and security cameras mounted at the entrance. Maybe I'd have better luck in the back. I circled around and found luck in the form of a supply truck parked right beside the restaurant. No driver, no cameras, no people. This was my way up.

I hoisted myself onto the hood and made my way up the windshield to the top of the truck. The gap between the truck and building was only two feet, so I made the easy jump. Soon as I hit the roof though, my phone started buzzing in my pocket. This wasn't an ideal time to take calls, so I let it ring out while I got on my hands and knees to crawl toward the atrium. When I got to the glass, I peered down at a buffet hall where six dozen carnivores were dressed for the upcoming Fourth of July weekend and savagely stuffing their smeared, sticky faces with brisket, thighs, and ribs. My stomach kicked at this familiar scene. I'd been avoiding the barbecue world for nearly fifteen years, and now that I was looking down on it like some divine creature, I remembered why I'd stayed away. Barbecue didn't just make my stomach mad. From my head to my chest to my teeth, it made me mad everywhere. But I didn't want to think about why. Not after what I'd done last night.

As I searched the crowd of meat eaters, I found Ginny, my target, at a table with her sister, her crutches against the wall. I raised my camera to my eye and focused on Ginny's face. She was teasing Sasha, lifting her brows and puckering her lips, and as she stuck out her tongue, a memory flashed in my head—I was a fourteen-year-old again in an inflatable pool of barbecue sauce with my cousin Annie. My hands shook, releasing the camera, but I jolted my neck back before the camera hit the roof.

That memory was another reminder why I should avoid smoked meat, but it made sense why the past was on my mind when Annie was the reason I was on this stakeout. She had filed her case to investigate Ms. Wolf with my agency yesterday afternoon. I had no idea, though, who this Ginny Wolf was to Annie as I placed the burning hot camera back on my face and snapped pictures of Ginny, her crutches, her gold pendant and butterfly tattoo, all material things identifying her. When she stood up for the buffet, leaving her crutches behind, I videoed the fraudster walking free and easy without them. As I'd thought, another liar.

My evidence secured, I returned to the restaurant's edge and jumped onto the supply truck. I wasn't loud, but I must have made noise inside the truck because the driver's door opened. When I saw who stepped out, I knew an apology wasn't cutting it. This was the largest man I'd ever seen. Not only was he around seven feet tall, with brisket-sized arms and an ugly blond bowl cut, his steely blue eyes were fixed on me like he wanted to rip my throat out.

"Hey," his tuba voice bellowed. "You taking pictures of me?"

"No," I said, but my answer didn't put him at ease because he jumped onto the hood to come after me. I didn't think it wise trying to fight a guy triple my size, so I rolled to the back of the truck, caught its back edge, let myself dangle, and released my grip. Soon as I hit the pavement, I sprinted.

I had a head start on the driver, but I'd only gone a few strides before I heard his monster feet slapping the ground behind me. Around my neck, my camera thumped like a heart against my chest. I tried to call out for Darnell, but the heat mixed with the running filled my lungs with hot air, making me choke. Behind me, the slapping feet were only getting closer. *You're not gonna make it.* And as I had this thought, my ponytail got yanked, and I was thrown to the pavement. I tried pushing myself up fast, but a boot crushed down on my spine first.

"Get off me," I gasped.

I strained to push up again, but the heel only dug deeper between my shoulder blades to cut off my breath. "I'll teach you not to spy on people," the voice said before my camera strap was snatched off my neck. "This is mine now. Better not see you here again." The boot then lifted, and the thug ran off.

I turned over and snapped my mouth open for air. "Darnell," I wheezed, choking to breathe.

Darnell heard me this time and opened his door. "Tori?" he called out. "Are you okay?" He ran over and helped me up.

"Yeah, thanks," I said, patting my chest.

Darnell's lip curled in distress at my arm. "Damn, what happened?"

I looked at where he was staring and saw my arm bleeding. Not the worst cut I'd had, maybe an inch long, but I could barely feel any pain. "That truck driver over there stole my camera." I pointed at the troll, now on the other side of the lot. "I'm getting it back." As I took a step forward, Darnell grabbed me by the shoulders.

"I don't think so," he said, like he was my dad. "You see the size of that guy? You're lucky he didn't crush your skull."

I tried to shake loose, but I was weak in Darnell's grip. "Please," I begged him, "my camera's priceless."

"Tor, your life's priceless." Darnell opened my door. "Now get in. I got something for your arm." I obeyed and climbed inside where Darnell wrapped my wound with paper towels. "That should help with the bleeding. Now you stay put while I charge that man with assault and theft."

I cleared my throat with protest. "You can't do that," I said.

"Excuse me?" Darnell's eyebrow ticked up at me. "Why not?"

"I was trespassing. If you charge him, he'll report me."

"So what? He's dangerous." Darnell opened his door, and I grabbed his arm with my uninjured hand.

"Do it and I'll lose my license."

His eyes widened with fury as he sucked on his teeth. "The things I do for you."

In case I didn't know Darnell was mad, he slammed his door and peeled out of the parking lot so fast my backpack flew to the floor of the car, spilling open at my feet.

I couldn't blame him for getting angry about this situation when I was even angrier. As I bent over to gather my stuff, my seat belt tight across my body, my teeth were grinding hard. *That asshole stole your camera.*

Darnell lit his fifth cigarette of the hour, and my phone buzzed in my pocket again. This time I pulled it out to check. "Great," I said. "My boss."

"Good, you can tell him how your assignment almost got you killed by an ogre."

I answered the call. "Hey, Kev."

"Hi Tori, got a minute?" Kevin sounded nervous or drunk.

"Sure, what's wrong?"

"Nothing," Kevin lied. "We got a request last night about an accidental death case. The widow's saying it wasn't an accident and specifically requested you, but I can give it to someone else if you'd still rather stick to fraud cases. Thought I'd ask you first."

"Why is she asking for me?" I said, my stomach hardening to prepare for a punch, though I knew the answer to my own question.

"I think it has to do with your last name. Aren't you related to Kansas City's Favorite Uncle?" Hearing that nickname made me gag like I'd smelled bacon. "Tori?" Kevin called out.

"Yeah, he's my uncle."

"Well, Luis Mendoza was a cook at the Uncle Charlie's location in Leawood. His widow claims she's getting death threats and that the police aren't looking into it . . ." Kevin's voice whirred beneath the *buh-dump* of my heartbeat. Turned out getting my camera stolen wasn't the worst part of my day. I just needed to stop hearing about this case before I smashed something.

"Don't want it," I said before hanging up and shoving the phone in my pocket. Darnell stayed quiet while I took staccato breaths. *You're fine. You're fine. You're fine.*

It wasn't until we reached Victory House, the sober house I was leaving for my aunt's, that Darnell turned to me and broke the silence. "So what did your boss say to get you so worked up?"

I was still in disbelief at my hysterical reaction that the words came out like I wasn't the one saying them. "He asked if I wanted a case at Uncle Charlie's."

"Uncle Charlie's? Man, good call turning that down. Your family's your worst trigger, and you've only been clean two years." Darnell reached into the backseat for a fresh Topo Chico, which, though warm, was still a Topo Chico. He handed me the bottle.

"Thanks," I said. With the black bottle opener ring I wore on my thumb, I popped off the cap and started chugging down the prickly bubbles. It wasn't a drug, but the sparkling water did calm me down.

"Was it about Luis Mendoza?" Darnell asked. I nodded while swallowing. "I remember that case," he said. "Memorial Day. Guy was on heroin, fell, hit his head, passed out in the cooker. Ruled an accident."

I sipped the bottle with more restraint. "Sounds like his widow doesn't agree with that story."

"Denial's the first stage of grief." Darnell smashed his cigarette into the ashtray he'd taped to the dashboard. "Guess she's stuck there."

"Yeah, you don't got to tell me about grief."

"You know," Darnell said, nodding at my bottle of water, "you shouldn't drink that so fast. You'll give yourself indigestion with all that carbonation."

"Don't worry, I've got my resources." From my bag, I pulled out an orange bottle and pointed to the label for my anti-narcotic prescription.

Darnell gave me an incredulous glance. "That stuff treats heartburn too?"

"What can I say?" I chased down two pills with a gulp of water. "It's a miracle drug."

As I chugged the bottle down to its bottom, my mind returned to Kevin's call and my foggy memory of what I'd done last night. It was after I'd read Annie's case request that I got so upset that I stole oxies from the girl next door and relapsed, hard. In consequence, I became even more boiling angry, looked up my treacherous extended family online, discovered Luis Mendoza's suspicious death at the drive-in only a month ago, and saw an opportunity to finally get revenge. That was why I'd submitted a case request to myself as Luis's widow. My plan was to investigate Uncle Charlie and bring him down. But last night I was wildly high, and in my present mildly drugged-up state, I could see the danger in my vision. Because even if my gut knew Luis didn't die by accident, it also knew with more clarity now that I couldn't investigate the truth. Like Darnell said, my family was my worst trigger. And seeing as I was already hiding my recent relapse from him and my aunt, I didn't need to make my situation any worse.

CamCat
Books

VISIT US ONLINE FOR MORE BOOKS TO LIVE IN:
CAMCATBOOKS.COM

SIGN UP FOR CAMCAT'S FICTION NEWSLETTER FOR
COVER REVEALS, EBOOK DEALS, AND MORE EXCLUSIVE CONTENT.

CamCatBooks   @CamCatBooks   @CamCat_Books   @CamCatBooks